"What brings you to Denver?"

"It's not important."

She didn't believe him. Whatever his reason for being at Brick's, he'd made an effort to find her. She felt cheated by the lie, just as she'd felt cheated in Abilene. "If it wasn't important, you'd answer the question."

"I know what I'm doing."

When he smirked, she saw the man who'd left her pregnant, alone and ruined. "You haven't changed a bit, have you, J.T.?"

His eyes were even bluer than she recalled, and his cheekbones more chiseled. The sun, high and bright, lit up his unshaven jaw and turned his whiskers into gold spikes. The man was untouchable, unreachable.

"That's right," he finally said. "I haven't changed a bit."

"I have," she said quietly. "What happened in Abilene is in the past. I'd appreciate it if you'd respect my privacy."

His eyes clouded with something akin to regret. "I understand," he said quietly. "You won't see me again."

His surrender shocked her to the core.

Victoria Bylin
and
Carla Capshaw

The Outlaw's Return
&
The Protector

LOVE INSPIRED
INSPIRATIONAL ROMANCE

LOVE INSPIRED®

INSPIRATIONAL ROMANCE

ISBN-13: 978-1-335-45478-2

Recycling programs
for this product may
not exist in your area.

The Outlaw's Return & The Protector

Copyright © 2020 by Harlequin Books S.A.

The Outlaw's Return
First published in 2011. This edition published in 2020.
Copyright © 2011 by Vicki Scheibel

The Protector
First published in 2010. This edition published in 2020.
Copyright © 2010 by Carla Hughes

This edition published by arrangement with Harlequin Books S.A.

For questions and comments about the quality of this book,
please contact us at CustomerService@Harlequin.com.

Love Inspired
22 Adelaide St. West, 40th Floor
Toronto, Ontario M5H 4E3, Canada
www.Harlequin.com

Printed in U.S.A.

CONTENTS

Victoria Bylin fell in love with God and her husband at the same time. It started with a ride on a big red motorcycle and a date to see a *Star Trek* movie. A recent graduate of UC Berkeley, Victoria had been seeking that elusive "something more" when Michael rode into her life. Neither knew it, but they were both reading the Bible.

Five months later they got married and the blessings began. They have two sons and have lived in California and Virginia. Michael's career allowed Victoria to be both a stay-at-home mom and a writer. She's living a dream that started when she read her first book and thought, "I want to tell stories." For that gift, she will be forever grateful.

Feel free to drop Victoria an email at VictoriaBylin@aol.com or visit her website at victoriabylin.com.

Books by Victoria Bylin

Love Inspired Historical

The Bounty Hunter's Bride
The Maverick Preacher
Kansas Courtship
Wyoming Lawman
The Outlaw's Return
Marrying the Major
Brides of the West

Visit the Author Profile page
at Harlequin.com for more titles.

THE OUTLAW'S RETURN

Victoria Bylin

The cowering prisoners will soon be set free;
they will not die in their dungeon,
nor will they lack bread.

For I am the Lord your God,
who churns up the sea so that its waves roar—
the Lord Almighty is his name.
—*Isaiah* 51:14–15

This book was the most challenging
writing experience I've ever had.
For that reason, it requires three dedications.

The first is to my editor, Emily Rodmell.
I'm beyond grateful for her insights into this story.

The second is to Sara Mitchell.
She's my dearest friend and a gifted writer.
I owe her more than I can say.

The third is to the people of
CenterPointe Christian Church
in Lexington, Kentucky. From the day
Mike and I first stepped through the doors,
you made us feel welcome. A special shout-out
goes to the ladies of the Flippin' Pages Book Club.
Let's hear it for Christian fiction!

Chapter One

Denver, Colorado
July 1876

When J. T. Quinn vowed to find Mary Larue, he never once imagined they'd meet on a perfect Sunday morning in Denver. On those long nights when he'd lain alone in his bedroll, he'd imagined seeing her on a stage in some high-class opera house. He'd pictured himself in a black suit and a white shirt leaning against the back wall with his arms crossed as he listened to her hit the high note only she could hit. Their eyes would meet and she'd recognize him. She'd miss a beat, but she'd pick up the song with even more power than before and he'd know…she still loved him.

That wasn't going to happen today.

It wasn't Saturday night, and J.T. wasn't wearing a suit.

It was Sunday morning, and he had trail dust in every pore. He also smelled like the inside of a saloon. He hadn't visited such an establishment for six months, but last night he'd walked past a gaming hall with a head full of memories. A drunken cowhand had stumbled out to the boardwalk with an open bottle of whiskey, and the contents had sloshed on J.T.'s trousers. The smell had sickened him in one breath and tempted him in the next. He'd have changed clothes, but the garments in his saddlebag were filthy. They stank, but not with whiskey. He'd resisted that temptation, and he'd done it because of his love for Mary Larue.

Heaving a sigh, he looked down at his dog. "What should we do, Fancy Girl?"

She whapped her tail against the boardwalk and looked up at him with her tongue lolling out the side of her mouth. J.T. didn't know what kind of dog she was, but they'd been best friends since he'd walked out on Griff Lassen at the Dudley place. They'd been running off Ambrose Dudley and his brother, squatters up in Wyoming, when the dog had charged at them and started barking. Griff had ordered J.T. to shoot her dead.

J.T. had done a lot of mean things in his life, but not even *he* could shoot a dog. On the other hand, he'd come close to shooting Griff. When the man aimed his Sharps at the mutt, J.T. had shoved the barrel downward. The bullet had ricocheted off a rock and creased Fancy Girl's head. J.T. had mopped her blood with his bandanna and fed her jerky from his pocket. When she'd followed him to his horse, he'd poured water from his canteen into a pot. She'd lapped every drop, and he'd filled it again.

He'd left the Dudley place with the job undone and Griff promising to get even, but the dog had followed him. That night he'd named her Fancy Girl because her fur reminded him of Mary's blond hair, and he'd made a decision. He didn't want to be the kind of man who hunted squatters and shot at dogs.

Over the past ten years, J.T. had sold his gun for money. He'd been nineteen when he'd first been paid to hunt down cattle rustlers, and next month he'd turn thirty. For a gunslinger, he had a lot of years on him. Today, standing outside a saloon and listening to Mary sing, he thought back on those years. He'd drunk oceans of whiskey and been with too many women. The whiskey had never failed to work its magic. The women, though, had lost that power, and it was because of Mary.

She'd been in his head for two years now, ever since Kansas, where they'd been a pair and she'd made him smile. Really smile. Not the sneer he usually wore. And not because she was generous with her affections. Mary made him smile because she believed he was a good man. He wasn't, but after the mess at the Dudley place, he wanted to try. Leaving that day with Fancy Girl, he'd decided to find Mary and make a new life. He had some money saved, enough to open a saloon, a place where she could sing and live the life she'd always wanted. He didn't plan to marry her. He'd changed, but not that much. Picking up where they'd left off seemed noble enough.

He and Fancy Girl had been searching for six months, and he'd finally caught a break. He hadn't touched a woman or a drop of whiskey since the mess in Wyoming, but he still had to eat. Last night he'd taken supper at the boardinghouse where he was staying with his dog. One of the boarders, an old man with bad eyes, had told him about a woman named Mary who sang like a nightingale.

You'll find her tomorrow morning at Brick's Saloon.

Not once had it occurred to J.T. that Mary would be singing a hymn in a makeshift church. His mind had gone in the opposite direction. He'd imagined her finishing up a night's work that involved more than singing. He'd been sick to think she'd fallen so low, but in the next breath he'd been relieved. No matter what Mary had done to survive, he still loved her. He wouldn't wish her the suffering of selling herself, but he rather enjoyed the thought of riding to her rescue. He didn't have much to offer a woman as beautiful and talented as Mary Larue, but he had plenty to give to a woman forced into prostitution. As a gunslinger, J.T. knew all about selling himself.

Mary's voice soared to a high note of a hymn. With that glorious sound, J.T.'s hopes crashed like a bird dying in flight. What did he have to give a woman who sang in church? Not a blessed thing. He didn't believe in God. The one time he'd cried out for mercy, the heavens had remained silent, and he had the scar to prove it.

Fancy Girl whined at his side.

"I know," he said. "We found her, but it's not going to work."

Inside the saloon, Mary's voice dipped and soared. As the hymn closed with a trembling "amen," Fancy Girl tilted her head. He could see where the bullet had left a lightning bolt between her ears. The dog had a keen intelligence and a way of reflecting J.T.'s thoughts. When she cocked her head, he saw the question he'd just asked himself.

"She doesn't need us, girl."

Fancy wagged her tail. *But you need her.*

"I know." He rubbed the dog's chin. "But she's happy now. She's got more than I can give her." He had a lot to offer a fallen woman, but a respectable one was beyond his reach. For all he knew, Mary could have found a husband. Did she have a baby of her own? Maybe a house with pretty curtains? J.T. didn't know, but he knew Mary had changed. The old Mary wouldn't have been caught dead singing a hymn. The new Mary sang the song with conviction.

If she'd been the woman he recalled, J.T. would have fought for her affection, but how could a man like him compete with God? J.T. certainly couldn't, though he could have given the devil a run for his money. The thought offered an old and lonely consolation. If he couldn't have Mary, why not buy a bottle of whiskey, a big one with a fancy label? Why not get drunk and sink into oblivion? J.T. fought the urge to go down that road, but he felt his grip slipping. Without Mary, he'd cleaned up his life for nothing. Finding a place to buy liquor on a Sunday morning wouldn't be easy, but he'd seen a mercantile that probably had a stash behind the counter.

He stopped scratching Fancy Girl's ears. "Let's go," he said to the dog.

She barked.

"Shhh," J.T. cautioned. The last thing he wanted was a nosy minister poking his head over the batwing doors. He took a couple of steps down the boardwalk, but the dog didn't budge. Instead of following him like she always did, she whined.

"I know how you feel," he said. "But we're not good enough for her." A man couldn't turn a sow's ear into a silk purse, and J.T. was definitely closer to a pig than fine fabric.

When the hymn ended, the minister called out, "Amen!"

Chairs shuffled and a woman called to the crowd. "We've got pie and coffee. Help yourselves, folks."

J.T. had skipped breakfast, and he had a sweet tooth

these days. Pie sounded good, but he had to go before the church folks started to leave. He aimed his chin across the street. "Come on, Fancy."

The dog perked her ears and tilted her head. J.T. considered the expression a smile, mostly because she got that look when he told her stories by a campfire. He did it to amuse himself, but mostly he liked the way Fancy seemed to listen. She had that look now. She seemed pleased, even eager to go inside the saloon, as if she expected a big bowl of water, maybe even a meal of scraps.

That's one thing J.T. could say for his dog. Fancy Girl had hope. J.T. had no such optimism. Mary had found a life better than anything he had to give. He had to leave before someone noticed him. "Come on," he repeated firmly to his dog.

The mutt looked at him as if he were an idiot, then she walked under the batwing doors with her tail wagging.

"Traitor," J.T. muttered.

Thoroughly annoyed, he leaned against the wall of the saloon, placing himself between the window where he'd peeked inside and seen Mary and the door that would put him directly in her line of sight. No way could he go inside, but neither could he leave his dog.

Surely a high-and-mighty minister would throw the mutt into the street. J.T. just had to wait for someone to notice her. Squinting against the sun, he leaned on the wall and crossed his arms. As soon as Fancy Girl learned her lesson, he'd throw away six months of hope. He'd find a place to buy whiskey, then he'd get his horses out of the livery and he'd leave Denver fast and forever. He'd find a tree by a stream, drink the whole

bottle and push Mary Larue out of his heart forever.
First, though, he had to get his dog back.

"A dog!" Mary declared. "It looks like she's coming to church."

"Maybe she is." Reverend Joshua Blue crouched
down and scratched the dog's ears. The service had just
ended, and the congregation was headed to the refreshment table. Mary glanced to see if her sister and brother
were behaving themselves. A month ago, their arrival
had turned her life upside down, and she was still reeling from the shock. Her father had been gone for years,
but her mother had died just a few months ago. Gertie
and Augustus had come to live with her. She spotted
them both in the back of the makeshift church.

Gertie met her gaze, then heaved a sigh worthy of
the actress she wanted to be. At seventeen, the girl
thought she knew everything. Mary had once had the
same illusion, but she'd learned some hard lessons in
her own acting days. She didn't want her sister to repeat her mistakes, but neither did she want to deny
her dream.

As soon as Gertie turned eighteen, Mary planned to
send her to New York to study with Maude Atkins, a
theater friend who had moved back East. Mary wished
she'd gone to New York, a city with classy theaters
and modern stages. Instead she'd traveled west with a
third-rate theater troupe. She'd made a name for herself,
but she'd also been disgraced. Two years had passed
since gunslinger J. T. Quinn had left her unmarried
and pregnant, but she hadn't forgotten the miscarriage
or the scandal that had erupted. People in Abilene had
known she and J.T. had a special friendship, and some
assumed the truth—that they were lovers. When she

became pregnant, she was desperate to keep the news to herself, but she miscarried just before taking the stage. The gossip about her turned into a full-blown scandal and she lost her reputation completely. When a drunken bounty hunter assumed she'd welcome his attentions, she'd shot him in self-defense. After an ugly murder trial, she'd cut all ties to Abilene and the theater.

Her friends at Swan's Nest knew she'd killed a man, but no one in Denver knew she'd been with child. Neither did the baby's father. She'd made her peace with God, but she had no illusions about people and gossip. She knew how it felt to endure stares and ugly talk. She cared deeply about her reputation, and she wanted to set a good example for Gertie. Her sister knew nothing about the scandal, and Mary intended to keep it that way. That's why she was sending Gertie to New York. If the girl pursued a stage career in Denver, she'd surely meet someone who knew about Mary's past. Someone would recognize Gertie's last name, the gossip would start and Mary would lose her reputation for the second time.

Her brother, Augustus, wouldn't understand the mistake she'd made, but he inspired other worries. He was twelve years old, thin as a bean and hadn't said more than "Yes, ma'am" and "No, ma'am" since he and Gertie had arrived from West Virginia. The boy was quiet because he stammered his words. As a singer, Mary had trained her voice. She'd tried to help Augustus control his breathing, but he'd only gotten more nervous with her attention. She didn't know what else to do, but she wouldn't stop trying to help him.

She loved her brother and sister, but her life had changed drastically the day they'd arrived. In some ways, it had changed for the better. In others, it had gotten so hard she wondered if God had stopped hearing her prayers.

Reaching down, she patted the dog. Its tongue fell to the side as it panted in the summer heat. "I think she's thirsty," Mary said to Josh.

"Hey, Brick!" the minister called to the saloon owner. "How about some water for our guest?"

Brick grinned. "Sure thing, preacher."

As the saloon keeper went to fetch a bowl, Mary traced the ridge of the white scar between the dog's ears. "I wonder where she came from."

"There's no telling," Josh answered. "But she looks well fed." He fingered the red bandanna tied around her neck. "She's also wearing her Sunday best."

As Mary laughed, Adie Blue, Josh's wife and Mary's best friend, approached with Stephen, her one-year-old son, balanced on her hip. Mary ached a little at the sight of them. If she hadn't miscarried, her baby would have been about the same age.

Adie patted the dog's neck. "The poor thing! It looks like a bullet grazed the top of her head."

"It looks that way," Josh agreed.

Glad to be distracted, Mary touched the scar. "Who would shoot a dog?"

Even if the mutt had been raiding a chicken coop, she didn't deserve to be shot. Strays did what they had to do to survive. Bending slightly, Mary scratched the dog's long chin. She had a thick golden coat, big brown eyes and an expression Mary could only describe as a smile. Tinges of black feathered above her eyes to make brows, and she was brushed and clean.

She rubbed the dog's jaw. "Where's your home, sweetheart?"

The dog cocked her head as if to say, *Right here.*

Mary knew the feeling. When she'd come to Denver, she hadn't known a soul until she'd found Swan's Nest, a boardinghouse for women in need. There she'd met Adelaide Clarke, now Adie Blue, and made new friends. If someone had told her two years ago she'd be singing hymns in church, she'd have laughed at them. But that's where she was today and where she wanted to be. A bit of a stray herself, Mary appreciated having a home.

She rubbed the dog's ears until Brick arrived with the water and set the bowl on the floor. As the dog lapped happily, Gertie sidled up to Mary. "Can we go now?"

"Not yet," she answered. "It's our turn to clean up."

"But—"

"Don't argue, Gertie." Mary sounded more commanding than she felt. She was ten years older than her sister, but they'd been close growing up. Disciplining Gertie didn't come easily, especially since Mary understood the girl's desire for excitement and fancy dresses. They'd grown up poor in a West Virginia town called Frog's Landing. Mary had been Gertie's age when she'd left in search of fame and fortune.

The fortune had been fleeting, and the fame had led to a broken heart. She'd never forget seeing Jonah Taylor Quinn for the first time. She'd finished her second encore at the Abilene Theater and had stepped backstage. He'd been leaning against a wall with his boots crossed at the ankle and a look in his eyes that could only be called scandalous. She'd blushed just looking at him, but then he'd greeted her with the utmost respect. He'd invited her to a midnight supper and she'd accepted. One meal had led to another, and they'd become

friends. As spring arrived in Kansas, they'd traded stories and kisses, and she'd fallen in love with him.

Then he'd left.... She still felt the sting of that midnight parting. *It's been good, Mary. But it's time for
me to go.*

But I have to tell you something. She'd paused to
gather her courage. Instead of telling him she was expecting a baby, she'd revealed her feelings. *I love you,
J.T.*

He'd smiled that wicked smile of his, then he'd
shrugged. *Love doesn't mean a thing, sweetheart.*

She'd slapped him. Before she could say a word, he'd
walked away. She couldn't bear to think about what
happened next, so she glanced at the dog. It had finished the water and looked content. "I wonder if someone's looking for her," she remarked to Adie.

"I've never seen her before."

"Me neither," Josh added.

Adie gave Mary a knowing look. "You're going to
take her home, aren't you?"

"Maybe."

Home for Mary was an apartment over the café she
owned thanks to a mortgage from the Denver National
Bank. She didn't have room for a dog, but neither could
she leave the animal to fend for itself. Mary had always
had a heart for strays. It didn't matter if they had two
legs or four. That inclination had caused trouble in
the past, but she'd learned her lesson. She loved children and dogs and wouldn't turn them away, but men
couldn't be trusted.

She looked again at Gertie and Augustus. Her
brother stood half-hidden in the corner, eating a piece
of pie. Gertie was giving her the evil eye. In another
minute, the girl would storm across the room and make

a scene. Mary hated arguing with Gertie, so she turned to Adie. "I'm going to start cleaning up."

"I'll do it," Adie volunteered. "You work hard all week."

"So do you."

Adie shrugged. "I have to wait for Josh. Besides, I have a favor to ask."

"Sure," Mary answered.

"When you come to supper this afternoon, would you bring a couple of loaves of that good sourdough? If I know Josh, we're going to have a crowd."

Sunday supper at Swan's Nest had become a tradition, one that had grown from a simple meal shared by the women who lived there to a feast for anyone who showed up. Josh made a point of inviting everyone from church, and today Mary had noticed some new faces. "I'll be glad to bring all you need," she said to Adie.

Her friend smiled. "While you fetch the bread, I'll take Gertie and Augustus to Swan's Nest."

"If you're sure—"

"I am." Both women knew Gertie could be difficult.

"Thanks." If Mary left now, she could squeeze in a few chores. She had to plan next week's menus and inventory the pantry. Absently she patted the dog's head. When it sniffed her hand, she smiled. Stephen wiggled in his mother's arms and made a *D* sound.

"Dog," Adie prodded.

"Da!"

Mary felt a stab of longing for the child she'd lost. She loved children, but she had no desire to marry. After what J.T. had done, she'd never trust a man again.

Absently rocking the one-year-old, Adie turned to her. "Are you going to take the dog?"

Mary looked down at her. "What do you say, girl?

Would you like to come home with me?" She didn't have a lot of space, but she had plenty of scraps.

The dog tipped its head.

"Let's go," Mary said to her.

As she crossed the room to speak to Gertie and Augustus, the dog followed her. Gertie fussed about going to Swan's Nest, but she didn't pitch a fit. Neither did Augustus, though Mary would have welcomed a tantrum in place of a nod. After waving goodbye to several members of the congregation, she left the saloon with the dog at her side.

She didn't immediately notice the man leaning against the saloon wall. It was the smell of whiskey that got her attention, then the rasp of a stifled curse. Expecting a cowboy with Saturday-night regrets, she turned to offer the man Christian charity and a slice of pie. Instead of a stranger, she saw J. T. Quinn. And instead of charity, she felt something else altogether.

Chapter Two

J.T. was thinner than she recalled and harder because of the leanness, a sign he'd been living on jerky and bad coffee. His brown hair had gold streaks from the summer sun, and his blue eyes still pierced whatever they saw. She felt the sharpness of his gaze and remembered.... She'd once loved this man, and she'd hated him when he'd left.

With the changes in her life, she couldn't give in to bitterness. She knew how it felt to be forgiven, and she had a duty to forgive others. She'd treat J.T. the way she'd treat a stranger, except he wasn't a stranger. She knew how he liked his coffee, and she'd seen the scars on his body from bullets and knives. None of those memories mattered. This man posed a risk to her reputation. If her friends saw him, they'd ask nosy questions.

She had to make him leave before someone else left the church. She gave him a curt nod. "Hello, J.T."

He tipped his hat. "Hello, Mary."

Unnerved by his husky drawl, she fought to steady her voice. "This is quite a surprise."

"Yeah." He eyed the batwing doors. "For me, too."

Was he surprised to see *her* or surprised to see her leaving a church service? Mary didn't know what to think. Why would he seek her out after all this time? On the other hand, what were the odds he'd visit Brick's Saloon on a Sunday morning by chance? One in a million, she decided. Josh's little church was unusual and well-known. Any saloon keeper in Denver could have told him she sang here on Sunday morning.

That meant he'd come to see her, but why? No one stirred up memories—both good and bad—like this handsome, hard-edged man. Ten minutes ago Mary had been singing "Fairest Lord Jesus" from the depths of her heart. Looking at J.T., she couldn't remember a single word.

Help me, Lord.

With the dog at her feet, she spoke as if nothing were amiss. "The saloon's not open. I was here for—"

"Church," he said. "I know."

"How—"

"I heard you singing." He glanced at the mutt at her side. "So did my dog."

"*Your* dog?"

"Yeah." He looked sheepish, as if he'd admitted something embarrassing. She supposed he had. A man like J.T. traveled with the clothes on his back and his guns. He'd carry bullets before he'd pack an extra can of beans, yet here he stood looking at a dog as if it were his only friend.

When he held out his hand, the dog licked his fingers. "You crazy thing," he murmured.

At the sight of such tenderness, Mary's forgot to breathe. In Kansas she'd seen J.T. beat the daylights out of a man who'd disrespected her. He'd worked as a hired gun to ranchers wanting to chase off rustlers, and he didn't think twice about it. He was hard, tough and mean, except with her. Then he'd been as soft as butter, tender in the way of a man who knew a woman's need for love while denying his own.

But then he'd left her. She'd forgiven him for leaving, but that didn't mean she'd forgotten the coldness of the parting. J. T. Quinn couldn't be trusted, not with her heart and not with knowledge of the baby. He'd disrespected her. She refused to allow him to disrespect a child that had never been born. In Abilene he'd left her in the middle of a conversation. Today she wanted answers. *Why are you here? What do you want?* Any minute people would start leaving church. Since Gertie and Augustus were with Adie, the café would be empty. She thought of yesterday's stew in the icebox. J.T. looked hungry, and so did his dog. She'd never been good at turning away strays.

"I own a restaurant," she said. "You look like you could use a meal."

"No, thanks."

He sounded confident, but he had the air of a boy trying to be tough. Her heart softened more than she wanted to admit. "Are you sure?"

"No, thanks, Mary. I just…" He shook his head, but the gesture didn't answer her questions.

A terrible foreboding took root in her belly. Had he heard the talk in Abilene? Did he know about the baby but not the miscarriage? She couldn't stand the thought of the scandal finding her again, nor did she want to open old wounds. Trying to appear casual, she tipped her head. "What brings you to Denver?"

"It's not important."

She didn't believe him. Whatever his reason for being at Brick's, he'd made an effort to find her. She felt cheated by the lie, just as she'd felt cheated in Abilene. "If it wasn't important, you'd answer the question."

"I know what I'm doing."

When he smirked, she saw the man who'd left her pregnant and disgraced. "You haven't changed a bit, have you, J.T.?"

His eyes were even bluer than she recalled, and his cheekbones more chiseled. The sun, high and bright, lit up his unshaven jaw and turned his whiskers into gold spikes. The man was untouchable, unreachable.

"That's right," he finally said. "I haven't changed a bit."

"I have." She lowered her voice. "What happened between us in Abilene is in the past. I'd appreciate it if you'd respect my privacy."

"Don't worry," he said. "You won't see me again."

His surrender shocked her to the core. She wanted to know why he'd given in so easily, but she couldn't risk lingering outside the church and being seen. To protect her reputation, she'd have to live with yet another unanswered question. With her head high, she stepped off the boardwalk. To her consternation, the dog followed her. In the middle of the empty street, she stopped and turned back to J.T. "Call your dog."

His jaw tightened. "Come on, dog."

Mary scowled at him. "You named her *Dog?* No wonder she's not obeying you!"

"That's not her name," he muttered.

"Then what is it?"

He looked straight at her. "Her name is Fancy Girl."

Air rushed into Mary's lungs. Fancy Girl had been his name for her. He'd called her his Fancy Girl, because she'd liked to dress up for the stage. She'd enjoyed the makeup and the flamboyant dresses, particularly the costumes that had freed her from the dullness of Frog's Landing. "You named her after *me?*"

"Yeah."

She should have been insulted. The fool man had named a dog after her! Yet she knew it hadn't been an insult. He loved his dog. A long time ago, even though he hadn't said the words, Mary had thought he'd loved *her*. She'd been mistaken. J.T. didn't love anyone. "It's been nice seeing you," she said in a courteous tone. "But I have to get home."

"I understand."

She doubted it. He didn't know her at all anymore. Reaching down, she rubbed the scar between the dog's ears. "Goodbye, Fancy Girl."

After a final scratch, she continued across the street. When the dog tagged along, J.T.'s voice boomed behind her. "Fancy Girl! Get over here!"

Hearing her old name in J.T.'s baritone stopped Mary in her tracks, but Fancy Girl ignored him. Mary rather enjoyed the dog's rebellion. People usually did what J.T. ordered. Occasionally they did it with a gun aimed at them, but mostly they obeyed because he spoke with authority. He wasn't in charge now.

As he called the dog a second time, a man came out of the church, looked long and hard at J.T., and went on his way. Any minute the congregation would be in the street and he'd be a spectacle in his black clothing. Needing to persuade him, Mary flashed a smile. "I promised Fancy Girl a plate of scraps. It looks like she's holding me to it."

His eyes twinkled. "She's a smart dog."

"Would you like to come with us?"

He snorted. "For scraps?"

"Scraps for her. Pot roast for you." She tried to sound businesslike. "I really do own a restaurant."

"Oh, yeah?"

"The best in town. It's called Mary's Café." She raised her chin. "It's mine, and I'm proud of it."

"You should be." Still he didn't move.

"Come on." She aimed her chin down the street. "Your dog won't take no for an answer."

A smile tipped on the corners of his mouth. "Sounds like you won't, either." Looking pleased, he stepped off the boardwalk and strode to her side. With Fancy Girl between them, they headed to the café with Mary hoping they hadn't been seen.

J.T. smelled like dirt and mistakes, and he knew it. Apparently so did Mary. Her nose wrinkled as he stepped to her side, so he widened the gap between them. Fancy Girl smelled better than he did. He didn't understand why his dog had taken such a strong liking to Mary, but he felt the same urge to follow her home.

As they walked down the boardwalk, she made small talk about the weather. J.T. responded in kind, but his mind wasn't on the July heat. He couldn't think about anything except the changes in Mary. She still had a saucy attitude, but the lines around her mouth had softened into an easy smile and her brown eyes had a sheen of happiness. She wore her hair differently, too. The curls were still honey-blond, but she'd tamed them into a simple twist. Her dress, a demure lilac, could have belonged to a schoolmarm.

Six months ago, he'd have mocked her plain dress and the prim hairstyle. He'd have teased her into being his Fancy Girl again, maybe into his bed.

Not now.

Not today. He thought back to how he'd left her and he had to wonder… What would have happened if he'd stayed with her? Would they be running a saloon with Mary singing and J.T. pouring drinks? He could resist the temptation to drink if it meant proving himself to Mary. His other worry—being called out by an old enemy, someone like Griff Lassen—would never leave, but time would ease the threat. Today, though, everything had changed. Mary didn't need him at all. With no reason to stay, he decided to buy supplies and ride west. Whether or not those supplies would include whiskey, he couldn't say.

With Fancy Girl in front of them, he kept pace with Mary as she turned down a side street. In the distance he heard the blast of a train whistle. They were near the depot, a good spot for business from hungry travelers. She indicated a storefront between a tailor and a telegraphy office. It was painted butter-yellow and had green trim. A sign read Mary's Café.

"This is it." She unlocked the door and pushed it open.

Stepping inside, he saw cream-colored walls, tables set with red-checked linens and an assortment of chairs that didn't match but somehow went together. Every surface sparkled, even the floor. A man could relax in a place like this. Apparently so could a dog. Fancy Girl ambled to a corner near an unlit potbelly stove, circled three times and curled into a ball.

J.T. took off his hat and hung it on a hook by the door. "You've got a nice place."

"Thank you." She raised her chin. "I've worked hard to get it started."

In her eyes he saw the old Mary, the one who'd fight for what she wanted. He also saw bluish circles fanning down her cheeks. She was still beautiful, but he'd never seen her look so weary.

How hard did she have to work? Did anyone help her with the cooking and the washing up? The woman he'd known in Kansas hadn't been the least bit inclined to kitchen chores. Thanks to J.T.'s faro winnings, they'd ordered lavishly at the Abilene Hotel and he'd bought her pretty things for the fun of it. She'd grown up poor, and he'd liked surprising her. He wondered how she'd gotten the money to open a restaurant. Was she beholden to the bank? Or maybe she had a business partner, a man with money. The thought made him scowl.

She'd clam up if he quizzed her, so he beat around the bush. "How's business?"

"Good." She indicated a table by a wall decorated with paintings of mountains. "Have a seat. I need to light the stove."

Instead of sitting, he followed her into the kitchen. In the crowded space he saw two massive iron stoves, a row of high tables against the back wall, three baker's racks full of pies and bread, and cooking utensils hanging from rods suspended from the ceiling. Basins were leaning against the back wall, clean and ready for the next load of dirty dishes.

J.T. saw the pride Mary took in her business, but he also saw hours of drudgery. In Abilene she'd slept until noon, even later sometimes. Judging by the aroma, she'd baked the bread before church.

Maybe he *did* have something to offer her. He couldn't promise her a life of leisure, but running a saloon would be easier than serving full meals. He wanted to blurt the invitation to come with him to California, but first he had to rekindle the old sparks between them. Leaning against the doorframe, he crossed one boot over the other and watched her set a match to the banked coals. When they caught fire, he shook his head. "You must work day and night."

She shrugged. "There's nothing wrong with hard work."

"No," he replied. "It's just…tiresome."

She gave him a quelling look, then removed a jar from the ice box, poured the contents into a pot and carried it to the stove. Facing him, she said, "This will take a few minutes. Let's sit out front."

As she stepped through the doorway, her skirts brushed his boots. He followed her to the table, then moved ahead of her and held her chair. He didn't know what it would take to sweep Mary off her feet, but fancy manners had always impressed her. He slid in her chair, then moved to sit across from her.

The instant he hit the chair, Mary popped to her feet. "You must be thirsty. I've got sweet tea or cider. Coffee is—"

"Mary, sit," he said quietly. "I don't want you serving me."

She sat, but she looked uncomfortable.

At last, J.T. had the upper hand. Hoping to put her at ease, he used the crooked grin that had never failed to charm her. "What brought you to Denver?"

She shrugged as if she didn't have a care in the world. "Denver is famous for its opera houses. I wanted to see it for myself."

Her gaze stayed steady, but he saw a flash of pain. He survived as a gunslinger because he could feel danger coming. What he saw in Mary's eyes troubled him deeply. "I'm surprised you're not singing somewhere."

"It didn't work out."

J.T. knew this woman. Short answers weren't her

style. Unless he'd lost his instincts, she was hiding something. He kept his voice mild. "But you love to sing. You're good at it."

She moved the fork a quarter inch. "I sing in church now. That's all there is to it."

"I don't think so."

Suddenly wary, she turned to the window and stared out the shining glass. When she didn't speak, J.T. thought back to the early days of his search and his visit to the Abilene Theater. The new manager had heard of Mary but didn't know where she'd gone, and her acting friends had moved on. When she'd left the rowdy cow town, she'd done it fast and quietly. He'd assumed she'd run from a broken heart. Now he wondered if she'd had another reason. "Talk to me, Mary."

She took a breath, a deep one. "You're right. There's more to the story. After you left, I had a run-in with Sam O'Day."

J.T. knew all about Sam and his brother, Harvey. They were bounty hunters, and they behaved like animals. "What happened?"

"I shot him."

"You *what?*"

"I shot Sam O'Day," she repeated calmly. "Do you remember the pistol you gave me?"

"Of course." The two-shot Deringer had over-under barrels, pearl handles and a gleaming nickel finish. They'd taken a buggy ride to nowhere, and he'd discovered she didn't know how to shoot. He'd taken the pistol out of his boot, taught her to use it and told her to keep it handy. They'd kissed for an hour and he'd pushed for more. She'd said no, but a month later he'd convinced her to change her mind.

With her chin high, she described the encounter with

O'Day. He'd been drunk enough to get thrown out of a brothel. When he'd seen Mary leave the theater alone, he'd called her names and cornered her in the alley. "He grabbed me," she said calmly. "I told him to let go, but he wouldn't."

J.T. saw the fear on her face, the determination that had enabled her to fight for her life. He knew how she felt, because as a boy he'd been pinned down in an alley with a knife against his scrawny chest. His older brothers had been vicious. "It's a bad feeling."

"It is." She took a breath. "I had your gun in my pocket. When he tore at my dress, I shot him. He died."

"Mary, I—"

"Don't say anything. What's done is done."

If J.T. had been around, O'Day wouldn't have dared to touch her. He should have been with her.... He should never have left. What a fool he'd been to go off with Griff Lassen. He'd been looking for a fight to keep his own rep from slipping. Instead he'd made an enemy of Griff. He'd gotten Fancy Girl out of the deal, but he lost everything else and so had Mary.

Feeling bitter, he forced himself to meet her gaze. "What happened after you shot Sam?"

"I went to the sheriff. He believed me, but I had to stand trial for murder."

He held in a cringe. "Did they lock you up?"

"For a time."

Twice J.T. had spent time in a jail cell. No one knew it except Mary, but dark, closed-in places gave him nightmares. As a boy he'd been abused in an alley by his older brothers, often with a knife. More than once, Mary had comforted him when he'd been jarred awake by a nightmare. "I know what jail's like," he said. "It's like being buried alive."

"It was awful," she admitted. "The jury ruled it was self-defense, but Sam's brother didn't agree. When he threatened to kill me if I stuck around, I decided to leave."

J.T. let loose with a curse. "I'll hunt him down. I'll—"

"Don't."

"But, Mary—"

"It's over and done." She looked into his eyes. "I worried for a while that Sam's brother would find me in Denver, so I traveled a bit before settling here. Harvey O'Day never found me, so I figured he went back to bounty hunting."

"That's most likely," J.T. confirmed.

"As for Sam, I forgave him a long time ago. Frankly, coming to Denver was the best thing that's ever happened to me. I made friends at a boardinghouse called Swan's Nest. I have supper there every Sunday. That's where I'm going next."

J.T. realized she hadn't answered his first question. "Why not perform here in Denver?"

"Those last days in Abilene were awful," she said mildly. "The theater world is small. If I act here in Denver, the talk will start again. I can't stand the thought."

He'd have chosen a whipping over the guilt he felt for leaving her. Not once had he considered Mary's reputation when he'd set out to claim her. When she straightened her fork for the second time, he reached across the table and gripped her hand. His gaze dropped to their knuckles—hers red and rough, his scarred from brawling—and he felt the rightness of what he wanted to say. "I'm sorry I left. I should have—"

"Don't waste your breath."

When she tried to take back her hand, he held it

tighter. "Leaving you was the biggest mistake of my life."

"I doubt that," she said, tugging again.

He had some convincing to do, and he had to do it with tenderness, not fighting. He let her go. "I don't expect you to believe me. Not yet. But I've missed you. That's why I'm here. Remember the dream we had about opening a saloon? Our own place in California?"

She bit her lip, but her eyes said she remembered.

"Come with me, Fancy Girl," he said in a hush. "We can pick up where we left off."

She didn't say yes to him, but neither did she slap his face. With his chest tight and his heart pounding, J.T. waited for her answer.

Chapter Three

$\backsim$

Mary had pulled out of J.T.'s grasp, but the warmth of his touch lingered. Two years ago she'd yearned for what he'd just offered. That dream had shattered the night he'd left, and so had her hopes for marriage and a family of her own. Memories kicked in the place where the baby had nestled for three short months.

She couldn't let J.T. see the memory in her eyes, so she blinked hurriedly. "The answer is no."

"Why not?"

Because you hurt me, and I'll never trust a man again. Because you broke my heart and left me with child. "I'm different now," she said simply.

"So am I."

She doubted it. He hadn't mentioned marriage and he wouldn't. A man like J.T. wasn't the marrying kind. She'd known that all along, but she'd foolishly believed she could change his mind. She spoke with deliberate calm. "What we had in Abilene is gone. All of it."

Even the baby.

Memories assailed her…the blood, the pain. The guilt had been worst of all. She hadn't wanted the baby until she'd lost it. That morning she'd woken up with cramps. Instead of staying in bed, she'd gone to the theater intending to perform as usual. She'd miscarried just minutes before she was supposed to take the stage, and the gossip had started instantly. Tears pressed into her eyes. If J.T. saw them, he'd know there was more to the incident with Sam O'Day.

Mumbling about the food, she hurried to the kitchen. Before she reached the door, he clasped her arms from behind. In Kansas he would have kissed her neck. She would have turned and gone into his arms. Today she felt trapped.

His voice came over her shoulder. "Come with me, Mary. It'll be good this time."

It had been good last time, but not good enough. Giving herself to this man had caused her nothing but grief. She'd lost her heart, her reputation and her career. She'd wept alone over their lost child, and that had hurt most of all.

As he tightened his grip, the smell of his unwashed skin reached her nose. She broke loose and faced him. "Leave me alone!"

He released her, but his eyes held her more tightly than his hands. "I need you, Mary."

"What you need is a bath!"

"I need more that," he murmured. "I need you."

"No, you don't."

"Mary, I—"

"Don't talk to me!" Turning, she clamped her hands over her mouth. The secret burned like fire in her belly. She wanted to punish him for what he'd done, but she couldn't. Not only did she have to keep the facts to herself, but she knew what it meant to need forgiveness.

As much as she wanted to blame J.T. for wooing her into his bed, she'd gone willingly, even eagerly. God had forgiven her—she knew that. She thought she'd forgiven J.T., but the memories left no room for mercy. She couldn't stand the thought of the scandal coming back to life. She desperately wanted J.T. to leave, but her anger left a sour taste in her mouth. They'd both sinned. If she sent him way in anger, she'd be a hypocrite. She took a breath to calm herself, then faced him. "I'm sorry. I shouldn't have shouted at you."

Relief softened his mouth. "I had it coming."

He stood still, waiting for her to make the next move. She glanced at Fancy Girl. She'd promised them both a meal, so she indicated his chair. "I'll get the pot roast. Fancy can have a bone when you leave."

"Thanks."

She escaped into the kitchen, dished his food and brought a plate to the table. He smiled his thanks, lifted his spoon and ate. In Abilene they'd lingered over supper with quiet anticipation. Today she used silence like a stage curtain. It hid her memories the way velvet drapes hid the audience, but thoughts of a curtain reminded her of the career she'd lost. Yesterday Roy Desmond, the new manager of the Newcastle Theater, had asked her to star in *The Bohemian Girl*. Because of the scandal, she had decided to turn him down. If her name showed up on Roy's fancy theater posters, people might become curious about her past. At the time she'd thought briefly of J.T. and blamed him. She couldn't possibly sing on stage again, even though she'd been impressed with Roy. An actor himself, he had managed a theater troupe on a Mississippi riverboat. She hadn't heard of him, but he'd been in Abilene and had heard her sing. He'd mentioned the trial and the gossip, then assured her he'd keep the information to himself. She trusted him.

J.T. finished the pot roast, then broke the silence with a contented sigh. "You sure can cook. I didn't know that."

"It's a family recipe." She reached idly to straighten the salt shaker.

His gaze dropped to her fingers, no doubt noticing the roughness. Her hands embarrassed her, but she refused to hide them. He arched one brow. "Are you sure I can't talk you into singing in that saloon in California? It's a long way from Abilene."

"I'm positive."

"Would you think about it?"

"There's no need." He'd push until he got what he wanted, and he wanted *her*. She had to give him another reason to move on. "My mother died a few months ago. I'm raising my sister and brother."

He didn't like children, so she figured he'd leave her alone. Instead he seemed interested. "How old are they?"

"Gertie just turned seventeen. Augustus is twelve."

He wrinkled his brow. "They're not that young. Gertie's practically grown. And Augustus—" He shook his head. "That's a dreadful name for a boy."

Mary didn't know what to make of his interest. "We've always called him Augustus."

"So give him a nickname."

"Like what?"

"I don't know." His eyes twinkled. "I bet we can think of something."

We? Mary had to set him straight. "Even if I wanted to go with you—*which I do not*—I have obligations.

I own this restaurant. I have a mortgage to pay and women who work for me. They need the money. Frankly, so do I. I'm saving to send Gertie to New York."

He scowled, a reminder that he'd been left on those crowded streets to fend for himself. "What's in New York?"

"Theaters. Gertie loves singing as much as I did."

"You still love it."

"Yes, but not the same way." She stood and lifted their plates. In Kansas she'd used his given name for only the most serious conversations. She used it now to make a point. "You're two years too late, Jonah. I wish you the best, but I don't want to see you again."

Dust motes hung in the light, swirling like ash from a burning bridge in a ray of sun coming through the window. The glare lit one side of his face and put the other in shadow until he pushed back the chair and stood. "I see."

When he looked at his dog, Mary remembered her promise to Fancy Girl. "I'll be right back."

She carried the plates to the kitchen, selected the meatiest soup bone she had, wrapped it in paper and carried it to the dining room. "Here." She handed it to J.T. "This is for Fancy."

He took it but hesitated before calling the dog. If the mutt refused to go with him, Mary didn't know what she'd do. With his brow tight, he spoke in a gentle tone Mary knew well. "Let's go, Fancy Girl."

When the dog ambled to his side, Mary breathed a sigh of relief. He took his hat off the peg and opened the door. With sunlight fanning into the room, he pulled the brim low and stepped outside, closing the door behind him. Mary blinked, and he was gone.

* * *

J.T. turned the corner, stopped and looked at his dog. "What now, girl?"

Fancy nudged the bone with her nose. J.T. wished his desires were as simple. He wanted a drink. The escape wouldn't last, but it would stop the ache in his chest. He'd wake up feeling even worse than he did now, but who cared? Without Mary, he had no reason to stay sober. As soon as he bought supplies, he'd leave town. Tonight Fancy could chew the bone in front of a lonely campfire.

"Come on," he said to her. "We're getting out of here."

He went to the livery for his horses, paid the owner and put the bone in a saddlebag. He secured the line to the pack horse, climbed on his buckskin and headed to the boardinghouse to fetch his gear. As the horses plodded down the street, he looked for a place to buy whiskey. He saw one closed door after another, then the gray wall of a large stone building. The granite gleamed white in the sun, and gargoyles jutted from the eaves. As he rounded the corner, he saw a sign that read Newcastle Theater.

"Hey, Quinn!"

He slipped his hand into his duster until it rested on the ivory grip of his Colt Navy, then he scanned the street for the person who'd called him. When he saw Roy Desmond, he wanted to spit. He knew Roy from the faro tables in Dodge City. The man cheated. Even worse, there was talk he'd killed a saloon girl. J.T. had no desire to speak with Roy, but he couldn't ignore him with Mary in Denver. The man had bragged about his life as an actor, and J.T. worried he'd seek out Mary.

She'd sent J.T. away, but he wouldn't leave until he knew what Desmond wanted.

"Hello, Roy."

"This is a surprise." The man flashed a grin. "It's been what? Three years since Dodge?"

"More or less." J.T. had known Roy before Abilene, before he'd been with Mary. "What are you up to?"

Roy indicated the stone building behind him. "You're talking to the manager of the Newcastle Theater. I'm a legitimate businessman now."

Only a snake like Roy would need to announce he'd become legitimate. J.T. took in the man's sack suit and pleated shirt. A gold watch dangled from his pocket, and his shoes were newly blacked. His hair was still dark but thinner than J.T. recalled, and deep lines framed his mouth. Nothing about Roy could be trusted, not his appearance and not the words dancing off his tongue. If Roy had any dealings with Mary, J.T. would have to think again about leaving Denver. He needed information, so he feigned interest in the man's venture.

"Legitimate, huh?" He grinned. "Does that mean no faro?"

Roy chuckled. "I've got other cards to play. In fact, you're just the man to help me play them."

It was just like Roy to speak in riddles. "What do you have in mind?"

"It involves a mutual friend of ours."

"Who?"

"Mary Larue."

Live or die, J.T. would do anything to keep Roy away from Mary. "What about her?"

The man indicated the door. "Come inside and we'll talk."

J.T. swung off his horse and tied off the reins. With

Fancy Girl at his side, he followed Roy into the opera house. Trying to look bored, he entered the cavernous foyer as if he walked around such places every day. He didn't, and the opulence stunned him. Thick carpet covered the floor, and the walls were crimson with gold stripes. Brass wall sconces caught the light from the open door and shimmered like flames. Even the air felt like velvet.

J.T. let out a low whistle. "Pretty nice."

"Nothing but the best." Roy led the way to a double door and opened it wide. "This is the stage."

With Fancy next to him, J.T. walked into the heart of the theater. At least fifty rows of upholstered seats fanned out from the stage, and a curtain the size of a barn hung from the ceiling. Five chandeliers formed the points of a star, and two balconies jutted from the wall. The last time J.T. had seen Roy, he'd been a two-bit gambler. How had he ended up among the Denver upper crust? And what did he want from Mary? He signaled Fancy Girl to sit, then surveyed the theater again. "This place is huge."

"It's the biggest opera house in town." Roy put his hands in his pockets. "Things are going well, but I've got a bit of a problem."

"Oh, yeah?"

"I manage this place for a group of investors." Roy's jaw twitched. J.T. had played cards with him and knew his mannerisms. The tic signaled a bluff. "Those men are expecting a solid return on what we've put into this place."

"Like sold-out shows?"

"Yes." His jaw twitched again. "There are two ways to make money in this business. Bawdy shows draw big crowds, but like I said, I've gone legitimate. Denver has money now. Big money, if you know what I mean."

"Yeah, I know." Denver was full of millionaires who'd made their fortunes from mining and the railroad. These folks wanted classy entertainment, not cheap burlesque.

Roy wiped his brow with a silk handkerchief. "My investors have high expectations, so I'm putting on an opera. That's where you come in."

"Me?" J.T. pretended to misunderstand. "I can't sing a lick."

Roy chuckled. "No, but Mary Larue can. Rumor has it you two were quite a pair in Abilene."

How did Roy know about Kansas? Was Mary already involved with him? J.T. fought to sound casual. "Who told you that?"

"I was in Abilene during the O'Day trail." Roy shook his head. "What a shame. It ruined her career. That woman sings like a nightingale."

J.T. hadn't pressed Mary for details about the scandal, but he didn't mind quizzing Roy. "What happened?"

"You don't know?"

"I left on business."

The theater manager propped his hips on the back of a seat. "The whole town was buzzing about the two of you. After you left, O'Day figured she was up for grabs. He followed her out of the theater and tried to—" Roy let his implication stand. "She shot him."

J.T. knew all that. "What happened after the trial?"

"She left town." Roy shook his head. "That's when the gossip got really bad, if you know what I mean."

"Yeah, I know."

Roy laughed. "You dodged a bullet, Quinn. Be thankful."

The remark struck J.T. as odd, but Roy was known for talking in circles. Even so, J.T. wondered…what bullet? Thinking about it, he decided Roy meant marriage. For once J.T. had to agree with him. He felt bad about leaving Mary, but he wasn't the marrying kind.

Roy's eyes glinted. "Mary and I have gotten to be friends. I asked her to star in my opera, but she turned me down. I'm hoping you'll help me change her mind."

J.T. looked around the theater with its chandeliers and velvet seats. The hall held the stuff of Mary's dreams, but she'd turned Roy down to keep the Abilene scandal a secret. He felt bad about the reason, but he liked her refusal. He looked Roy in the eye. "Mary said no. It's her choice. Not mine."

"I thought you might have some influence. From what I hear, you had her wrapped around your little finger."

No man wrapped Mary around his finger. She'd been good to him because she'd cared about him, and he'd taken advantage. The memory shamed him. "Mary's her own woman."

Roy's eyes gleamed like black stones. "So you don't have a claim on her?"

"What are you getting at?"

"If you're done with her, I'll take her for myself."

J.T. gripped Roy by the collar, squeezing until the man's jugular pressed against his knuckles. "You touch Mary and you're dead." Fancy stood silent at his feet, ready to attack if he gave the word.

Roy held up his hands. "Hold on, Quinn! I was thinking about Mary, what I could give her."

"No, you weren't."

"I swear it." Sweat beaded on Roy's brow. "I could make her famous. Rich, too. That's all. Okay?"

J.T. set Roy down, but he didn't believe a word the man said. Lust showed in his eyes. So did greed. J.T. forgot all about buying whiskey. He forgot about leaving Denver. He had to warn Mary about Roy. The man said he had investors, but J.T. sensed a lie. Had Roy's so-called investors given him money, or had he cheated them out of it? If he'd cheated them, what kind of payback did they want? J.T. saw a lot of self-proclaimed justice in his line of work. People paid him to administer it. Looking at Roy, he saw the familiar look of a man without shame. He matched the theater manager's stare. "Stay away from Mary Larue."

"Sure," he said too easily. "She's all yours."

She wasn't, but J.T. didn't mind Roy thinking along those lines. He paced out of the opera house with Fancy Girl at his heels and rode straight to Mary's café. There he slid out of the saddle and pounded on the door. When she didn't answer, he peered through the window and saw the table where he'd eaten pot roast. It was already re-laid with silverware and a clean plate. It looked as if he'd never been there, as if she'd erased him from her life. Maybe she had, but no way would he leave her a second time to deal alone with someone like Sam O'Day or Roy Desmond.

J.T. figured she'd left for the Sunday supper she'd mentioned at a place called Swan's Nest. Mary didn't want him around her friends, but he had to warn her about Roy. Annoyed, he looked at his reflection in a dark window. Mary was right about that bath. He'd clean up, then he'd track her down. He'd do his best not to embarrass her, but he couldn't leave until she promised to keep away from Roy Desmond.

Chapter Four

By the time Mary reached the iron gate marking Swan's Nest, she'd pushed J.T. out of her mind. At least that's what she told herself until the hinges creaked and she jumped. Walking up the manicured path, she looked at the stained-glass window above the covered porch. Pure and white, a swan glistened on a pond of turquoise glass. It didn't have a care in the world, but Mary did. She'd gone from nearly a soiled dove to a swan when she'd become a Christian, but she couldn't erase the past. If the scandal found her in Denver, gossip would start and men would hound her. Worst of all, she could lose Gertie's respect. Things could get ugly fast, and then where would she be? Silently she prayed that no one had seen J.T. leave.

As she climbed the porch steps, the door opened and she saw Adie. Her friend beckoned her inside. "We have to talk."

Mary worried about her sister. "Is it Gertie?"

"She's fine."

"Then what—"

"It's about you and that man I saw."

Mary's cheeks turned cherry-red. "You saw us?"

"I sure saw *him*." As Adie lifted the basket of bread, Mary wondered if she'd been impressed by J.T.'s good looks or his black duster and guns. She scolded herself for not being prepared for questions. She should have realized someone would look out the window. She wouldn't lie to Adie, but neither would she confide in her friend completely. Secrets were a burden, not a gift. "I knew him in Abilene." She tried to sound matter-of-fact. "It was a long time ago."

"You looked worried," Adie spoke in a hush. "That wasn't Sam O'Day's brother, was it?"

Mary had told Adie about the murder trial, but she'd never mentioned her relationship with J.T. "There's no connection."

"Then who was he?"

"No one special. He liked my singing."

Adie's brows rose. "The man I just saw—the one in black with guns on *both* hips—he tracked you down because he likes *music*?"

Mary felt chagrined. "Well, he liked me, too."

"Are you sure it wasn't more than *like*?"

"It wasn't." If he'd loved her, he would have stayed. He might even have married her.

Adie touched her arm. "Just so you're okay."

"I'm fine." She had no desire to have this conversation, not with a crowd in the garden, so she lifted the basket. "We better get supper ready."

"Sure."

Relieved that Adie didn't press, Mary carried the bread to the kitchen. Caroline, a brunette with a heart-shaped face, greeted her from the stove. Bessie, her sister and older by several years, was frying potatoes and teasing her sister about baking too many pies.

The routine of cooking helped Mary relax. As she

tied an apron, Adie told her Augustus and Gertie were in the garden with the other guests. Mary felt a familiar lump of worry. Her brother avoided people because of his stammering, and Gertie had taken to putting on airs. "I wish they'd make friends," she said as she sliced the bread.

Caroline stirred the gravy. "Gertie's with Bonnie Reynolds. Last I saw, they were looking at a *Godey's Lady's Book*."

Bonnie was a year older than Gertie and had a good head on her shoulders. Mary liked her. She didn't feel the same way about the other girl Gertie had met. Katrina Lowe was older by five years and had traveled alone from Chicago. She worked in a dress shop and dreamed of designing theater costumes. She'd been raised in a well-to-do family and had excellent manners, but she also had a defiant way about her.

Mary worried about Gertie because of her ambition. She worried about her brother because of his shyness. "What about Augustus?"

Caroline kept stirring the gravy. "I haven't seen him."

Bessie chimed in. "I sent him outside with a bowl of apples."

"Maybe he's with the other boys," Adie said hopefully.

Doubting it, Mary untied her apron. "I'd better check on him."

As she headed for the door, Caroline spoke over her shoulder. "You might wander by the rose garden."

"Why?"

She grinned. "I saw a new man at church this morning. He's single *and* handsome."

Ever since she'd caught Pearl Oliver's wedding bouquet, Mary's friends had been conspiring to find her a husband. She wished Caroline had caught the bouquet. *She* wanted a husband. Mary didn't. All men weren't as untrustworthy as J.T., but she'd never take that chance. She tried to sound lighthearted. "I don't care about a husband. I've got Gertie and Augustus."

"You *did* catch the flowers," Bessie reminded her.

"And I wish I hadn't!" she laughed. "You're all impossible!"

Closing the door behind her, Mary stepped into the yard. Her friends didn't realize it, but the teasing stirred up memories of J.T. and the miscarriage. She needed to shake off the upset, so she put on a smile as she approached the visitors in the garden. She saw a group of boys playing tag, but Augustus hadn't joined them. Disappointed, she approached Gertie and Bonnie, who were seated on a bench under a crab apple tree. "Have you seen Augustus?"

"He left," Gertie replied.

Worry shivered up Mary's spine. "Where did he go?"

"I don't know." Gertie indicated the street. "The last I saw him, he had some apples and was walking that way."

Mary saw horses hitched to the fence. Maybe Augustus had gone to give them treats. "Thanks, Gertie."

As Mary headed for the street, Bonnie called to her. "Miss Larue?"

"Yes?"

"I saw some boys with him about twenty minutes ago. One of them was Todd Roman. He's older, and he's not very nice."

"You saw him talking to Augustus?"

"Sort of." Bonnie knew the boy stammered. "I don't know why, but Augustus went with them."

"Where did they go?"

"I didn't see."

"Thank you, Bonnie." Mary hurried to the gate and worked the latch. Her brother would never leave without telling her, nor would he have willingly gone with a group of boys he didn't know. Determined to find him, she stepped out to the street and called his name.

With his hat pulled low, J.T. guided his horse down the road that led to Swan's Nest. After leaving Roy, he'd returned his pack horse to the livery and gotten directions to the mansion, bought fresh clothes and gone to a bath house for a good scrubbing. Bay rum wafted off him, and he'd never had a closer shave. If he looked respectable, maybe Mary would believe him about Roy.

"What do you think, girl?" he said to the dog trotting at his side. "Is Mary in as much trouble as I think?"

Fancy Girl looked at him with a doggy grin, a reaction that gave J.T. comfort. For a while he'd been worried the mutt was going to trade him for Mary.

"S-s-stop it!"

The cry came from behind a wall. High-pitched and quavering, it sent J.T. back to a filthy alley in New York and his brother beating him for losing four pennies. Judging by the tone of the voice and the way it cracked, it belonged to a boy nearing adolescence...a terrified boy who needed help.

"Come on, Fancy."

J.T. turned the buckskin and dug in his heels. The horse wheeled and broke into a run. At the end of the wall, he reined the animal to a halt and leaped out of the saddle. Fancy Girl arrived at his side, growling and ready to attack if he gave the word. At the sight of a boy up against a brick wall, his nose bloody and tears staining his cheeks, J.T. wanted to rip into the attackers himself. The boy being beaten had blond hair and no muscle on his bones. The ones doing the hitting were older, heavier and mean enough to laugh at the boy's whimpering. Two of them were holding him spread-eagle against the wall, while a third threw a punch hard enough to crack a rib.

"Hey!" J.T. shouted.

The boys doing the attacking glared at him, but they didn't release the blond kid. The kid tried to pull away, but he didn't have the strength.

"L-l-l-let me go," he whimpered. "P-p-p-lease. I—I—I—"

The stuttering made J.T.'s throat hurt. The boy doing the hitting laughed. "Wh-wh-what d-d-did you say, Au-au—"

"I heard him just fine," J.T. dragged the words into a growl. "He said to leave him alone."

The boys holding the kid's arms watched him nervously but didn't budge. The third one—the leader, J.T. surmised—held his ground. With his small, dark eyes and lank hair the color of coffee, he had the look of a buzzard determined to pick the boy's bones—or his pockets—clean. He stared at J.T., then lowered his chin. "This ain't your fight, mister."

"It is now."

The boy's eyes gleamed with a compulsion to fight. J.T. would be glad to oblige, but not in the way the boy expected. He paced toward the two holding the blond kid spread-eagle, letting them see his knotted fists and cold stare. In unison they stepped back and raised their hands in surrender. The boy who'd been beaten groaned and slid into a heap.

"Get outta here!" J.T. shouted at them.

The two sprinted for their lives. J.T. turned to the third one. He looked closer to manhood than the others, maybe sixteen or so, and he'd stood his ground. He spat, then glared at J.T. "Get lost, mister."

With his duster loose and his gun belt tight on his hips, J.T. walked straight at him.

The boy didn't budge.

J.T. kept coming. When he got within a foot, he saw sweat on the boy's brow. "You want to fight?" he said in a singsong tone.

The kid said nothing.

He had no intention of using his fists, but this boy-man didn't know that. J.T. smirked, tempting the kid to take the first punch. It would be unwise and they both knew it. J.T. was faster, stronger and meaner. He didn't twitch, didn't blink. He simply waited.

The boy swallowed once, then again. When he blinked, fear showed in his gaze. The boy knew J.T. outmatched him, just as *he'd* outmatched the blond kid.

"How does it feel?" J.T. said in an oily voice.

"Wh-what do you mean?"

"N-now who's afraid?"

"Look, mister—"

"Shut your mouth." He grabbed the kid by the collar. "I could have you on the ground in two seconds and you'd be dead in three." He shoved him back and out of reach. "You leave my friend alone."

The boy answered by glaring.

J.T. strode toward him as if he were going to kick him. Instead he kicked up a cloud of empty dust. "Come on," he shouted. "Take a swing at me."

Just as he expected, the boy scrambled to his feet and ran. He got twenty feet away and turned. "I don't know who you are, mister! But you'll be sorry." He jerked a finger at the boy slumped against the wall. "So will you, Au-au-gustus!

The stutter mocked the boy who'd been beaten, but it was J.T. who felt punched in the gut. Mary's brother was called Augustus. How many boys in Denver would go by that awful name? Looking at the kid again, he saw Mary's wheat-colored hair and distinct cheek bones. He watched to be sure the boy who'd done the bullying kept running, then he turned back to Augustus. The resemblance couldn't be denied. "Do you know Mary Larue?"

"Sh-she's my s-s—" The kid sealed his lips.

J.T. took the stammering for yes. "I knew her in Kansas."

Augustus wiped the blood from his nose with the sleeve of his white shirt, probably his Sunday best. He sniffed, then looked at J.T. again. "Th-th—" *Thank you.*

"No problem, kid." The stammering hurt in ways J.T. had never experienced. He held out his hand to shake. "I'm J. T. Quinn."

The boy leveraged to his feet, then fell to the ground unconscious. Crouching at his side, J.T. rolled him to his back. The boy had probably fainted from shock, but he couldn't be sure. A blow to the head could cause bleeding in his brain. A busted rib could puncture a lung. He shook the boy's shoulder. "Hey, kid."

Augustus didn't move. He didn't twitch. Nothing but a shallow breath came from his parted lips. Fancy Girl put her cold nose on his cheek. No response. With fear pooling in his gut, J.T. lifted the boy's eyelid. The pupil shrank against the light, a good sign. "Come on, Augustus. Talk to me."

Nothing.

J.T. didn't know where to find a doctor, but he knew where to find Mary. He lifted her brother onto his horse, climbed up behind him and galloped to Swan's Nest.

Chapter Five

Mary walked to the end of the street and called her brother's name for the fifth time. When he didn't answer, she went back to Swan's Nest and looked for him again in the garden. Without a sign of him, she paced back to the street. A rider and a cloud of dust caught her eye and she stopped. The man's black duster billowed behind him, and he'd pulled his hat low against the wind. A dog ran at his side.

"Fancy Girl," she murmured. J.T. had tracked her down, and he was approaching at a gallop. What could he possibly want? She couldn't stand the thought of speaking with him in front of her friends. As he rode closer, the blankness of his silhouette took on color and shape. He was clutching something against his body. Not *something,* she realized. *Someone*…a boy with blond hair and a bloody white shirt.

"Augustus!" Hoisting her skirts, she ran to them.

J.T. reined the horse to a halt at the iron gate. With the boy limp in his arms, he slid from the saddle. "He needs a doctor."

"I'll fetch Bessie." A trained nurse, the older woman had served in the War Between the States. If she couldn't help Augustus, Mary would send Gertie for Doc Nichols. She flung the gate wide. "Take him to the parlor."

She waited until J.T. passed with the dog at his heels, then she raced by him and opened the front door. "Bessie!" she called down the hall to the kitchen. "Come quick!"

Wearing a white apron and drying her hands, the nurse hurried down the hall. "What is it?"

"It's Augustus. He's hurt."

J.T.'s boots thudded on the polished wood floor. "Where do you want him?"

"On the divan," Bessie ordered. "Who are you?"

"A friend of Mary's."

The nurse nodded, an indication Adie had shared her curiosity with Bessie before Mary arrived. It hadn't been gossip, just friends caring about each other, but Mary still felt uncomfortable.

With the boy cradled in his arms, J.T. strode across the room where only moments ago Mary had stood with Adie. He lowered Augustus with a gentleness she remembered from Abilene, then he stepped back to make room for Bessie. As he tossed his hat on a chair, Fancy Girl walked to his side and sat.

Bessie pulled up a chair and started her examination. Terrified, Mary hovered over her shoulder. Bruises on Augustus's cheek promised a black eye, and he had a bloody nose and split lip. Her gaze dropped to his shirt. Red smears in the shape of knuckles testified to what had happened. Her brother had been beaten.

She whirled to J.T. "Who did this?"

"We'll talk later," he said in a low tone.

She wanted answers now, but mostly she wanted her brother to wake up. She turned back to his limp body and saw Bessie taking his pulse. The nurse lowered his wrist, but her expression remained detached. "Get the smelling salts," she ordered. "And water and clean towels."

"Will he be all right?" Mary asked.

"I don't know yet."

Her eyes darted to J.T. Adie and Caroline were outside, and she needed help. "Come with me."

He followed her down the hall, his steps heavy on the wood while hers clicked. She wanted to know why he'd been near Swan's Nest, but she didn't dare ask. Augustus had urgent needs, and she didn't want to breathe a word of the past in front of anyone. In the kitchen she opened a cabinet with medical supplies and found the smelling salts. Next she filled a bowl with hot water and fetched clean towels from a shelf. J.T. lifted the bowl and carried it down the hall. Mary followed with the towels and smelling salts.

Bessie uncorked the bottle of ammonia carbonate and held it under Augustus's nose. She waved it once, twice. His nostrils flared, then his eyes popped open. Groaning, he rolled to the side and vomited. Bessie held a bowl under his chin and caught the mess. Mary saw streaks of blood and gasped. Was he bleeding inside? Were his ribs cracked? Bessie needed to know, so Mary turned again to J.T. "You've got to tell us what happened."

He shook his head.

How dare he withhold information! She raised her voice. "I want to know who did this."

He put one finger to his lips. It had been an old signal between them, a warning to guard her mouth around people he didn't trust. Considering the circumstances, it infuriated her. "Talk to me."

"I'll explain later." He looked disgusted with her. "The boy fought hard. Give him his pride."

Mary saw his point. Embarrassed by her outburst, she dipped a towel in the hot water. While Bessie checked for broken bones, Mary wiped the blood from her brother's face and neck. When the nurse poked his ribs, he groaned.

"Do you think they're broken?" Mary asked.

"I'd say they're bruised."

Furious, Mary set the towel on the rim of the bowl and lifted a dry one. For her brother's sake, she had to stay calm. Augustus was twelve years old, but his stammering made him seem younger. In her heart, he'd always be the baby brother she'd rocked to sleep in Frog's Landing. Looking down, she smoothed his hair from his damp brow. "How are you feeling?"

"I—I hurt."

His lips quivered with the need to say more, but he sealed them in frustration. If she pressured him, the stammer would get worse. She had no choice but to wait for Augustus to calm down or for J.T. to enlighten her. With her lips sealed, she watched as her brother craned his head to look at the man in the corner. What she saw on his bruised face could only be described as awe. She didn't blame him a bit. It seemed that J.T. had come out of nowhere to help him. She didn't know who had attacked her brother, but Augustus's expression told her J.T. had stopped the beating. She owed the man her gratitude. She didn't want to owe him anything, but he'd been good to Augustus.

Bessie finished checking for broken bones then looked into Augustus's eyes. She held up three fingers. "How many do you see?"

The boy held up his hand to indicate three.

"Good," Bessie replied

Mary thought of the red-streaked vomit. "I'm worried." She indicated the bowl. "What about the blood?"

"It's from the nosebleed."

Fear drained from her muscles, leaving her limp. "So he's going to be all right?"

"I'd say so." Bessie looked at Augustus. "You took quite a beating, young man. I think you fainted from shock. Your ribs are badly bruised, and you're going to have a black eye. We'll get ice for that in a minute. I'm also going to bind up your ribs."

"Th-th-thank—" He bit his lip.

"You're welcome," Bessie replied. "You should stay in bed for a few days, then you can move around as much as you're able." The nurse patted his skinny shoulder, then left to fetch the wrapping for his ribs.

Mary took Bessie's place on the chair. "I'm so sorry this happened to you."

Her brother looked down at his feet. She'd never seen him look so defeated. Had he been bullied because of his speech? It seemed likely. He'd been teased about his stammering all his life, but people in Frog's Landing had known him. In Denver, a city populated by strangers, he'd become an outcast.

J.T. crossed the room. When he reached boy's side, he offered his hand. "Hello, Augustus. We met, but you might not remember. I'm J. T. Quinn."

"I—I remember."

Augustus took the man's hand and shook. Mary had never seen her brother do anything so grown up, or J.T. do anything so kind.

Augustus tried to sit up, but J.T. nudged him flat. "Don't torture those ribs. I've busted mine a couple of times. It hurts a lot."

The boy nodded vigorously.

J.T. pulled a side chair from the wall and positioned it next to hers at an angle where Augustus could see him. He dropped down on the seat and hunkered forward. "We gotta talk, kid."

Figuring J.T. didn't know about the stutter, Mary cringed for her brother. "He has trouble speaking."

"I know that."

"You don't understand," she continued. "He—"

"He's fine." J.T. kept his eyes on Augustus. "All things considered, you handled yourself well."

In Mary's experience, her brother turned into jelly when kids bullied him. She looked at J.T.; then wished she hadn't. They were side by side, so close she could smell the bay rum on his newly scraped jaw. When she'd seen him earlier, he'd been unshaven and reeking of whiskey and sweat. Now he looked presentable. More than presentable. Blinking, she recalled the man she'd met backstage in Abilene, the handsome stranger who'd pursued her with a look.

J.T. met her gaze and held it, signaling her with a mild glint to be quiet. She bristled, then realized he knew far more about the episode than she did. She didn't understand boys at all, and Augustus with his silence presented an even bigger challenge. She knew he needed a man in his life. She'd been asking God to send a grandfatherly sort of man from church, but the prayer had gone unanswered.

When she stayed silent, J.T. turned back to Augustus. His lips tipped into a smile. "There's nothing I like better than chasing off a bully. Thanks to you, I got to run off three of them."

When Augustus rolled his eyes, Mary realized J.T. was telling the story for her benefit.

"Yeah, they were big," he continued. "Mean, too. You're going to have a glory of a shiner."

Augustus made a face.

Instead of offering pity, J.T. laughed. "Welcome to the club, kid. You'll be fine in a few days, but I've been wondering... Has this happened before?"

Augustus looked down at his feet. "S-s-sort of."

Shivers ran down Mary's spine. "It has to stop. We'll go to the sheriff."

J.T. looked exasperated. "Don't waste your breath."

"We have to try," she insisted.

"Fine," he answered. "But there's not going to be a deputy in the alley next time Augustus gets waylaid. We need to solve this ourselves."

He'd said *we*. He didn't have that right. Her eyes snapped to his profile, but he was looking at her brother. She knew he could feel her gaze. He was dismissing her the way he'd walked out on her in Abilene. She wanted to tell him to leave Swan's Nest *now*, but the situation with Augustus complicated everything.

The boy kept his eyes on J.T. "They w-w-ant me to steal from..." he looked at Mary, pleading with her to understand.

She repeated for him. "They want you to steal from...?"

"Y-you!"

"Me?" Her brow wrinkled.

J.T. kept his focus on her brother. "Let me take a stab at this. Those guttersnipes know you're Mary's brother, right?"

"Yes," Augustus managed.

"They know she runs the café."

The boy nodded.

"They want you to take money out of that cash box she keeps just inside the kitchen."

Mary frowned at him. "How do *you* know about that box?"

"I saw it." His smirk reminded her that he'd ridden with the Carver gang before he'd become a hired gun. J.T. would never steal from her, but he knew how to do it. "You work hard, Mary. Put that box somewhere else."

"I will."

He turned back to her brother. "Do you know who these bullies are?"

In fits and starts, he described how they'd cornered him one day when he'd been running an errand. They'd threatened to beat him up unless he brought them five dollars. He refused, and for the past week he'd been afraid to leave the café. Today they'd followed him to Swan's Nest.

Mary's heart bled for him. "Sweetie, why didn't you tell me?"

He jerked his head to the side, but not before she saw hurt in his eyes. She smoothed his hair. "I'll fix it, Augustus. I promise. I'll talk to their parents. I'll—"

"Stay out of it," J.T. said quietly. "This is your brother's fight."

"But he's so young," she argued. "And he's small for his age. He can't protect himself."

"I say he can," J.T. replied. "He just needs to learn a few things."

She agreed, but he didn't need to learn them from an outlaw-turned-gunslinger. What could J.T. possibly teach the boy? How to beat someone into pudding? How to gamble and lie? How to charm a woman and break her heart? She didn't want him anywhere near her brother. Augustus was a gentle, tenderhearted boy who liked to whittle and play checkers. He didn't need J. T. Quinn in his life. He needed an older man who'd teach him to be respectful.

J.T. looked at her for five long seconds, then he sat back in the chair and studied the boy. "Those lessons are starting right now."

She gasped. "Now wait just a minute—"

J.T. stayed focused on Augustus. "We'll start with your name. From now on you go by Gus."

"Gus?" The boy copied him.

"That's right." J.T. shifted his boot to his knee. "No more of this 'Augustus' stuff. It's a terrible name. Half the time even *I* can't say it."

The boy giggled. Mary refused to crack a smile, though her lips quivered. J.T. had a point. For a boy who stuttered, *Augustus* was a torture.

J.T. shook his head with mock drama. "How'd you get such an awful handle anyhow?"

The boy shrugged, but Mary knew. "He was born in August. Our mother loved the summer."

The man grimaced. "It's a good thing he wasn't born in a girly month like June."

"Or-or J-Januar-r-r-y!"

The three of them laughed until Gus hugged his ribs. "It h-h-hurts!"

But Mary knew it felt good, too. She hadn't heard her brother laugh in a long time.

Breathing light, the boy turned to the man. "Th-thank you, Mr. Quinn."

"Call me J.T." He sounded gruff.

Mary wanted to forbid the friendship, but she couldn't deny the excitement in her brother's eyes. For the first time since he'd arrived in Denver, confused and hurting after their mother's passing, he'd connected with someone.

J.T. pushed to his feet. "Get some rest, Gus. I need a word with your sister."

"S-sure."

Mary needed a word with him, too. If he thought he could weasel his way into her life by helping her brother, he'd be wise to think again. She had to keep this man as far from her family and friends as she could. Since he'd found Gus close to Swan's Nest, it was evident he'd been coming to see her. She wanted to know why.

"I'll be back," she said to Augustus—Gus now.

As she stood, J.T. offered his hand as if the boy were a grown man. "I'm proud to know you, Gus."

Her brother gripped J.T.'s fingers and shook hard. "I—I—uh—M-me, t-too."

J.T. let go and put his hands on his hips, pulling back the duster enough to show his guns. "Every man takes a beating now and then. Sometimes he wins, sometimes he doesn't. Those jerks today were bigger than you—older, too. You didn't steal the money like they wanted, so stand tall."

Instead of the man who'd hurt her, Mary saw Gus's hero. Her heart softened, but she steeled herself against any fondness. She had to remember J.T. had hurt her. The other feelings he inspired—the good ones—made her weak in the knees.

Bessie came through the door with a tray holding strips of cloth. "I'll bind his ribs now. Why don't you two get some supper?"

J.T. met her gaze. "Thank you, ma'am. But I need a word with Mary, then I'll be on my way."

"Whatever you'd like," Bessie replied.

Mary didn't know what to make of J.T.'s consideration. She'd have to answer questions when he left, but he'd saved her from being a spectacle in the garden. He picked up his hat and together they headed to the doorway. As he passed Fancy Girl, the dog pushed to her feet and followed. When they reached the hall, he clasped Mary's arm and steered her to the door. "We need some privacy."

"Yes, we do."

With her heart pounding, she followed J.T. to the porch. As she expected, he paced to the railing and looked up and down the street. She saw the gunfighter who never let his guard down, but below the surface lived the boy who'd been brutalized by his own brothers. J.T. had hurt her, but life had hurt him first. It had hurt her, too. Not until she'd come to Swan's Nest had she found a measure of peace.

When she'd been brash, her friends had been kind.

When she'd been arrogant, they'd been patient.

She knew the value of that kind of love, and she tried to share it with others. She'd *thought* she'd been tested by Gertie and her haughty airs, but it seemed the Lord had sent someone else to try her patience... the man who'd hurt her more than anyone on earth. Even for Gus's sake, she couldn't risk J.T. staying in Denver. No matter the cost, she had to convince him to leave town tonight.

Chapter Six

J.T. didn't often get a chance to be kind. People paid for his meanness, and they got their money's worth. He counted saving Fancy Girl as his one act of goodness. Befriending Gus would be the second. He genuinely liked the boy, but he saw another benefit to helping the kid. He'd hurt Mary when he'd left her in Abilene. Teaching Gus to defend himself would help pay that debt.

If someone didn't teach the boy how to fight, he'd end up dead or mean. J.T. couldn't let that happen. He had to convince Mary to let him help her brother, so he dropped his hat on a low table and propped his hips on the railing, watching as she considered the porch swing but remained on her feet. If things had gone as he'd hoped when he'd arrived, he would have enjoyed sitting with her. He'd have put his arm around her and nudged her head down to his shoulder. They'd been a perfect fit in that way. Enjoying the memory, he indicated the swing. "Have a seat."

"No, thank you."

She gave him the coldest look he'd ever gotten, and that said a lot considering his occupation. If she wanted to fight, so be it. He'd always enjoyed sparring with her. Leaning back on the railing, he supported his weight with his hands. The duster fell open, but he didn't think much about it. Mary knew he wore his guns all the time.

He got down to business. "I'm gonna stay in town as long as your brother needs help."

"That's not necessary."

"I say it is." He spoke so softly he barely heard himself. "Gus needs me."

"He'll be fine."

"Like I was *fine* in New York?"

She knew about the scar on his shoulder and how his brothers had beaten him. He'd told her the stories when they'd been alone in the dark, when his heart had been softened by her touch and she couldn't see his embarrassment. She'd held him after more bad dreams than he cared to recall.

Her eyes said she remembered, too. But her voice came out hard. "I understand the situation. Augustus is—"

"You mean Gus."

"All right," she said too amiably. "*Gus.* You're right about his name. You're also right about him being able to defend himself. I'll ask a man from church to talk to him."

"Talking isn't enough."

"It has to be."

"It's not." J.T. decided to take a chance. "Fighting is like kissing. You can talk all you want, but eventually you've got to do it."

She opened her mouth to argue, but nothing came out. Judging by the sudden blush, she remembered their kisses as well as he did. He wanted to go farther down that road, but first he had to prove that Gus needed him. "Your brother's a good kid, but he's puny and he stutters."

"I know that."

"If he doesn't learn to fight, he's going be bullied his whole life. Is that what you want for him?"

"Of course not."

Tense, she dropped down on the bench and pushed off. The chains began a steady, irksome squeak. "I know Gus needs help. I just don't think you're the one to teach him."

"Sure I am." He knew as much about fighting as anyone. "What are you worried about?"

Instead of the boldness he expected, he saw a guardedness that didn't fit Mary at all. In Abilene she'd spoken her mind freely. Today she looked nervous, even scared. He wondered why, but she wouldn't tell him even if he asked. He'd have to puzzle it out for himself. He lowered his arms, hiding the guns beneath the duster. "Do you think I'll teach Gus my bad habits?"

"Yes," she said. "Exactly."

"You don't have to worry, Mary." She truly didn't. J.T. wanted Gus to be a good man, not a hired gun like himself.

She lifted her chin. "Considering how you left me, why should I trust you with my brother?"

"Because I've changed. I haven't had a drink in six months, and it's been so long since I gambled, I don't remember how." Not exactly. He remembered, but he needed to make a point. "There's more. Do you want to hear it?"

"No." She pushed to her feet. "It doesn't matter, because I don't want you in Gus's life. He's fragile. You'll hurt him."

He touched her arm. "Are we talking about Gus or you?"

"Gus!"

"I don't think so." She was close enough to kiss, and her lips were trembling. She wasn't just angry with him. He'd opened old wounds and they were bleeding. "I'm sorry, Mary. I'm sorry I left you, sorry I..." He shook his head. He'd used her like he used liquor, and he owed her amends. "You deserve to know something else. I haven't been with a woman since I quit drinking."

"J.T., don't—"

"Listen to me. Please." His voice dropped to a hush. "Just one more time, Fancy Girl. I need to say this to you."

A tremor passed from her arm to his hand. If she told him to leave, he'd do it. But he needed to make this confession. She closed her eyes and lowered her head. When she finally looked up, he saw a bleakness that troubled him, but she nodded yes. "All right. I'll listen."

He indicated the swing. She sat, but her face had lost its color. Leaning against the railing, he dragged his hand through his hair. "I don't know where to start, exactly. Back in Abilene—"

"I don't want to talk about Abilene." She sounded panicky and he wondered why. "Tell me about Fancy Girl. How did you find her?"

"It's more like she found me." He told Mary about the mess at the Dudley place and how he'd made an enemy of Griff Lassen. Feeling both silly and proud, he glanced at his dog, then looked at Mary with an apologetic smile. "Imagine that... J. T. Quinn going soft over a dog."

She said nothing, but her eyes said she could imagine it just fine.

The thought gave him hope. "That night I knew I had to find you. I went to Abilene, but no one knew where you'd gone."

Her cheeks flushed. "I left in a hurry."

"So I figured."

"It's been a long time."

The way she said it, he wondered if it would ever be long enough to forget the shame she'd endured. J.T. knew just how long—or short—a span of time could be. "It's been six months since I've tasted liquor." He paused, because his next words were personal for them both. "Getting drunk hurts the man doing it. Using a woman hurts *her*. I know how that feels, because I sold my gun as surely as a prostitute sells her body. You weren't that kind of woman to me, Mary. I cared about you, but I hurt you just the same. I'm sorry."

He wanted her forgiveness.

He needed it.

A bird twittered in a nearby tree. Laughter drifted from the crowd in the garden. Someone rang a dinner bell, startling them both. Silent as a lamb, he waited for her to speak. When she didn't say a word, he knew she'd send him away. She wouldn't let him near Gus, and neither would she believe him about Roy Desmond. If he told her about Roy now, he'd push her in the man's direction. Maybe he'd send her an unsigned letter from another town, or he could shove a note under her door. With everything lost and nothing else to give, he put on his hat, pulled it low and walked down the steps.

His boots thudded on the risers, then kicked up dust on the path. Fancy Girl followed him without being called, a consolation that eased the hurt but didn't erase it. As he lifted the latch on the gate, he heard the creak of the swing and Mary's footsteps hurrying down the path.

"Wait!" she called.

He turned and saw her running to him. She stopped a foot away, looking harried and confused and as beautiful as ever. Her eyes were shiny with tears, and her cheeks had turned from ashen to pink. Sunshine turned her hair into gold, while the brightness cast their shadows side by side.

"I forgive you," she said.

"You do?"

"Yes." She swallowed hard. "I forgave you a long time ago. It's just…" She bit her lip. "No one here knows everything that happened in Abilene. After you left, people called me a loose woman. The gossip was awful. If it started here, I'd—" she shook her head "—I'll deal with it if I have to, but I worry about Gus and Gertie."

He'd come to Denver to rescue her, not to make her life hard. "No one needs to know about our past. What's done is done."

"Yes."

Judging by her expression, she saw the flaw in his logic as plainly as he did. Their memories couldn't be erased. He knew how she felt in his arms. He'd laughed at her silly jokes and seen her wipe her nose when she had a cold. On the flipside of the coin, she knew him even better than he knew himself. He wanted that closeness again, though he knew he had to earn it. "I won't hurt you, Mary. I promise. I just want to help you."

"It doesn't matter what you promise." She clipped the words. "I don't trust you, J.T."

"I understand." And he did, perfectly. "I wouldn't

trust me either just yet. But someday you will. It's up to me to change your mind."

She looked peeved.

"We'll start with Gus." He let his eyes twinkle as if they were in Abilene again. Though he had been ready to leave earlier, he couldn't bear the thought of never seeing Mary again. "Does he like to fish? I could take him—"

She frowned. "We need some rules."

"Sure." He usually looked at rules as things to break. For Mary, he'd obey them. "What do you have in mind?"

She stood as straight as a measuring stick. "No cussing."

"Agreed." He wouldn't be accountable if he stubbed his toe, but he'd try. He didn't cuss much anyway.

"And spitting." She wrinkled her nose. "I abhor spitting."

He put his hand over his heart. "My dear Miss Larue, have you *ever* seen me spit in front of a lady?"

She blushed. "No, but I want to be clear."

Feeling bold again, he clasped her arms to hold her in place. The gesture had come from the past and she stiffened, but he didn't regret it. He wanted her to feel his sincerity. "You can trust me, Mary."

To seal the promise, he kissed her on the forehead. She could make all the rules she wanted, but he'd gotten what he'd wanted for six months. He had a chance to win her back. He also had a good reason to stay in Denver, where he could keep an eye on Roy Desmond. *And* he'd be able to prove himself by helping her brother.

He released his grip and stepped back. "I'll visit Gus tomorrow."

"That's too soon."

"Then Tuesday." He didn't want to wait. He'd get bored, and boredom led to thoughts of liquor and cards.

Mary shook her head. "The café is busy that day. I close early on Wednesday. You can come for supper."

He'd have three days to endure, but he nodded. "Wednesday it is."

He stepped through the gate with Fancy Girl trotting at his heels and a smile playing on his lips. He liked the idea of taking a boy fishing, so he decided to ride out of town to find a good spot. The buckskin wanted to run, and J.T. needed to burn off the rush in his blood. He and Mary had a long way to go, but today had been a good start.

Mary watched as J.T. pivoted the buckskin, tipped his hat and took off at a gallop with Fancy Girl barking for the fun of it. When he turned the corner, she let out the breath she'd been holding. The kiss had been a vow of sorts, an apology for the past and a promise to mind his manners, but it stirred memories of other kisses, the ones she'd given to him freely. This time J.T. had done the giving, and she didn't know what to think.

She stared down the empty street, wondering where he'd go and realizing he hadn't told her why he'd been near Swan's Nest. She wanted to know, but she wouldn't go looking for him now. She hated the thought of him in Denver, but even worse had been the guilt she'd felt when he'd walked away thinking she hadn't forgiven him. Whether she trusted him or not, she couldn't hold a grudge. His offer to help her brother had stunned her. She had no doubt he'd be good for Gus. In spite of the threat to her reputation, Mary couldn't deny her brother's need for a man in his life.

She needed to think about what she'd tell her friends,

so she headed back to the swing and sat. Adie would respect her reluctance to talk, but Caroline would ask a hundred questions. People who saw her with J.T. would speculate, and the gossip would begin even if Mary said or did nothing. She massaged her temples. *Please, Lord. I need help.*

"Mary?"

She looked up and saw Adie coming up the steps with two plates of food, one for Mary and the other presumably for J.T. Caroline stood behind her, looking both curious and kind. Mary managed a wry smile. "You found me."

"Is everything all right?" Caroline sat next to her on the swing.

"I think so."

Adie handed her a plate, set the other on the table and sat on the chair by the steps. "Where's Mr. Quinn?"

"He's gone."

"For good?" Caroline asked.

"No, he's staying in Denver." Mary trusted her friends, but secrets had a way of leaking into everyday conversation. She wouldn't dodge their questions, but neither would she tell the whole story. Uncovering the plate of chicken, she feigned a wry smile. "My past just caught up with me, I'm afraid."

Caroline, an uncontrollable matchmaker, had a sparkle in her eyes. "Bessie said he's good-looking."

"Oh, he is," Mary said casually. "A woman knows J.T.'s in a room, but he's not likely to stay there." She wanted to bite into the chicken to feign normalcy, but her stomach knotted. She set the plate on the table, looked at Adie and then Caroline. "I've never told anyone about J.T."

Caroline touched her arm. "Did you love him?"

Yes! With everything in me. I was carrying his child. I wanted to marry him. How foolish she'd been. How naive about men. Lowering her gaze, she whispered, "I thought I did."

Caroline gripped her hand. The brunette had lost a husband after the War Between the States. He'd been a man of color, and she'd kept the marriage a secret from everyone except Bessie. She'd understand if Mary blurted the truth about J.T., but Mary couldn't take the risk.

Adie offered a hankie. Mary took it and wiped her eyes. "I expected too much from him."

"No, you didn't," Adie said gently. "You wanted what most women want. A husband. A family of her own."

Mary thought of the baby she'd lost and the hole it had left in her life. Adie didn't know about the miscarriage, but she would have understood the pain of an empty womb. She and Josh had Stephen, their adopted son, but they'd been married a year and Adie hadn't conceived. Mary wished she could share her story. Instead she focused on the obvious. "J.T. hurt me terribly, but I should have known better than to fall in love with him."

Caroline squeezed her hand. "We can't choose whom we love."

"No," Mary agreed. "But I should have been careful. I should never have…" She shook her head. "I don't want to talk about it."

"It might help," Adie prodded.

The more Mary talked, the more her friends would want to know. But if she said nothing, they'd wonder. "He's a gunfighter," she finally said. "And he gambles, or he used to."

Caroline sat back in the swing, causing it to rock. "He came looking for you. You must matter to him."

"A little," she admitted. "But not enough."

Adie watched her. "You said he's staying."

"He is, but only to help Augustus." She grimaced. "He had the nerve to tell my brother to change his name to Gus."

"It's about time!" Adie declared.

Caroline laughed softly. "Didn't you say you were praying for a man to help your brother grow up?"

"Yes, but—"

Adie chuckled. It wasn't rude, just annoying. "I don't know why God does what He does, but I'd say He answered your prayer in a *very* interesting way."

"Me, too." Caroline smiled.

Interesting wasn't what Mary wanted her life to be. Dull and ordinary suited her fine. So did running the café and forgetting the past. She had no desire to dance on the edge of the truth, but that's what she'd be doing until J.T. left Denver.

As he neared the stream where he planned to take Gus, J.T. slowed his horse to a walk. Fancy Girl came up to him running and barking at the same time. He knew how the dog felt. Mary had forgiven him, and he wanted to shout to the world.

High and bright, clouds skittered past the sun in a way that sent shadows running from him. Raising his eyes to the sky, he wondered what a good woman like Mary saw in a mongrel like himself. Forgiving him had cost her something. She didn't want him in Denver, yet she'd honored his request. She'd always been generous to him, but today she'd been merciful.

How could she be so kind when he'd hurt her so

badly? J.T. thought of his brothers beating him in that New York alley. A few years ago he'd learned that all three of them had died from cholera. Old feelings had come back, and he'd cheerfully spat on their graves. He'd wounded Mary as surely as his brothers had hurt him, yet she'd forgiven him. He had to admire her kindness.

He looked down at his dog, panting and happy from the run. "You look thirsty, girl. Let's find water."

He nudged the buckskin onto the stream where he'd camped a couple of nights ago. He'd eaten his fill of trout and so had Fancy Girl. The spot was perfect for what he had in mind for Gus.

The way J.T. saw things, the boy needed confidence more than he needed to know how to fight. If Gus didn't know how to handle a gun, they'd do some target practice. He'd teach the boy how to throw a punch, but mostly he wanted Gus to carry himself with pride. Bullies were like wolves. They cut the weakest animal from the pack and took it down. If Gus stopped being a weakling, the bullies would find other prey.

As J.T. approached the stream, Fancy trotted on ahead of him. He followed more slowly, checking out the terrain for signs of drifters and men like himself. Near an old fire pit he saw a pile of cigarette butts. He didn't want Gus to consider tobacco a good habit, so he climbed down from his horse and ground them into the dirt. Looking around, he saw broken branches where horses had been tied. He checked out the hoofprints and decided the spot had been used by a lone man with two horses, someone much like himself. J.T. worried all the time about old enemies, but the rider had moved on. The spot would be fine for camping with Gus.

"Come on, Fancy," he called to his dog.

When she barked, he rested his hand on his gun. When she barked a second time, he worried she'd gotten stuck in the willows lining the stream. Approaching cautiously, he saw her in the middle of the water, looking down with her ears pricked and her tail wagging. When she pawed at something, a trout escaped her grasp with a small leap. J.T. laughed out loud. How many dogs knew how to fish? He called her again and she came bounding to him, her chest wet and her eyes full of triumph. He dropped down to his knees and hugged her hard. He hoped that someday Mary would come as willingly into his arms.

Chapter Seven

On Monday morning, Mary saw Roy Desmond walk into the café for breakfast. He took his usual table in the corner, greeted Gertie with a debonair smile and ordered ham and eggs. She wondered if he'd made his selection for Arline, the lead character in *The Bohemian Girl*. Gertie had been nagging her to accept the part, and she wouldn't let up until Roy picked someone else. There was a lull in the crowd, so Mary dried her hands on her apron and went to say hello.

Roy saw her coming and stood. "Good morning, Mary."

"Hello, Roy."

He indicated the chair. "Would you care to join me?"

"Yes, but just for a minute." She sat before he could hold her chair, making small talk so that she didn't look anxious. When the moment seemed right, she brought up the new opera. "How's the casting going?" she asked.

"Just fine," he said. "Except for Arline. I'm still hoping you'll change your mind."

The role of Arline, a gypsy princess, appealed to Mary in every way. The music soared, and she liked the girl's bravery. Until Roy filled the part, she'd yearn to take it. "I hope you find someone soon."

He held her gaze. "The role's yours. Just say the word."

"No. But thank you."

"At least look at the audition poster." He put his elbows on the table, laced his fingers and leaned slightly forward. "Do you recall the advertisement for your show in Abilene?"

"Of course." Chill bumps erupted on her arms. She had no desire to remember those days, especially not with Roy.

"The same artist did the drawing." He lowered his voice to a murmur. "Of course, that was before the trouble you had with O'Day."

Had Roy meant to assure her that he'd keep her secret, or was he using the old scandal to blackmail her into playing Arline? Mary didn't know, but she didn't take kindly to threats. The thought of the scandal erupting made her tremble, but threats made her fighting mad. Which had Roy intended? She needed to find out, so she looked him in the eye with deliberate poise. "I'm sure the poster is lovely."

"It is."

"I appreciate your interest," she said. "But my singing career is over.

He lowered his chin. "That's a tragedy."

"It's my choice." It had been, sort of. If she hadn't lost her reputation, she would have never left the stage. "I have a good life now. I'm happy."

He teased her with a smile. "You'd be even happier singing for me."

Laughing, she stood to leave. "No one will be happy if I don't get back to the stove. Have a good day, Roy."

"One more thing." He stopped her with a hand on her forearm. "I ran into a mutual friend of ours."

She thought of the dozens of people she'd met in her acting days. Even a distant acquaintance could stir up gossip about the scandal. Her stomach churned. "Who?"

"J. T. Quinn."

She felt relieved. J.T. wouldn't talk. "I saw him on Sunday."

"Just thought I'd mention it," Roy added.

Mary excused herself and headed to the kitchen. Whatever worries she had about Roy disappeared. Considering his knowledge of her past, warning her about J.T. had been considerate. If she could have taken the role of Arline, she would have done it. Instead she grabbed the three new orders Gertie had left on the counter and went back to the hot stove.

It was Tuesday, almost night, and J.T. had slept away the afternoon. He'd woken up five minutes ago, sweating and tense. He didn't like small places, and this room could have been a closet. He'd taken it because it was close to a side door. He wanted a private exit for himself, and Fancy needed to go out at night to do her business. Irritable, he looked out the tiny window high on the wall. Night was coming fast. He had to light a lamp or get out before the darkness grabbed him.

He couldn't stand the thought of another evening with nothing to do. Feeling twitchy, he stood and reached for his hat. "Come on, Fancy. Let's take a walk."

The dog ignored him in favor of the bone Mary had given her. She'd gnawed it clean and was still enjoy-

ing it. J.T. had no such comfort. What did a man do
with himself when he didn't drink, smoke or gamble?

He slept.

He ate.

He thought too much. "Come on, girl," he said with
more excitement than he felt.

Fancy looked over her shoulder. With her tail wagging and the bone between her paws, she tipped her
head at him, then went back to chewing with an intensity J.T. saw in himself.

"You've got a one-track mind," he said to her.

The dog's thoughts were on the bone. His were on
places he couldn't go and things he didn't do anymore.
He needed to get out of the tiny room, and he needed
air that didn't smell like the sauerkraut cooking in the
kitchen. The smell reminded him of the food he'd scav-
enged from garbage cans in New York when he was
a child. He hated cabbage and always would. He'd eat
somewhere else tonight.

"Okay, Fancy. You can stay." He put on his gun
belt and duster, scratched the dog's head and left the
boardinghouse.

The day had cooled with the setting sun, and he
welcomed the fresh air. He *didn't* welcome the temptation nipping at his heels. *Just one drink...just an
hour of faro.* He walked faster, but his thoughts kept
pace. He wished he'd taken Fancy Girl with him. Most
saloons didn't appreciate four-legged customers, and
having her at his side made it easy to walk by the
open doors.

One street led to another until he found himself on
the corner of Market and Colfax Avenue. A whisper
of conscience told him to stay on Colfax, but his feet
turned down Market. A block later he was surrounded

by saloons and dance halls. Pianos filled the air with tinny music, and girls in skimpy dresses were giving him easy smiles. He looked away, but his toe caught on a warped board and he stumbled. Off balance, he found himself staring through the open door of a saloon. Two men were standing at a counter. Between them a bottle glistened amber in the lamplight. One had an empty glass, the other a full one he was raising to his lips. J.T. could taste the poison, feel it running down his throat. A faro dealer sat at a table shuffling cards. The rasp called to him like the morning crow of a rooster.

As much as he missed the oblivion of liquor, he missed faro even more. Beating the odds gave him a thrill. So did winning big. If he made a bet or two, he could double the money in his saddlebag and secretly give it to Mary. If he gambled tonight, it would be for a good cause. He put his hand on the half door and pushed. As it moved, a fight broke out in the street. He turned and saw a cowboy sprawled on his back. Two men were going after him, shouting and kicking and cussing. The cowboy had blond hair, and in his drunken state he couldn't put words together.

J.T. came to his senses in a rush. As much as he liked faro, he cared more about helping Gus fight off bullies. Needing to get away from temptation, he walked away from the saloon at a rapid pace. In the distance he saw the Newcastle Theater and decided to walk by it. It wouldn't hurt to remind Roy that he had his eye on Mary.

When he reached the theater, the doors opened and the crowd began to go inside. Among the wealthy couples, he spotted Roy speaking to a girl in her late teens. Dressed in pink, she had cinnamon hair and a spar-

kle that reminded him of Mary. Next to her stood a
brunette wearing a crimson gown with gold trim. He
guessed her to be in her twenties and far more sophisticated than the girl. He was sure of it when Roy made
the younger girl blush with just a look.

J.T. didn't know the girl at all, but he wanted to drag
her home to her family. What was she doing at the
theater without a chaperone? The thought surprised
him, because he didn't like chaperones. The ones he'd
encountered had been nosy old women who'd gotten
in his way. Watching Roy with this girl changed his
mind about the custom. She was smiling too brightly,
encouraging him without knowing the nature of his
thoughts.

J.T. recognized that innocence. He'd been seventeen
when Zeke Carver recruited him to be the lookout on
a bank job. He'd done well and had ridden off with
them. That night he'd gotten drunk for the first time.
He didn't remember much, but it had been the start
of his worst years. With regret thick in his throat, he
watched the girl and her friend enter the theater. Roy
watched them with too much intensity. J.T. stared hard
at the man, willing him to look at him instead. It took a
long minute, but the man finally turned and their eyes
locked. Roy smiled.

J.T. didn't.

Smirking, Roy followed the last of his guests into
the theater and closed the door.

More distrustful of the man than ever, J.T. walked
past the building. Near the doors he saw a poster in a
glass case. Below a drawing of a gypsy woman, it read:

Coming Soon!
The Bohemian Girl

Auditions for the role of Arline
Saturday, August 3rd at 2 p.m.

Did the sign mean Roy had given up on Mary? J.T.
didn't think so. Knowing how much she loved to perform, he saw the poster as bait. Tomorrow after supper
she'd get an earful about Roy.

As he entered a quieter part of the city, he slowed
his pace. To his surprise, he ended up in front of the
saloon where he'd found Mary a few days ago. Instead
of the shuffle of cards, he heard fiddle music. And in
the place of whiskey, he smelled chili so hot it stung
his eyes. Mary used to tease that he didn't know good
food when he had it, because he'd burned off his taste
buds. Maybe he had. He'd burned a lot of things in his
life—bridges, women, even friends. His life was one
big pile of ash, but a man still had to eat.

With his stomach rumbling, he pushed through the
door. He glanced at the fiddler, an old man playing
"Buffalo Gals," and headed for the counter. The barkeep, a large fellow with red hair, greeted him with a
nod. "What can I get you, friend?"

"A bowl of chili."

The man indicated a stool. "Have a seat."

J.T. ambled to the far side of the counter and sat
where he could see the door. The place wasn't busy, and
he wondered why. Maybe the owner served cheap whiskey, or maybe he didn't serve whiskey at all. He looked
behind the bar. Instead of bottles, he saw a hodgepodge
of canned goods, tin plates and a row of glasses. A
mirror hung on the wall, reflecting both the room and
J.T. himself. Six months ago, he'd had deep crevices at
the corners of his mouth, and his eyes had been blood-

shot. The man staring at him now looked almost young, though J.T. felt as burdened as ever.

The barkeep put the chili in front of him. "That stuff's hot. Want something to put out the fire?"

Beer. "Just water."

"Got some sweet tea," he offered.

"Sure."

After the barkeep left, a man with the look of a gun-fighter walked into the saloon. He was wearing dark clothing and he was surveying the room as J.T. had done. J.T. glanced at the man's waist. When he didn't see a gun, he guessed him to be a preacher, maybe the one who'd spoken here on Sunday. He'd expected the man to be older, maybe with a paunch and gray hair. The fellow who pulled up a stool was his age or younger. If life had marked him, it didn't show.

The barkeep returned with the sweet tea and a plate of jalapeños. He put the items in front of J.T., then poured coffee for the reverend. J.T. ate his meal, half listening as the men discussed the progress on a church they were building. The sides were going up fast, and they needed to get the roof in place. J.T. didn't think much about the talk until the minister mentioned a familiar name.

"You know how Roy Desmond is," he said to the barkeep. "He's not happy about having a church next to his theater."

"What did he say?" the barkeep asked.

"He wants to buy the property." The minister sipped his coffee. "He offered us a lot of money, too."

"What's he want it for?"

"A hotel."

J.T. nearly choked on a chili bean. If Roy opened a hotel, it wouldn't be reputable.

The barkeep dried a glass on his apron. "Maybe we should sell to him and build somewhere else."

The minister shook his head. "I want to be in the heart of the city."

"So do I, but—"

"We aren't selling." Judging by the minister's tone, he'd build that church or die trying. J.T. understood the feeling, because he felt that way about protecting Mary. J.T. had no interest in churches, but he and the minister had a common enemy in Roy Desmond. They also had needs that fit like a handshake. The minister needed someone to put a roof on the church, and J.T. needed to keep an eye on Roy. Working on the roof would give him a bird's-eye view of the theater manager's activities.

J.T. set down his spoon and spoke to the minister. "I heard you say you needed a roofer."

"That I do."

"I can swing a hammer, and I don't mind heights." Small dark places were another matter. "I'd be interested in the job."

The man named a wage that struck J.T. as pitiful, but he didn't care about the salary. If he could keep an eye on Roy, he'd have the pay he wanted. Neither did he balk at the man's description of the steep roof and bell tower. The minister gave him a steady look. "That's the job. It's yours if you want it."

"I'll take it."

He walked up to J.T. and offered his hand. "I'm Reverend Joshua Blue. Call me Josh."

J.T had a hunch the man would recognize his name because of Mary. He gave him a look that dared him to judge, then held out his hand. "I'm J. T. Quinn."

"You're Mary's friend."

"The same."

The minister's grip tightened with a warning. *Hurt Mary, and you'll answer to me.* "She's a good woman."

"The best," J.T. replied, squeezing even harder. It was easy to imagine the reverend staring down the devil himself, a fact that gave J.T. comfort. He was glad Mary had people who cared about her.

The man's lips tipped upward. "I'm glad we understand each other, Mr. Quinn."

"Yes we do," he answered. "Call me J.T. When do I start?"

"How about tomorrow?"

"Sounds good."

"Do you know where the church is?" Josh asked.

"You said next to the Newcastle."

"That's right." The reverend indicated the barkeep. "This is Brick."

The man studied J.T.'s face as if he were matching it to a Wanted poster. "I know about you, Quinn. You rode with the Carver gang."

J.T. had no desire to recall those days. "It was a long time ago."

The man's eyes narrowed. "How long?"

"Years." *A lifetime.*

"So you weren't there for that silver heist in Leadville?" His tone accused J.T. of more than stealing silver, a sign he'd been harmed by the Carvers.

J.T. had heard such accusations before. He'd spent three years with the gang before he'd gone off on his own, but he still carried the stench of that time. Not only had the Carvers robbed banks and stagecoaches, they'd been cruel about it. J.T. would never forget Zeke tormenting a scrawny old man while his daughter watched. He'd left the gang soon after that job. If he was going to stay in Denver without getting shot, and without embarrassing Mary, he needed to stop Brick from digging up the past.

"I rode with the Carvers before Leadville," he admitted. "Those were ugly times and I want to forget them." He also wanted to forget his time with Griff Lassen. J.T. didn't think Lassen cared enough to hunt him down, but the man might take a shot if he had the chance.

The reverend spoke with a Boston accent. "We all have things we want to forget."

"Some of us can't." Brick spat the words.

J.T. knew the feeling. Confident, he looked the barkeep in the eye. "I don't want trouble, Brick." He used the man's given name to take control, but he said it kindly. "I owe Mary Larue a favor. I'm going to be in Denver until that debt is paid. That's all."

The man scowled. "You better mean it."

"Yes, sir. I do."

Brick heard the "sir" and relaxed. "All right, then."

Josh interrupted. "We'll leave the past buried. But to be clear, gentlemen, I don't mind a little trouble for a good cause."

J.T. wondered what cause the reverend would call "good." The ministers he'd known had all been gutless. The worst had been the old man in New York. He'd given J.T. and his brothers food when their mother died, but he'd done nothing when the landlord threw them into the street. Looking at Reverend Joshua Blue, J.T. had a hunch he'd fight for orphans, even ornery ones.

The minister said goodbye and left, leaving J.T. to finish his supper. He chewed a jalapeño, swallowed and then sat, rather amazed that he'd just taken an ordinary job. Not only had he become a working man, he'd be helping to build a church. J.T. finished his supper and headed back to the boardinghouse. He didn't know what tomorrow held, but he felt a pleasant mix of possibilities.

Chapter Eight

"**Y**ou're late!" Mary cried as Gertie came through the back door to the café.

It was nine o'clock, and her sister had promised to be home in time to help serve breakfast to the crowd that arrived on the morning train. In the dining area, travelers filled every seat, and a dozen were standing outside the door. Enid, the other waitress for the morning, had threatened to quit unless Mary hired more help. Older and fighting rheumatism, she didn't hesitate to complain. In the chaos, Mary had nearly set fire to a pound of bacon.

Gertie grabbed an apron hanging on the back wall. "I'm so sorry, Mary. I—uh—I… I overslept."

When Gus dragged out his words, Mary ignored it. When Gertie hesitated, she suspected her sister of twisting the truth. Turning from a bowl of half-scrambled eggs, she took in Gertie's appearance. She'd pulled her cinnamon-colored hair into a hasty coif, but Mary could see remnants of elaborate curls. She also smelled traces of expensive perfume, something a woman would wear on a special occasion.

Gertie had spent the night with Katrina supposedly

to help finish a dress. It seemed they'd had time to do other things. Exactly what, Mary didn't know. But whatever those things were, they'd put a determined gleam in Gertie's eyes.

Mary beat the eggs harder but she kept her voice casual. "What did you and Katrina do last night?"

"We…" Gertie fumbled with the apron strings. "It's a long story. Could we talk later?"

Mary would be taking lunch to the workers at the church, and J.T. was coming for supper. The thought made her nervous enough without having to contend with Gertie. Neither did she want to give her sister time to scheme. "Now is fine."

Gertie pulled the apron strings tight. "You're going to be mad, but I'm not sorry. Katrina and I went to the Newcastle last night."

"You *what*?" Mary stopped beating the eggs.

"I knew you'd be upset," Gertie said. "But I *had* to go! Oh, Mary. It was wonderful. The music—"

"I know about the music." She dumped the eggs in a pan. "Gertie, we've talked about this. You're too young. You promised—"

"I know, but—"

Enid steamed through the doorway with an armload of dirty dishes. "There you are!" she said to Gertie. "Get movin', girl! We've got a trainload of hungry people out there. They're going to eat *me* if we don't get 'em fed."

"I'm sorry, Enid." Gertie gave Mary a defiant look, then lifted a notepad and pencil from a standing desk. "I'll get busy right now."

Mary watched as her sister paced into the dining room. They had a plan, the best one Mary could imagine. But Gertie had no patience. Mary needed to know what had happened last night, but first she had to finish serving breakfast.

Sighing, she added a rasher of bacon to the frying pan. Gertie had as much sense as Mary had had at that age, but she also had an older sister who'd protect her. That meant keeping Gertie at home until she was eighteen, then sending her to study acting with Maude. They'd had this argument before. This morning they'd have it again.

When the breakfast crowd thinned, Mary told Enid to write Closed on the chalkboard in the window. As the last customer paid Gertie, Mary took off her apron and looked at Enid carrying an armload of dirty dishes. Gus usually helped with the washing, but Mary had kept him in bed. He'd improved and wanted to get up, but she figured he needed the rest.

"I hate to ask," she said to the waitress. "But could you finish the dishes? I'll pay you extra, or course." She needed to hire a dishwasher, but she was reluctant to pay another salary when she needed money for Gertie.

Enid looked peeved. "I'll do it for you, Mary. But that sister of yours—"

"I know."

"One waitress can't handle the train crowd." Enid rubbed her back. "Especially *this* waitress. If it happens again, you'll have to find *two* new waitresses, because I'll quit."

"I'll speak to Gertie," Mary promised.

"It's not just my achin' back." Enid made no effort to lower her voice. "I don't like getting the evil eye from people we've kept waitin'. Word'll get out that you're slow, and folks will go somewhere else."

"I understand."

"That sister of yours—"

"Yes, Enid." Mary had heard enough. She respected Enid for her age and her hard work, but she didn't need a lecture about Gertie. Nor did she want Enid listening when she spoke to her sister. "Why don't you go on home? I'll do the dishes myself." She'd do them after she'd made sandwiches for the men at the church.

"Don't mind if I do, miss."

The older woman took off her apron and waddled out of the restaurant. When the door clicked shut, Mary went into the dining room where Gertie was placing fresh napkins on a table she'd wiped clean. The girl usually balked at helping in the café, but today she'd done a good job.

"We need to talk," Mary said.

Gertie straightened the last napkin, then looked up with rebellion burning in her eyes. "I know I should have asked for permission to go to the show at the Newcastle, but you'd have said no."

"That's right."

"I don't understand." Gertie's voice trembled. "We live in a city with a dozen theaters. I could—"

"You're too young," Mary answered. "Maude Atkins can teach you things."

Gertie put her hands on her hips. "*I* know someone who can help me right now."

"Who?"

"You know him, too."

Mary hated it when her sister played coy. Instead of seeming sophisticated, she sounded like a brat. "And just who is this man?"

"Roy Desmond."

She should have guessed. Gertie usually waited on his table, and he enjoyed telling her stories about his acting days. Mary liked Roy and didn't mind the distraction, but she'd begun to worry about Gertie thinking too highly of the man. She needed to choose her words carefully to keep her sister from defending him. "I like Roy, too. But New York has far more opportunity."

"But I don't want to wait," Gertie protested. "I know what you've done for me, Mary. I love you for it, but I don't want to wait *a whole year!*"

"It's not forever…just until your birthday.'

"That's eleven months!"

Gertie marched into the kitchen with the empty napkin tray. Mary heard the clang of the wash basin, then the splash of water from the pump. Enamel plates slammed together as Gertie scraped the remnants into a slop bucket.

Mary didn't blame Gertie for being upset. Who wouldn't choose singing on stage over running a restaurant? If she could have taken the role of Arline for herself, she'd have done it. But performing in Denver was out of the question, both for herself and Gertie. She went into the kitchen where the girl was scrubbing dishes with a vengeance. Mary stepped to her side, lifted a towel and dried a plate. "I know how much you want to audition. Really, I do."

The dish in Gertie's hand sank to the bottom of the murky water. She wiped her teary eyes with her sleeve, then looked at Mary. "Have you seen the Newcastle on the inside?"

"No." She avoided the building.

Gertie stepped back from the basin. "It's beautiful. The chandeliers are like diamonds floating in the sky, and the seats are so velvety it's like sitting on a throne. I've never seen anything like it."

Neither had Mary. She'd performed in theaters

all over the West, but nothing could compare to the opera houses in Colorado. Denver didn't even wear the crowning jewel. Some of the best theaters were in Crescent City and Leadville, mining towns with gold and silver pouring out of the ground. Mary didn't want to think about the luxury right now, not with a dish towel in her calloused hands.

"I'm sure the theater's lovely," she replied

"It is." Gertie bit her lip. She'd had that habit since she was small, and Mary knew what it meant. Her sister wanted something she shouldn't have. The girl looked at her with owlish eyes. "I have a favor to ask."

"What is it?"

"Katrina and I spoke with Mr. Desmond last night. We talked about *Bohemian Girl*."

Mary imagined herself as Arline and swatted the picture away. "What did he say?"

"You know he wants you to play the lead." Gertie let the temptation tangle. "He'd give me a part, too."

Mary wiped the plate more vigorously. "Gertie, no."

"He just wants to *talk* to you."

"Didn't you hear me?" Mary stopped wiping the plate. "I said *no*."

"I don't understand!" Gertie flung the dishrag into the water. "I know you think I'm too young, but you'd be with me."

"Gertie—"

"Do you know what I think?" The girl turned from the basin. "I think you're afraid of something!"

"That's not it!"

"Then what is it?"

You don't know the risk. Mary sealed her lips, but she couldn't stop a sudden grimace.

Her sister's eyes widened. "You're hiding something, aren't you?"

Mary shook her head. "My concern is for *you*, Gertie. I know what theater life is like."

"What does *that* mean?"

Gertie had hit a nerve, and she knew it. She'd push until she got an answer. Mary had to confide in her sister or make a concession. The thought of Gertie at the Newcastle filled her with dread. The theater world was small. Someone was sure to know about Abilene. They might connect her and Gertie. They might think Gertie was like Mary had been. The men might try to take advantage. As long as Gertie's last name was Larue…but Gertie didn't *have* to be Gertrude Larue. She could take a stage name. She could be Gertrude Jones or Penelope Smith.

Mary didn't want Gertie acting at such a young age, but neither did she want her sister asking questions. Mary had to guard her secret, and that meant giving in—just a little—to Gertie. She'd have to convince the girl to use a stage name, but she suspected Gertie would agree to anything.

Even with her sister using a different name, Mary had to be cautious. She'd agree to meet with Roy to pacify Gertie, but she wanted to see the posters outside the Newcastle. If she recognized the names of the actors, she'd have to back out of the meeting no matter how hard Gertie pushed. Until now, Mary had avoided the theater as much as possible. Today, when she took the lunches to the church with Gus, she'd scan the posters for familiar names.

Pulling herself together, she faced Gertie. "I'm not saying I've changed my mind, but we can meet with Mr. Desmond."

Gertie bounced on her toes. "What are you doing this afternoon?"

"Why?"

"I told him we'd meet him at two o'clock."

"Gertie!" Mary didn't like being pushed. "I bring lunch to the church today. Besides that, Mr. Quinn's coming to supper." And Gus had been nagging her for two days to bake a chocolate cake.

"I know," Gertie said quickly. "I'll help with everything. I'll clean the apartment, whatever you need. Just name it."

Mary raised one brow. "How about being on time for work in the morning?"

"I will," she promised. "I'll do anything. Roy said—"

"Roy?" Mary's brows snapped together. Since when did her seventeen-year-old sister get to use the man's given name?

Gertie blushed. "He said all the actresses call him Roy, and that I should, too."

Mary didn't like Roy's familiarity at all. Not only had he overstepped a polite boundary, but he'd put a wedge between Gertie and herself. She felt manipulated and didn't like it. "What time will he be here?"

"He won't." She grinned. "We're going to the Newcastle. Isn't that grand?"

Mary's stomach flipped. While looking at the posters put her at risk, going inside the theater meant entering a lion's den. "He should come here."

"But it's all arranged."

Mary thought for a minute. If she protested going to the theater, Gertie would ask why. It was the middle of the week and the middle of the day. The theater was dark on Wednesday, so the chances were good the actors wouldn't be around. She also saw a chance to bargain with Gertie.

"All right," she agreed. "I'll meet you at two o'clock, but there's something I want from *you*."

"What is it?"

"Until I say so, you'll address Roy as Mr. Desmond. Do you understand?"

"No," she said with a saucy look. "But I'll do it."

Gertie would have agreed to anything at the moment. She needed to understand why Mary had to insist on proper conduct. "It's more than manners, Gertie. Roy is older. He's experienced in ways you're not."

The girl huffed. "I know that."

Mary held in a sigh. "I don't think you do."

"You worry too much."

When it came to Gertie, Mary didn't think she could worry enough. Wanting to keep peace between them, she faked a scowl. Gertie laughed and they hugged. With her eyes closed, Mary remembered being seventeen and unafraid. She'd never have that innocence again, but she could protect Gertie. Mary knew all about the temptations of theater life. If her sister was as ambitious as Mary had been, Gertie would do anything to win the best roles. She'd flirt with theater managers and flatter them. She'd taste her first drops of liquor, and she'd wear clothing that revealed too much. More than anything, Mary wanted to protect her sister from going down that empty road. She thought of J.T. coming for supper and shuddered. Looking at him, she'd remember the compromises she'd made, then she'd think of the baby and wonder.... Would the child have been a boy or a girl? Would it have had his eyes or hers?

J.T. had promised to mind his manners, but the sparks between them had always been obvious. If

Gertie sensed more than an old friendship, Mary would have some explaining to do. She hoped J.T. would be on his best behavior. As for herself, she'd play the role of "old friend" perfectly. It would be the performance of her life, but she had to protect her brother and sister from any threat of the old scandal, and that meant protecting her reputation.

Four hours later, Mary and Gus were walking down Sixteenth Street with a handcart full of sandwiches and cobbler for the workers at the church. The sun couldn't have been brighter, but she couldn't stop worrying about what she'd see on the posters. To build her confidence, she'd worn the blue suit and lace jabot she saved for special occasions. Her best hat was pinned at a fashionable angle, but she felt none of its boldness.

When she and Gus reached the front of the theater, she indicated a spot of shade. "Wait here," she said to him. "I'll be right back."

"S-sure."

She walked alone to a glass case displaying the poster for the current show. Five performers were listed, and she didn't recognize a single name. Allowing Gertie to take a small part, if Roy agreed and she used a stage name, seemed like a reasonable compromise. Turning, she spotted the poster for *The Bohemian Girl*. The drawing of Arline shot her back to the day she'd left Frog's Landing with a satchel full of dreams.

In St. Louis she'd met Maude and joined a traveling theater troupe. While touring the West by train, Mary had done everything from selling tickets to mending costumes. The shows ranged from burlesque to Shakespeare, and she'd loved every minute. Her big break had come on a humid night in Dodge City. When the star of the show fell ill, she'd filled in. In a theater full of cowhands and ruffians, she'd closed the show with "Home Sweet Home." There had been no applause, not even the squeak of a chair, and she'd thought she had flopped.

Then a man sniffed.

Someone murmured, "Amen."

A cowpoke jumped to his feet and broke into applause. The crowd rose in a wave, clapping and stamping their feet until she thought the walls would tumble to the ground.

She'd loved every minute of the applause.

She'd basked in the compliments.

When a reviewer called her a sensation, she'd read the newspaper story a hundred times. She'd gained a name for herself that day, and later she'd signed a contract to star at the Abilene Theater. There she'd met J.T., and there her career had ended.

Feeling melancholy, she walked back to Gus. The boy was standing by the cart, nervously looking up and down the street. After speaking with him, she was certain Todd Roman was among the boys who'd bullied him. Yesterday she'd visited Deputy Beau Morgan. He'd promised to keep an eye on the streets near the café, but as J.T. had predicted, the law couldn't do much else. She walked to Gus's side. "How are you doing?"

"G-good."

"I'm glad." She tousled his head. "You should lie down after lunch."

"I d-don't *want* to l-l-lie down."

Mary liked her brother's spunk, but she worried about his tone. He needed to be strong, but she didn't want to lose the sweet boy he'd always been. "Just don't overdo it," she said mildly.

Frowning, he shoved the handcart down the board-walk. As they passed the corner of the theater, he pointed to the top of the unfinished church. "L-l-look!"

Near the peak of the roof she saw a man darkened by shadow, balanced on scaffolding as he hammered wooden planks onto the rafters. He had long legs, broad shoulders and a fringe of brown hair sticking out from his hat. Lean and muscular, he looked as comfortable as a mountain lion lazing on a tree branch. When he reached into the nail bucket, the light shifted and she recognized J.T.

She forgot about the sandwiches in the cart.

She forgot about the jugs of tea and the cobbler she'd brought.

She forgot everything except the man on the scaffolding thirty feet above the ground, out of reach but in the middle of her life. How had someone like J.T. ended up on the roof of a church with a hammer in his hand? It made no sense…none at all. What had he told Josh? If he'd revealed any of the details from the past, she'd be furious.

She turned to Gus. "Set up the cart. I have to speak with Pastor Josh."

As her brother headed for a patch of shade, Mary went into the unfinished building. She spotted Josh standing at a table, making notes on the building plans with a stubby pencil. Sunlight filtered through the rafters, then turned to full shadow as she stepped under the planking. Aware of J.T. working above them, she walked quietly to Josh's side. He looked up and smiled. "Must be time for lunch."

"It is."

"Good, I'm starved."

She wanted to ask him about J.T., but the hammering would force her to shout. Frustrated, she glanced up. J.T. had moved a few steps, giving her a view of his legs through the rafters as he pounded nails in a steady rhythm. Before she could look away, he shifted his feet to the right where the boards had yet to be placed. His upper body came fully into her view. So did the gun belt hanging from his trim waist.

Look away, she told herself.

But she couldn't do it. Seeing J.T. on the roof of a church left her stunned and gaping. Instead of his usual dark clothing, he was dressed in dungarees and a blue shirt that matched the sky. He didn't look anything like the gunslinger who'd left her in Abilene, nor did he appear to have gambled all night while indulging in liquor. He looked rested, healthy and sober.

He glanced down, maybe to speak to Josh, and saw her startled expression. Even with the height of the church between them, she saw a twinkle in his eyes. He'd surprised her, and he'd enjoyed doing it. Mary didn't know what to make of the feelings rushing through her. J. T. Quinn was a handsome man, and she'd once loved him. Her feelings had died, but she couldn't deny the leap in her belly at the sight of him. She quickly squelched her feelings. This man had broken her trust. She didn't want to feel anything for him. Not anger. Not love. She wanted to feel…nothing.

She gave a courteous nod. "Good afternoon, Mr. Quinn."

"Good afternoon, Miss Larue."

When a smile lifted his lips, she felt as if they were meeting for the first time. *Nothing* suddenly turned into *everything.* She recalled seeing him for the first time in Abilene and how he'd looked at her. He had that same recklessness now, and it took her back to their first kiss…their first everything.

Josh shouted up to J.T. "Come on down. Mary makes the best cobbler in town."

"I know."

And he did. In Kansas they'd taken a buggy ride to nowhere. She'd brought a picnic lunch with cobbler made from the recipe she'd used this morning. They'd traded stories, and he'd kissed her for the first time. She hoped the memory didn't show in her eyes, but she saw it plainly in his. In the past they'd traded secrets with just a look, and she'd enjoyed the closeness. Today she feared it.

She lowered her eyes as if she hadn't seen him at all, but she heard every creak as he climbed down the scaffolding. When the noise stopped, she turned to Josh. "You hired J.T.?"

"I met him at Brick's last night." He told her about offering J.T. the job and how he'd been willing to work on the roof. "I was glad to hire him. Is there a problem?"

"No," she said. "I'm just surprised."

"Surprised I hired him, or surprised he said yes?"

"Both, I guess." She wanted to know what J.T. had said to Josh, but she couldn't pry without looking anxious. She settled for the obvious. "He's not exactly a churchgoer."

"Maybe that'll change."

"There's more." Did Josh realize he'd hired a gunfighter? J.T. had killed fourteen men. "He's done things, bad things. As far as I know, he's not sorry."

Josh considered her words, then spoke in a hush. "I don't know what's in J.T.'s heart, Mary. I *do* know God brought him here. I also know J.T. carries a gun, and I'm sure he's used it."

"He has."

He swatted a fly away from the drawings. "Every man has regrets. It's how he deals with them that matters. It seems to me J.T.'s in the right place."

"He is. It's just—" she shrugged. "I don't know."

"You're afraid," Josh said simply.

Mary's cheeks burned. No one knew exactly what had happened with J.T., but she wondered if Josh and Adie suspected. Their adopted son had been conceived out of wedlock by Josh's sister. Josh had judged the woman harshly, and he'd paid a terrible price for his lack of compassion. He and Adie wouldn't hold Mary's mistake against her, but other people would. She didn't know what to say to Josh, so she said nothing.

He lowered his voice. "Stay strong, Mary. If you're confused about J.T., talk to Adie."

"I'll think about it." But she already knew her decision. If she told her secret to anyone at all, she'd lose control over it.

Josh indicated the doorway. "Let's get lunch before it's all gone."

They left the building with Mary leading the way. The workers had helped themselves to the meal, so she searched for J.T. and Gus. She found them leaning against the wall of the opera house, holding sandwiches and grinning as Fancy Girl did tricks at J.T.'s command. She'd never seen her brother so happy, and she couldn't help but be touched when J.T. gave the dog half his sandwich. The man she'd known in Abilene wouldn't even pet a dog. She could have been indifferent to the old J.T., but the new one inspired other feelings altogether. If she'd met him today for the first time, she would have welcomed him to Denver. She'd have smiled and even flirted a little.

No way would she go down that road. She'd forgiven J.T., but she'd never forget the pain of his betrayal. She knew how Josh had met him, but she still didn't know why J.T. had taken the job. Was he trying to impress her? Did he need the money? She didn't know, but the facts couldn't be denied. Instead of gambling and drinking, he was sharing his lunch with a hungry dog.

The changes in J.T. counted as the second biggest surprise of her life, the first being the changes she'd experienced for herself. Who'd have thought an actress with a scandalous past would sing in church and love it? If she could change, so could J.T. If he'd changed as much as it seemed, where did that leave the rebellious leap of her heart? Mary didn't know, and she didn't want to find out. J.T. had ruined her life once and he could do it again.

She couldn't love this man because he'd betrayed her, and she couldn't hate him because of her faith. That left being his friend. She fetched another sandwich from the cart and headed in his direction. The gesture didn't mean a thing. Neither did the blush on her cheeks or the eager thrum of her pulse.

Chapter Nine

J.T. saw Mary and nudged Gus. "Looks like your sister found us."

"Yeah."

The boy didn't sound happy about it, but J.T. was. He'd been looking forward to seeing her from the moment Josh mentioned she'd be bringing lunch. Watching her now, he saw a sparkle in her pretty brown eyes and the tilt of a smile. He'd also seen her hesitate at the handcart. He'd have to watch carefully to read her feelings, but he didn't mind. She looked beautiful in a blue suit that nipped in at her waist, and her golden hair was up in fancy twist.

He wanted to think she'd dressed up for him, but of course she hadn't. Earlier he'd surprised her and he'd enjoyed doing it. Looking at her now, he wondered why she'd dressed so formally to serve lunch to a work crew. He considered quizzing Gus, but the boy couldn't answer fast. By the time he managed the words, Mary would be at their side.

She approached with a smile and a paper-wrapped sandwich. "If I'd known Fancy was going to be here,

I'd have brought her a bone." She offered J.T. the sandwich. "This is for you."

"I had one."

"You gave the entire thing to Fancy," she said, scolding him but not really.

"Thanks," he said as he took the food. "I'm half-starved."

Mary shifted her weight. "I have to admit I'm surprised to see you. How did you end up working on the roof?"

He'd just taken a bite. Chewing, he decided to tell her the bald truth. "I'm so bored I can't stand myself. Pounding nails gives me something to do."

"Is that all?" She looked baffled.

"More or less." He decided against mentioning Roy. Explaining his concern required a lengthy conversation, and he didn't want to talk in front of Gus. He planned to speak to Mary tonight.

She looked at him thoughtfully. "Are you enjoying the work?"

"Yeah, I am." He indicated the peak of the roof. "I like being high up."

Not only could he keep an eye on Roy, also he enjoyed being away from danger and temptation. Watching the clouds wander across the sky, changing shape and moving at the whim of an invisible wind, he felt a yearning to put down his guns. What would it be like to live without that burden? J.T. didn't know, and he'd never find out. A man had to protect himself, because no one else would. He also intended to protect Mary and her family.

Standing in the sun, Mary reached into her drawstring bag, took out a hankie and dabbed at her forehead. "It's warm today, isn't it?"

J.T. agreed, but it wasn't the heat that had his attention. He recognized Mary's bag from Abilene. She'd used it for special occasions—like auditions. His gaze went to the fluttering hankie, then to the white lace gloves covering her hands, and the delicate ribbons tied at her wrists. The pieces of the puzzle slammed together. They were standing in the shadow of Roy's opera house, and he'd seen her studying the poster for *Bohemian Girl.* Did Mary have plans to meet with the theater manager? It seemed likely.

Gus smiled at his sister. "F-F-Fancy does tricks. W-w-ant to see?"

"Sure," she answered.

J.T. wanted to question her, but not with Gus there. Showing off Fancy Girl would give the boy what he needed, then J.T. could speak with Mary. "We'll start off easy." He focused on Fancy. "Okay, girl. Sit."

The dog sat.

"Roll over."

The dog rolled in a full circle and popped to her feet. Gus laughed and so did Mary. J.T. had never heard such a lovely sound. He wanted to hear it again, and Fancy had plenty of tricks. With nothing to do at night, he'd spent hours teaching her, both to amuse himself and to keep her safe. If someone came after him, he wanted the dog to take orders. Not only did she respond to his voice, she followed hand commands.

"Sh-she's smart," Gus said.

"There's more." At J.T.'s command, Fancy sat up, shook hands, played dead and woofed. Last, he dropped to a crouch and said, "Kiss goodnight." The dog enthusiastically licked his face.

Both Mary and Gus applauded, but Mary spoke

for them both. "She's wonderful, J.T. You're a good teacher."

He'd never thought of himself in that light. "She's a smart dog."

Gus sighed. "I—I—I wish I c-could m-make her s-s-sit."

"You can," J.T. replied. "Watch this."

He pointed to the ground and Fancy sat. He flattened his hand and made a cutting sign. She dropped down and played dead. Last, he gave the dog a thumbs-up. She jumped to her feet, watching diligently for his next command. Gus's eyes were as wide as saucers.

"You try," J.T. said. "Start with pointing to the ground."

When Gus pointed, Fancy hesitated, but only slightly, then she sat. Gus's face lit up. He still had a whopper of a black eye, but his grin was even bigger. For the next few minutes, J.T. taught Gus the hand signals, with Fancy Girl obeying perfectly. J.T. felt proud, and the boy and dog looked even happier.

He clapped the kid on the back. "You did a good job."

"It—it worked!"

"Sure it did," J.T. replied. "You gave Fancy the right signs, and you did it like you meant it."

Gus beamed at his sister. "I—I want a dog!"

"We'll see," she said, smiling.

For the first time in years, J.T. felt genuinely good. The feeling was on the inside, not because of whiskey or winning at cards, and he didn't want it to leave. How did a man hold on to such goodness? He didn't know, but he wanted to try.

He broke off a bite of the second sandwich for Fancy

Girl. As she licked his fingers, Mary gave him a stern look. "I brought that for you."

"I figured I'd fill up on cobbler."

Her cheeks turned pink, a sign she remembered that picnic in Kansas as plainly as he did. Their eyes stayed locked—his daring her to remember, and hers filled with something akin to fear—until she turned to Gus. "Would you get cobbler for J.T.?"

"Sure."

As the boy left, Mary turned to him. "Thank you for helping Gus."

He considered mentioning the camping trip he had in mind, but he wanted to speak to her out of Gus's earshot. "I haven't done much."

"You've done more than you know." She patted his dog. "So has Fancy Girl. She's amazing."

They chatted about the dog, an easy subject for them both, until Gus came back with two bowls of cobbler. He gave one to J.T. and offered the second to Mary. She refused it, so he happily claimed it for himself. She touched the boy's shoulder. "Collect all the dishes when you're done eating, then wait with Pastor Josh until I get back, okay?"

Gus's brow wrinkled. "I—I—I don't want to wait with P-P-Pastor Josh. I—I'm not a baby!"

"I know, sweetie."

J.T. would have given his left thumb to hear Mary call him sweetie, but he wasn't a twelve-year-old boy with something to prove. He punched Gus playfully on the shoulder. "Hey, kid. How about you get the dishes and then work with me?"

"Really?"

"Sure." He indicated the scaffolding. "Do you mind heights?"

Gus's eyes lit up, but Mary frowned. "It's too dangerous."

J.T. understood her concern, but Gus needed to do something manly. Climbing high would give him a reason to brag. "I'll keep an eye out for him. It's high, but the scaffolding's wide."

Gus looked at his sister with a silent plea. She must have felt the urgency, because she smiled at him. "Are you sure you want to climb that high?"

"Y-yes."

"All right. But do what J.T. says."

"I will."

He had to speak with Mary alone about Roy, so he gave Gus a job. "See that bucket over there?" He pointed to the bottom of the scaffolding. "It's for nails and it's empty. Ask Josh where you can fill it."

As Gus ran off, J.T. turned to Mary. "You look pretty," he said, meaning it and hoping to disarm her at the same time.

"Thank you."

"Are you going somewhere?" He tried to sound matter-of-fact, but worry sharpened his tone.

She arched her brows. "I don't think that's any of your concern."

Oh, yes, it was! She'd dressed up for something— or someone. He pushed back a surge of jealousy, but it leaked into his voice. "It sounds like you're visiting a secret admirer."

She glared at him.

Eye to eye, they each waited for the other to crack. J.T. vowed it wouldn't be him, but looking at Mary and standing close, seeing the curve of her lips and the tilt of her chin, he felt the hammer of the past. This woman made him feel tender inside. He had to work to sound tough. "You're not going to tell me, are you?"

"No, I'm not." She took the longest breath he'd ever seen her take, then she lifted her chin. "My life is *none* of your business."

"It used to be," he said quietly.

The look she gave him was scathing. No matter what she wanted to believe, or what she wanted *him* to believe, J.T. knew she wasn't indifferent to him. She cared far more than she wanted to admit to herself or to him.

"Mary!" Someone shouted from the street.

He turned and saw the girl with cinnamon hair. Flushed and nervous, she was wearing a fancy getup and walking in their direction.

Mary sighed. "That's my sister."

The girl called out again. "Hurry! We're going to be late."

Not bothering to hide his upset, J.T. squared off with Mary. "Are you meeting with Roy Desmond?"

"What if I am?"

He wished he'd told her about Roy sooner. "You have to trust me. He's not who you think he is."

Before she could react, Gertie reached her side. "It's two o'clock. We have to go *now*."

Mary turned to her sister. "Mr. Desmond won't mind if we're a bit late."

"*I* mind!" Gertie declared. "I'm so nervous I can hardly think!"

"Take a deep breath," Mary instructed. "It'll calm you."

J.T. needed calming, too. But breathing wouldn't do the trick. Nothing short of throwing Mary over his shoulder and carrying her away from Roy and his opera house would take away the burning in his gut. He gave her a hard look. "I know Roy. He's dangerous."

She arched a brow. "I don't believe you."

He deserved the jab, but he cared about her and Roy didn't. "Mary, you have to listen—"

"This is none of your business," she insisted.

Gertie studied him, pulling back as if he were a toad. "Who are you?"

He looked her dead in the eye. "I'm J. T. Quinn, and you're too young to be going to the theater without your sister."

"I beg your pardon!"

"I saw you last night." He didn't want Mary siding with Gertie, so he calmed his voice. "Mr. Desmond spoke to you for quite some time."

"Yes, but—"

"Don't trust him, Miss Larue." He was old enough to call her Gertie, but he wanted her to feel the weight of being a grown woman. "I know Mr. Desmond better than you do."

"You have no business—"

Mary broke in. "Gertie, don't be rude. I'll handle Mr. Quinn."

The girl didn't argue, but she shot him a look of pure contempt. J.T. turned to Mary. "What's this meeting about?"

She hesitated. "He wants me to star in *Bohemian Girl*. There's a part for Gertie, too."

J.T. smelled twice the trouble he'd sensed earlier. Roy had upped the ante by involving Mary's sister. Unless J.T. found a way to influence Mary, he'd lose her to Roy and the theater. He needed more time. "Have that meeting, Mary. But I want you to promise me something."

"What?"

"Don't give him an answer today. We were friends once. Give me a chance to prove I'm right."

"I don't owe you anything."

"I know," he said quietly. "I'm asking a favor." J.T. rarely asked for anything. He usually took what he wanted, but Mary's trust had to be given freely.

"All right," she finally said. "We'll talk tonight."

"That's all I'm asking."

She said goodbye to Gus, took Gertie by the arm and headed for the theater. No harm would come to them today. The danger lay in Roy convincing Mary to trust him and then taking advantage. J.T. worried about her, but he worried about Gertie even more. The girl had all the sense of a child playing dress-up. Tonight he'd speak his mind, and he wouldn't give up until Mary cut all ties with Desmond.

As Mary and Gertie approached the theater, Roy opened the door with a sweep of his arm. "Good afternoon, ladies! Welcome to the Newcastle."

"Hello, Roy," Mary replied.

Gertie nodded a bit too graciously. "Good afternoon, Mr. Desmond."

Mary stepped into the foyer with seeming calm, but the quarrel with J.T. had unnerved her. She'd seen honest worry in his eyes, but she also knew J.T. to be overly cautious. She felt certain he was overreacting to Roy's interest in Gertie, but she'd agreed to his request because she'd once respected his judgment. For all his faults, J.T. was a good judge of character. Today she'd gauge Roy's conduct for herself. Tonight she'd weigh the risks and make a decision.

Roy gave her a warm smile. "This is your first time in the Newcastle, isn't it, Mary?"

"Yes."

"Let's start with a tour." He raised his arm to indicate the foyer. "As you can see, my investors have spared no expense."

Mary had been in dozens of theaters, but none of them had been draped in velvet and gilded with gold. The burgundy carpet squished beneath her best shoes, and she smelled traces of the expensive perfume worn by the women at last night's show. On the sides of the foyer, staircases swept up to the balcony that held a mix of plush boxes and less expensive stalls.

She felt Roy's eyes on her face and instantly schooled her features. "It's lovely."

"I'm glad you like it." He looked at Gertie and made a hook with his elbow. "Shall we show your sister the stage, Miss Larue?"

"Oh, yes!" Blushing, Gertie took his arm.

Mary didn't like her sister's reaction, but she couldn't find fault with Roy's manners. Mildly uncomfortable, she followed them through a set of doors that led into the main part the theater. A few steps behind them, she stifled the shock of seeing hundreds of seats waiting to be filled. She turned to the balcony and saw even more seating. She'd sung in front of large crowds but never in a building of this size. Overhead, chandeliers reflected sunlight pouring in through windows framed by open drapes. The high walls were covered in the newest flocked wallpaper, and the window frames were painted gold. The stage boasted even more grandeur. A red velvet curtain hung in secretive folds. Behind it lay music, a story. She'd always loved the moment just before the curtain opened, when she could feel herself sliding into being someone else, into a world of make-believe and adventure.

"Mary?" Roy's voice broke into her thoughts.

"Yes?" She couldn't take her eyes off the curtain.

"You seem impressed."

"I am," she admitted. From the time she could talk, she'd imagined herself in faraway places. Performing had brought those dreams to life a few hours at a time. Looking at the stage, she felt that call with a yearning she'd forgotten.

Gertie touched her arm. "It's even more amazing with an audience."

"I'm sure it is," she murmured.

"There's more," Roy said. "Follow me."

As he led them down the center aisle, she felt as if she were in a trance, caught between a brilliant dream and a drab reality. She knew where Roy was taking them. In a moment they'd walk past the stage. He'd lead them through a hidden door and they'd be in a hallway that led to the place of dreams and make-believe. Just as she expected, Roy opened a concealed door and they emerged into a backstage area full of scenery. Mary smelled paint for the backdrops, sawdust, powder and face paint.

Gertie scampered to a rack holding costumes in an array of colors. "They're beautiful!"

"They're for *Bohemian Girl*." Roy lifted one and offered it to her. "This is for a peasant girl. I believe it's your size, Miss Larue."

Holding the dress to her shoulders, Gertie spun to face a full-length mirror. "Mary, look!"

She blinked and saw herself ten years ago. "You look beautiful."

Roy startled her with a polite hand on her back. "This way," he said, turning her to the stage.

Mary let him guide her across the wooden platform. The curtain blocked her view of the seats, but she could imagine the music and the applause.

"Stay here," he instructed. "And look straight ahead."

He left her alone center-front on the stage. She heard the glide of ropes and the whoosh of velvet as the curtains parted. The air stirred, and she saw seats stretching into the darkness under the balcony, and then up in the balcony almost to the ceiling. She'd never seen any place so glorious.

Roy crossed the stage and stood slightly behind her. "Is it as wonderful as you imagined?"

She couldn't lie. "Yes."

He motioned to Gertie. "Miss Larue, come and join your sister."

Gertie set down the gown and came to stand next to Mary. Excitement rippled off the girl's skin as she took in the velvet seats and the beams of light from the windows.

Roy stayed behind them. "The role of Aline is yours, Mary. There's a role for Gertie, too." He sounded sublime, even generous.

Her sister clutched her arm. "Say yes. It's the answer to everything."

She yearned to accept Roy's offer, but the risk of reigniting the scandal was too great, especially with J.T. in Denver. In order to provide a good life for Gertie and Gus, she had to protect her reputation.

Roy spoke over her shoulder. "Shall we discuss the terms of the contract in my office?"

"Not today." She'd made a promise to J.T., and she'd

keep her word. "I'd like an evening to think things over."

Gertie huffed. "But Mary—"

"Shhh." She hated treating her sister like a child, but she was acting like one.

Roy smiled at Gertie like a father. "Your sister needs time, Miss Larue. It's perfectly understandable."

Gertie calmed down instantly. "Yes. Of course."

Mary appreciated Roy's intervention. "Thank you. You've been very understanding."

He smiled. "Whatever you want, Mary. It's yours."

What Mary wanted, Roy couldn't give. She wanted to be free of secrets and scandals. She wanted her brother to speak normally and for Gertie to be patient.

Her sister turned to Roy. "Excuse me, Mr. Desmond. But what time should we come tomorrow?"

"I'll come to the café. We can finalize the arrangements when you're done serving breakfast."

Mary appreciated his thoughtfulness. "I'll give you my answer then."

After exchanging goodbyes, the women left the theater. As they passed the church, Mary looked up at the scaffolding. J.T. must have been looking for her, because he stopped hammering as soon as she came into sight. He tipped his hat, then said something to Gus. Her brother set down the nail bucket and waved, smilingly so wide that his teeth glistened in the sun.

She'd never seen Gus so pleased. Neither had she seen J.T. so determined. Tonight they'd talk about Roy's offer, but Mary knew what she had to do. She couldn't say yes for herself, but she could make Gertie's dream come true. She acknowledged Gus and J.T. with a wave, then turned to her sister. "We might be able to work something out with Mr. Desmond."

Gertie gasped. "Do you mean it?"

"I do, but Roy might not agree with what I have in mind." She prayed silently that Gertie wouldn't press her for details. "I'm done performing. With the café and Gus, I have no desire to go back to the stage. But you're younger. You're just getting started."

Gertie nodded furiously. "That's right."

"*If* Mr. Desmond agrees to give you a role without me as Arline, I think you should choose a stage name. Gertrude is old-fashioned."

The girl grabbed Mary had hugged her. "I *hate* 'Gertrude'! And 'Gertie' is for a little girl. I want to be Emmeline. That's my middle name… Emmeline Larue!"

Mary shook her head. "Larue confuses people. They'll think you speak French. How about Emmeline Duncan?" Duncan was their mother's maiden name.

Gertie thought for a minute. "I like it, and it would honor mama."

Mary liked it, too. "Then it's settled. I'll speak with Roy tomorrow. If he agrees, you can take a *small* part."

Gertie hugged her hard. "Thank you, Mary. You're the *best*!"

With her secret buried, though not as deeply as she would have liked, Mary walked arm in arm with Gertie to the apartment, where she'd bake a chocolate cake. She'd promised Gus, and she owed J.T. for his concern. She wouldn't let him sway her about Roy, but she'd do him the courtesy of listening.

Chapter Ten

Seated in front of a nearly empty checkerboard, Gus raised his arms in triumph. "King me!"

J.T. had to hand it to the boy. They'd played five cutthroat games of checkers, and Gus had won four of them. With each win, the kid had signaled to Fancy Girl and she'd given a victory bark. J.T. had enjoyed every minute. Grinning, he offered a handshake. "Congratulations. You're good at this."

Gus gripped his fingers hard. "Thanks."

"He's the best," Mary said proudly.

She was standing behind him, drying her hands on a towel that fanned the air with the lingering aroma of chocolate cake. Earlier she'd served fried chicken and potatoes, corn and biscuits as light as the clouds he'd watched all afternoon. High on the scaffolding, he'd enjoyed pounding nails with Gus. They hadn't spoken at all, not because Gus stammered but because they didn't need to talk.

J.T. had enjoyed the quiet, but he'd also liked the chatter at supper. After his run-in with Gertie, he'd expected her to give him a cold shoulder. Instead she'd been friendly. While he played checkers with Gus,

Mary and her sister had done the dishes, quietly conspiring in female tones he rarely heard and greatly enjoyed. He hoped the cheerfulness meant that Mary had
no intention of arguing with him about Roy. With a little luck, she'd seen the man's true character for herself.

"All right," she said to Gus. "It's bedtime."

"B-but—"

J.T. stood. "Your sister's right, kid."

Satisfied, Gus swept the checkers into a box, said
good-night and went down the hall with Fancy at his
heels. Gertie had excused herself earlier, leaving J.T.
and Mary alone in the front room. When she sat on
the divan, he positioned himself next to her but not
too close. Once they were done talking about Roy, he
hoped to stay awhile longer. While working with Gus,
all sorts of thoughts had filled J.T.'s head. He'd had his
fill of drifting and killing, and he'd started to wonder.... What would it be like to start a new life?

If anyone could understand, it was Mary. In Kansas she'd been as wild as he'd been, yet now she had a
home and a business...and faith, he reminded himself.
Of the three changes, the last one surprised him the
most. Earlier today he'd considered the odds of a man
like himself putting a roof on a church. A year ago,
he'd have said they were a million to one. J.T. hadn't
thought much about God except to dislike Him, but
Mary felt otherwise, and he wanted to understand her.

He leaned back on the divan. "Thanks again for supper. I had a good time."

"I did, too."

He felt at home tonight, something he'd never experienced before, though he'd often visited her hotel suite
in Abilene. There she'd had two rooms, a sitting area
and her bedroom. The bed had been soft. The divan

in the sitting room had been short and stuffed to the point of being uncomfortable. He wasn't uncomfortable now. The divan felt as familiar as his saddle, and the room was pleasantly cluttered with Mary's treasures. He recognized a vase he'd given her in Abilene. She'd filled it with dried sunflowers like the ones they'd seen on that buggy ride to nowhere.

He wished now that the ride had gone somewhere, anywhere, as long as he'd gone there with Mary. He wanted to rekindle that closeness, but first he had to finish with Roy. He draped a boot over his knee. "How did it go this afternoon?"

"Good."

When she took a breath, he got a bad feeling. "You took the role, didn't you?"

"No," she said firmly. "My career's over, but there's a part for Gertie. I'm keeping my promise to hear what you have to say, but I'm inclined to let her give acting a try."

"Mary, no." The evening had been nice…too nice, he realized. Gertie had been on her best behavior, because she wanted something from her sister. Mary had kept the evening light, because she wanted him to accept her decision.

J.T. figured he had double the trouble. He still had to worry about Roy's interest in Mary, and now Roy was using Gertie to manipulate them all. Mentally he kicked himself for not telling her about Roy sooner, but she didn't trust him enough to take his word. He couldn't stand the thought of Mary dealing with Roy. He wanted to block the door with his body, keeping her in this land of checkers, fried chicken and sunflowers dried into a memory.

In a burst of clarity, one like the moment on the

roof, he realized he wanted to be locked in this room with her. The admission startled him in one breath and infuriated him in the next. What did a fool like him have to offer a woman like Mary? She was smart not to trust him, but he knew Roy's intent. He needed to convince her to keep Gertie away from the Newcastle, so he stood and offered his hand. "Let's take a walk."

Her brows lifted. "A walk?"

"Yeah."

"Where to?"

"I don't know," he replied. "But I don't want to have this talk with Gertie's ear pressed to the door."

He'd caught Mary by surprise, and she laughed. "That's exactly where she is."

He kept his hand steady, waiting and hoping, until she clasped his fingers and allowed him to guide her up and off the divan. The touch connected them, not in the past but in the present. J.T. put on his gun belt, then he led Mary to the door, lifted her shawl from a hook and draped it over her shoulders. Other nights came back in a rush of memory, the times he'd walked her to the hotel after the show and they'd kissed…the times he'd followed her upstairs to her suite of rooms.

He couldn't fix the past, but he could protect her from Roy Desmond. Maybe someday she'd trust him again…. Maybe someday she'd let him back into her life.

Mary followed J.T. down the outside stairs, saying nothing because she didn't know what to say. She'd expected a quarrel. Instead he'd swept her into the night for a walk. She needed the air to clear her head, and he'd been right about Gertie eavesdropping. Mary had no intention of going back on her word to Gertie. Roy might say no, but she'd try to get Gertie a role. If she broke her promise to her sister now, the girl would ask too many questions. She loved Gertie and wanted her to be happy.

She doubted strongly that J.T. could say anything that would change her mind. She wasn't completely comfortable with Roy, but she trusted the theater manager more than she trusted J.T., though tonight he'd been wonderful with Gus. He'd boosted her brother's confidence in a dozen small ways.

You carved these animals? They're really good.

You've got a lot of books. You've read 'em all? I wish I'd done that.

By the end of the meal, Gus had been sitting tall and eating enough for two boys his size. J.T. had been just as respectful of Gertie, calling her Miss Larue as he showed Gus how to pull out his sister's chair. The old J.T. had been as approachable as barbed wire. The new one had grinned when a boy beat him at checkers. She wondered if he let Gus win, then decided he hadn't. Gus played a good game, and she'd seen the competitive glint in J.T.'s eyes. He had wanted to win, and he wanted to win now. What the prize was, she didn't know.

When they reached the bottom of the stairs, he pointed to the center of town. "Let's go this way."

She didn't ask him where they were going. She doubted he knew, and she was content to listen to the matching rhythm of their steps. Her problems seemed insignificant beneath a sky full of stars. Unconsciously, she started to hum.

"Is that from Roy's show?" he asked.

"No, it's a hymn."

As she tipped her face in his direction, his lips curled

but not into a sneer. Neither was he smiling. He looked befuddled. Turning slightly, he met her gaze. "I guess that's one I haven't heard."

Come to church and I'll sing it for you. The words danced on her tongue, but she bit them back. She didn't want J.T. to be a part of her life, yet how could she not invite him to church? Not only would the refusal be self-serving, but she'd be a hypocrite. Not that it mattered.... He'd surely refuse the invitation. Feeling safe, she looked up at him. "Come to church on Sunday, and I'll sing it for you."

"Let's go right now."

Mary laughed. "You're kidding."

"No, I'm not." He reached for her hand. "I'll show you what Gus and I did today. Besides, the building's a good place to talk about Roy."

His fingers felt warm on hers, strong and tender in the way she remembered. It was also dark, and the boardwalk had as many warped boards as it did flat ones. The silence between them felt gentle, the way it did between old friends who'd talked themselves out, but Mary felt nothing akin to friendship for this man. Her feelings—both sweet and painful—ran too deep. She'd vowed to never trust him again, but she hadn't expected to be having a conversation in a church. As they neared the unfinished building, moonlight turned the raw pine into silver beams. Behind the framework, she saw the stone wall of the Newcastle.

J.T. guided her through the opening left for the door, then indicated the table at the far end of the building. The two chairs had been tucked in place, and a lantern stood waiting to be lit. She didn't know what to think as they walked across the diagonal floor planks. God didn't need walls and a roof to be present, nor did He turn His nose up at men with bad habits and blood on their hands. Mary felt that same compassion for J.T., but she couldn't trust his judgment. At the same time, she trusted God, and somehow He'd brought J.T. to Denver. For what purpose, she didn't know. Nervous, she walked with him through the bar-like shadows formed by the open rafters. When they stepped beneath the solid portion of the roof—the portion J.T. had hammered into place— he pulled back a chair. "Have a seat."

She dropped down on the chair, watching as he struck a match and lit the lantern. With the light casting his shadow against the wall, he pulled the second chair out from the table and sat facing her. "You're not going to like what I have to say about Roy, but you've got to believe me."

"I said I'd listen." She indicated the empty church. "Here we are."

He sat straight with his hands on his knees, his spine rigid and his eyes as hard as gunmetal. "You know I saw Roy talking to Gertie. She's too young to read a man's signs, but I know what he was up to."

Mary sighed. "I don't think—"

He dug his fingers into his knees. "I'm telling you, Mary, Roy ogled Gertie like a wolf stalking a lamb. If you let her take that role, Roy will pressure you both in all the wrong ways."

Roy had always been polite to her. She knew him. "That's a bit extreme."

"It's not."

"I know you mean well." She spoke quietly to calm him. "But why should I believe you? Roy's a customer—a good one. He's been a friend." She didn't mention that he knew about the miscarriage and the murder trial and that he hadn't shared the information with anyone in Denver.

J.T. looked her in the eye. "I know what I saw. I also know what I heard."

"What?"

"Do you mind if I speak plainly?"

J.T. never asked permission for anything. The respect startled her. "Go ahead."

"After I left you on Sunday I ran into Roy." He told her about going inside the theater and how Roy had asked him to influence her to take the role of Arline. She didn't like Roy's attempt to manipulate her, but she could understand his need to pay off his investors. Unlike J.T., she believed Roy to be a real businessman.

She interrupted him. "I haven't heard anything that makes me worry. He manages a theater. He wanted me to sing—"

"He wants more than that." The words came out in a growl. "He said he *wants* you, and he didn't mean just for the stage."

She'd stopped trusting J.T. two years ago. She saw no reason to start now, especially with such an unseemly observation. "I don't believe you."

"You've *got* to."

"Why should I?"

"Because he told me straight out." He took both her hands in his and held them like he'd never let go. "He looked me in the eye and said, 'If you're done with her, I'll take her for myself.'"

Sam O'Day had made a similar remark when he'd trapped her in the alley. In the days before she'd left Abilene, even men she knew to be honorable had given her disturbing looks. Roy knew the gossip about her, what she'd done. She wanted to deny J.T.'s claim, but she couldn't. How well did she really know Roy? Not as well as she knew J.T. He was suspicious by nature, smelling smoke where there wasn't fire, but he was also a shrewd judge of character. Shaking inside, she pulled out of his grasp and paced to the side of the church closest to the theater. Looking up at the dark windows, she prayed. *Help me, Lord. Should I trust J.T. or not?*

Her heart cried no.

Her common sense said otherwise. He had no reason to lie to her, and deep down she'd been troubled by Roy's attention to Gertie. If there was even a remote chance Roy would use Gertie for improper purposes, Mary couldn't allow it. But the cost… She stared up at the dark theater. If she went back on her word to Gertie, her sister would demand to know why. Just as threatening, Roy could destroy her good name with a single rumor. What would Gus do when other boys called his sister ugly names? A lump pressed into her throat.

"Mary?"

J.T.'s voice came over her shoulder. He was standing behind her, close enough that she could again smell the bay rum that had tickled her nose all evening. She needed to tell him what she'd decided, even thank him for protecting her, but she didn't trust her voice.

Stepping closer, he put his hand on her arm. "There's more."

She shook her head. "I've heard enough."

"Roy killed a saloon girl in Dodge." His fingers tightened. "If he gets near you or Gertie, I'll—"

"Stop!" She couldn't stand another word. "I'll tell Gertie no. I'll never speak to Roy again."

How many times did she have to pay for what she'd done in Abilene? And why did Gertie have to suffer with her? She pressed her hands against her cheeks to hold back a flood of tears, but a sob broke from her throat.

J.T. clasped her elbow. Turning her slowly, he drew her fully into his arms until she nestled her head in the familiar crook of his neck. Her lips were an inch from tender skin she'd once kissed. She could hear the whisper of his breath, his baritone as he crooned to her. She wanted to hate this man for hurting her, but he knew her in ways no one else did. She'd shared her dreams with him, the shame of growing up poor. He knew how much her career had meant to her. What he hadn't understood was that *he'd* meant more to her than anything.

He bent his neck so that his cheek brushed the top of her head. "It's just not right," he murmured. "I wish… I wish all sorts of things."

For two years she'd lived silently with her shame. Tonight the tears refused to stop. J.T. was smoothing her hair and murmuring about wishes and regrets. When his lips brushed her temple, she felt the tenderness to her toes. She hadn't been held in a very long time. She felt protected, and that made her cry all the more.

"It'll be all right," he murmured. "I won't let anyone hurt you."

The next thing she knew, his mouth was an inch from hers. She expected him to kiss her, but instead he shifted his lips to the shell of her ear. "I've missed you, Mary…so much."

"J.T. I—"

"When I'm with you, I can believe there's good in the world, maybe even some good in me."

Stroking her hair, he tilted his head to match the angle of hers. She knew the look in his eyes, knew the purpose of it and what he wanted. It wasn't just a kiss. He wanted things she had no power to give. He wanted peace. He wanted hope. Only God could meet those needs. She had to stop him from kissing her, but she couldn't find the words, couldn't move her limbs.

In Abilene he'd have taken the kiss without asking. Tonight he stopped an inch from her mouth, waiting for her to signal her willingness. Regardless of her feelings. She had to be wise for them both.

Cupping his jaw, she whispered, "No, J.T. Not again."

Releasing her abruptly, he turned and walked into the shadows. In the dark, he put his hands on his hips, raised his face to the half-finished roof and muttered something not meant for her ears.

With J.T., defeat always turned to anger. She braced herself for it now.

Standing in the dark, beyond the glare of the lamp and Mary's reach, J.T. figured he had a choice. He could let her push him away, or he could fight to win her back. He knew she cared about him. She'd been gentle when she'd cupped his jaw, and even more tender when she'd held him back. She wanted to kiss him, and she didn't kiss a man casually, so what stood between them? Who did he need to fight?

A year ago he'd have waged the battle with Mary. He'd have tempted her until she gave in. Tonight that scheme struck him as wrong, even evil. It was the kind of thing Roy would do. J.T. didn't see the theater manager as a rival. An enemy, yes. But Roy wasn't standing between them in this half-finished church. What stood between them, he realized, was the past. *Who* stood between them was her God. The faith she'd once had in J.T., she now had in someone he couldn't see. A dry laugh scraped his throat. He'd fought a lot of hard men in his time, but he'd never taken on someone invisible.

How did he do battle with this kind of enemy? J.T. didn't know, but for Mary he was willing to find out. With his jaw tight, he glared at the sky above the unfinished roof and muttered in his head. *If You're hiding up there, show Yourself!*

Nothing happened.

Lightning didn't flash.

No one dropped dead.

But deep in his chest, J.T. felt a pounding he couldn't explain. He'd called out enemies before. Not once had he felt the trembling that plagued him now. He wasn't afraid. He couldn't be, because fear killed men like himself. If a shootist hesitated, he died. Mentally J.T. pulled the quiver into a tautness of mind. To win Mary, he had to learn a whole new game. If he tempted her with kisses, she'd dig in her heels. If he treated her right, she just might trust him again.

He liked the idea, but it came at a cost. Considering her beliefs, treating her right meant marrying her, and marriage meant giving her children. J.T. liked Gus, but squalling babies were another matter. He'd never pictured himself as a father, and he still didn't. When it came to marriage, he had nothing to offer. Mary had been wise to remember his failings before he'd kissed her the way he wanted.

Like the scoundrel he'd been in Abilene, he leaned against a post, crossed his arms and faced her. "Was that, 'No, I'll never kiss you again,' or 'No, but I'll think about it'?"

Instead of getting riled, she looked at him as if he were Gus's age and acting tough. "It wasn't either."

"Then what was it?"

"It was, 'No, but I wish I could.'"

"Oh, yeah?" He'd wanted to sound wicked, but his voice came out hopeful. Embarrassed, he turned his head to the doorway, an opening that provided a way in *and* a way out. He had that choice now with Mary. He could play tough, or he could talk to her like he'd imagined when he was on the roof looking at clouds. When he finally spoke, he was still looking at the door. "I did some thinking today."

"About what?"

"Clouds, mostly." He finally looked at her. "And us. I know I hurt you, Mary. What would it take to earn back your trust?"

"You can't."

He didn't want to believe her. "I've got a long way to go, but I'm hoping you'll give me a chance. I'd like to do something for Gus."

She hesitated. "Like what?"

"A camping trip. We wouldn't be gone long, just four or five days."

She didn't say no right away, but neither did she look eager. "Where would you go?"

"The stream a mile or so past the Slewfoot Mine. It's loaded with trout." If he proved himself with Gus, she would have to admit he'd changed. He still had worries about marriage, but the thought wasn't as awful as it had been two minutes ago. He had to convince her. "Gus is a good kid. Did you see him working today?"

"A little bit."

J.T. smiled at the memory. "He filled the nail bucket so full he needed two hands to carry it. The boy's determined to grow up."

"I know, but he's so young."

"Not that young." J.T. had spent his twelfth birthday

stealing food for his brothers. He'd spent his thirteenth hiding on a train bound for St. Louis. He hadn't celebrated since then, though he privately marked each year with amazement that he'd lived so long.

Mary bit her lip. "If I say yes, will you tell me something?"

"Sure."

She gave him a long look that pinned him in place. Whatever she asked, he'd have to be truthful, and she knew how to get to him. She waved her hand to indicate the church. "Why are you here?"

"In Denver?"

"No, *here*." She meant the building. "You don't need the job, and you don't like to work. You don't belong—" she bit her lip, then said, "You've never been to church in your life."

"You were going to say I don't belong here."

She looked at him with sad, guilty eyes, a sign of the chasm between them. Earning her trust would take more than being nice to Gus or warning her about Roy. He needed to understand the woman she'd become.

She looked pained. "You belong here as much as I do. Anyone who comes through that door is welcome."

He smirked. "Not me, apparently."

"No," she said. "You, especially."

She hadn't meant to sound so earnest, but J.T.'s denial had hit a chord. When she'd first come to Swan's Nest, she'd felt unworthy of singing in church. Josh had set her straight, and she wanted to show others the same goodwill. She didn't doubt J.T. belonged under this roof. Whether he belonged back in her life was another matter. She'd realized how much he'd changed when he hadn't kissed her. It seemed that the old J.T.

had died. The new one had been conceived six months ago but was yet to be born. She couldn't trust him fully, but neither could she send him away.

He needs You, Lord. What do I do? What do I say?

She didn't have a perfect command of Scripture, but she had a story of her own and she could tell it. They were facing each other in the circle of light. Blinking, she turned down the wick to hide her churned-up feelings. Instead of putting distance between them, the circle tightened like a lasso drawing them together. She felt the rightness of the moment and it made her bold. "I think I know how you feel."

His lips curved into a sneer, but his eyes were bleak. "I doubt it. You've never killed anyone."

"Yes, I have," she reminded him. "I shot Sam O'Day."

The bleakness drained from J.T.'s eyes, making way for annoyance. She'd bested him, and he didn't like it. "Sam doesn't count."

"Why not?"

"It was self-defense."

"That's true," she acknowledged. "But I still watched him die, and I was the cause."

She understood guilt far better than J.T. realized, but not because of Sam O'Day. She'd always wonder if she'd caused the miscarriage by going to the theater instead staying in bed. She considered telling him about the child she'd lost, but she doubted he'd console her. His reaction would likely be relief. She'd never tell J.T. about the baby. It would hurt too much to see his disdain, but he needed to know she understood him. She thought back to shooting Sam and how it had changed her. The baby had changed her more, but remembering

Sam served her purpose. "I won't ever forget that night in the alley. I couldn't get away from the talk, so I left."

He said nothing, but she knew he understood. He'd walked away from the Dudley place as surely as she'd left Kansas.

"Leaving Abilene was like jumping off a cliff," she continued. "I didn't know what would happen. I just knew I couldn't do what I'd always done."

"That's it," he murmured

"I hit the ground at Swan's Nest." She'd been weak and broken, but with time she'd healed. "You jumped off a similar cliff. You're still falling, and you're looking for a branch to grab."

He looked at her a long time. "When did you get so wise?"

"I'm not wise at all." She waved off the compliment. "I'm just someone who jumped off a cliff and found a branch."

She hoped J.T. would grab the same one she had. Her faith sometimes faltered, but the branch wouldn't break. Was he reaching out the way she had? It seemed possible, even likely. They were standing in a half-finished church. He owned a dog, and he'd been generous to Gus. She wanted to encourage him, so she smiled. "I'd be glad for you to take Gus camping."

"He's a good kid."

"The best."

"I'll be careful around him," he said. "He can't talk right, but someday he'll be a good man."

Mary's throat tightened. "There's good in you, too."

"I don't think so."

"I mean it."

She recalled the scar she'd seen on his shoulder, a reminder of the time his brother had cut him because he'd refused to steal. He hadn't had an aversion to steal-ing, he'd said. He'd been as hungry as they were, but he'd been terrified of getting caught and being sepa-rated from them. The confusion of it, the desperation, still put tears in her eyes.

She blinked them back. "I see the good in you, J.T., because God loves people, everyone, even you."

She ambled to the side of building, leaving him in the light while she stood in the shadows. As she ex-pected, his expression turned wry. "Considering my bad habits, that's hard to believe."

She wished she had Josh's command of the Scrip-tures. She wished she was like the apostle Paul with his education, or Peter, who'd been renamed "The Rock." She supposed she was closest to John in temperament, the apostle who wrote about love. Her good intentions would have to suffice. "This is what I know," she said simply. "God knows about every mistake I've made and every ugly thought I've had. He still loves me."

J.T. huffed. "It can't be that simple."

"It's not," she acknowledged. "I could talk about sin and mercy, but the branch I grabbed was love. He loves you, too. J.T. You've done terrible things. You know it, and you want to make things right. That's the good I see in you."

He shook his head. "You're a fool, Mary. A blessed fool…."

"No, I'm not."

His eyes locked with hers in a dance she recog-nized from Abilene. He wanted something from her. In Kansas, it had signaled physical desire. Tonight she saw a longing for more than pleasure. He wanted hope. Six months ago he'd started a desperate search. If he looked long enough, he'd find answers…eventually.

She couldn't trust him yet, maybe not ever, but she could pray for him. She crossed back to the table and held out her hand. "Let's go. If Gus is awake, you can tell him about the camping trip."

J.T. took her hand. "I'd like to finish the roof. How about next week?"

"That would be fine."

They walked back to her apartment in companionable silence. If anyone could give Gus confidence it was J.T. She trusted him fully with her brother. Whether she could learn to trust J.T. with her heart, and whether J.T. could learn to trust God, remained to be seen. Until then, she'd keep her feelings and her memories tucked safely away.

Chapter Eleven

On Sunday morning, J.T. put on his best clothes and went to church. He wanted to think he'd come to see Mary, but he knew otherwise. Since their talk, he'd felt like a stranger in his own skin. This morning when he'd shaved, he'd seen a man he didn't know anymore. He looked younger, almost happy. He was more excited than Gus about the camping trip, and yesterday he'd caught himself humming "Pop Goes the Weasel" while he pounded nails.

Something crazy was happening to him, and he didn't like it. If he lost his edge, he'd be a dead man. Yesterday on the roof, he'd glared at the clouds and muttered a foul word just to prove he could do it. It had sounded hollow, and he'd felt an emptiness that had nearly knocked him to his knees. He'd muttered a second oath. *If You're real, God, I want to know it.*

Nothing.

Silence.

He'd felt the weight of his guns and made a decision. If God wouldn't show Himself, J.T. would go hunting for Him. That's why he was sitting in Brick's Saloon on Sunday morning, cleaned up and smelling a little too good because he'd come to see Mary, too. He'd arrived early to be sure he got a seat near the back. Fancy Girl lay at his feet, the recipient of a special invitation from Josh. He smiled at the memory of the minister telling him God loved all creatures great and small, and that Fancy would be welcome anytime.

Keeping an eye on the back door, he saw all sorts of folks coming to church. He recognized a couple of men from the building, three ladies who'd brought lunch and Bessie from Swan's Nest. The nurse had come in with another woman, a brunette who had to be her sister. Bessie saw him, waved and took a seat near the front.

Josh came out of a back room and strode to the podium. A fiddle player struck up a melody and the room quieted. J.T. hadn't seen Mary since Wednesday, and he wanted to know what had happened with Gertie and Roy. Gus had been coming with Josh to work on the roof, but J.T. hadn't quizzed him. It would have been unfair to the boy.

With no sign of Mary, his nerves prickled. He was about to leave for the café when Gus, squeaky clean but out of breath, pushed through the doors.

J.T. motioned to him. "Hey, partner."

The boy's face lit up. "C-c-can I sit with you?"

"Sure." J.T. appreciated the company, another sign he wasn't himself.

As Gus joined him, Gertie sauntered in with her nose in the air. Mary rushed in behind her, looking more harried than he'd ever seen her. Gertie slipped into a seat in the corner opposite from him and put on a pout. Mary walked to the front of the church and whispered something to Josh, probably an apology for arriving late. The minister said something back, maybe asking if she needed time to compose herself. When she shook her head, Josh nodded to the fiddler. The musician raised his bow high, then brought it down with a slash that began a storm of beautiful music. J.T. sat riveted, both by the melody and by Mary. When the sharp notes trickled to silence, she began to sing.

He didn't pay attention to the words, but the tune matched the one she'd been humming on Wednesday night. The music connected him to her, but he didn't see the Almighty anywhere in the room. Josh was the same man who'd hired J.T. and got annoyed at crooked nails. His eyes wandered to Bessie and her sister. They were singing the words, but they were still just people.

Mary finished the song with a long "Amen." On a signal from Josh, the congregation rose to its feet. J.T. stood out of respect for Mary and Josh, not reverence for God.

"Ladies and gentlemen," Josh said in a full voice. "Let's pray." The minister thanked God for the glorious day. J.T. had to agree. The July morning couldn't have been nicer, but so what? Next Josh prayed for God to bless his sermon. Fine, J.T. thought. He'd listen, but he didn't expect much.

After a hearty "Amen," Josh looked up. "Our next hymn is 'Come Thou Fount of Every Blessing.'"

When the fiddler played a run, Mary took a breath. In the same instant, she saw J.T. and paused with surprise. He thought of the dream he had, the one where she was singing on a big stage on a Saturday night—the dream where she sang just for him. The moment matched exactly, except they were in a church instead of a theater. And instead of a flashy dress, she had on the lilac gown she'd worn last week. She didn't look like a schoolmarm today, and she no longer seemed harried and worn out. She couldn't have been more beautiful to him. Just like in his dream, she smiled and began to sing.

J.T. didn't understand the words about streams of mercy. They made no sense at all, but then he heard a voice coming from the seat next to him. It belonged to Gus, and the boy wasn't stammering. J.T. looked at him, amazed at the clear tones. Gus couldn't talk right, but he could sing perfectly. In the boy's eyes, J.T. saw the innocence of a child and the marks of suffering. He saw himself in those depths. He also saw something that scared him half to death. He saw the goodness Mary saw in *him*.

He saw the love of God.

Had the Almighty just shown Himself? It seemed so, but J.T. couldn't believe it. A God with any sense would have been spitting fire at a man like him. He wanted to fight with an enemy. Instead he was looking at Gus with a brotherly love he'd never felt before. The boy needed him, but J.T. needed the boy just as much, maybe more. Gus gave him a purpose, a reason to be an honorable man.

The next words of the hymn made a little more sense. *Jesus sought me when a stranger, Wandering from the fold of God.* J.T. didn't know if he'd wandered from God or not. Could a man wander from someone he'd never known? His mother had owned a Bible and she'd read it, but it had been lost when he and his brothers had been tossed out of their meager apartment. He'd never forget that awful day. A minister with droopy eyes had tried to take J.T. to an orphanage, separating him from his brothers because he'd been the youngest. He'd fought and so had his brothers, though later he'd wondered why.

The stealing had started right away. The fighting got

worse and his oldest brother had cut him with a knife.
With the blood running down his scrawny chest, J.T.
had made a decision. He'd kill before he'd be killed;
he'd hurt others before they hurt him. For close to
twenty years he'd lived that way with great success, but
today he felt like that boy pinned to the hard ground.

He turned to the front of the room with a scowl.
When Mary finished the song, he sat. Josh went to the
podium, greeted him with a discreet nod and started
talking about love. The minister didn't dwell on the
love of a man for a woman or brotherly love. He'd
talked about the love that made a man willing to die
for others, to make sacrifices and stay decent even
when others weren't. Because of his feelings for Mary,
J.T. felt the truth of every word.

The truth stopped when Josh got to the part about
forgiving his enemies. "We can forgive others because
God forgives us," the minister said.

J.T. had no desire to forgive his brothers. Why would
he? They'd beaten him black and blue. He refocused in
time to hear Josh talk about turning the other cheek.
No way on earth would J.T. let someone beat him up,
or worse, beat up someone he cared about. Hadn't Josh
seen Gus's black eye? Clearly the man didn't know how
it felt to be held down and kicked in the ribs. When J.T.
had refused to steal, his oldest brother had pressed the
knife into his shoulder and twisted it until he screamed.

He'd come to church today to smoke out the Almighty. Instead he'd been introduced to a fool. With
his muscles taut, he stopped listening to Josh and stared
at Mary, wondering what had happened with Roy and
Gertie and what she'd say when he insisted on walking
her home. Just as he'd once vowed to hurt others before
they hurt him, he made a mental promise to keep Mary

and her sister safe from Roy Desmond. If Mary's God didn't want the job, J.T. would gladly take it.

When she finished the opening hymn, Mary sat in the front row with Adie. Could her life be any more complicated? God had created the world in seven days. J.T. had been in Denver for the same amount of time, and her world had gone to pieces. She and Gertie weren't speaking, and yesterday Caroline had quizzed her about J.T. Mary hadn't given her the details about what had happened in Abilene, but her refusal only added to the air of mystery around him.

Today she expected the talk to get worse. J.T. had come to church looking both handsome and skeptical. At the end of the sermon, Josh would invite everyone to Swan's Nest for supper. If he came, her friends would see them together. Good-natured or not, she dreaded the speculation. To end it, she'd be J.T.'s friend today and nothing more.

Another threat to her secret came from Roy. Three days ago she'd turned down his offer. Instead of accepting her decision graciously, he'd taunted her in a sly tone. Predictably, Gertie had been furious.

But why! You said—

I know what I said. I made a mistake. I got carried away. You're too young.

It's because of what J. T. Quinn said, isn't it? Who is he, anyway? He's practically a criminal!

To her shame, Mary had said nothing in J.T.'s defense. He'd acted honorably, but she couldn't defend him to Gertie. Her sister would ask too many questions…questions Mary didn't want to answer. She desperately wanted to put Gertie on the next train to New York, so yesterday she'd gone to the bank to borrow money. The banker had turned her down, kindly suggesting that patience was a better investment. If only Gertie had agreed. The girl hadn't spoken to Mary in two days. She'd come to church this morning, but only because Gus had asked.

Mary tried to focus on the sermon just as Josh closed his Bible. As expected he invited everyone to Swan's Nest, then motioned for Mary to come forward for the closing hymn. She sang the same song every week, so the words came easily even though her thoughts remained scattered. After the last note, the crowd broke apart. As men put back the chairs, the women drifted to the refreshment table.

Mary spotted J.T. and Gus at the back of the room. The boy looked happy, but the man had an angry gleam in his eyes. Gertie was heading for the door, and she looked smug. Mary couldn't stop her sister, so she approached J.T. and Gus.

J.T. scowled at her, but Gus smiled. "H-h-h-i!"

"Hi, there," she replied. His hair had fallen in his eyes. She itched to smooth it back but stopped herself. J.T. was right. Gus needed to grow up.

"W-watch this." He gave Fancy the signal to sit. When the dog obeyed, he fed her a cookie.

Mary smiled at J.T. Instead of enjoying his dog's talent, he looked ready to kick a chair across the room. "You don't look happy," she said mildly.

"I'm not."

He was glowering when Caroline approached. "I haven't officially met Mr. Quinn," she said to Mary.

She did *not* want Caroline asking questions *or* playing matchmaker. "J.T., this is Miss Caroline Bradley. Caroline, this is Mr. J. T. Quinn."

J.T. lost the scowl. "It's a pleasure to meet you, Miss Bradley."

"Call me Caroline. I hope you're coming for supper."

J.T. looked peeved. "I don't think so."

"Jake plays a mean jig," Caroline said with a teasing air. "You should see Mary dance."

"I've had the pleasure," he replied. "We were acquainted in Abilene."

Mary was the actress, but J.T. delivered the explanation of their past in a perfectly casual tone.

Caroline smiled at him. "I'd love to hear more about those days. Mary has such a beautiful voice. I bet she was famous."

Infamous had been more like it. She traded a look with J.T., one that would have seemed bland to an observer but held all the ties of the past. *Please don't reveal anything. Please keep quiet.*

Looking almost bored, he turned to Caroline. "Mary had quite a career. But like she said, it was a long time ago."

Caroline wasn't appeased. "How did you two meet?"

Annoyed, Mary cut in. "We met at the theater. That's all there is to it."

"That's right," J.T. said mildly.

Bessie approached from the side. "Good morning, Mr. Quinn. I hope you'll join us for supper this afternoon."

He shook his head. "I don't think—"

Gus interrupted. "P-p-lease, J.T.? It'll be f-fun."

A week ago her brother had been silent and sullen. Today he had spunk. J.T. shot her a look. He had no desire to go to supper, and he knew his presence would raise questions for her, but he also wanted to please Gus. To keep the talk to a minimum, they needed to appear to be friends. Mary offered a warm smile. "You're more than welcome, J.T."

"All right," he said. "I accept."

Bessie, always a nurse, tipped up Gus's chin and looked at his black eye. "You've got quite a shiner."

"Yeah."

"How's the rest of you?"

"G-g-good." He wanted to say more but couldn't.

J.T. filled in. "Gus is working with me on the new church."

When Mary smiled her appreciation at J.T., Caroline saw and got a mischievous look. The woman was an unstoppable matchmaker. Mary could have been angry, but her heart ached for her friend. Of the five women from Swan's Nest, Caroline had been the most eager to have a family of her own. A young widow, she'd suffered in ways no one else had. No matter what Caroline did, Mary loved her.

Bessie indicated three men leaning against the wall. "I believe those gentlemen need refreshments, Caroline. Shall we?"

"I—I—I want more, too," Gus added.

"Then let's get you some." Caroline motioned to Gus, and the three of them left. Fancy stayed with J.T.

Frowning, he scratched the dog's ears. "Sorry about going to supper. I hope it's not awkward for you."

"We can handle it." *We.* When had they gone from enemies to allies? Mary didn't know, but she appreciated his consideration.

Still looking down, he spoke to his dog. "What do you say, Fancy? Can we handle supper with church folk?"

When the dog wagged her tail, J.T. chuckled. "I guess so." He looked back at Mary. "I'll do my best to keep talk away from Abilene, but Caroline's determined to find out what happened between us."

"I know." She grimaced. "If you want to back out, I'll make excuses for you."

"Not a chance," he muttered. "Gus needs to know a man keeps his word." His tone implied that *she* needed to know he'd keep *his*.

Her brother came back with more cookies. "Wh-where's Gertie?"

"She went home."

He turned to J.T. "My s-s-sister's mad."

"Yeah, I saw."

Mary couldn't go into details with Gus present, but J.T. deserved to know she'd taken his advice. "I told Roy no for both of us."

"I want to hear about it," he said casually. "I'll walk you home."

She didn't want to be seen leaving with him. "I wish I could say yes, but—" she indicated the crowd in the room "—well, you know."

"Yeah. I understand." He sounded snide. "I'll go with Gus. You can deal with Gertie."

"That would be nice."

The boy grinned. "We can teach Fancy a new trick."

Had she imagined Gus's smooth speech, or had the stammering eased? J.T. looked at him with the same question, then he turned to her. "I'll see you in a while. Be ready, because I want answers."

"You'll get them."

Somehow she had the feeling he was talking about more than her dealings with Roy. He'd come to church today, something she'd never expected. He'd also been gracious to her friends and careful with the past. It was getting harder not to trust this man. With a final nod, she left him and went home to smooth the waters with her sister.

Chapter Twelve

J.T. watched Mary pass through the door, silently wishing her luck as she went to check on her sister. He'd seen the girl leave the church, and he'd been struck by the cocky tilt of her chin. Gertie had Mary's fire but none of her experience. She'd be easy prey for Roy, a thought that filled J.T. with familiar bitterness. He didn't want Gertie or anyone else to have scars like his own.

It was a long walk to Swan's Nest, so he decided to fetch his horse from the livery and ride double with Gus. After he spoke with Mary about Roy, he'd get ready for the camping trip. Yesterday he'd finished the roof except for the bell tower, which required a batch of smaller shingles that had to be cut. Josh had been pleased to hear about the trip with Gus and had offered to loan them fishing poles.

Until this morning, J.T. had liked the minister, even respected him. While working on the church, Josh was just… Josh. He laughed when other men laughed, and he sympathized with their troubles. That man had preached today, and he'd thrown down some hard words. Halfway through the sermon, J.T. had been so angry he'd stopped listening. "Come on," he said to Gus. "Let's get out of here."

They were close to the door when Josh blocked their path. "Good to see you, J.T."

J.T. scowled. "Reverend Blue."

Josh's lips tipped up. "I wear a preacher's collar for church, but that's the only difference from the rest of the week. I'm still Josh. Do you have a minute?"

"Nope." He turned to leave, but the minister gripped his arm. No one stopped J.T. from leaving, and he indicated that fact to the good Reverend Blue with a steely look. "What do you want?"

Josh released his arm. "A minute of your time."

"What for?"

"You started snarling halfway through the sermon. I want to know why."

J.T. put a hand over his heart. "You gave a *fine* sermon, reverend. It was downright glorious, chock-full of sweetness and light. I was blessed indeed to hear you talk about turning the other cheek."

Josh raised one eyebrow. "You're good at sarcasm."

J.T. said nothing.

"There's more to this message," Josh said in a firm tone. "Next Sunday we're going to talk about when it's right to fight. I suspect you know something about that."

"I do."

"Good," he said. "Come back. You can tell me if I'm getting it right."

The minister was toying with him. Fine. If Josh wanted to argue, J.T. would give him an earful at Swan's Nest.

As the man stepped aside, J.T. muttered, "See you later," and headed for the door. Gus, imitating him, repeated his words and they left, walking in silence until they got to the livery. The old man running the place saddled J.T.'s horse, brought it out and accepted a tip. J.T. swung into the saddle and pulled Gus up behind him. He could feel the buckskin prancing as they passed the alley where Gus had been attacked.

The boy tensed. "L-l-ook!"

Turning, J.T. saw the three boys who'd beaten Gus, no doubt lying in wait for him. He reined the buckskin to a halt. "What do you want to do, kid?"

"I w-w-want them d-d-dead!"

J.T. knew the feeling. He also wanted Gus to become a far better man than himself. He thought of Josh's sermon about cheek-turning and his mention of a time to fight. How did a man put the pieces together? J.T. didn't know, but he knew one thing with certainty. He didn't want Gus to be like him. Before he influenced the boy for the worse, he needed to puzzle out what he'd heard today.

He spoke more to himself than Gus. "Maybe later, kid."

"Yeah, later."

As they rode past the alley, J.T. felt none of the rage that should have spurred him on. What kind of mess had he gotten himself into? Not only had he given up liquor and cards, he'd lost some of his meanness. A month ago he'd have bullied the bullies with pleasure. Today the rage was a mountain in the distance, no less real than the dirt below his feet but somehow less personal. The thought made him ornery. By the time they arrived at Swan's Nest, he wanted to fight someone. Gus slid off the buckskin first, followed by J.T., who tied his horse to a fence. His gaze skipped the front porch and went to a garden where he heard conversation.

Gus scampered down a narrow path. "Th-this way."

J.T. followed him past a vegetable garden, then to a cut in a hedge of blooming rosebushes. The sweet fragrance filled his nose, but he refused to enjoy it. Gus indicated the house. "I—I have to h-help carry food."

"Go on ahead," J.T. replied.

With Fancy Girl at his side, he looked around the garden. Tables and chairs had been set up, but what caught his eye was a white marble bench. It reminded him of the gravestones he'd seen in a New York cemetery, not the paupers' field where his mother had been laid to rest but the church cemetery two blocks away. Covered in lush grass, it had been surrounded by a black iron fence two feet taller than he'd been. Behind it he'd seen markers the color of the bench in this garden. When he'd asked why his mama couldn't have a nicer resting place, the minister who'd buried her told him there were different places for rich people.

That day J.T. decided that the Almighty didn't deserve respect. If his mother wasn't welcome in that sacred place, he wanted nothing to do with the God who owned it. He still felt that way. Looking at the bench in Josh's garden, he saw swirls of gold in the white marble. Superior and unwelcoming, the stone gleamed in the heat of the day.

Feeling smug, he walked to the bench and sat on it. As Fancy laid at his feet, the heat of the stone went through his trousers. It was a bit too hot, but he stubbornly stayed in place. No one, not God or the sun, was going to tell him where to sit. Hunkering forward, he looked at the people chattering to each other. Josh had spotted him and was coming at him with a glass of lemonade.

The preacher bit off a grin. "Comfortable?"

"More or less."

"That bench gets a tad hot this time of day." He held out the dripping glass. "Have some."

The lemonade looked delicious, but J.T. hesitated. He didn't want to talk to Josh, not with his backside on fire. He wished he hadn't sat down. He wished other things, too—that Josh hadn't talked about turning the other cheek, and that his mother had been buried in a cemetery with an uncomfortable bench. He hadn't been expecting such thoughts. They'd come from nowhere, but he couldn't shake the old anger, or the picture of that droopy-eyed minister telling him the nice cemetery was for rich folks.

He was thirsty, so he accepted the glass with a snide look. "Hoop-di-doo. Christian charity." He raised the lemonade in a mock toast. "Thanks, preacher-man."

Josh had the nerve to look pleased. "The sermon got to you, didn't it?"

He could say no and hide behind the lie, or he could admit that the sermon had upset him. Neither choice appealed to him.

Josh stepped slightly to the side, casting a shadow across J.T.'s face. Memories spun through his mind, joining with fragments of the past week to create a disjointed picture of his entire life. He thought of the good times with Mary and then about the men he'd killed. He thought of Gus, then about Fancy Girl and playing fetch with a stick, and how he used to wonder if she'd really come back. When he thought of his mother's last breath, and then his brothers holding him down and the knife cutting his flesh, his thoughts turned black.

He shoved to his feet. With his hands dangling as if ready to draw, he squared off with Josh. "Tell me, preacher-man. Why all this?" He waved his arm as if swatting away his life. "Why can't Gus talk? Why do mothers get sick and die, and why do brothers hurt each other?"

Sadness filled the minister's eyes, but they were still blue like the sky. J.T. didn't usually notice such things, but he felt as if the sky were falling down around him.

Josh spoke in a hush. "You've seen a lot of life."

"You bet I have," he said, dragging out the words. "I've seen way too much to believe in turning the other cheek."

"I know."

"No, you don't." He was close to shouting. He never shouted, but he couldn't stop his voice from rising. "Tell me, preacher-man. Have you been pinned like a bug on your back? Maybe shot or cut with a knife?"

"No knives," Josh acknowledged. "But I've been shot and beat up."

The answer caught J.T. off guard. He thought of Gus wanting to kill the boys who'd hurt him. For Gus's sake, he'd give the preacher a chance. "What did you do?"

"I protected Adie." He stared hard at J.T. "I'll choose talking over fighting every time I have a choice. But if a woman's being hurt, or a child, I'm going to protect that person any way I can. If it means inflicting a bit of pain, I'll do it. If it means dying to save them, I'm willing."

J.T. felt the same way about Mary.

The minister's eyes turned to blue fire. "It's a choice a man makes on the fly. I've made it. You have, too. Don't think God doesn't understand. He knows more about justice and suffering than you or I ever will."

J.T. didn't know what to make of Josh's little speech, especially the mention of justice. J.T. survived by selling his gun. That didn't strike him as especially wrong, but his feelings about it did. He'd enjoyed every battle, every bullet that had drawn blood.

The minister removed a chapbook from his coat pocket and handed it to him. "Here."

J.T. took it and looked at the cover. He saw a picture of a lamb and a title he didn't recognize. "What is it?"

"The Gospel of John. It's a piece of the Bible."

J.T. didn't want it, but he was tired of arguing. Scowling, he tucked it inside his vest next to the Deringer he kept hidden.

A little girl called in their direction. "Pastor Josh! Miss Adie wants you."

"I better get moving." The minister shook his head as if he were henpecked, but J.T. saw through him. Josh loved being needed by his wife. J.T. wanted Mary to need *him* the same way. He expected her any minute, so he kept his eye on the path from the street. Fancy Girl lay at his feet asleep in the shade of the bench. She'd been napping a lot lately, and he was beginning to think they were both getting soft.

Brick walked over and asked how the roof was coming along. J.T. didn't mind chatting with the man, and it helped to pass the time. When the barkeep moved on, Caroline brought him another glass of lemonade and asked if he'd be staying for the fiddle music. J.T. accepted the tea to be polite, but he had no desire to stick around for the music. He wanted to speak to Mary and leave.

Another five minutes passed. Adie and Caroline were bringing food out to the tables, trading whispers and glancing at him until Adie finally walked up to him. They hadn't been officially introduced, so she offered her hand. "I'm Adie Blue, Josh's wife."

"Yes, ma'am," he replied. "I'm J. T. Quinn, Mary's friend."

"Is she here?"

"No, but I'm expecting her."

"Me, too." Adie glanced around the garden. "It's not like her to be late. Would you mind checking the café?"

"I'll go right now." He'd had the same thought. "Will you tell Gus?"

"Sure."

He wasn't coming back, so he woke up Fancy. "Come on, girl."

She jolted awake and followed him to his horse. Eager to be gone, he rode at a gallop until he neared the train depot. Wagons and carriages slowed him down, but his thoughts were running at full speed. Something had kept Mary away from Swan's Nest. It probably involved Gertie, which meant the trouble harkened back to Roy.

J.T. turned on the street where the café sat like a buttercup in row of weeds. Leaping off his horse, he saw that the café windows were dark, so he took the stairs to the apartment two at a time. At the top, he heard Mary weeping. He didn't bother to knock or call her name. He walked straight into the apartment, where he saw her huddled on the divan. Before she could protest, he pulled her into his arms and did what he should have done in Abilene. He held her like he'd never let her go. "Tell me what you need," he crooned. "Whatever it is, I'll find a way."

Chapter Thirteen

She needed a handkerchief, but she doubted J.T. had one. She tried to lift her head to say so, but he held her close, smoothing her hair with the touch she'd enjoyed in Abilene. How could a man capable of such violence be so tender? Through her tears, she saw Fancy Girl drop down in a beam of sunlight and stretch, a reminder that J.T. had changed from the hard man who'd left her.

As her tears dampened his shirt, she smelled bay rum and cotton made warm from his skin. When he'd held her in Abilene, she'd inhaled deeply and enjoyed the scent of him. Today it sobered her and she pulled back, wiping her eyes on her sleeve. She couldn't let him hold her like this. She trusted him with Gus, but her feelings were another matter. If she lost her heart to him, she'd have more heartache than she did right now, which was plenty in light of Gertie's letter. The two-page missive was on the table.

J.T. reached inside his vest and pulled out a bandanna. "Here you go, honey."

She took it and dabbed at her eyes, the endearment echoing in her mind. "You shouldn't call me that."

"I know," he said quietly. "It just slipped out."

She couldn't hold it against him, not when she'd enjoyed hearing it. Deep down, she wanted to hear the sweet name again. It was a foolish notion considering the past, but she couldn't deny the pleasure of being in his arms. They fit well together. They always had.

As he gauged her reaction, she felt the dampness of her tears. Gertie's letter had filled her with guilt, and every regret had come out in a flood. She wished she'd never been with J.T.... She wished she'd told Gertie everything he'd revealed about Roy. But the cost... Gertie would demand to know why Mary believed him, and she'd have to tell her sister everything. She'd have done it in an instant to protect Gertie, but the shame had silenced her. So did the fear that she'd lose Gertie's respect and what little influence she had. She also had to worry about Gus. If Mary told Gertie the truth and Gertie shared the secret with Katrina or anyone else, the gossip would burn like wildfire. Mary's good name would be ruined in Denver, and Gus would be the brother of a scarlet woman.

J.T. studied her as if she'd been injured. "You don't cry easily. What happened?"

"It's Gertie." She handed him the letter.

He took it and shifted forward, holding the pages with both hands. As he read, she recalled walking into her apartment. She'd felt the stillness, gone to the bedroom and flung open the wardrobe. Her own dresses had been untouched, but Gertie's side had been empty. Mary had found the letter on her pillow and read it. Seated next to J.T., she skimmed it again.

Mary,
 Forgive me, dear sister. After all you've done for me, a letter is a cowardly way to tell you

what I've decided. I should tell you to your face, I know, but I can't bear to see the disappointment in your eyes. Neither do I want you working your fingers to the bone so I can go to New York, especially when it's not necessary.

Something wonderful happened. I auditioned for the role of Arline and I got it. Roy says I sound just like you. That's high praise indeed. He made it clear you were his first choice, that I'd be your understudy if you changed your mind, but he has high hopes for me. He knows so much about the theater. I'm sure I can learn from him as surely as I could have learned in New York.

I love you, Mary. But I have to take this opportunity. Katrina has invited me to live with her. I hope you and I can be friends.
Your sister,
Gertie
P.S. I'd be honored if you'd come to opening night.

Mary finished reading and looked away. J.T. set the letter on the table. "Roy's using her to get to you."

A shiver rippled down her spine. "I can't sit here and do nothing. Maybe I should take the role." The scandal was likely to find her, but she could keep an eye on Gertie.

"Don't do it," J.T. said, bossing her.

She didn't like his tone. "You don't have the right to give me orders."

"Maybe not, but I'm going to anyway."

"That's ridiculous!"

"It's smart. If you give Roy what he wants, he'll want

more. Don't think for a minute he'll leave Gertie alone. He'll use her to manipulate you. Mark my words."

He'd spoken like the cold, calculating man who hired out his gun for money. "I don't want to be around Roy, but I have to find a way to protect Gertie."

"I'll talk to her."

"You can't." Gertie would ask questions. "I don't want her to know about us. She'll tell Katrina everything." And Katrina would tell her customers.

"That's a fact." He looked into Mary's eyes. "I failed you in Abilene. I won't do it again. We'll deal with this together."

She felt protected, but J.T.'s presence would throw kerosene on even a hint of the old rumors. Neither could she risk J.T. learning about the baby and the miscarriage. "I appreciate the thought, but I know Gertie better than you do."

"And I know Roy," he countered. "I won't leave you, Mary. Not with your sister acting crazy. Roy's going to use her as bait. I'm sorry to disappoint Gus, but we won't be going on that camping trip. I need to stay in town."

"That's not necessary." She hated to let her brother down, but mostly she wanted J.T. to be out of the way in case she changed her mind about confiding in Gertie. "Gus is excited."

"He'll understand."

"Yes, but it's not fair." How did she balance Gus's needs with Gertie's? And what about J.T.? She suspected the camping trip meant as much to him as it did to her brother.

Mary faced him. "Do you think Gertie's in danger right now?"

"Not yet." He sounded businesslike. "As long as she's useful, he won't harm her."

"That's not much of a comfort, but I want you to go with Gus."

He thought for a minute. "All right, I'll take him. I don't like Gertie being around Roy, but she might grow up a little. Maybe she'll decide going to New York is best."

"That would be wonderful, but I don't have enough money to send her yet."

"How much do you need?"

"Fifteen hundred dollars." The amount would cover train fare, several months of living expenses, fashionable clothing for Gertie and something for Maude. Mary had some money saved, but it wasn't nearly enough.

J.T. lifted her hand in his and squeezed. "I've got five hundred dollars. It's not enough, but it's yours."

The gesture touched her to the core. "I can't take your money."

"Why not?"

"Because it wouldn't be right."

Suddenly tense, he loosened his grip on her hand, paced to the window and stood with his back to her and his arms crossed as he looked out the glass. When he turned around, his eyes were like blue stones. "So my money's not good enough for you. It's tainted, and so am I. Is that it?"

"Tainted?"

"Yeah." He smirked. "We both know how I earned it."

Mary finally understood. By rejecting J.T.'s money, in his mind she was rejecting *him*. "That's not it." She stood and went to his side. "If I worried about how my customers earned a living, I'd have to quiz each one at the door. If you feel bad about the gambling, give the money to charity."

"I do feel bad," he said quietly. "I want to give it to *you*."

Her heart stretched with each beat, making room for this man who failed her but wanted to make things right. She couldn't change the past, but she could respect his effort to be a good man. "Do you mean it?"

"I do."

"In that case," she said. "I accept."

He took her hand again and kissed her knuckles. "I'll find a way to get Gertie to New York before Roy does any real damage. I just need some time."

She knew how J.T. made a living. Worry wrinkled her brow. "Time for what?"

"To earn the rest of that fifteen hundred dollars."

She held his hand tight. "Promise me something."

"What?"

"That you won't go gambling for any more of it. That's money I won't take."

He squeezed her hand in reply, but he didn't make the promise. Did she trust him, or should she pressure him to give his word? She couldn't do either, and she wouldn't breathe a hint of his gift to Gertie. J.T. had made a rash promise, and she didn't want her sister to be disappointed if he failed to keep it. The possibility— even the likelihood—of J.T. going back to his old ways had to be considered. Bristling, she went to the divan and sat. Gertie's letter lay neatly on the table, a testament to her sister's naiveté and her own back in Abilene. "I wish Gertie could see what Roy's doing."

"So do I."

She barely heard him. "She's going to make the

same mistakes I did. She'll wear costumes that reveal too much, and then she'll wear costumes that reveal more. Men will look at her, and she'll feel beautiful. She'll think she's in love, and then she'll—she'll—" She shook her head to chase away the shame.

"Mary, don't."

Silhouetted by harsh light, he stood tall and bossy and as handsome as ever. "Don't what?" she cried. "Don't remember what *I* did?"

"Don't blame yourself for Gertie's choices." He paused. "Or for what *I* took from you. You were innocent. I wasn't."

She couldn't hear this, not now. "It's over, J.T. *Over.* I'm forgiven. I forgive you. That's enough."

"Not for me."

"It should be," she said angrily. "We sinned. I regret it. Apparently so do you."

"I do." He paced across the room and stood in front of her. "I pressured you. It was gentle, but it was still wrong."

She'd given herself to him freely, but he was right. She'd been naive. She hadn't expected to conceive, and she wondered now what he'd say if she told him about the miscarriage. She didn't know, and she was afraid to find out. Hurting for them both, she reached for his hand. "We can't change the past, but we can put it behind us."

He looked at their fingers laced in a pledge of sorts. "Do you really believe that?"

"I do."

He shook his head. "I wish I could."

"You can," she said gently. "It's a choice."

"What is?"

"Starting over."

"Not for me." He looked into her eyes with a bleakness she'd hadn't seen in Abilene, then he released her hand. "Do you really think I can hang up my guns? That I can just *decide* to be someone new?"

"I did," she said. "You're situation is more complicated, but no one knows what tomorrow holds."

"That's a fact." He looked around the room, taking in the trinkets of her life both past and present. His eyes lingered on a vase she'd brought from Abilene, then he studied the animals Gus had carved and an embroidered sampler of a Bible verse. It had been a gift from Josh and Adie. Without her faith, her family and her friends, her apartment would have been a very different place, and J.T. knew it.

She'd given him all she had, so she held out her hand. "Let's go to Swan's Nest."

He hesitated, then clasped her fingers. "I was going to skip supper, but I'm feeling hungry after all."

As he helped her off the divan, Mary noticed Fancy Girl lying on her side in the sun. Her belly was round and firm, and...moving.

J.T. looked at the dog with affection. "I've been in town too long. She's getting fat and lazy."

Mary touched his arm. "I don't think that's it."

He watched Fancy Girl, scowling until her tummy did a little roll. He looked closer, then his eyes widened. "Well, I'll be. She's having puppies." He walked to the dog's side, dropped to a crouch and put his hand on her belly. Mary stood watching, feeling the warmth along with him, then the beginning of new life when a puppy moved and a smile spread across his face. She'd seen J.T. smile before, but it had been nothing like the one she saw now. It came from the inside, some place hidden but full of life.

He pushed to his feet, then looked at her with awe. "I've never felt anything like that."

"It's amazing, isn't it."

"Yeah." He chuckled. "I wonder when it'll happen."

"I'd guess a week or two." She'd grown up around farm animals.

J.T. rubbed his neck. "Will she be all right with Gus and me on this trip?"

"I think so."

He blew out a breath. "If that doesn't beat all. My dog having puppies... Can Gus keep one?"

She felt rosy inside. "We'd both like that."

J.T. clicked his tongue to the dog. Fancy lumbered to her feet, and the three of them left the apartment. Mary saw his horse in front of the café. "I don't want Gus or Adie to worry. Why don't you ride ahead?"

He gave her a look that bordered on scathing. "There's no way I'm leaving without you. We'll both walk."

"That's silly."

His eyes flared with a spark she knew well. "Are you feeling a tad bit bold?"

"Why are you asking?"

"You can ride with me. We'll take a back street so no one sees your petticoats."

She hoisted her lilac skirt above her ankles, put her foot in the stirrup and pulled herself into the saddle. "Hurry up," she teased.

He untied the reins, climbed up behind her and reached around her waist. "How fast do you want to go?"

In Abilene she'd trusted him to lead, and they'd galloped down long and twisting trails to nowhere. Today the path would lead to Swan's Nest, but they could take the long way or a slower one. "You decide," she said, feeling wistful.

He kept the buckskin at a walk until they turned the corner that led to the railroad tracks and a back way to the mansion. With the road empty, he eased the horse into a lope that wouldn't strain Fancy Girl. When they arrived at Swan's Nest, he slid off the buckskin and lifted her out of the saddle. She landed facing him with her hands on his shoulders. The scent of bay rum tickled her nose, and laughter from the garden filled her ears. Rising to her toes, she kissed his cheek.

His gaze hardened, but in a good way. "What was that for?"

"For everything," she said. "For Gus. For Gertie..."

He held her a bit tighter. "I'm watching out for them. I'm keeping an eye on you, too."

A week ago she had given J.T. the cold shoulder. Today she wanted—needed—to trust him. If he hadn't come to Denver, she might have stepped into Roy's trap. Not only did her siblings need this man's influence, but she felt the stirrings of the old attraction. She wanted to hold him close. She yearned to comfort him and lean on him, but she knew how quickly he could disappoint her. She stepped out of his grasp. "Let's find Gus."

Side by side they walked into the garden with Fancy at J.T.'s side. They found Gus finishing his supper and told him about the puppies.

"C-c-can I keep one?"

J.T. grinned. "You get first choice."

Mary left the two of them talking about dogs and camping while she searched for Adie. She found her friend in the house, putting Stephen down for a nap in the nursery. When the boy settled, Adie led Mary to the bedroom she shared with Josh. There she sat on the settee while Mary swayed in an old rocking chair, telling Adie about J.T.'s talk with Roy, Roy's insistence she play Arline and his influence on Gertie.

"I'm terrified for her," Mary finished. "She has no idea what she's doing."

"No, she doesn't." Adie looked peeved. "We want Gertie to come home, but you can't force her."

Mary agreed. "She'd run away again."

"Have you considered talking to her plainly?" Adie meant about the scandal.

"I think about it all the time, but I can't trust her to keep it to herself. And I'm ashamed. I want to be a good example for her. What will she think if she knows the things I've done?"

"It's a tough choice, but one you're going to have to make." Adie straightened a pillow on the bench. "Whatever you decide, Gertie's not the only person you have to worry about."

"There's always Gus—"

"I'm not talking about your brother." She nudged the pillow again. "I want to hear about that handsome man who's obviously in love with you."

"Adie!"

"Well, he is," she said plainly. "Are you in love with him?"

Mary shook her head. "Absolutely not."

"I saw you riding with him." Adie didn't have Caroline's matchmaking instincts, but she could separate truth from wishful thinking with a shrewdness that came from experience. "You looked happy about it, too."

"I was, but I don't want to be. He hurt me terribly. I can't trust him."

"You're trusting him with Gus and Gertie."

"That's different."

"It's also a start," Adie said quietly.

"I will *not* fall in love!" Mary rocked harder in the chair. "Not with J.T. or any other man."

"I said the same thing a year ago. So did Pearl Oliver, and look at her now."

"That's different."

"Is it?" Adie asked. "Do you really think you can choose whom you love?"

Mary wanted to say yes, but she couldn't deny the stirring in her heart. "I don't know."

"God isn't blind to what's happening between you two."

"I don't want *anything* to happen," she insisted. "I don't trust him. Besides, he's not a Christian."

"Neither was I before I met Josh." Adie looked wistful. "He loved me anyway…as a friend."

A lump pushed into Mary's throat. The thought of trusting J.T. even as a friend terrified her. So did the sight of a baby blanket lying haphazardly on the settee and the glide of the chair where Adie rocked her son to sleep. She couldn't love J.T. until she trusted him, and she couldn't fully trust him until she told him her secret. She stared out the open window, listening to the chirp of a sparrow. "It's not that simple."

"Why not?"

The words spilled out before she could stop them. "I was with child when J.T. left me. I lost it."

"I'm so sorry." Adie reached for her hand. "Does he know?"

"No, and I can't tell him. He'd say something mean, and I'd hurt all over again."

"He might surprise you."

He already had. What he'd done for Gus had left her
in awe, and he'd been smart about Gertie. Mary knew
how to cope with hurt feelings. J.T.'s good intentions
unnerved her.

"Pray about it," Adie advised.

Mary didn't want to even *think* about it, but she had
to be willing. "I'll try."

"That's enough."

Mary could have stayed in the quiet room for hours,
but Gus and J.T. would be looking for her. "We should
go back."

The women returned to the garden, where Mary
found J.T. seated with Bessie and Caroline, polishing
off a meal. The next two hours passed in a blur. She
expected him to be remote, but instead he entertained
her friends with stories of his travels. He'd been all
over the West, everywhere from Texas to Montana, and
he'd seen everything from a line of twisters eating up
the prairie to a cattle drive bigger than Rhode Island.

Near the end of the afternoon, Caroline and Jake the
fiddler coaxed Mary into singing some old favorites.
She had a grand time, but the real stars of the day were
Gus and Fancy Girl. As the boy showed off her tricks
with hand signals, Mary couldn't decide who looked
more proud—Gus or J.T.

The last surprise came as they stood to leave. When
Josh offered to stable J.T.'s horses at Swan's Nest, J.T.
agreed and thanked him. Not once in Abilene had the
man accepted a favor from anyone.

They said their goodbyes, then she and J.T. headed
down the street, with Gus and Fancy Girl walking several feet ahead of them. If they'd been in Abilene, she'd
have been expecting a kiss. She felt the anticipation
now, and it was pleasant. She couldn't trust J.T. with

her heart, but did the battle have to be won before she kissed him? Common sense told her yes, but he deserved to know she appreciated the changes in him.

When they reached the café, Gus was waiting on the third step. She reached in her pocket and handed him the key. "Go on up. I'll be right behind you."

He hugged Fancy Girl so hard that Mary thought the dog would pop. J.T. watched with a smile. "Hey, girl. Kiss goodnight."

He'd spoken to the dog, but his eyes were on her as Fancy licked Gus's face with abandon.

"Good night, Fancy," Gus said easily.

J.T. offered his hand to the boy and they shook. "Get some sleep, partner. We're leaving early."

The boy raced up the steps, leaving her alone with this man who confused her and dusk falling like a curtain. She knew J.T.'s ways. If she stayed, he'd kiss her. With streaks of pink coloring the horizon, a kiss seemed like a precious gift, a reminder that love trumped a man's mistakes. She couldn't trust J.T. completely, but he needed to know people cared about him. Feeling shy, she tilted her face up to his. He looked into her eyes like he'd done in Abilene, but he didn't move. Instead he inhaled softly, then he kissed her on the cheek. "Good night, Mary."

She'd expected more, wanted more. "You're leaving?"

"Yeah."

She didn't know what to think.

"Go on, now," he murmured. "Get upstairs before I kiss you the way I want."

She couldn't move her feet, couldn't think beyond the shock of J.T. resisting the kiss she'd been willing to give. If he'd kissed her, her heart would have sped up. Without the kiss, it wanted to fly out of her chest. Instead of taking the gift she had freely offered, he'd chosen to protect her from possible regrets. She'd been ready to forget herself. Tonight J.T. had been strong.

She cupped his cheek. "There's goodness in you, Jonah. I see it."

He looked like he wanted to argue. Instead he murmured, "Good night, Mary. Pleasant dreams."

She turned and went up the stairs, his presence gentle in her mind as he waited for her to step inside the apartment. She closed the door, then went to the window and looked down. Her eyes found his, and he acknowledged her with a nod. Touching the glass, she whispered a prayer for him, then watched as he walked down the street. She prayed for him until he vanished from sight, then she kissed her fingers and pressed them to the window, leaving a mark on the glass shining darkly between them.

Chapter Fourteen

Early the next morning J.T. had breakfast with Gus at the café, then the two of them rode to the stream past the Slewfoot Mine. They spent the day shooting at cans and laughing at stupid jokes, then they fished for their supper. They caught enough trout to feed themselves and Fancy Girl, burned a can of beans and ate all the biscuits Mary had tucked into Gus's pack.

Full to the brim and tuckered out, Gus spread his bedroll on one side of the fire and climbed in. Fancy was stretched at his side. Yawning, the boy stared up at the stars. J.T. wasn't ready to settle down. Sitting on a rock by the campfire, he refilled his coffee cup. The day had left him pleasantly worn out, but he was worried. When he and Gus first set up camp, he'd found two whiskey bottles, a sign someone had camped here last night. Whoever he was, he'd used the brand preferred by Griff Lassen. J.T. had tossed the bottles aside, but the smell had reminded him of the things he'd denied himself. In particular he was thinking of last night's kiss...the one he'd held back.

In Abilene he'd have kissed her until she told him to stop, and he'd have made sure she didn't want to stop.

Last night he'd stopped for them both. It made no sense. For six months he'd imagined holding her close. She'd given him the chance and he'd stepped back. He had to be crazy or stupid, maybe both. He picked up a rock and heaved it into the dark.

Gus turned over in his bedroll. "A-a-are you all right?"

"Sure."

"Y-y-you look mad."

"Nah." He dumped his coffee to do something. "I was just thinking about stuff."

"Yeah. Me, too." Looking slightly nervous, the boy propped himself on one elbow. "C-can I ask you something?"

"Sure."

"It's about…where p-p-uppies come from."

"Puppies?" J.T. almost stammered like Gus. "You mean like…where babies come from?"

"Sort of."

No one ever got the jump on J.T., but Gus had caught him completely off guard. He had no desire to have this particular talk, but he also saw a need. What twelve-year-old boy wanted to ask his sister about such personal things? J.T. saw a chance to man up and do something good. He tossed a second rock. "So you want to know about babies and stuff."

"S-s-sort of."

The boy stammered more when he was worried, so J.T. took the bull by the horns. "It's nature's way, kid. A man and a woman—"

Gus shook his head. "I—I—I already kn-n-ow *that* part."

Relief washed over J.T., until he realized Gus's real

question might be even harder to answer. "What do you want to know?"

"I know where b-b-babies come from. I just don't know *why*."

"Why what?"

"Why it happens."

Six months ago, J.T. would have said nature took its course. Tonight he recalled *not* kissing Mary, and he knew he had to give Gus an honest answer. What he said would influence the boy for the rest of his life. J.T.'s own education on the matter had come from his oldest brother, and it had been crude. Even at a tender age, he'd known his brother was wrong-minded about women.

He saw a chance to give Gus something better. "The best way it happens is when a man and woman love each other and get married." He didn't bother telling the boy about the other ways it happened, or the worst ways.

"Wh-why do they love each other?"

"That's a mystery to me, too." He tapped his fingers on the enamel cup. "A man meets the right lady, and it just happens."

"H-h-has it happened to you?"

The meaning of the question hit J.T. hard. For six months, he'd thought about finding Mary and being with her. He'd recalled how she'd cared for him in Abilene and how she'd made him smile. Not once had he thought beyond giving her a place to sing. Marrying hadn't been in the plan, and neither had giving her children. He'd been too selfish to think about anything except his own wants. Last night when he hadn't kissed her, he'd done it for her…he'd done it for *them*. The meaning of that choice hit him hard.

He kicked the dirt. "Yeah, I've been in love."

"Do you l-love m-my sister?"

He saw *that* question coming. Looking stern, he stared at Gus across the fire. The boy stared back with a daring J.T. had to admire. Instead of telling Gus that some questions were too personal, he laughed out loud.

Gus glared at him. "Well, do you?"

He knew better than to involve the boy. Yes, he loved Mary. He could admit it to himself, but what did he have to give her? His guns, two good horses and a talent for faro. And his bad name. No woman in her right mind would want J. T. Quinn for a husband, but he felt a yearning he couldn't deny. He wanted to spend the rest of his days with Mary Larue, and he wanted to give her the respect of a wedding ring.

He felt Gus's eyes on his face and hoped the boy couldn't read his thoughts. He picked up another rock and hurled it at a distant shadow. "If I talk to anyone about that, it should be your sister."

"But you like her, don't you?"

"Yes, Gus. I do. I like your sister a lot." He felt a lot more than *like*, but *like* would do for a twelve-year-old. "It's late, and we're hunting rabbit tomorrow. You need to get some sleep."

"Yeah." The boy hunkered down in his bedroll.

J.T. spread his own blankets, then stretched flat and stared at the sky. He didn't doubt his love for Mary, but what could he do about it? Even if he found a way to make a living—he enjoyed roofing—other differences kept them apart. She believed in God, and he didn't. No way would J.T. ever turn the other cheek to an enemy. Looking at the patchwork of clouds and sky, he began to wonder—did it matter what he thought about God? He couldn't share her faith, but maybe he didn't need to compete with it. All couples had their differences. She liked rhubarb and he didn't. He liked his coffee hot and strong. She ruined hers with cream. Did their differences really matter? He'd cleaned up his life. He was willing to die for her. Surely that was enough to earn back her trust.

He was pondering the possibility when he heard scuffling in the brush. Bolting upright, he grabbed his gun and took aim. Fancy Girl jumped to her feet and growled. When the noise faded completely, he uncocked the hammer.

Gus sat upright. Sleepy but wide-eyed, he looked at the gun in J.T.'s hand. "Did you hear something?"

"Just a coyote."

The boy patted Fancy Girl, then glanced at the sky. He looked nervous, and J.T. regretted scaring him. It would have been worse, though, if someone had snuck up on them.

Gus looked at him from across the dead campfire. "C-c-an I asked you another question?"

"Sure." It couldn't be worse than the ones about love.

"D-do you ever pray?"

He was wrong. This question was harder. Gus looked up to him. What he said would matter, and J.T. didn't want the boy to be like him. He also had to be honest, because anything less would insult them both. He put the gun back under the blanket he used for a pillow. "I prayed when I was your age."

"What about now?"

"Not much." *Not ever.*

"I-it's not hard." Gus sounded confident. "M-my mama taught me special words to s-s-ay, but mostly I th-think them."

J.T. had no idea what to say, but he wanted to encourage the boy. "That's good."

"I—I don't stammer when I t-t-talk in my head."

What would that be like, J.T. wondered, to hear yourself right but have the words come out wrong? Every man had flaws, but Gus lived with constant failure. It had to hurt.

The boy seemed to be talking to the dark. "M-ary says my stam-m-mer doesn't m-m-matter to God, but I w-wish i-it would stop."

"I know the feeling, Gus." J.T. had wishes of his own. "I've never had a stammer, but there are things about myself I don't much like."

He had no desire to share his regrets with Gus. The boy had been far too protected to understand J.T.'s choices. To his relief, Gus lay back down. So did J.T., but he felt as if the stars were pinning him down. Since he'd dared God to show Himself, he'd had been pestered by clouds and curious boys, hot benches, friendly people, puppies and most dangerous of all, the notion of being in love. If the Almighty had taken J.T.'s challenge to show Himself, He'd done it in curious ways.

Gus's voice came out of the dark. "J.T.?"

"Yeah?"

"Do you think G-God listens?"

A week ago he'd have said no. Tonight he was asking the same question. "I don't know."

"I do," Gus said with certainty.

As if that were enough, the boy fell asleep, leaving J.T. to stare at the sky. He shut his eyes to hide the stars, but he couldn't shake the feeling he was being watched, or watched over, so he opened them again. A falling star shot across the black expanse, leaving a trail that faded to nothing. He imagined his own life ending the same way. He wasn't afraid of dying. He wasn't afraid of anything.... Except he was. He was terrified of small dark places and being pinned on his back. He was worried about Fancy Girl having puppies, and he feared what Roy Desmond would do to Gertie. And Mary. He was afraid he'd lose her again before he could fully earn her trust.

A cloud obscured the top half of the crescent moon. As the shadow passed, Fancy Girl lumbered to her feet and came to him. Leaving Gus to his dreams, she took her usual spot and rested her head on his chest.

"Hi there, girl." He scratched her neck the way she liked, then rested his hand on her belly. The puppies were quiet now, but he could feel the promise of life and it humbled him. There were things a man could do, and things he couldn't. J.T. could take a life, but he couldn't give it back. He hoped Mary would be around when Fancy's time came. The dog would do all the work, but he knew that birth and death were a breath apart.

"Rest up, girl," he murmured. "You're going to be fine."

The dog's tail whapped.

"I know," he said to her. "Strange things are happening to both of us."

J.T. didn't have new life growing in his belly, but he felt the stirrings just the same. With Fancy at his side, he closed his eyes and thought of what he'd do with Gus tomorrow. They'd hunt rabbit so the boy could practice with a rifle, then they'd do some more boxing. Lost in pleasant thoughts, he fell into a deep and comfortable sleep.

On Wednesday morning Mary finished cleaning up after breakfast, locked the café and went to Swan's

Nest to borrow a buggy. In her arms was a picnic basket, and in her pocket was the map J.T. had left to the stream where they'd be camping. He'd given it to her without being asked, and she'd been impressed. After a chat with Adie, she left Denver with a sense of pleasant anticipation.

She'd had plenty of time to think about her feelings for J.T. She didn't feel ready to tell him about the miscarriage, but she liked the idea of being his friend. Adie had helped to open Mary's eyes, but sadly so had Gertie. While praying for her sister, Mary had seen herself even more clearly in Gertie's determination to ignore the facts about Roy. Mary couldn't deny that J.T. had changed.

She'd seen the evidence for herself and no longer questioned his good intentions, but his place in her life was another matter. Regret changed a man's heart, but faith changed his ways. With faith, a man could love a woman more than he cared about himself. Without it Mary couldn't trust J.T. fully, but she hoped they could be friends. To show him she'd crossed a line, she'd packed a picnic lunch with cobbler and other goodies, and she planned to surprise him at the stream.

With the sun bright, she passed the Slewfoot Mine and turned down the road that led to Cherry Creek. It wound past boulders and cottonwoods, around a bend and ended at a clearing. She saw ashes in the fire pit, bedrolls, neatly stacked cookware and their horses grazing nearby. J.T. and Gus had to be close, so she climbed out of the buggy. Heading toward the creek, she heard J.T. making playful threats, Gus's high-pitched shouting and the furious splashing of a water fight.

Enjoying the happy sounds, she ambled down the trail until the sparkle of amber glass stopped her in her tracks. Looking more closely, she saw a whiskey bottle in the brush. Not just one bottle, but two. Trembling, she bent down and inspected them. They were both clean, unmarked by rainwater or dirt. One of them had no odor, but the other still reeked and was marked with fingerprints. It hadn't been there long. Maybe hours... no more than a day or two.

J.T. had let her down...again.

She wanted to go back to the buggy and leave, but she couldn't leave Gus in the care of a drunken gun-fighter.

Furious, she picked up the bottle and marched to the stream. From the top of a small rise, she saw the man and the boy waging war with water and buckets. She saw J.T.'s shaving tools on a rock, his shirt hanging on a willow branch and Gus's shirt next to it as if they were cut from the same cloth. She stood with the whiskey bottle in her hand, watching and crying and wishing J.T. had never come back to Denver.

With her eyes on J.T.'s face, she navigated between the rocks and weeds. He didn't see her and neither did Gus. She watched her brother dump a bucket of water over J.T.'s head. The clear liquid sparkled on his hair and face, then ran in streams down his chest, washing him clean but not really.

"Why, God?" she murmured. "Why did You bring him back just to fail me?"

As if to answer her question, J.T. suddenly spotted her and smiled. Gus took advantage and knocked him off his feet. He went under and came up sputtering and laughing and happier than she'd ever seen him. With a disgusted look, she held up the whiskey bottle. She waved it for him to see, threw it as far as she could and went back to the buggy to wait.

Chapter Fifteen

J.T. didn't see the bottle until it flew out of Mary's hand. Sloshing out of the stream, he shouted at Gus over his shoulder. "Stay here, kid. This is between your sister and me."

Dripping wet, he grabbed his shirt and charged barefoot up the steep incline, dragging his shirt over his head as he chased her. A thorn dug into the sole of his foot, but he ignored it. At the top of the hill, he saw her twenty feet away. "Mary, wait! It's not what you think."

She whirled and faced him. "Yes, it is. It's whiskey."

"It's not mine."

"Do you expect me to *believe* you?" She laughed bitterly. "I smelled the bottle. It's fresh. It has fingerprints on it."

"I know. I threw it away."

She huffed. "Of course you did."

"You've got to believe me." He paced closer, a step at a time, giving her a chance to back off if she was going to run. Crowding her wouldn't help his cause. She had to come willingly. She had to choose to give him a chance. Fighting both the fear that she'd run and the anger of being falsely accused, he held his arms to the side to open himself fully to her view.

"Do I look drunk?" he said mildly.

Her eyes dipped to his bare feet, dirty now and stinging from the thorn. She took in his wet trousers and the damp shirt, and finally she looked into his eyes. J.T. knew they were clear and bright. They were also full of hope, because he really did have a clean conscience. It felt good.

He took a step closer. "Am I slurring my words?"

"No." She bit her lip. "I want to believe you, but I saw the bottle. I smelled it."

He took another step, a larger one.

Mary stayed in place.

He came closer still, holding her gaze until they were a foot apart. If she wanted to smell his breath, the choice was hers. Understanding his intention, she leaned slightly forward and inhaled. So did J.T. He smelled the rosy soap Mary used in Abilene and sun-warmed cotton. When her eyes went wide, he lowered his arms. "What do you smell?"

"I smell…water."

He wanted to kiss her for the joy of it, but he settled for enjoying her surprise. "I found the bottles by the fire pit. I tossed them so Gus wouldn't find them."

The next thing he knew, Mary had her hands on his shoulders and was clutching his shirt. The wet cotton dragged against his back, pulling them closer as she matched her mouth to his in a kiss that erased every thought except one—he loved this woman. She didn't seem to care that he was sopping wet, so he put his arms around her and drew close. When she made the kiss bolder, so did he. Her straw hat was in his way, so he loosened the ribbons and took it off her head.

He wanted to give more than he took, but he wouldn't give more than Mary wanted. He matched her breath for breath but offered nothing more. She ended the kiss with a sigh, then rested her head on his shoulder. He thought of his demand that God show Himself. This was forgiveness. This was mercy. Mary trusted him again, but now where did they go? He wasn't the only person who had to decide, so he loosened his arms enough to see her face. She looked like a woman who'd been thoroughly kissed and now regretted it. Troubled, he used both hands to put the hat back on her head.

"What happens next?" he asked.

"I don't know." Backing away, she hastily tied the satin ribbons. The patches from his wet shirt showed on her dress, leaving an imprint of the embrace. The sun would dry the dress in minutes. The kiss couldn't be so easily erased, but Mary looked like she wanted to try. She finished the bow with a snap, then squared her shoulders. "I shouldn't have kissed you."

"Oh, definitely not," he said, teasing her.

"I mean it." She started to pace. "I came out her to tell you how much I appreciate what you've done for Gus and Gertie. I brought bread and chicken and…and cobbler. I thought we could be friends, but that kiss—" Groaning, she turned her back. "You've *always* done that to me. It's just not fair!"

"It's fair, all right."

"Oh, no, it's not!"

He walked up behind her. "You do the same thing to me, probably even stronger." He wanted to turn her around, but the choice to come into his arms belonged to her.

"I'm so confused!" she said to the sky. She pressed

her hands to her cheeks, moaned, then lowered her arms and faced him. "I have to be honest with you."

"I'm listening."

"Kissing you was as wonderful as ever."

He'd been expecting her to call him a good-for-nothing. Instead she'd given him a compliment. "I can say the same to you."

"Some things don't change," she said quietly. "But others do. I can't kiss you again. Not like that. I was caught up in the moment. It shouldn't have happened."

"Why not?"

"Because I'd be lying."

"Lying?" He didn't understand at all.

"I don't want to repeat the past, and right now that's all we have." She looked stronger now, as if she'd found her purpose. "I'm not the woman you knew in Abilene. It might not look like it from the outside—"

"It shows," he interrupted. "I see the changes."

"They're on the inside, too." She lifted her chin even higher. "My faith is important to me, but I'm human. I like kissing you, but we can't be more than friends. The differences between us matter."

When he finally understood, his eyes narrowed. "You love God and I don't." He calmed his voice. "I don't see why it's a problem. You can go to church all you want. It doesn't bother me a bit."

Her expression told him that he'd missed the point.

He felt like throwing a rock at a cloud, climbing up to one and pummeling it into smoke. He cared about Mary. He loved her. He'd have told her if he thought she'd be happy about it, but loving her only added to the wedge between them. He was beginning to feel like a puppet on a string, and he didn't like it. He was also starting to worry about Gus. The boy had seen the start of the quarrel and would be concerned. "This needs to wait," he said coldly. "Gus is still at the creek."

Mary looked pained. "I didn't forget him."

"Neither did I."

She lifted her chin. "He'll be hungry. We can still have lunch."

J.T. wanted to get away from her, but she had a point. "I'll get him. Wait here."

"I'll go," she insisted. "I want to see him."

"No!" He'd had all he could stand. "I'm soaking wet, and I've got a thorn in my foot. You accused me of getting drunk in front of Gus, then you kissed me like you meant it, but you didn't. And *now* you want to give me cobbler. Right now, all I want is to put on dry clothes and *not* talk."

With that, he headed for the stream to get Gus.

As Mary handed out sandwiches, she couldn't stop remembering the picnic in Kansas. That day she and J.T. had talked for hours and kissed like fools. Today they weren't speaking to each other. Instead they each focused on Gus. She listened to the boy's tales about shooting and boxing lessons, while J.T. ate in silence except to praise her brother. After the cobbler, Gus asked J.T. if they could go home today instead of tomorrow. He agreed, and together they packed while Mary washed dishes at the stream.

With the water rippling around the rocks, she thought of her decision to be J.T.'s friend and the kiss that revealed her deeper feelings. Adie was right. Love wasn't a choice, and she loved J.T. She couldn't tell him, though. Not only did her faith matter, but she'd didn't trust him with her feelings about the past.

A lean shadow fell on the sand next to her. Abruptly,

she turned and saw J.T. several steps away. "We're packed and ready."

She had one more plate to rinse. "I'll be up in a minute."

She hoped he'd linger so they could patch up the quarrel, but he walked away. She finished scrubbing the last dish with sand, rinsed it, then gathered the plates and went back to the campsite. To her surprise, the buckskin was tied to the buggy, and J.T. was waiting with his hat pulled low. Gus, mounted on J.T.'s extra horse, looked pleased. When she reached the rig, J.T. took the basket, shoved it under the seat and then offered his hand. "I'm driving you home."

"You don't have to."

"Tell that to Gus," he said drily. "He accused me of not being a gentleman."

She gave J.T. a sympathetic look and then took his hand and climbed into the buggy. He motioned for Fancy Girl to jump in next to her and then walked around the rig and joined her, the seat squeaking with his weight. He took the reins, and off they went.

One mile of silence.

Two miles of silence.

Three miles of silence. Fancy Girl leaned against Mary, pushing her into J.T.'s ribs. If he'd put his arm around her, they'd have been as close as they'd been in Abilene. Instead, he kept his spine rigid, and so did she. The silence troubled her even more than the kiss. They couldn't be in love, but she wanted to be his friend. She was close to bursting when he shifted his boots and their feet touched. When he didn't pull back, neither did she. The touch wasn't the conversation she wanted to have, but it was a start.

"Any word on Gertie?" he finally asked.

"I haven't seen her." She stared down the empty road. "If I don't hear from her soon, I'm going to visit her."

"We need to get her to New York."

"I wish I could."

His eyes glinted with the toughness she recalled from Abilene. "Give me a few days."

That was all he said until they arrived at the café. He unloaded Gus's things, then he and the boy cleaned the guns they used, including a .22 rifle he gave to Gus to keep. They talked about bullets and whatnot until J.T. left to return the buggy to Swan's Nest with Fancy Girl riding next to him.

As he rode off, Mary wondered if his plan to get the money for Gertie included a turn at a faro table. He knew how she felt about gambling, so she said nothing. The decision to gamble belonged to J.T. The choice to refuse the money was hers, and that's what she intended to do.

At Swan's Nest J.T. cared for his horses and put up the buggy. No one pestered him, so he finished fast and went straight to Sixteenth Street in search of a faro parlor. He'd earn that money for Gertie and he'd do it tonight. He knew Mary objected to gambling, but he hoped she'd take the winnings for Gertie's sake. After today's craziness, he felt more compelled than ever to keep his promise. With his saddlebag over his shoulder—the bag with his clothes and all his money—he pushed through the door to a gaming hall called the Bull's Eye.

"This won't take long, girl," he said to Fancy.

He had his whole stake with him. With a little luck, he'd triple it in an hour…

Two hours later, he walked out the same door shaking his head. He'd never had such awful luck. The dealer hadn't minded Fancy Girl at all, especially once J.T. started losing. To make up for the losses, he'd upped his bets. He'd quit before he lost everything, but he had less than half of what he'd started with.

The run of bad luck made him mad. Being mad reminded him of Mary and how she'd kissed him and backed away. What did she want from him, anyway? Whatever it was, he didn't have it to give. With his saddlebag lighter, he headed to the boardinghouse and went to his room. Leaving the door wide to catch the light in the hall, he dropped the saddlebag on the floor and lit the lamp. Once it flared, he shut the door and locked it.

Fancy headed for a corner she never used, dropped down and looked at him with sad brown eyes.

"I know." He grumbled. "I made a fool of myself."

Thoroughly annoyed, he plopped down on the bed. Faro dealers were notorious cheats, and J.T. was rusty. He considered trying a different faro parlor, but he didn't want to leave Fancy Girl alone. Trapped and too angry to sleep, he wedged a pillow against the wall and sat up on the bed. He needed something to do. Even a button to sew would have been a distraction. Something to read would have been better, even a stupid dime novel.

Desperate, he glanced around the room and saw the chapbook on the nightstand. He blinked and was on the white stone bench in Josh's garden. If he didn't fill his mind with something, he'd end up in that alley in New York, on his back and feeling his brother's knife. Even with the light on, the room felt small and tight. Needing to escape—in his mind, since he couldn't leave

Fancy—he opened the chapbook. His thumb pointed to a single sentence. *And the light shineth in darkness; and the darkness comprehended it not.*

J.T. knew the power of darkness. He knew how it felt to be trapped by it, caught between walls and rendered helpless and blind. It was light that befuddled him. He didn't understand where it came from, but he could see it. He'd seen the light in the way Fancy Girl loved him. He'd seen the light in Gus, too. Today he'd seen the brightest light of all in Mary. She'd taken back the kiss, but not before she'd come willingly into his arms. The light, he realized, was love. Not only had he seen the light…he'd felt it. He loved Fancy Girl and Gus. He loved Mary most of all, and today he could believe she loved him back.

Him, J. T. Quinn, a killer by trade and a gambler by choice. A man who'd spilled blood and enjoyed it. Mary cared for him. How could that be? He read more of the little book, comprehending just enough to know that he wanted to know more. He didn't understand most of what he read, but Mary did. The light lived in her. More than anything, he wanted to feel the brightness for the rest of their lives. He'd do anything to earn that privilege, but how? What did he have to do? A thought came out of the blue, and he smiled. Tomorrow Mary would get a surprise.

J.T. set down the book. As he turned down the lamp, Fancy Girl jumped on the bed and curled against his leg. With his hand on her belly, he thought about puppies and cobbler, kisses, love, cheating faro dealers and the strange twists of a hard day.

Chapter Sixteen

"**W**here are the aprons?" said a male voice.

Mary turned from the stove and saw J.T. and Fancy Girl both looking at her with concern. She'd been racing around the kitchen, and her cheeks were flushed. The waitress she'd hired to replace Gertie hadn't shown up, and Enid was complaining loudly. *And* the train had arrived early, filling the café with hungry patrons. "What are you doing here?" she asked.

"I'm your new dishwasher."

"You're *what?*"

"I'm washing dishes for you." He cast a wary eye at a tub full of dirty plates. "You need help. Here I am."

She didn't know everything he was thinking, but she recognized his effort as a peace offering for yesterday's quarrel. As much as she needed help, she worried about his commitment to finishing the church. "Isn't Josh expecting you?"

"Not today."

She smiled at him. "In that case, the job's yours. In fact, I'm grateful. The aprons are next to the pantry."

Fancy found a comfortable corner, and J.T. went to the row of hooks with kitchen apparel. He selected a white bibbed apron, tied the strings over his gun belt and went to work on a stack of greasy plates. Between the sizzling bacon and the clatter of dishes, Mary thought about yesterday. The kiss had to be forgotten, but she needed to talk to him about earning the money for Gertie. Yesterday she'd let him leave without speaking her mind. This morning she felt compelled to bring up the matter.

She spoke to him from the stove while flipping hotcakes. "We need to talk about Gertie and New York."

When he didn't reply, she looked over her shoulder. Not many men could wear an apron tied in a bow and still be menacing. Somehow J.T. looked as if he were commanding the dishes to wash themselves. Mary wished she could control Gertie with that kind of authority, but her sister would have stared back.

She added a rasher of bacon to a pan. "I want to be sure you know, I won't take new gambling money."

He still didn't respond.

"It wouldn't be right," she insisted. "I'd feel—"

"You don't have to worry," he said, almost growling at her. "I lost my shirt at the Bull's Eye. I won't be going back."

"Oh, dear." She felt both bad for him and relieved. "How much did you lose?"

"A lot."

She didn't want to embarrass him, but she needed to understand. "Are you washing dishes because you need the job? I'll pay you."

He faced her with a dripping plate in one hand, a rag in the other and a stare that would have made a wolf cower. "I'm not doing this for money."

"I just thought—"

"I didn't lose everything." He plunged the plate in

the soapy water. "I failed you, Mary. I didn't get drunk, but I gambled and lost half of what I had. Instead of getting Gertie to New York, I made things worse."

"No, you didn't." His method had been all wrong, but she couldn't ignore his good intentions. She saw the losing streak as a blessing and smiled. "The way I see it, I got a dishwasher out of the deal." She winked at him for fun. "A handsome one at that."

His brows snapped together. "Don't tease me."

She turned red.

"I like it too much," he muttered. "And losing's no fun."

"I'm sorry." She should have considered his pride. "It was thoughtless of me, but I'm not sorry you had a bad night at faro. Winning would have hurt you more than it would have helped Gertie."

He shook his head. "I feel like a fool."

She crossed the room and stood in front of him, clasping his biceps as she looked up. "You made a mistake, Jonah. It'll be okay."

His hands, dry but still warm from the water, came to rest on her waist. Neither of them took the kiss dangling between them. It hung like hard, green fruit, full of promise but far from ripe. With her eyes bright, she kissed his cheek and went back to the stove.

"Mary?"

She looked over shoulder. "Yes?"

"Thank you."

"For what?"

"Understanding." Silent again, he dipped a plate into the rinse water.

For the next two hours, they worked as a team with Enid serving, Gus clearing tables and Fancy Girl getting scraps from Gus. When the last customer left,

Mary began scraping grease from the stove. Gus came up behind her. "G-Gertie's here."

The stove could wait. She reached around her back to untie the apron. "I'll be right there."

Gus paused. "Sh-she's with th-that man."

Mary wanted to lock Gertie upstairs and give Roy a piece of her mind, but the strings had turned into a knot. Before she could untie it, J.T. had removed his own apron and wadded it into a ball. "You're not going out there alone."

"But—"

"The four of us need to have a civilized conversation," he said amiably. He looked at Gus. "Take Fancy Girl upstairs."

"Sure."

The boy left with the dog, and Mary spoke briefly to Enid. The waitress promised to bring a friend to help serve lunch and went out the back door.

J.T. indicated the entry to the dining hall. "Shall we?"

"Certainly."

She stepped into the room with J.T. behind her. Gertie's eyes widened at the sight of him, but it was Roy's expression that told a story. He clenched his jaw, then put on a smile. The surprise gave Mary an advantage, and she intended to keep it by being hospitable. She crossed the room as if she'd been expecting them and greeted Gertie with a hug.

"Shall we sit?" she said graciously.

Gertie feigned a dignified nod. Roy looked less agreeable, but he helped the girl with her chair. J.T. seated Mary next to Gertie, then pulled out a chair for himself.

Mary smiled a bit too cheerfully. "I'm done serving breakfast, but I can offer coffee or tea?"

Gertie squirmed, then shared a glance with Roy that sent bolts of fury down Mary's spine. She did *not* want her sister trading secretive looks with Roy. She shot a look of her own at J.T. He seemed completely at ease, except that he was drilling Roy with his eyes.

The theater manager cleared his throat. "Gertie asked me to call on you today, Mary. She says you're worried about her joining my theater troupe, that you think she'll grow up too fast. I can assure you, I'll treat her like my own daughter."

He'd said the right words, but his dark eyes had no life. How could she have trusted this man?

Gertie smiled at him gratefully and then faced Mary. "There's no reason for me to go to New York. Roy's been so kind, and I'm learning from the other actresses. I want you to be happy for me."

Mary knew her sister. Gertie would rebel if she spoke her mind, but neither could Mary offer the approval the girl wanted. She had to tell the truth. "I will always love you, Gertie."

"I know, but—"

Mary shook her head. "There are no 'buts' when it comes to family. I want you to go to New York. It's just a question of when."

Gertie pulled back from Mary and faced Roy. "I told you she wouldn't understand."

"But I do," Mary countered.

"So do I," J.T. added.

Glaring at him, Gertie took a hankie from her reticule and dabbed at her moist brow. Mary didn't recognize the fine linen and wondered if Roy had given it to her. The theater manager looked pointedly at J.T., then took the girl's hand. "It'll be fine, Gertie. I promise."

Mary wanted to give Roy a piece of her mind, but J.T. looked as cool as January. It was easy to imagine him killing Roy in cold blood, a thought that horrified her. If he harmed Gertie, she'd want justice to be served but only by the law. She turned to her sister. "I care about you. You *know* I want what's best for you."

Gertie sniffed.

Roy pushed to his feet. "I think it's time we left."

J.T. stood but said nothing. Gertie rose more slowly and so did Mary. She wanted to hug her sister, but the girl paced to the door. Mary followed, vaguely aware of Roy saying something to J.T. Gertie left without a goodbye, her shoes tapping angrily on the boardwalk.

Roy followed her, stopping in front of Mary and leaning too close. "Take the role, and I'll leave your sister alone."

"How dare you!" she hissed. "She's a *child*!"

"She's old enough. Just remember, you can change your mind anytime you want."

"I won't."

An ugly smirk curled on his lips. "It would be a shame to have word get out about your sordid past. I wonder what little Gertie would think about you and J. T. Quinn?"

An actress at heart, Mary feigned disinterest. "That's old news, Roy. No one cares but you."

"I doubt that." Looking smug, he walked out the door.

Mary wanted to throw a plate. "The nerve of that man!"

J.T. had stayed at the table, and he stood there now with a look of cold disdain. How could he be so calm?

Mary wanted to drag Gertie home by her hair. Instead she massaged her temples. When she remembered Roy had spoken to J.T., she stopped rubbing at the headache and looked up. "What did he say to you?"

"He wants to talk to me alone."

"About what?"

"I'll find out tonight. We're meeting during the show."

"At the theater?"

"His office," he replied.

She hated giving Roy an advantage, even a territorial one. "I want to go with you."

He lowered his chin. "No."

"But—"

"He's a snake, Mary. You go near him, and he'll bite you."

"But he's got my *sister*." If she told Gertie everything—her own secret and what J.T. had said—maybe the girl would listen. It was her last resort.

He crossed the room and stood nose to nose with her. "If you go *near* that theater, I'll throw you over my shoulder and carry you home."

He was teasing, sort of. "You wouldn't dare."

"I'd dare, all right." The playfulness left his eyes. "Whatever it takes to keep you away from Roy, I'll do it."

She felt the weight of his words, the caring in them. She trusted J.T. with Gus and Gertie, even her own life, but her heart was another matter. "You're right," she murmured. "I won't go near the Newcastle."

Stepping back, he indicated the weapon that never left his hip. "My gun is staying right here. If Roy harms you or Gertie, I'll use it."

Mary abhorred violence, but she valued his protection. "If you fire that thing at Roy in self-defense, I might not mind. But I hope you don't have to."

"Me, too."

His answer surprised her. In Abilene he'd been quick to shed blood. "Do you mean that?"

"I do." His mouth leveled into a line. "I'm tired of fighting, but that doesn't mean I can stop."

"Why not?"

He shook his head. "A man's reputation stays with him."

So did a woman's. Mary knew that fact well. "I made a fresh start. So can you."

"Not with men like Griff Lassen after me." He looked more tense than ever. "It'll be a long time before they all forget I'm alive."

Mary had the same problem. People would talk about the Abilene scandal as long as someone would listen. "I understand. It's why I'm so careful with my reputation."

His jaw muscles tensed. "If anyone pesters you, they'll regret it."

He'd always been protective of her. "Thank you."

"The same goes for Gertie. If Roy touches her, he'll pay."

Mary believed in justice, not cold-blooded killing, but she'd be as quick as J.T. to protect Gertie. "Let's hope nothing happens to her."

He got down to business. "Tonight I'll hear what Roy has to say. I have a feeling something happened we don't know about."

"What makes you say that?"

"He came here to bargain with us. That means he's not getting what he needs from Gertie. You didn't give in, and we know he needs money for his so-called investors. Now he wants to talk to me." J.T.'s eyes took on an amused light. "Since I can't sing a lick, there's got to be another angle."

"Like what?"

He took his gun from the holster, spun it fast and dropped it back in place. "Maybe he wants someone dead."

"J.T., no!"

He acted as if he hadn't heard her. "We'll talk after I see him, either tonight or tomorrow."

"Tonight," she insisted. If Roy and J.T. tangled, she wanted to know about it. And if he had news on Gertie, she needed to hear that, too.

"I better go," he said. "I've got a little work left on the roof. Mind if I take Gus?"

"I'll get him."

Mary went up the stairs. She saw her brother sitting with Fancy Girl in a dark corner. Unless Mary missed her guess, the dog would have her puppies in a day or two.

She spoke to Gus. "J.T.'s waiting for you. Tell him I'll watch Fancy while you two work."

"O-okay."

Gus left in a hurry. Mary took an old blanket from under her bed and gave it to the dog for a nest. Rubbing Fancy Girl's belly, she remembered her own few months of being with child. She didn't feel ready to tell J.T. about the baby they'd lost, but Roy's threat to expose the scandal put pressure on her. She also knew Roy would keep her secret as long as it gave him an advantage. She had time to decide, and she wanted to take it. She needed J.T.'s friendship too much to risk losing it.

"What do you think?" she said to Fancy Girl. "Do you think he'll understand?"

The dog sighed, then closed her eyes. Mary had the same inclination.

As J.T. approached the side door to the Newcastle Theater, he passed the scaffolding he'd climbed this afternoon while working on the roof with Gus. Moonlight lit up the planks where he'd stood with the boy, giving them the look of a ladder to the sky. He liked being high, but tonight he had to go low, as low as Roy Desmond.

This afternoon he'd seen Gertie sashay into the theater. He'd also observed other actors as they'd come and gone, and they'd mocked her unmercifully. The girl didn't have Mary's talent. Roy needed Mary, which meant Gertie was bait. Like a worm on a hook, she'd be sacrificed in Roy's quest to satisfy his investors. J.T. didn't have the details, but he figured Roy had two options. He could pay the money he owed, or he could eliminate the threat of someone coming to collect it.

Applause burst from the open windows of the theater. J.T. glanced up, then knocked on the side door. Roy opened it immediately, a sign he'd been waiting and didn't want to be seen.

"Come in, Quinn."

J.T. stepped into a long hall lit by six wooden sconces. In the distance he heard an actor's booming voice and an answering rumble of laughter. He wondered if Gertie was backstage or in the audience, and if she'd come to the theater alone or with Katrina. Roy opened the door to his office, a square room with a massive desk, a sideboard set with crystal and whiskey and a divan upholstered in red velvet. He indicated the divan. "Have a seat."

"No, thanks."

"Whiskey?"

The liquor didn't tempt him at all. "Not tonight."

Roy poured a glass for himself. "I guess the rumors are true."

"What rumors?"

"That you've gotten soft."

If J.T. lost his reputation, he'd be an easy target for any young buck wanting to prove himself. The thought shook him up, but he put the reaction aside. He had to focus on Mary and Gertie. "What do you want, Roy?"

"I have an offer for you." Seated behind the desk, Roy swirled the whiskey and downed the contents. Men drank for a lot of reasons, including for courage. Something had put Roy on edge. If the right person was making the man nervous, J.T. would have an ally.

Roy set down the glass with a thud. "You don't like me, Quinn. And you don't want Mary Larue singing in my theater."

"That's right."

"She doesn't want her baby sister here, either."

"Right again."

"I propose a trade." He steepled his fingers over his chest, tapping them in a rhythm meant to make J.T. nervous.

It wouldn't work, because J.T. refused to let it. "I've been working all day, Roy. Say your piece or I'm gone."

"You won't leave."

"And you don't want me to. Get on with it."

"All right." He leaned forward. "I told you I have investors. That's not exactly true."

"I figured."

"I won a considerable amount of money playing poker on Mississippi riverboats. I figured I could go legitimate." The man looked pale. "I'm not getting any younger, and I like the idea of settling down, even taking a wife."

J.T. had had similar thoughts.

"Contrary to what you think," Roy continued. "I'm very fond of Mary Larue."

"So am I. "

"I figured that out. Don't worry, Quinn. You can have her."

J.T. felt no relief. The man still had a hold on Gertie. "What do you want?"

"I need someone to do a job for me."

He had no desire to do Roy's dirty work, but he liked the idea of negotiating to keep him away from Gertie, maybe for the money to send her to New York. "What kind of job?"

"The kind that requires your particular talent. The men who lost to me on that riverboat didn't do it graciously. They said I cheated."

"Did you?"

"Maybe."

Of course he'd cheated. J.T. had seen Roy do it in Dodge. He wasn't a good enough gambler to earn enough to invest in a high-class theater. No man liked being cheated. A rich one had the power to seek revenge, sometimes by hiring a man like J.T. to do the job. "What do you want from me?"

"Someone's looking for me, and he's in Denver. I got wind of it from one of my actors. The fellow's a hired gun like yourself."

"Who is he?"

"Griff Lassen."

J.T. could have lived the rest of his life without seeing Griff. He weighed the odds of the man already knowing he was in Denver and decided it wasn't likely. J.T. had spent less than two hours in a single gaming hall. Otherwise he'd been pounding nails at a church and washing dishes. Griff wouldn't find him easily, but the possibility had to be considered.

"I know Griff," he said to Roy.

"He's a mean one."

"So I've heard."

Roy got up and poured more whiskey. "If you kill Lassen, I'll pay you well."

J.T.'s conscience twitched, but not because of Lassen. The man deserved to die. Not only had he wanted to kill a dog, J.T. had seen him torment an expecting woman until J.T. stopped him. Lassen had no scruples, but J.T. had acquired some of his own. What would Mary think if he took this job? He'd demand enough from Roy to get Gertie to New York, but he doubted she'd take the money.

On the other hand, who could object to letting two scorpions sting each other? If J.T. did nothing, Griff would take care of Roy. The theater manager would end up dead with no help from J.T. He'd have to stay low until Lassen did the dirty work, and he'd have to keep a close eye on Mary and Gertie, but the idea had merit. In no way did it violate Mary's beliefs. The longer he waited to give Roy an answer, the more time Lassen had to do his job.

J.T. stood. "I'll think about it."

"I want an answer tonight."

"Tomorrow."

Roy hesitated, then nodded because he had no choice. "Tomorrow it is, but know this, Quinn. If you don't do what I'm asking, Gertie Larue is going to find out more about men than she's ready to know."

"Are you threatening—"

"You bet I am." He looked as filthy as his thoughts. "The girl's worthless to me. I might as well get some use out of her."

J.T. wanted to beat Roy to a pulp. Turn the other cheek to a man who'd abuse a young girl? No way. Seething inside, he blanked his expression. "I'll give you an answer when I'm ready."

Roy gave him a critical look. "I hope it's not true about you."

"What?"

"That you've lost your edge."

"I haven't." Keeping his eyes on Roy, he left the office. Satisfied the man wouldn't try something, he turned down the hall and left the theater.

In the shadow of the church, he considered Roy's claim that he'd lost his edge. He hadn't fired at anything more threatening than a tin can in six months. Suddenly jittery, he headed for the café. With his boots thudding, he thought about Mary and how she'd trusted him with Gus and Gertie, and how she believed there was good in him. Here he was, a cynical man charged with protecting Mary and her family. He had no interest in a God who ignored boys in alleys, but he could respect a God who cared about good women and kids who stammered, foolish girls and dogs having puppies. It was almost enough to make him grab the same branch Mary had grabbed when she'd come to Denver.

As he neared the apartment, he saw her in the upstairs window. She dropped the curtain and disappeared into the dark. Before he reached the steps, she flung open the door. "Hurry, J.T.! It's Fancy Girl. The pups are coming, and she's in trouble."

J.T. bolted up the steps. If God cared, he had a terrible way of showing it.

Chapter Seventeen

J.T. hurried to Fancy Girl and dropped to his knees. He examined her with his eyes but didn't touch her. "How long has she been laboring?"

"Too long."

She told him about the past five hours. Fancy had gone into labor in the later afternoon, and she'd been panting and tense without giving birth. Looking into the dog's eyes, he saw the glaze of pain. Did dogs fear death? He didn't know, but he deeply feared losing her.

Mary took his hand. "I sent Gus to fetch Bessie."

J.T. rubbed Fancy's ears, crooning to her until his voice cracked. He wanted to scoop her into his arms and carry her to someplace bright and safe. Instead he watched as she panted with another contraction. When it passed, she raised her head to him and whined. Fancy never whined.

Mary put her arm around his shoulders. "I'm praying, J.T. It's all I can do."

Needing to give comfort as well as receive it, he cradled Mary's head against his chest. They were like two birds huddled against the cold, lifelong mates sharing warmth and hope and the love he was tired of holding back. Together they dropped to a sitting position. Staying close to him, Mary rested her palm on Fancy's belly.

"Come on, sweetheart," she pleaded. "Push those puppies out."

J.T. would have given anything to command the dog to give birth the way he told her to sit. A hand signal, a few words. But he didn't have that ability. He could take a life, but he couldn't order the puppies to be born. Looking at Fancy, her belly tensing as she panted and suddenly pushed, J.T. felt a jolt of understanding. The puppies would emerge from darkness into light. He was making a similar journey and fighting every step just as they were. Why would he stay in the dark when the light was just a breath away?

The puppies had no idea what goodness awaited them. Their mother's milk would nourish them. Fancy would lick them clean with her rough tongue. In a few weeks they'd be tumbling all over each other, and one special pup would belong to Gus and be loved more than it could imagine. J.T. wanted these puppies to be born. *He* wanted to born again, in much the same way.

Tears leaked from his eyes. "Please, God," he murmured. "Help my dog…. Help me."

Mary gripped his hand…his shooting hand. She squeezed so hard she nearly broke the fingers, and he didn't care if she broke them all. He touched Fancy's belly and felt a contraction. The dog stopped panting and started to push. She pushed and pushed…until life emerged from the darkness of her womb into the light. At the sight of the sac holding the puppy, J.T. couldn't move. Fancy turned and licked, breaking the covering and then licking the puppy until it breathed. He started sobbing like a baby, and he didn't care.

With Mary next to him, he watched as Fancy gave

birth to four more pups for a total of five. Three of them had her blond coloring. The other two were black and white. Wondering about the father, he thought of his talk with Gus about babies. A man had responsibilities to a woman, but dogs would be dogs.

"Are there more?" he asked Mary.

"I think she's done."

They sat side by side, sharing the miracle while J.T. got a hold of his emotions. Finally, he said, "Something amazing just happened."

"Yes."

"I don't mean just the puppies," he said in a hush. "I prayed to your God and He listened. I guess that makes Him my God, too."

Breathing softly, she put her palm on his jaw and turned his face to hers. He felt the warmth against his day-old whiskers. When she spoke, her voice quavered. "I'm happy for you."

"I love you, Mary."

He wanted to hear the words back. Instead she sealed her lips. He'd never needed to be loved before, but tonight he needed *her*. She pressed her fingers tight against his jaw. In return he matched his mouth to hers. They'd kissed before, but it hadn't been like this. He desired her as a woman, yes. But tonight he wanted to belong to her…. He wanted to marry her. The commitment scared him, but not as much as losing her.

Full of hope, he deepened the kiss. To his dismay, Mary pulled back. "I don't know what to say."

Say you love me. Say you trust me. Instead, she seemed troubled. Hadn't he just crossed the last hurdle between them? At the stream, he'd earned back her trust. Tonight he'd embraced her faith. What more did he need to do? He didn't understand. "What's wrong?"

She stared at Fancy, sleeping now with the puppies tight against her belly. "This has been quite a night."

If she needed to beat around the bush, he'd wait for her. "Yeah."

"Fancy's a mother." Her eyes took on a curious light. "I wonder who the father is."

"Just some mutt." The pieces of the puzzle didn't fit. "It doesn't matter. The puppies belong to Fancy."

She rubbed the dog's neck. "It doesn't seem fair."

"What doesn't?"

"She does all the work, and the father gets off scot-free." She looked at him. "Do you think that's right?"

"It is for dogs."

He was more confused than ever. What did dogs and puppies have to do with them?

Mary opened her mouth to say something else, but Gus burst into the apartment. "H-how is she?"

"She's fine." Mary pushed to her feet, stepping away when he wanted to have his arm around her.

Feeling slighted, he stood next to her but kept his hands loose. Bessie came through the door behind Gus, followed by Josh and Adie. J.T. hadn't heard the carriage, and he counted it as a mistake. Was Roy right? Had he lost his edge? The night had been full of changes, and he'd hadn't even told Mary about his talk with Roy.

She stepped away from him to make room for Bessie. "Fancy had the puppies on her own. I think everything's fine."

The nurse smiled. "I'm glad to hear it."

Adie congratulated J.T. as if he were a father and then joined the women. They started talking about Fancy, with Bessie asking questions about medical things that J.T. did *not* want to hear about. Josh looked

just as pinched. Gus stayed with them, clearly count-
ing himself as one of the men. J.T. clapped the boy on
the shoulder. "Thanks for getting Bessie."

"When I went to g-get her, I s-s-saw those b-boys."

He meant the bullies. "What happened?" J.T. asked.

"The b-b-big one told me to stop, but I k-kept running. If they'd followed me, I'd have f-fought them all."

Ten minutes ago J.T. had cried out to God for mercy.
Now here was Gus, stammering and afraid. Had anything really changed tonight? Suddenly solemn, the
boy studied the five puppies. "I—I want one that looks
like F-Fancy."

Josh glanced at J.T. "Pretty amazing, isn't it?"

"That it is, Reverend."

The minister raised an eyebrow. "You said reverend
like you meant it."

"I do." J.T. turned to Gus. "Keep an eye on her,
okay? I need a word with Josh."

Heading for the door, J.T. caught Mary's attention.
"I'll be back. Then we'll talk about Gertie."

"All right."

She sounded guarded, and he wanted to know why.
He'd told her he loved her, and she hadn't said it back.
He didn't understand her reaction at all. He wanted to
throw everyone out of the apartment and talk to her, but
he had business with Josh—both personal and profes-
sional. He followed the minister down the stairs. When
they reached the bottom of the steps, Josh sat on the
third one up while J.T. roamed to the street, looked up
and down out of habit, then faced the minister. "My
dog almost died tonight."

"I hear it was close."

"Too close. I've seen death."

"Me, too."

"I prayed." His jaw tightened. "I don't understand why, but God was merciful. I'm done fighting Him. What do I have to do?"

Josh stood and bowed his head. J.T. had never bent his neck to anyone, but he did tonight. In a conversational tone, the minister asked God to forgive J.T. of his sins and to welcome him into the Kingdom. When Josh said "Amen," J.T. echoed him. He didn't feel anything new, but he understood that he'd made a decision that mattered. As long as God didn't get in his way, J.T. figured they'd get along just fine.

The minister stepped back. "I feel compelled to warn you about something."

"What?"

"Becoming a Christian is like lighting a stick of dynamite. If the fuse doesn't fizzle out, it goes off with a bang."

J.T. didn't care about dynamite. He had business with Roy, and he wanted Josh's help. "The *bang* I want most is one that'll get rid of Roy Desmond."

Josh's eyes glinted. "What's new with Gertie?"

J.T. described his meeting with Roy. "With Griff Lassen in the picture, there's been a shift in what Roy wants. Instead of getting Mary to sing and earn him a pile of money, he wants me to take care of Lassen. If I do his dirty work, he'll leave Gertie alone."

"And if you say no?"

"He'll hurt her." J.T.'s blood turned to ice. Maybe he hadn't lost his edge after all.

Josh's expression hardened. "What kind of man threatens a seventeen-year-old girl?"

"An evil one."

"Gertie needs to come home *tonight*."

"If she will." J.T. had seen her stubborn side. "When we finish here, I'll take Mary to find her."

Josh eyed him thoughtfully. "Then what?"

A smile played on J.T.'s lips. "We let Lassen take care of Roy."

Josh clapped him on the back. "You know that stick of dynamite I mentioned?"

"Sure."

"Get ready, because it's burning fast. Have you told Mary any of this?"

"Not yet."

"It's up to her to convince Gertie to come home. While we're waiting for Lassen to strike, we'll both keep an eye on Roy."

Tomorrow J.T. would be working on the bell tower. It rose even higher than the Newcastle and gave him a perfect view of the surrounding streets. He'd see Roy coming and going. He'd also be able to spot Griff Lassen if he approached Roy. "I'll be watching."

"So will the Lord," Josh added.

J.T. believed God had saved his dog's life, but he had a hard time imagining Him anywhere except in the clouds. In general he preferred to work alone, and that's what he intended to do.

"We better get inside," Josh said. "Mary needs to have that talk with Gertie."

And J.T. needed to speak with *her*. She'd kissed him like she meant it, then she'd backed away for the second time. Before the night ended, he intended to find out why.

Chapter Eighteen

With the men outside, the women were sitting at the kitchen table. Adie and Bessie were chatting about the puppies and Gus, but Mary barely heard them. Her thoughts were on J.T. How could a woman's dreams come true and die in a single moment? When he'd prayed, she'd felt the sincerity and wept. Fancy had lived and Mary had been ready to tell him about the baby they'd lost…and then he'd spoken glibly about dogs being dogs. If she told J.T. about the baby and he mocked her, her fragile trust would be shattered. Yet if she didn't tell him, the trust would be incomplete.

She needed time to build her courage, but she had another problem. J.T. hadn't told her about the meeting with Roy, and this morning's confrontation with Gertie had filled her with guilt. Would her sister come home if she knew about Abilene? Confessing to Gertie could ruin the good life she'd made for herself and her siblings, but not confessing was risking Gertie's future.

Adie touched her arm. "You're a million miles away. What's wrong?"

"It's Gertie."

"Has there been any word from her?" Bessie asked.

Mary told them about this morning's visit. "I'm scared to death for her. I'm thinking about telling her more about why I left Abilene." Adie already knew about the miscarriage. Bessie didn't, so Mary told her about her affair with J.T., the miscarriage and how she'd killed Sam O'Day when he'd forced himself on her, calling her a loose woman and worse. "I lost my reputation, and I'm terrified of going down that road again, especially with Gus and Gertie. People would treat them badly because of me."

Bessie's silvery eyes took on a shine. "With Gertie in danger, it's a chance you have to take."

But the cost… She could lose customers and go out of business. How would she support her brother and sister? She'd be called ugly names, and Gus would hear them. The thought disgusted her, but she'd gladly sacrifice her good name to save Gertie. Even if her sister failed to understand, Mary loved the girl too much to do nothing.

"You're right." She didn't want to wait another minute. "I'll talk to Gertie first thing in the morning."

The women commiserated until the men came inside. Josh escorted Adie and Bessie to the carriage, leaving J.T. and Mary alone. They both sat on the divan, but not too close. His declaration of love was dangling between them, but she ignored it. "Tell me what happened with Roy."

He looked annoyed. "I'd rather talk about us."

"I know," she said. "But I'm not ready."

"Ready for what?"

"For anything." *Or everything.* She pleaded with her eyes. "Can we please talk about Gertie?"

He gave her a long look and then took pity on her.

"Sure," he said, reaching for her hand. "The meeting with Roy had some surprises."

He told her about Griff Lassen, Roy's offer and the man's threats to Gertie. Mary wanted her sister home tonight, not tomorrow. If it meant pounding on Katrina's door, she'd do it. If Gertie refused to listen, she'd ask J.T. to make good on his promise to carry her home like a sack of flour. She stood and snatched her shawl from a hook by the door. "Let's go."

J.T. stood more slowly. "It's late. Are you sure?"

"Positive."

"If people see us, they'll talk."

Bless him, he was thinking about her reputation. "It won't matter after I speak to Gertie. I'm going to tell her everything about Abilene. If I do, maybe she'll believe me about Roy." And after she spoke to Gertie, she'd tell J.T. about the baby.

He looked worried. "I'll tell Gus we're leaving for a while."

He strode down the hall and opened the door to her brother's room. When he spoke in a hush, the comfort of it rocked Mary to the core. This could be her life— a home with J.T. and her siblings and Fancy Girl. Everything depended on his reaction to her revelation. If Gertie's situation hadn't turned dire, she'd have told him now. Instead, she followed him out the door, setting a fast pace as they walked to the women's hotel where Katrina lived.

"I hope we can get in." She doubted a clerk worked this late.

"I'll break down the door if I have to."

Mary felt the same urgency, but embarrassing Gertie would make the situation worse. She needed to convince her sister, quietly but with a full accounting, to come home right now. The hotel loomed in the distance. A three-story building made of brick and mortar, it had the look of a fortress. When a carriage halted in front of the hotel, J.T. tugged her into the shadows. "We'll wait here."

Tucked behind him, she watched a driver climb down from the seat and open the door. A man emerged. As he turned to offer his hand to a fellow passenger, she recognized Roy. Next she saw the hem of a shimmering gold gown, then the elegant reach of a woman's arm. Katrina emerged and glided to the boardwalk.

Roy turned back to the carriage and again offered his hand. Gertie followed in Katrina's steps, except she wobbled instead of moving gracefully, and instead of wearing the pink dress befitting her age, she was draped in a purple evening gown with a low-cut diamond neckline. Giggling, she lost her balance and swayed against Roy. As he steadied her, the three of them laughed far more than the situation justified.

"She's drunk," J.T. observed.

Furious, Mary fought the urge to run to her sister. Instead, she watched Roy position himself between the two females. With his elbows bent, he escorted them to the hotel entrance. He said something that made Katrina smile, then he turned to Gertie. Mary couldn't see her sister's face, but she recognized the lift of her chin. The foolish girl was inviting a kiss. When Roy obliged, Mary tried to push past J.T.

He caught her by the waist. "Not yet."

"But—"

"Be patient," he advised. "Roy's leaving."

The girls stayed on the porch, waving as if Roy were a departing king. As soon as the carriage took off, J.T. stepped out of the shadows and she followed. When they were within earshot of the girls, he called out in a full voice. "Good evening, ladies. It looks like you've been to the theater."

Katrina, having never seen him before, wisely didn't reply. She put an arm around Gertie and turned the doorknob.

"Katrina, wait," Mary called. "It's me."

Off balance and wobbly, Gertie struggled to focus her eyes. "Mary?" She slurred the word to mush.

"Yes, sweetie. It's me." She felt no anger toward Gertie, only pity. The girl had never touched alcohol in her life. Judging by the fruity smell, Roy had given her heavy red wine. Naive and determined to hide it, Gertie had consumed far too much.

Mary approached with J.T. behind her. Katrina glared at him. "Who are you?"

"A friend of Miss Larue's," he replied. "If you'll excuse us, we'd like a word with her sister."

"It's late." Katrina looked a bit unsteady herself. "Come back tomorrow."

"That's not acceptable," Mary countered.

J.T. broke in. "We'll speak to Mary's sister *now*." He shifted his gaze to Gertie. "Is that all right with you, Miss Larue?"

"I—I don't know." She looked positively green. "I think I'm going to be—" She heaved into the bushes.

"Sick," J.T. finished for her.

Katrina stepped back in disgust. Mary ran to Gertie's side and held her head as she lost the contents of her stomach. When she finished, Mary wiped her sister's mouth with her hankie. Groaning, Gertie tumbled into a heap and passed out. They wouldn't be having that talk about Roy tonight. Mary called to J.T. "Will you carry her home?"

"Sure." He climbed up the steps, giving Katrina a sharp look as he passed her, then he dropped to a crouch. Katrina gave Mary a look of her own. "Gertie lives here now. I'll help her upstairs."

"No, you won't." J.T. scooped her into his arms, straightened and gave Katrina a look full of pity. "Good night, miss. If you're smart, you'll keep away from Mr. Desmond."

He turned and strode down the street with Gertie hanging from his arms like a rag doll. Mary gave Katrina a pitying look of her own, picked up Gertie's reticule and followed him.

"You can't do this!" Katrina cried.

Mary turned on her heels, speaking as she back-pedaled away from the younger woman. "Yes, I *can* do this, Katrina. And I'm doing it. Roy isn't who you think he is."

The girl smirked. "You're just jealous."

"Hardly."

"Gertie won't listen," she shouted back. "She's going to be a great actress, and I'm going to design all her costumes. You can't stop us."

"Maybe not," Mary countered. "But I can try."

Facing forward, she lengthened her stride to catch up with J.T. Tomorrow she'd have that talk with Gertie. She needed to have a similar conversation with J.T., but she wouldn't do it tonight. Her sister would need her full attention.

J.T. had a lot of sympathy for Gertie. He knew all about the dry heaves and headaches. He'd gone down that road alone, and he'd done it often. Gertie had Mary at her side, and she'd done it just once. He hoped she'd learned a lesson. She was home and safe, so he didn't have to give Roy an answer about Lassen right away. Stalling to give Lassen a chance to work offered the best shot at protecting the future J.T. wanted with Mary and her siblings.

While Mary put Gertie to bed, he waited in the front room with Fancy Girl, watching the puppies as they nuzzled and slept. He'd never seen anything so beautiful and so remote from his own experience.

"J.T.?"

He turned and saw Mary in the hall entry. Bluish circles fanned beneath her eyes. "You look done in," he said.

"I am."

He indicated the divan. "Sit with me." She could rest her head on his shoulder.

Mary stayed in the hall. "It's late. You should go."

He didn't like the idea at all. He wanted to know why she hadn't told him she loved him, and why she'd stopped a perfect kiss, but he wouldn't make demands. "All right," he agreed. "I'll head out. We can talk tomorrow."

Looking reluctant, she nodded.

J.T. wanted to kiss her good-night, but she didn't budge. He settled for patting Fancy Girl. The new mother raised her head and gave him a doggy smile. "You did good," he murmured.

Closing her eyes, Fancy lowered her head and slept. J.T. pushed to his feet and headed for the door. Mary finally crossed the room, and he hoped for an explanation, but she stopped two feet away. "Thank you for helping Gertie tonight."

He wished she'd appreciated his love as much. "She's a handful, but she's still a good kid."

Mary didn't move.

Neither did he.

What's wrong, Mary? Tell me. He pleaded silently until she let out a breath. "Will I see you tomorrow?"

"First thing," he said.

She smiled, but her mouth looked pinched. "Good night, J.T. Thank you again."

After a nod that should have been a kiss, he walked alone to the boardinghouse. When he reached his room, he unbuckled his gun belt and draped it over a chair. Usually he missed the weight of it. Tonight he experienced a lightness he didn't understand. Without his dog or a living soul to distract him, he sat on the bed and pulled off his boots. Pictures of the day played through his mind—Roy's threats…kissing Mary…the moment he thought Fancy would die.

Unable to sleep, he picked up the chapbook and read slowly, taking in the words a few at a time and seeing himself among the thieves and the lost. When his eyelids drooped, he blew out the lamp. Darkness filled the room, but tonight it had no power, and he slept like baby.

J.T.'s contentment lasted until six o'clock the next morning. After rising from the narrow bed, he washed and put on dungarees in preparation for dishwashing duty. As always, he strapped on his guns. Griff Lassen could come through the door. Roy could go on the attack. Trusting God to heal his dog was one thing. Trusting Him to watch out for Mary and Gertie struck J.T. as crazy.

He also had to figure out how to earn a living. He'd come to Denver to rescue Mary, not to be tied to her apron strings. Everything seemed wrong as he headed for the café. He'd cut himself shaving, and he missed

Fancy Girl trotting at his side. By the time J.T. walked through the back door to the café, he felt more prickly than a cactus. The irritation increased when Mary saw him and didn't smile.

"Good morning," she said formally.

He grumbled a greeting and went to the cupboard to get an apron. Tying it around the gun belt, he felt like a wolf with feathers. He half filled the wash basin at the pump, lifted a kettle from the back of the stove and poured the boiling water into the cold. Mary was busy cracking eggs in a bowl. Trying to be civil, he spoke over the crunch of the shells. "How's Gertie?"

"She's sleeping." She tossed a shell in the scrap bucket. "I haven't spoken to her yet."

Gertie could argue with Mary, but she'd have a hard time putting *him* in his place. "Maybe we should do it together."

"I'll do it," she said too quickly.

Feeling useless, he whittled soap into the basin. Enid entered the kitchen with the first load of dirty plates. She didn't know what to make of J.T., so she ignored him. He didn't blame her. He didn't know what to make of himself. The man who sold his gun for hundreds of dollars was scrubbing egg slime. Working on the church had more dignity—he planned to finish the bell tower shingles today—and he could hold his own as a gunsmith, but neither occupation appealed to him.

"H-h-hi"

He looked over his shoulder and saw Gus. "Hey, kid."

The boy fetched a towel from a shelf and started drying the clean plates. As they worked, he told J.T. about Fancy and the puppies. They were doing well, and Fancy had consumed two bowls of water and eaten ham for breakfast. For the next hour they joked about names for the puppies, finally agreeing on Eeny, Meeny, Miny, Moe and Isabel, just because Gus liked the name and thought that was the puppy he'd keep.

Mary interrupted. "Gus? Would you empty the garbage pail?"

"Sure."

It was Gus's regular chore, but there were still dishes to put away. The boy knew better than J.T. where they went, so J.T. indicated the plates. "Finish up here. I'll handle the garbage."

Gus grinned. "Lucky you! It stinks."

J.T. lifted the pail with one hand and opened the door with the other.

Whomp!

Something hard bounced off his chest. He set down the bucket and stared down the alley. This time he saw the rock coming. Only it wasn't aimed at him. The kid who'd thrown it—one of the boys who'd attacked Gus—had targeted Mary's window. The rock missed the glass but hit the siding.

Gus raced through the door, saw the boys and stopped in his tracks. "Th-that's them!"

A second boy threw a rock at Gus. Gus ducked, but the rock ricocheted off the wall and hit J.T. in the neck.

No one messed with J.T. or the people he loved. He'd sunk to washing dishes, but he could still scare the daylights out of a group of punk kids. That's what he intended to do. Gus was shouting and scrambling to find a rock to throw back. J.T. knew how he felt, but then he recalled Josh's advice to turn the other cheek. J.T.'s insides were boiling, but he saw a chance to turn a page in his life.

"Let's try a different strategy," he said to Gus.

"Wh-wh-what?"

"We're going give these boys breakfast."

"B-b-breakfast?"

"I know. It's peculiar." The old J.T. would have already put the rock throwers in their place.

Gus finally nodded, so J.T. called out to them. "Hey, are you guys hungry? The meal's on me."

Gus looked wary, but J.T. had the upper hand. The boys would either run away or they'd stay because they were hungry and surprised by the offer. He saw them gather across the alley behind a wood pile. "We've confused them," he said to Gus.

"G-g-good."

One of the boys who'd held Gus against the wall showed himself. "Do you mean it about breakfast?"

"Sure."

A second one came out from behind the stack of wood. He murmured to his friend. He couldn't look J.T. in the eye, but they both came forward.

"There were three of you," J.T. called. "Bring your friend." The third kid had been the meanest, the one who'd pummeled Gus.

The boys looked at each other, then indicated the opposite side of the alley. J.T. spotted the older boy under a stairwell. He looked scrawny, dirty and mean. J.T. didn't know who these boys were or why they'd turned into alley rats, but he'd once been like them. He also knew they'd brutalized Gus. Justice had to be served, or else Gus would be mad the way J.T. had stayed mad his entire life. He and Gus had turned the other cheek by offering a meal, but something had to be said about what these boys had done, and J.T. planned to say it. By speaking up, he hoped to teach Gus a lesson that worked better than hitting before you got hit.

"Come on," he called. "I'm serious about breakfast."

The oldest kid finally stepped into the alley. "It's a trick, isn't it?"

"No, it's not," J.T. answered. "I want you to apologize to Gus. If that's a trick, there it is."

The three boys looked at Gus. Gus glared at them, then looked at J.T. "I—I—I hate them."

He touched Gus's shoulder. "I know, kid. You've got every right to stay mad, but take it from me—you won't feel any better if you do. Let's try this Josh's way." If it didn't work, he and Gus would deal with the brats later.

"All right," Gus managed.

The third boy approached slowly. The two youngest looked sheepish, while the oldest wore a scowl that put crevices in his youthful face. J.T. stopped them all at the back door. "You," he said, pointing at the oldest one. "You beat up my friend. We're willing to put that aside, but you owe him."

The boy-man stared at J.T. "What do you want?"

J.T. turned to Gus. "It's your call."

When Gus's eyes widened, J.T. remembered the stammering and wished he'd been more careful. He couldn't backtrack without embarrassing Gus, so he silently hoped—prayed—the boy would speak clearly.

Gus looked the bigger kid in the eye and stared the way J.T. did when he wanted to look mean. The boy took a slow breath and then said, "I want an apology."

The words came out just fine. J.T. wanted to clap him on the back, but he settled for adding a hard look to Gus's request.

"Sorry," the two boys muttered.

"And—" Gus took another breath. Rather than seeming hesitant, it made him foreboding. "I want a promise. *Leave me alone.*"

J.T. looked at the three boys. "You owe him that much, even more."

The oldest kid narrowed his eyes. "Who are you, anyway?"

"J. T. Quinn."

The kid went pale. "*You're* J. T. Quinn?"

"The same." He offered his hand.

The boy stared at him for a good five seconds. In that silent moment, the two of them shared a sad truth. J.T. knew what he was talking about, and the boy knew it. The boy shook J.T.'s hand, then turned to Gus. "I'm sorry for what we did."

Gus said nothing. He didn't want to risk stuttering, but neither did forgiveness come easily. He was still scowling when Mary opened the back door.

"There you are!" she said. "I thought you'd— Oh. You're Todd Roman. I've heard about you."

The boy looked sheepish. What he saw in Mary, J.T. didn't know. But something had knocked a bit of the cockiness out of him. The boy's cheeks turned as pink as a girl's. "I'm sorry about what happened, Miss Larue. My mama would be ashamed of me."

Mary didn't soften. "You owe my brother an apology."

Todd didn't look pleased, but between Mary and his mother's memory, he was outnumbered. "It won't happen again," he said to Gus. "I'm sorry."

"Me, too," said one of the other boys.

"Same here," said the third.

J.T. thought of his own brothers hurting him in the alley. He'd once vowed to never forgive them, but some of the malice left as he watched Gus stand tall.

"J-just don't do it again," he said firmly.

Everyone ignored the slight stammer. Feeling proud,

J.T. traded a look with Mary. He wanted to trade more looks like this one, but she still had a formal air, and he still needed a job. Before he thought too much about the future, he had to settle matters with Roy, and he needed to find a job that didn't require an apron.

"What do you say?" He punched Gus's arm. "Shall we see who can eat the most hotcakes?"

"Sure."

"I'll get busy." Smiling, Mary went back in the kitchen. The boys followed her, with J.T. bringing up the rear. As he stepped over the threshold, he saw Mary waiting for him at the wash basin. She touched his arm. "That was wonderful."

"Gus did the hard part."

"Yes, but you're good with kids."

"Not really." He didn't know anything about babies and little girls, except that they terrified him. "I know boys and I know men, that's all."

He couldn't read her expression, so he took her hand and squeezed. "What is it, Mary? Talk to me."

"I have to get to the work." She sounded business-like again. "We've got four boys who want hotcakes."

He let her go, but he followed her with his eyes to the stove. Whatever she was hiding, it posed a threat he didn't understand. Movement in the doorway caught his eye, and he saw Gertie in the purple dress she'd worn last night. With her head high, she walked straight to Mary. "How dare you drag me home like that!"

J.T. saw red. "Now wait just a minute—"

"J.T., no!" Mary's voice came out in a shriek. "This is between Gertie and me."

The girl gave him a look more superior than the one she'd used on Mary. "You have a lot of nerve to criticize Roy."

"He's dangerous, Miss Larue."

"And you're not?"

"Not like Roy." He had to convince her of Roy's true character. "He's not good to women."

She laughed, but it had an ugly sound. "You abandoned my sister when she was *with child*, and you think Roy is bad?"

Gertie's accusation hit him like the first drops of rain from a coming storm. *Mary with child...his child.* The drops turned into a torrent. A baby...his baby... their baby. Where was it? What had happened after he'd left Abilene? He thought Mary had come to trust him, but he was wrong. Could he have hurt her any more than he had? He didn't think so. Whatever Gertie had to say, she could say to both of them.

Chapter Nineteen

Forgetting the hotcakes, Mary whirled to face J.T. The anger he'd felt toward Gertie turned to stark confusion directed toward her. She felt the same churning, maybe more because she loved Gertie, and her sister had betrayed her. She wanted to scream at the foolish, bratty girl to shut up. She also wanted desperately to tell J.T. in private about the baby. Their future hung on his reaction, and she didn't want to blurt the story in front of Gertie.

She gave him a look that begged for patience, then she turned back to her sister. "How dare you!"

"Roy told me *everything*. You act all prim and proper. But you're not, are you? You're a trollop!"

Mary gasped.

J.T.'s voice boomed. *"That's enough!"*

Gertie spun in his direction. "Oh, no, it's not! You're a worthless piece of trash, Mr. Quinn. Get out of here."

Mary couldn't argue with J.T. and Gertie at the same time, so she concentrated on Gertie.

The girl had turned back to her and was screeching like a wet cat. "I want to act and you won't let me because you're selfish! It's not my fault you ruined your life. Do you know what I think? I think you're a hypocrite, and so does Katrina."

The hotcakes started to smoke. Flipping them frantically, Mary heard the thud of J.T.'s boots on the wood floor. She turned and saw that he'd whipped off the apron and was approaching Gertie with a steely look in his eyes. Mary couldn't stand the thought of the two of them tangling. She wanted to deal with Gertie on her terms, not his.

"Not now," she said as he reached the stove. "This is between Gertie and me."

He stopped in his tracks and stared at her. "Do you mean that?"

"Yes." She couldn't cook and deal with Gertie at the same time. The bacon was about to catch fire, and the biscuits had to come out of the oven *now*.

Enid came through the door. "Those boys want their hotcakes." She left an order and went back to the dining room.

"Please," Mary begged J.T. "Just go. We'll talk later."

"When?" he insisted.

The bacon spattered and she shrieked. Gertie headed for the door. "I'm leaving."

He blocked her path. "No, you're not. You're going to have a talk with you sister, and if you're smart you'll listen to her." He indicated the spatula in Mary's hand. "Give me that. I'll finish the cooking."

Mary held it away from him. "It would be best if you left."

"You need help."

"Please," she said again. "Leave this to me." In Abilene she'd wanted him to stay. Today she wanted him to go.

He studied her with sad, angry eyes. "Is that what you want?"

"Yes."

She hurriedly turned a strip of bacon and motioned to Enid in the dining room. The waitress hurried back through the door. "What is it, miss?"

"Finish up." Mary handed her the spatula. "I have to speak to Gertie."

The waitress shook her finger at the girl. "You're nothing but trouble, young lady. If you were my daughter, I'd—"

"Enid, no." Berating Gertie would only make her more rebellious. Mary gripped her sister's arm and dragged her to the back door. J.T. watched with a cool expression and then left through the door to the dining room. She had no idea where he'd go or what he'd do. She only knew the past had been opened like a grave.

She steered Gertie out the door and into the alley. It stank of garbage, and the morning heat promised a scorcher of a day. With no place to sit, she faced her sister standing up. They were equals in height but not experience, though Gertie wouldn't agree.

"It's true about J.T. and me," Mary told her. "We were more than friends, and I conceived. I lost the baby before I came to Denver." She told Gertie about the scandal, the miscarriage and the murder trial. "That time of my life was ugly and awful. I don't want you to make the same mistakes."

"Of course I wouldn't," she said, more naive than ever. "Besides, I'm old enough to know what I want. You're holding me back."

"I'm protecting you."

"No, you're not. I'm paying for *your* mistakes."

"That's not true." Her throat ached with the effort

to be calm. "Theater life is more challenging than you know."

"It's *wonderful*."

"Yes, it is." Mary had loved being onstage. "But if you love it too much, you'll forget what's really important."

"That's ridiculous."

Losing hope, Mary pulled out her last weapon against Roy. "I know you don't trust J.T., but he knows Roy better than you or I do." She told Gertie about the dead saloon girl and Roy's debts. "He's using you to manipulate me. He threatened you."

"I don't believe you."

Gertie hadn't even asked how he'd threatened her, a sure sign that she'd been taken in by Roy and her own ambition. Roy hadn't seduced her yet, but Mary feared he'd try and succeed. Even more frightening, he'd use Gertie to get what he wanted from J.T.

Gertie shrugged. "I don't care what Roy supposedly said to J.T. I know Roy, and I trust him."

"But he's *using* you," Mary insisted.

"I don't care." Looking all of seventeen, Gertie lifted her chin. "Some people would say *I'm* using *him*."

Mary gave up. Stepping back, she spoke to her sister as if she were the adult she wanted to be. "No matter what happens, Gertie. I love you. You can come home anytime."

"I love you, too."

They'd be sisters forever, so Mary hugged Gertie tight. She didn't want to let go, but the girl broke away with a slight push. Looking foolish and brave, Gertie walked past the stinking garbage cans to the edge of the café. Without glancing back, she cut between two buildings and went to the street.

Alone in the growing heat, Mary thought about J.T. She'd told him to leave and he had. She needed to speak with him, but Gertie's betrayal posed an immediate threat. The gossip about her would start the minute someone set foot in Katrina's dress shop. Needing to pick up the pieces of her life, Mary headed to Swan's Nest without bothering to change clothes or even remove her apron. Enid would close the café for her.

As for J.T., she wondered where he'd gone and what he'd do. It was just like Abilene, except this time she'd ordered him to leave, and it was up to her to do the explaining.

J.T. had gone to the dining room, but he had no intention of leaving the café. He couldn't get the picture of a child—*his* child—out of his head. Had Mary given the baby away? Was she paying someone to raise it? He counted the months and years in his head. A baby would be over a year old. Did they have a son or a daughter? Could it walk yet?

He couldn't imagine Mary giving up a baby, but what choice had he given her? At the thought of an orphanage, he wanted to put his fist through the wall. His own child abandoned just as he'd been abandoned. The thought shamed him. So did the misery he'd inflicted on Mary. Other thoughts came unbidden. Not all babies were born. He'd been in enough brothels to know that desperate women did desperate things. Other times nature took its course. Babies came too soon and died, or they didn't come at all. Whatever had happened to Mary and their child, he had to know the truth.

He wanted to go after her now, but she needed time with Gertie. He settled for sitting down with Gus and the boys from the alley. Judging by Gus's hard look,

he'd heard Gertie's accusation. J.T. didn't want the kid
to have him on a pedestal, but neither did he want to
lose Gus's respect. He spoke in a tone just for them.
"We'll talk later."

Glowering, the boy stabbed a hotcake. J.T. made
small talk with the other boys, but he couldn't stop
wondering about Mary and Gertie. His gut told him to
go to her, but he had to honor her request to deal with
Gertie alone. The boys polished their plates, thanked
him for the food and left with friendly words for Gus.
J.T. felt good about the meal, but the trouble with Mary
put him on edge. He wanted to go after her, but Gus
needed an explanation, and J.T. didn't want Enid to
hear it.

"Wait here," he said to the boy.

He went into the kitchen, where Enid was scrubbing
the stove. "Go on home. I'll finish up."

She looked at J.T. as if he were vermin. "If what I
heard is true, Mr. Quinn, you need to do right by Miss
Larue. She's a fine woman."

"Yes, she is."

Enid put her hands on her hips. "If you ask me, men
are nothing but trouble."

J.T. had to agree. Mary had lost everything—a baby,
her reputation, her career—while he'd run off like the
father of Fancy's puppies.

Enid gave him another hard look, then wadded up
her apron and walked out the door with her words echoing in J.T.'s mind. He wanted to do right by Mary, but
he had nothing to offer except his bad name. He had
no way to support her, and he cared about such things.
Even if he asked, would Mary have him? Not telling
him about the baby meant she didn't trust him after all.
J.T. didn't know much about forgiveness, but he knew

he had to ask for it again with full knowledge that he'd left her with child.

He went to the back window, parted the curtain and searched for Mary and Gertie in the alley. When he didn't see them, he figured they'd stepped out of sight or gone to the apartment. Frustrated, he went back to the dining hall. The boys had left, but Gus was standing by the kitchen door with his arms crossed, looking closer to a man than a boy and ready to hold J.T. accountable. If the situation hadn't been so serious, J.T. would have enjoyed the boy's audacity.

Gus stared at him. "W-w-we need to t-talk."

"Yes, we do." Wanting to give the boy the respect he deserved, J.T. sat so that Gus had the advantage of height. Knowing the stammer would be out of control, he spoke for them both. "You heard what Gertie said."

"I-i-is it true?"

"Yes, it is." The admission shamed him. "I didn't know about a baby until now, but that's no excuse. I need to square things with your sister."

Gus's blue eyes burned into him. "Are y-you going to m-m-marry her?"

"It's up to her."

"B-b-but you're going to ask." It was an order, not a question.

J.T. recalled the conversation they'd had while camping. "I love your sister, Gus. She's the reason I came to Denver. But it's not that simple. Do you remember asking me about loving a woman?"

The boy nodded.

"I made a mess of your sister's life. I'm doing my best to clean it up, but exactly how I do that is up to her."

Gus uncrossed his arms, but he still had the look

of a riled brother protecting his sister. If he'd had a shotgun, J.T. might have been worried…or grateful. He wanted to make Mary his wife, but it felt wrong to ask her when he had nothing to give. He'd eat all the crow Gus or Mary could serve, but he needed a way to pay for the crow.

Still scowling, Gus started stacking the dirty plates. "Y-y-you need to f-fix things with her."

"You're right." Their child hadn't been conceived in the best way, but he wanted to give the baby and Mary a good life. He just didn't know how to do it. "I'm not leaving until she comes back."

"G-g-good."

The boy scowled again. Even with the stutter, he'd learned how to be menacing. Unable to hold back a proud grin, J.T. held out his hand. "Congratulations, Gus. You stood up for your sister like a grown man. I'm proud of you."

Stoic, the boy shook back hard. J.T. couldn't help but be amazed. A stammering twelve-year-old had gotten the best of him. Surprisingly happy about it, he indicated the dishes. "I better get busy. I don't want your sister walking into a messy kitchen."

For the next two hours, he and Gus washed dishes, scrubbed pots and swept the floor. With no sign of Mary, J.T. wondered where she'd gone. Maybe she'd convinced Gertie to come home and they'd gone for the girl's things. He thought about going to Katrina's hotel, but his presence would make matters worse. He also had to consider the impact of last night on Roy and his threats. J.T. had promised the man an answer about Griff Lassen. With Gertie back in harm's way, J.T. couldn't stall. As soon as he finished his business with Mary, he'd take Roy's offer, but just to buy time. First, though, he had to find out about the baby.

He needed to stay busy, so he found some vinegar and washed the windows. He wiped down the tables again and even dusted the pictures on the wall, but there was still no sign of Mary.

When the café couldn't be any cleaner, Gus had an idea. "Want to play checkers?"

"Sure."

He wanted to see Mary the instant she showed up, so he told Gus to bring the game to the dining room. Ten games of checkers later, J.T. couldn't stand the waiting, but neither could he leave.

"Hey, Gus," he said as they put away the pieces. "I need a favor. Will you see if your sister's at Swan's Nest?"

"Sure."

The boy ran off, leaving J.T. to sweep the boardwalk and the stairs. When Gus came back, he had news J.T. didn't understand. "She was there, but she left with Adie."

Knowing she was safe, he settled in to wait some more. He'd wait all day if he had to. He'd wait all night…all week…all month. He'd wait forever if that's what it took for Mary to come to him. He went outside to the stairs to the apartment and sat on the third one. As soon as Mary came home, they'd be searching together for the child he'd never known but wanted to love.

"I can't do it," Mary said to Adie.

"Yes, you can."

After hearing Mary's story, the minister's wife had looped her arm around Mary's waist and dragged her upstairs to change her clothes. "Like I said, we're going calling this afternoon."

Mary stopped in the hall. "That's the *last* thing I want to do!"

"Which is why we're going to do it," Adie said simply. "Right now Gertie is telling Katrina everything, and they're making up what they don't know or understand. Every woman who steps into that dress shop is going to hear a half-made-up story. You can do nothing and let the rumors catch fire, or you can do what a fire chief would do."

Mary saw a glimmer of hope. "I can light a back fire."

"Exactly," Adie replied. "We're going to tell every woman we know the truth before she hears the gossip. It's the only way."

"Are you sure?"

"Yes."

Mary's pride balked. "But it's so private." Wasn't it enough that she'd made peace with God in her prayers?

"I wish Gertie would keep quiet, but she won't. Sharing what happened is embarrassing for you, but it might help someone else." Adie's hazel eyes turned misty. "You're not the first woman to give herself to a man too soon. Josh's sister crossed the same line. He'd give anything to change what he said to her."

Mary knew the story. Josh had said terrible things to his sister, and she'd fled Boston in disgrace. When she'd died giving birth, Adie had adopted the child as her own. She and Josh had found happiness, but Mary had her doubts about J.T.'s reaction to the miscarriage. If he said "good riddance," she'd feel rejected all over again. And if she didn't address the gossip, she'd again be a victim of the scandal. The thought disgusted her.

She'd worked hard to start a new life. If she had to fight to protect it, she'd do it. And if J.T. had the gall to disrespect her feelings about the baby, she'd fight him, too.

Mary looked at the massive wardrobe against the wall. Adie used it for storage now, but it once held the dresses Mary brought from Abilene. "I can't go in this greasy apron. Do you have something that will fit me?"

"I think so."

Adie flung open the double doors, fanning the air and stirring the yellow curtains. The scent of cedar filled the room and mixed with light coming through the window. Breathing in the familiar smells, Mary thought back to the first days she spent in this room. It was here she'd mourned the loss of the baby and grieved her career. It was here she'd uttered her first desperate prayers. The room had been a place of healing, a place of hope.

She hadn't left any clothing at Swan's Nest, but she and Adie were close to the same size. Approaching the wardrobe, she saw a gown that *had* been hers. It was the dress she'd been wearing when she'd left Abilene. She'd hadn't taken it to the apartment, because she couldn't bear to wear it. Today the stylish gown matched her mood. Jade green with satin trim and pagoda sleeves, it had a round lace collar and a pleated overskirt. The dress was bold, brave and just plain pretty.

"This is perfect," she said to Adie.

Together they dressed and did their hair. Wearing fancy hats and even fancier gloves, they climbed into the buggy and Adie drove to the impressive home of Rosalie Cates. A widow, Mrs. Cates attended church at Brick's because she liked Josh's Boston accent, not because she enjoyed the humble surroundings. She also frequented Katrina's dress shop.

A butler ushered Mary and Adie into a parlor and offered refreshments. Rosalie entered the room a moment later. Obviously curious, she looked from Adie to Mary, then back to Adie. "It's a pleasure to see you. And a surprise. I'm guessing the church is having a fundraiser?"

"No," Adie answered. "We're here to talk about gossip."

Rosalie masked her expression. "Am I the subject of it?"

Mary saw herself in the woman's sudden wariness, the lift of her chin and the donning of a mask that hid her feelings.

"It's not about you," Adie replied quickly.

Mary met the woman's gaze. "It's about me. I'd like to tell you the truth before you hear rumors."

"Of course." Rosalie indicated a brocade sofa littered with satin pillows. "Please sit down."

Mary saw sympathy in the woman's eyes…and sadness. The glimpse into Rosalie's heart gave her courage, and she told the story with an ease she hadn't expected. Somehow the details were less dramatic than they'd been in the alley with Gertie. "That's it," Mary finished. "I made a mistake and I regret it. I've also made a fresh start. I hope to continue to give my brother and sister a good home."

"Of course you do." Rosalie looked Mary square in the eye. "I admire you."

"You do?"

"Yes." The older woman pulled a hankie from her sleeve and twisted it. "My sister didn't have your courage. She was twenty-three and unmarried when she told me she was expecting. To this day, I don't know who fathered the child, if she'd been attacked or had gone to the man willingly. I only know she hanged herself."

Adie gasped.

So did Mary.

Rosalie shoved the hankie back up her sleeve. "Tell your story to everyone who'll listen. If Katrina insists on spreading rumors, I'll make sure she loses customers."

And so began a day full of surprises.... Rosalie insisted on accompanying them on the rest of their calls. As a trio, they visited eight women and heard eight different stories. No one shunned Mary, and four of them offered to join Rosalie in finding a new dressmaker. By the end of the day, Mary felt both humbled and awed. Her deepest fear had turned into a blessing that stretched beyond herself.

With dusk settling, she relaxed in the buggy with Adie. "That was easier than I thought."

Adie kept her eyes on the street. "It seems to me there's one more person you need to call on."

"I know." The time had come to face J.T. "He's staying at a boardinghouse off of Market. Would you take me?"

Adie immediately turned the buggy. "What are you going to tell him?"

"Everything."

"Can I give you some advice?" she said softly.

"Of course."

"J.T.'s a hard man. Don't be surprised if he says all the wrong things."

Mary heart sped up. "That's what I'm expecting." And that's what she couldn't bear. Saving her reputation had given her a measure of peace, but Gertie's betrayal had opened all her old wounds, especially the one from losing the baby. Adie chatted mildly about men, likening them to mules and mustangs. Some were hardworking. Others were wild and unpredictable. J.T. fit the latter description, though he'd worked like a mule washing dishes. She loved all sides of him, but his toughness could hurt her.

When they reached the boardinghouse, Mary turned to Adie. "He might not be here. Would you wait?"

"Sure."

Mary went to the door, spoke to the landlady and learned that J.T. had been gone all day. Discouraged and a little miffed, she went back to the buggy. "He's not here," she told Adie.

"Do you want to look for him?"

"I wouldn't know where to start." He could have gone to Brick's for supper. He could have been dealing with Roy or Griff Lassen. If he'd lost his moorings, he could have gone to a saloon or a gaming hall. Discouraged, Mary looked straight ahead. "Would you take me home?"

"Of course."

The streets were empty now, and the sunset had faded to dusky blue. Adie didn't speak, and neither did Mary. Her throat hurt from the day's conversations, and her chest felt heavy with dread. Gus had heard Gertie's accusations. She'd have to speak with him. She'd also left the café without doing the cleaning, and she doubted Enid's goodwill extended to sweeping floors.

As they approached the restaurant, Mary looked at the windows. This morning they'd needed washing, but now they sparkled. The boardwalk had been swept, too. Wondering if Gus had stepped up to help her, she turned her attention to the stairs to her apartment. Instead of Gus, she saw J.T. sitting on the third step and watching her with a glint in his eyes. As the buggy halted, he approached without a word and offered his hand, palm up and expectant.

Mary hugged Adie and whispered, "Pray for me."

"I will."

Turning, she accepted J.T.'s hand and stepped down from the buggy. Adie drove off, leaving them alone with hard questions that had to be answered. Gripping her hands in both of his, J.T. asked the hardest question of all. "What happened to the baby?"

Chapter Twenty

Mary tried to gauge his reaction, but his eyes were as hooded as hers. She pulled out of his grasp. "I don't want to have this talk on the street."

"Fine. We'll go upstairs."

"But Gus—"

"He'll understand." When he looked up at the window, she followed his gaze and saw Gus watching them. J.T. jerked his chin and the boy stepped away, presumably to go to his room to give them privacy. J.T. had obviously spoken with her brother, but he didn't seem to be have much patience with *her*.

"How long have you been waiting?" she asked as they climbed the stairs.

"Since morning."

"That's all day."

"I know," he grumbled. "I'd have waited all night if you hadn't come home."

She looked at him from the corner of her eye, remembering the windows and the clean boardwalk. Not only had he waited for her, but he'd done what he could to help her. Her blood thrummed with hope. In another minute she'd know if she could trust him with her deepest feelings. At the top of the landing, he reached around her waist and opened the door. She crossed the threshold, and he closed it behind her with a soft click. Standing in the light from a single lamp, he took off his gun belt and hung it on chair. In a dark corner, Fancy Girl greeted them by wagging her tail. The puppies lay at her side, their eyes still sealed as they suckled.

Turning abruptly, Mary faced him. "I lost the baby."

"*Lost* it?" He sounded like he was talking about a missing pocketknife.

Was he callous or confused? Mary's insides trembled. "I had a miscarriage. The baby was never born."

He let out a slow, even breath. "That's a relief."

Just like in Abilene, he'd hurt her. This time she wanted the satisfaction of telling him to leave for good. "Get out of here!"

"*What?*"

"I said *leave*!"

"No way." His voice came out in a growl.

"I will *not* let you disrespect that child!" For two years Mary had stifled her anger and hidden her grief. Tonight she had nothing to hide. "That baby was part of me. It was part of *us*. I was scared at first, but I wanted it. I loved it." She turned her back on him and stared out the window. "If you can't understand how I felt, I don't want you in my life."

"Oh, I understand," he said with deadly calm. "You're the one who's misinformed."

"I doubt that."

He walked up behind her, stirring the air with his long stride. "I'm not relieved you lost the baby. I'm relieved it's not living in an orphanage somewhere."

Turning slowly, she looked into his eyes. They were full of violence and bitterness and a possessiveness that gave her chills. She wanted to believe he cared, but she could only see the anger.

Glaring at her, he put his hands on his hips. "Do you know how I spent the day?"

"You cleaned the café." The answer struck her as inane, but it showed that he cared.

"That's right," he said. "I mopped and scrubbed and *worried* that *our* child was alone in this world. I thought *all day* about a child growing up like I did, eating garbage and stealing and getting punched and cut and—" He sealed his lips. Turning abruptly, he hid his face from her. "I can't stand the thought of it."

She put her hand on his shoulder. steadying him and absorbing the soft trembling that ran up her arm. "Neither could I. I was so scared—"

He turned and pulled her against him. "I should have been there. I should have—" He stopped short, but she imagined the declaration she'd once dreamed of hearing. *I should have married you.* He hadn't said the words, and she was glad. She didn't want him to speak out of guilt or obligation. They were new people, and she wanted a new beginning. The silence turned into a wall. Needing air, she turned to the window, where she saw the reflection of his face. He rested his hand on her shoulder, curling his fingers against the satiny fabric of her dress. His eyes dipped down the glass, taking in the gown he was likely to remember.

"When did it happen?" he asked.

"A month after you left." She spoke to his reflection. "I'd had pain all day, but I ignored it. I was about to go onstage when the bleeding started. I'd made the mistake of confiding in Ana." She'd been Mary's best friend at the time, and J.T. knew her. "She let it slip, so the rumors were already flying. When I couldn't go on stage, everyone knew for certain I'd been carrying your child."

"I'm sorry," he said ever so gently. "I'm sorry for the scandal, and I'm sorry you lost the baby."

She turned at last. "I am, too."

The air thickened with their mingled warmth. He cupped her face but didn't kiss her. Neither did he speak. The future beaconed like a baby's first smile. He'd made peace with God, and he'd told her he loved her. Earlier he'd almost made a declaration, but now he looked remote. Mary wanted to tell him she loved him and trusted him fully, but as she parted her lips to speak, he lowered his hand.

As if he'd come to his senses, he headed to the divan and sat with hands dangling between his knees, tapping his fingers in an annoying rhythm.

He wanted to ask Mary to be his wife, but a man had his pride. He couldn't propose marriage without a way to support her. He wanted her hands to turn soft again, not be callused from cooking and pushing a broom. He also figured babies would come, and he refused to bring a child into the world if he couldn't provide a good home. Unwilling to let Mary go completely, he looked at her standing by the window in a gown he recognized from Abilene.

"I remember that dress," he said. "You were wearing it the night I left."

"That's right."

"And you weren't wearing it this morning." He'd waited for her all day. "Where'd you go?"

"Adie and I went calling." She showed off the skirt with both hands. "I'd left this at Swan's Nest."

Her eyes were dancing and he loved the boldness. "Who'd you call on?"

"Eight women who will support me in this town." She told him about the visits and how she'd been received with dignity. "Even if the gossip starts, I'll be fine."

"That's good."

Her boldness had paid off, but J.T. wanted to give her even more assurance. Once he had the means to support her, he'd marry her. First, though, he had to find a way to make a living…a way that didn't involve guns or cards. His gaze drifted to Fancy Girl, and he thought of the ways God had shown Himself. Did the Almighty know how badly he needed a job? He had a little bit of work to do on the roof, but the church would be finished in a few weeks. He knew a lot about guns, but being a gunsmith would keep his reputation alive.

Mary was looking at him expectantly. They'd covered a lot of ground tonight, but more trouble lay ahead. He couldn't ask her to be his wife, but she needed protection, and so did Gertie. "I'm going to see Roy tonight. I have to give him an answer about Lassen."

Her eyes filled with worry. "Are you going after him?"

"No. I'm just buying time. I'll give Roy what he wants, and we'll wait for Lassen to make a move."

Footsteps pounded up the stairs. He heard a woman—no, a girl—sobbing uncontrollably. It was the sound a child made when it was hurt and had no pride, the sound *he'd* made when his brother cut him. He strode to the door and flung it wide. Gertie stumbled blindly into the room. He caught her shoulders and saw blood on her face and gown. Her nose was swollen, and a torn sleeve hung like a broken arm.

"Who did this?" J.T. demanded, though he already knew.

Mary flung her arms around her sister. Gertie fell against her, sobbing out the details of Roy inviting her into his office, offering her whiskey and touching her and—J.T. stopped listening. Roy Desmond needed to die.

Why, God?

Yesterday he'd trusted the Almighty and Fancy had lived. Tonight Gertie had been attacked. It made no sense at all. What a fool he'd been to trust Mary's God. No way would he turn the other cheek to a man like Roy Desmond. On the church roof he'd dreamed of taking off his guns. Looking at Gertie in her bloody dress, he vowed to wear them until the day he died.

"I'll be back," he said to Mary.

"No!" she cried. "Stay here."

Ignoring her, he snatched his gun belt off the chair. *No one* messed with J. T. Quinn. Not his own brother. Not Roy Desmond. Not even God.

Mary grabbed his arm. "You're too angry to go out there."

Telling him he was too angry made him even angrier. "I'm going, Mary. You can't stop me."

"We need to pray," she said desperately.

"I'm done praying." No way would he sit around like a little girl. He pointed to Gertie, bloody and weeping. "Are you willing to let this go?"

"No, but—"

"I'm going after Roy, and I'm going to kill him."

Shrieking, Gertie buried her face in her hands and wept even harder. J.T. wondered if Roy had done worse than hit her, but he didn't want to embarrass her by asking. He knew how it felt to be humiliated, so he looked to Mary for an answer. Glaring at him, she murmured in her sister's ear.

"No," Gertie murmured. "But he tried. I should have listened to you. I should have—"

"It's over now." Mary rocked her sister in her arms, patting her back as if she were small. "Let's get some ice on your face."

With one eye on Mary, J.T. pulled the Colt and checked the cylinder, watching as Mary wrapped a hunk of ice in a towel. As he holstered the pistol, she held the ice to Gertie's swollen nose. Her tenderness met a need; his toughness would meet a different one. Healing and vengeance sometimes did a macabre dance.

Mary looked him in the eye. "I'm going to help Gertie clean up, then we'll decide, together, what to do. Do *not* leave until I get back. Do you hear me, Jonah?"

The old J.T. would have walked out and taken care of business. The new one had a vague sense of Someone watching and waiting to see what he'd do. That same presence had *watched* him get cut as a kid. That Someone had *watched* Gus take a beating and Gertie being punched in the face by Roy. Every time she looked in the mirror, she'd remember tonight. That same Someone had also spared Fancy Girl's life, but J.T. counted the score as 1-3. He narrowed his eyes until they twitched. "I can't stay here and do nothing."

"Yes, you can."

She'd used the bossy tone she used on Gus. He didn't like it all. He glanced at Gertie and saw himself in her bloody, broken face. Being attacked made a person think they somehow deserved it. She didn't. No matter what stupid things she'd done, no woman deserved a beating, and neither did a child. Wanting to help her, he softened his voice. "I'm sorry this happened to you, Miss Larue."

Her lips quivered. "I feel so stupid."

Mary held her tighter. "You made a mistake. We'll go to the law in the morning."

J.T. huffed. "A lot of good *that* will do."

Gertie wiped at the tears and the blood. "You were right, both of you. The other actors mocked me, but I believed Roy. He told me things—"

"He tickled your ears," J.T. said. "That's how he works."

"I know that now." Gertie's eyes had the flatness of stones. Looking older than her seventeen years, she shuffled down the hall.

Mary challenged him with a look. "I have to go to her. *Do not leave.*"

In his heart he'd left five minutes ago. "I can't do it, Mary. I can't turn the other cheek."

"Maybe not," she acknowledged. "But you can wait ten minutes before you walk out. I know what you're thinking, Jonah. You think God doesn't care."

"You don't know *half* of what I'm thinking." She was too good inside, too full of kindness. He wanted to lash out at someone, but not at Mary. He'd never hurt her intentionally, not even her feelings. On the other hand, he had no sympathy for her God.

"I'm going after Roy," he said calmly. "Since I'm a reasonable man, I'll give him a choice." It wouldn't be a real choice. Roy would die for hurting Gertie, but Mary didn't need to know.

"What's the choice?" she asked.

"He can pay for Gertie's trip to New York, or he and I can square off outside of town."

The old coldness settled into his bones, a sign he'd

gotten his sharpness back. Mary stared so long he wondered if he'd become a stranger to her. He felt colder with every beat of his heart, sharper and more clear-headed, until the chill went so deep he felt nothing.

Mary broke the silence. "It's not your place to kill Roy. Vengeance belongs to God. We have laws—"

"I'd say vengeance belongs to Gertie."

"It doesn't," she insisted. "If you kill Roy in cold blood, you'll be a murderer."

"So what?" He'd already killed fourteen men.

"Just one night," she pleaded. "Maybe Lassen will take care of Roy."

Or maybe Lassen would come after *him*. J.T. was tired of twiddling his thumbs. "I'm leaving."

"I'm begging you—"

"No!" He'd enough of her foolishness. "I'm doing what I should have done two days ago."

He looked at Mary a long time, taking in her tears and her determination, the pretty green dress and the way she stood her ground. They'd come a long way from Abilene, but somehow they were back at the beginning. He was going to leave her, and she wouldn't like it. This time, though, he wanted to come back. "I'll find you when I'm done with Roy."

Slowly, as if her body had turned to clay, she shook her head no. "If you leave now, we have no future. Every time you walk out a door, I'll wonder if you're coming back."

He held out his arms to show off his guns. "This is who I am."

"It's who you *were*. Give God a chance—"

"I'm done with God," he said without feeling. "If you're done with me because of it, I understand."

Breath by breath, her silence built a wall. It thick-

ened with the tick of the clock. J.T. felt the weight of
his guns. The belt rode high on his hips, embracing
him and pulling him into the dark where he'd find
Roy and kill him. He didn't have to go. He could take
off his guns and do nothing, but he'd never be the man
Mary deserved, or the God-fearing man she wanted.
He glanced at Fancy Girl and the puppies. If he killed
Roy, he'd have to leave Denver without her. He'd never
see his dog again. And Gus...he'd have to leave without saying goodbye. Was killing Roy worth the cost?
His heart said no, but if he didn't protect Mary and her
family, who would?

Just like in the alley in New York, God had blinked
and a child had been hurt. Justice had to be served, and
J.T. intended to do it. He looked at Mary a long time,
etching her face in his memory the way he'd done on
that first day in Denver, then he walked out the door.

She watched through the window as J.T. paced down
the street. She touched the glass with a silent plea, but
he didn't turn around. A door opened in the hallway.
Turning, she saw her brother.

"Wh-what happened?" he asked.

"Gertie got hurt." She stepped away from the window. "I'm going to get Bessie."

"Will she be okay?"

"I think so." She told Gus about Gertie's nose and
Roy's threats. A week ago he'd have reacted like a
frightened child. Tonight his eyes blazed with a man's
instinct to protect the women in his home. He looked
around the room. "Where's J.T.?"

"He's gone."

"I heard you b-both shouting. Is he c-coming back?"
Gus had hardly stammered a single word. He'd

grown up this week. If J.T. didn't return, the boy would learn another hard lesson. Surely she and Gus meant more to him than killing Roy, though she understood the desire for vengeance. If Gertie's nose didn't heal right, she'd be marked for life. If J.T. had stayed, she could have sent them both to get Bessie. Instead she had to rely on her brother.

"He's not coming back tonight." *Maybe not ever.* "Would you get Bessie?"

The boy put on his shoes and hurried out the door. "I'll be fast."

Mary went to the bedroom, where she saw Gertie at the vanity, dressed in a pink wrapper and examining her nose in the oval mirror. "It's broken. It'll be crooked forever."

"Maybe not." She told Gertie that Gus was getting Bessie, then she pulled a pin from the girl's disheveled hair. "Do you want to tell me what happened?"

Tears filled her eyes. "I can't bear to think about it."

"It'll help to talk."

Mary pulled a second pin, then another. Gertie's hair came loose, and the story tumbled out of her. As Mary brushed away the elaborate curls, she listened to a story that could have ended with far worse than a broken nose. Roy could have raped her and then murdered her to ensure her silence. Trembling for her sister, Mary combed out the last tangle. "This doesn't have to ruin your life. You can still go to New York when you're eighteen."

Gertie shook her head. "I don't want to go."

Dreams didn't die that easily. Mary gripped her sister's shoulders. "Why not?"

"I don't have talent."

"Who says?"

"Everyone." Tears filled the girl's eyes. "I made a fool of myself. The other actresses laughed at me. I heard them. And now my nose is a mess."

"You've had a terrible experience." Mary spoke to Gertie's reflection and her own. "There's no shame in quitting if that's what you really want, but how about waiting until you're older before you decide?"

A sheepish smile curved on Gertie's lips. "That's probably smart. Maybe my nose will heal straight."

"Let's see what Bessie says."

Being careful of Gertie's bruises, Mary laced her hair into a braid. As she tied the ribbon, Bessie stepped through the door with Caroline at her side. The nurse set her medical bag on the bed, then pulled up a chair next to Gertie. "How badly did he hurt you?"

"My nose is broken."

"Anything else?" She touched the girl's arm.

Gertie understood the question. The fear that filled her eyes broke Mary's heart. "He tried, but I got away."

"Good girl." Bessie studied her nose with a clinical air. "It's broken, but I don't think it's displaced."

"Are you sure?" Gertie sounded hopeful

"As sure as I can be with all that swelling." Bessie pinched the bridge of her nose. "I don't feel a bump."

Caroline nudged Mary. "Where's J.T.?"

"He left."

Before Mary realized what her friend intended, Caroline steered her into the parlor and guided her down on the divan. "Is he going after Roy?"

"I'm afraid so."

Caroline gripped her hand. "Maybe he'll calm down before he does something stupid."

"I hope so." Mary slipped away and went to the window. She looked for J.T., though she didn't expect to see him. "If he comes back, there's a good chance he'll have blood on his hands."

"Oh, Mary."

"I've never seen him so angry."

Caroline came to stand next to her. "Keep praying. That's all you can do."

"I know. It's just—" She started to cry. An hour ago, J.T. had earned her complete trust. The last barrier to loving him had been shattered tonight. She hadn't said the words, but she'd given him her heart and he'd already broken it again. Forgiveness had come easily for what he'd done in Abilene, but tonight she felt bitter. "He left. How can I trust him?"

"Maybe that's not the right question," Caroline said.

"Then what is it?"

"Can you forgive him? And I don't mean just more time." The brunette looked past the street to the sliver of moon. "You know I was married once. I loved Charles with everything in me, but not a day passed that I didn't have to forgive him for something. The day he died was the worst. I begged him not to go that night. I knew something awful would happen, and it did. In the end, I had to forgive him for dying."

. Mary's chest tightened. "How did you do it?"

"Just like you'll forgive J.T. I did it one hurt at a time."

"I don't know." Her voice quavered. "If he goes after Roy, he'll be guilty of murder. He might not come back."

"Give him time," Caroline advised.

"How long?"

"As long as it takes."

Mary smiled at her friend. "Thank you."

She couldn't always count on J.T., but she could depend on the women of Swan's Nest. Through the dim glass she saw a thousand stars. She didn't know how long J.T. would be gone, but she'd be waiting when he returned.

Chapter Twenty-One

Without Fancy Girl at his side, J.T. felt as if he'd stepped back in time. The night air cooled his face but not his blood as he headed for the Newcastle. Tonight he had a job to do.

The stars followed him without blinking, and not a cloud could be seen for miles. Refusing to look at the unfinished church, he went to the side door of the theater, kicked it down and strode to Roy's office. Wall sconces lit his way, flickering as he passed them. When he reached Roy's door, he kicked it down and found more darkness. He didn't know where Roy lived, but he had a good idea where to find him. Attacking Gertie would have fired his blood. Market Street offered women, liquor and cards, just what Roy would want to satisfy his lust.

J.T. headed back down the hall. Stepping over the splintered door, he saw the scaffolding against the church wall. He'd never climb it again. Someone else would have to finish the bell tower.

With only vengeance in mind, he turned down Market Street. Peering into saloons and dance halls, he searched for Roy while intending to avoid Griff Lassen. He spotted Lassen in a busy saloon, ducked out of sight and crossed the street to a place called the Alhambra. At the counter he saw Roy sipping whiskey. A smear of blood showed on his cuff, and he had a scratch on his jaw. J.T. approached him without a hint of anger. "Hello, Roy."

"Quinn."

J.T. signaled the barkeep. "Whatever my friend's drinking for him. Whiskey for me." He wouldn't drink it. The liquor was a sign to Roy that he meant business. He kept his eyes straight ahead. "You jumped the gun with Gertie Larue."

"You were dragging your feet." He meant J.T.'s promise to stop Lassen.

"I told you I'd get back to you today. Here I am."

"You were stalling."

"I was being careful."

"I don't believe you, Quinn."

The barkeep set down the glasses and poured. J.T. ran his finger along the rim, distracting Roy as he slid his other hand inside the duster, resting it on his gun. "You've upped the price. I want two thousand dollars."

Roy laughed. "For that little brat?"

"Don't test me." He dug the Colt into Roy's side. "Bring the money to the Slewfoot Mine tomorrow at noon. You pay me off, and I'll finish with Lassen. If you don't—" he cocked the hammer "—I'll kill you for what you did to Gertie."

Slowly Roy turned his head. "The little trollop's just like her sister."

If they'd been in a lawless cow town, J.T. might have shot Roy on the spot. The only thing stopping him was the likelihood of getting caught. He needed his horse for a fast getaway, so he settled for twisting the gun hard enough to leave a bruise. "Do you want to die right here?"

Roy let out a breath. "Tomorrow it is."

J.T. eased the hammer back in place. "The Slewfoot at noon," he repeated. "Don't be late."

He holstered his weapon and stood. Tomorrow Roy would die. When he showed up with the money, J.T. would challenge him to a duel. He'd win, of course. But Roy had enough skill to call it a fair fight.

He paid for the drinks, left the saloon and headed to Swan's Nest to get his horses, taking a longer route to avoid Mary's apartment. When he reached the mansion he went around the back to the carriage house. Working in the dark, he saddled the buckskin. Rather than take the pack horse, he decided to leave it for Gus. When he got back to the boardinghouse, he'd write a note to the boy. It wasn't much of a goodbye, but it would have to do.

He led the horse into the yard, climbed on and rode down the street. A block later he passed a buggy coming in the opposite direction. He recognized Caroline and Bessie and hunkered down. Suspicious of a lone rider, Caroline nudged the horse into a faster walk and passed without looking at him. He'd become nothing to them, a stranger. Soon he'd be nothing to Mary. She'd be wise to forget he'd ever come to Denver. Gus wouldn't forget him, but now the memories would hurt. He couldn't bear to think about his dog. Fancy Girl wouldn't understand at all.

He could still change his mind. Instead of killing Roy himself, he could go to the law. He could apologize to Mary and trust God for justice. The thought sent bile up his throat. Tonight the Almighty had shown His true colors. He didn't care, and He couldn't be trusted.

At the boardinghouse, J.T. tied his horse out back and went to his room. As always he left the door open until he lit the lamp. Light flooded the tiny space, revealing both the contents and the emptiness as he shut the door and locked it. He missed his dog. He missed Mary. His gaze fell on the chapbook he'd left on the nightstand. Ignoring it, he took gun oil and a rag out of his saddlebag. It had been a long time since he'd prepared his weapons for battle, but he did it now the way a man greeted an old friend.

When he finished, he wrote the note to Gus on paper the landlady provided along with bedding and a washbowl. Tomorrow, when he finished with Roy, he'd deliver the note and the money to Swan's Nest and then leave town. He hoped Mary would keep the two thousand dollars. Not only was it Gertie's due, but he had nothing else to give her. He considered writing down his wishes, but talking about money seemed cold when he wanted to tell her he loved her.

Resigned to losing her, he put the note for Gus in his saddlebag, packed his things and then stretched on the bed and slept.

Morning came hard and bright.

So did hunger.

So did the knowledge he wouldn't be washing dishes for Mary ever again. He swung his feet off the bed, looked for Fancy Girl out of habit and felt melancholy. He tried not to think about Mary.

He shaved and washed, put on dark clothes and went to the kitchen for breakfast. He ate quickly and in silence, then returned to his room, where he put on his guns and duster. He'd told Roy twelve noon, but he wanted to arrive first. J.T. knew the road to the Slewfoot Mine well. He'd ridden it a week ago with Gus, and two weeks ago when he'd arrived in Denver with foolish dreams. The ride to the mine glistened with memories of the camping trip. It was by the dying fire that he'd come to understand love. It was in the same spot he'd won back Mary's trust and dared to hope for a future with her.

His hope was dead, and the old J.T. was back in business. Riding slowly, he approached the played-out mine. Someone had boarded up the rectangular entrance, but time had eroded the planks and a man could get inside. Overhead the sky burned with a blue heat broken only by billowing white clouds. Today he felt no wonder at their distant beauty, only an awareness that clouds came and went. He rode past a hillside covered with gravel-like rock, then looked to the right where scattered boulders offered cover. The mine loomed in front of him. Knowing it led to a maze of dark tunnels, he turned away from it.

"Quinn!"

The raspy voice didn't belong to Roy. It belonged to Griff Lassen, and he sounded as mean as ever. J.T. was high on his horse in open space. He needed cover and he needed it now, so he backpedaled the buckskin to a lone boulder. Sliding out of the saddle, he gripped his Colt and sized up the terrain. He didn't like what he saw at all. The apron of rock above him would give neither cover nor purchase, and the road he'd just ridden stretched for a quarter mile before it turned. A couple of cottonwoods offered protection, but not much. Aside from the mine, he had nowhere to go.

He'd picked this place so he could see someone coming. Instead he'd ridden into a trap. He felt like a fool. Instead of Lassen doing in Roy, Roy had tricked J.T.

into facing off with Lassen. There was bad blood between J.T. and Griff, but today they had a common foe in Roy. Before J.T. did anything, he needed to know where he stood with his former partner. "Is that you, Griff?"

"Yeah, it's me," he called back. "I can't say I was expecting you. Desmond's supposed to show up with the money he owes some friends of mine."

Griff sounded downright pleasant. Maybe he'd forgotten about Fancy Girl and the squatters. "Funny you'd mention Desmond," J.T. called with equal friendliness. "He's got business with me, too."

"Maybe we should come out from behind these rocks and talk."

"I don't know, Griff." If J.T. moved, Griff would have a clear shot. "You weren't too happy with me about that dog incident."

"I know."

"I left you in a lurch." He wouldn't apologize, but Griff would get the drift.

"Forget it, Quinn. I say we let bygones be bygones. Come on out."

As a precaution, J.T. took off his hat and put it on a stick. "Here I come," he called, waving the hat.

A bullet went through the brim. Pivoting around the boulder, J.T. jammed the hat on his head and fired back.

In the volley of gunfire, Griff cursed. "You're a traitor, Quinn! That squatter in Wyoming put out my eye. You're going to pay for that."

J.T. had no intention of dying, but he'd gotten himself in a bind. The entrance to the mine offered cover, but he'd be trapped in the maze of tunnels—dark tunnels that went nowhere. He turned and looked down the road he'd just taken. It offered no protection at all. His best chance lay in making a deal with Lassen.

"Let's talk," J.T. shouted. "You want Desmond. So do I."

"I don't need your help."

"Sure you do."

Lassen answered with a low laugh. "Face it, Quinn. You're about to die." He fired to prove his point.

J.T. counted to three, twisted around the boulder and fired back. He caught a glimpse of Lassen and fired again, but not before Lassen got off a shot of his own. The bullet ricocheted off the rock an inch from J.T.'s face. He'd die if he didn't make a move, so he broke for the mine, firing as he ran at full speed until his foot landed in a hole and he stumbled.

He heard a crumbling like dead wood, and then he was falling…falling…falling into a black hole without a bottom. Cool air rushed by him. His shoulder banged on the side of the shaft and he lost his grip on his gun. Rocks and dirt tumbled with him until he landed on his back thirty feet below the surface. Pain shot through his chest and shoulders. He couldn't breathe, not even a gasp. Vaguely he realized he'd fallen down an air shaft and landed in the belly of the mine. His thoughts formed an unwilling prayer.

Dear God, what have I done?

He'd gone off today like a stupid kid. He'd left Mary and Gertie at Roy's mercy, and now he was going to die. Silently, he endured the pain in his body, not crying out because he couldn't make a sound.

He managed a small, painful breath. Then another. Finally he could breathe a little and he realized he wouldn't be dying in the next ten seconds. Lying flat on his back, he took stock of his injuries. He'd had the wind knocked out of him, and he couldn't move his right shoulder without knife-like pain. He checked it with his good hand and decided it was dislocated and not broken. His head hurt so bad he couldn't focus his eyes. He tried to sit up, but the pain forced him down.

Staring at the circle of blue sky, he thought of his horse. Lassen would steal it and take the money in the saddlebag. He'd also look for J.T.'s dead body and maybe fire down the shaft to finish the job. No matter how much it hurt, and how much he hated the dark, J.T. had to take cover. Swallowing bile, he dragged himself six feet into the pitch-black. Twice he nearly passed out, but he made it to the chiseled rock wall. Cradling his arm, he sat up and vomited. Whether the nausea came from the knock to his head, the pain or fear, he didn't know. He could only hope the mine had another way out.

Looking up, he saw a waterfall of light but not the mouth of the shaft. As a shadow erased the glow, a small landslide of dirt and rock tumbled over the edge. "You down there, Quinn?"

J.T. held in a curse. He couldn't let Lassen know he'd survived the fall.

"I saw you go down." Lassen's chuckle echoed down the shaft. So did the click of a gun being cocked. "The mine caved in a year ago. There's no way out."

Sweat poured down J.T.'s back. He wanted to scream, but he couldn't let the man know he'd survived. If he did, Lassen would shoot into the shaft. He didn't have a clear shot, but bullets could ricochet. Instead of leaving, Lassen pulled the trigger of his gun. The bullet hit two feet from J.T.'s thigh. By a sheer act of will, he didn't shout. Lassen fired again and again. The bullets flew and ricocheted until he'd emptied his pistol. Roaring with laughter, he holstered the weapon and walked away.

J.T. didn't have lead in his belly or his head, but sweat was pouring out of him in rivers. He could breathe almost normally, but his bones felt as if they'd been crushed. Sitting up, he spotted his Colt six feet away in the circle of light. A lot of good it would do him. No one except Roy knew where he'd gone, and Roy wanted him dead. He'd never been more alone in his life. He stared at the gun a long time, then crawled to it and put it in the holster still tied to his thigh.

The walls closed in on him. So did the dark. He had to get out. There had to be a way.... Panting with pain, he leveraged to his feet and hobbled into what seemed to be a tunnel. He moved forward cautiously, dragging his good hand along the wall. Dirt collected under his nails. With each step, the mine grew colder. He sniffed for fresh air but smelled only dust and sweat. Ten paces later he reached a dead end. He backtracked and stumbled on a downed timber. He circled the area again, then a third time, and still there was no way out.

Cold and bleeding, he limped to the light. With his pulse thundering, he looked up at the sky and screamed for help at the top of his lungs.

Chapter Twenty-Two

Mary didn't expect J.T. to show up to wash dishes, and he didn't. She served breakfast as usual and then went upstairs to check on her sister. When Adie arrived with a box of chocolates for Gertie, she told Mary that J.T.'s buckskin was missing from the carriage house, but that he'd left his pack horse.

"Maybe he just went for a ride," Mary said hopefully.

"I don't think so." Adie's eyes filled with sympathy. "Someone kicked down the side door to the Newcastle."

It had to be J.T. Mary imagined Roy dead at his desk with a bullet between his eyes. She hated the man, but she couldn't tolerate murder. She braced herself for bad news. "Has anyone seen Roy?"

"Josh saw him this morning."

Relief flooded through her, but it disappeared in a wave of fresh worry. Had Roy bested J.T.? It was possible but unlikely. She'd been about to bring Gertie a lunch tray, but she set it down and headed for the door. "I have to find J.T."

Adie gripped her arm. "You can't go after him."

"Why not?"

"Roy might try to hurt you the way he hurt Gertie. Josh is talking to Deputy Morgan right now, then he'll go to J.T.'s boardinghouse. Brick offered to check Market Street, and some of the other workers are looking, too."

J.T. had friends, and he didn't even know it. Mary felt a bit calmer, but nothing could ease the burden of having parted with angry words. She'd thought a lot about Caroline's story. She could forgive J.T. for anything, and she loved him enough to wait for him to come to his senses. She might not always trust J.T.'s judgment, but she could trust God. She just had to be patient.

Adie broke into her thoughts. "Do you have any idea where J.T. might be?"

She thought for a minute. If Roy was walking around Denver, J.T. would have stayed in town to watch him. Was he lying low until Lassen made a move? Perhaps he was setting up a ruse of his own for Roy and Griff Lassen. The other possibility, that he was dead or dying, scared her to death.

"He could be anywhere," she admitted to Adie.

Her friend squeezed her hand. "When J.T.'s ready, he'll come to you."

"I hope so."

"He loves you," Adie said with confidence. "He'll be back."

Mary wanted to believe her, but she knew life could be unkind. She didn't always understand God's ways, but she could pray for J.T. with every breath. It was the best and only thing she could do.

The remainder of the first day passed with J.T. trying to climb out of the air shaft. He found a rope, but it crumbled in his fingers. Even if it had been strong, what could he have done with it? His shoulder was hanging like a broken wing, and he'd fallen too far.

He took off his gun belt and set it on the ground. Of all the useless things to have…he needed water and food, a blanket and clothes that weren't soaked in sweat. He needed someone with a rope and a horse to pull him out, but no one knew where he'd gone. He controlled his fear by looking up at the circle of sky, but dusk brought total darkness. He preferred physical pain to the panic, so he decided to try and fix his shoulder.

Lying flat, he maneuvered the arm forward and back. His groans echoed in the shaft, but he worked the joint until it popped into place. Relief from the pain was instant, but the panic made him sweat again, and sweating reminded him of how badly he needed water. He tried to moisten his lips, but his tongue felt sticky and dry. A man couldn't go long without water, and J.T. had consumed just one cup of coffee at breakfast. The day before he'd been so worried about Mary that he hadn't eaten anything, and he didn't recall drinking more than a few sips of water while cleaning the café. The coolness of the mine worked to his advantage, but he didn't have more than three days, maybe four, before he'd be a corpse.

Fighting to stay calm, he searched the patch of sky for even a single star. A white dot emerged from the gloom, growing brighter as he stared. He wanted to pray, but he'd pushed God away. Mary had pleaded with him to wait before going after Roy, and he'd pushed her away, too. Now he was buried alive and Roy was walking around Denver, a threat to Mary and her family. He wanted to shout and break things, but no one would hear him and he had nothing to hit. Instead, he closed his eyes and recalled the nights Fancy Girl had warmed his toes. He remembered his talk with Gus about babies and love, and mostly he thought about Mary. For a short time, she'd carried his child. He couldn't think of a more generous gift, and what had he given her in return? Nothing but heartache.

His leg cramped, a sign of needing water. Straightening it to kill the pain, he opened his eyes and looked again at the star. It hadn't moved, and he drew comfort from the point of light. He'd have given anything to climb out of the hole, but he could only lie in the dark, dreaming of Mary and wishing he'd done things differently.

On the second day, Mary woke up early and dressed for church. She'd never seen Gus so glum, and Gertie's mood matched the plum-colored bruises on her face. The girl didn't feel ready to answer questions, so she asked to stay home from the Sunday service. Gertie needed time to heal, so Mary hugged her sister and left with Gus.

They arrived at Brick's place early. Instead of an empty saloon, she found Josh in a circle of men, quizzing them for news about J.T. Brick had made another tour of Market Street, and he'd learned J.T. had met with Roy at the Alhambra. The meeting had seemed amiable to the barkeep, and the men had left separately and an hour apart. Mary didn't know what to think. Had J.T. set up a future confrontation with Roy? And what had happened to Griff Lassen? No one knew what he looked like, which made finding him impossible.

Just as disheartening, Josh had made a second visit to J.T.'s boardinghouse. This time he'd asked the landlady to unlock the door and he'd inspected the room. Wherever J.T. had gone, he'd taken his things.

When people started arriving for the service, the meeting broke up. Mary took her place in the front row, but she couldn't stop turning to the door with the hope she'd see J.T. She sang the usual hymns, but today they brought no comfort. She could believe J.T. would do something stupid to Roy, but she couldn't believe he'd leave without a final goodbye. He loved her. He loved Fancy Girl, and he cared about Gus. Nor would he have left Denver with Roy still a threat.

At the end of the service, Josh led a prayer for J.T.'s safety, ending it with a hushed "Amen." He gave the usual invitation to supper at Swan's Nest, but Mary made excuses and left. Alone and scared, she walked the streets, looking in every crevice and corner for the man she loved, until her feet were sore and her knees were throbbing. At the end of the day, she dragged herself up the steps to her apartment.

Gus came out of his room. "Is he coming back?" he asked.

"I hope so."

But with every minute, she grew more convinced he was dying or dead. Aching inside, she went to the window and stared at the horizon. Clouds towered in the west, boiling and churning as thunder announced the coming of a storm. Mary bowed her head. "Please, Lord," she said out loud. "Keep J.T. safe. Show Yourself to him, and remind him that You love him."

Choking on tears, she whispered, "I love him, too." She'd have given anything to have said the words before he left. Instead she'd let him leave in bitter silence. Tomorrow she'd look for him again. She'd search until she found him, just as he'd been looking for her when he'd come to Denver.

J.T.'s second day in the mine began with a shift in the light from black to gray. His belly ached with hunger, and his throat felt as dry as sand. Predictably, his head hurt worse than yesterday. He could move his shoulder but not easily. As the hours passed, the pain sharpened his thoughts to the simplest of facts.

He was going to die here.

He'd left Gus without saying goodbye.

He'd never see his dog again.

Worst of all, he'd left Mary twisting in the wind. Not only had he left her in danger from Roy, but she'd never know what had happened to him. They'd quarreled, but J.T. didn't doubt she cared for him. By dying in this hole, he'd done the unthinkable to the woman he loved. He'd left her to worry and wonder forever.

"Mary, forgive me," he whispered.

He closed his eyes and pictured her face. Two days ago he'd earned back her trust. He'd had hopes for marriage and had wanted to find a decent way to make a living. He'd dared to believe that God cared. Then Gertie had been attacked, and again he'd lost confidence in anyone but himself. Prideful and sure, he'd dug this grave with his arrogance.

For hours he stared at the circle of sky. As the sun rose to high noon, the pale glow turned into hot gold. It warmed his face and blinded him with the same light. He couldn't see, couldn't blink. He felt the goodness of the light and almost wept. He wanted to be a man, not a squalling child, so he took a breath to steady himself. It worked, but just barely.

More hours passed. His mouth turned to cotton and

he felt feverish from lack of water. He thought of Fancy Girl and the puppies and how she'd licked them into life. He relived the camping trip with Gus and the water fight, the way he'd fallen back in the stream and how the water had rushed over him. He imagined Mary singing songs he'd heard in Abilene, then the hymn she'd been singing when he'd found her in church. Two weeks had passed, but it seemed like a lifetime.

He tried to moisten his lips, but he didn't have enough spit. He wished he'd stayed with Mary. He wished he'd done things her way instead of his own. His belly hurt with hunger, but the thirst plagued him far more. He had the shakes and his legs wouldn't stop cramping. He didn't have much time, maybe a day or two. The end would come soon. He'd go crazy and soil himself like a baby. He'd die alone and without dignity.

His gaze slid to his gun belt. He looked at the Colt for several minutes, then he stretched his arm and curled his fingers around the ivory handle. He slid the pistol from the holster, pulled it to his side and closed his eyes. He imagined the gun barrel in his mouth. It would taste like metal and gun oil, smoke and traces of sulfur. He knew exactly how far to cock the hammer, how gently to pull the trigger for a clean, quick shot.

He opened his eyes wide and stared at the patch of sky, refusing to blink as the blue vanished behind a cloud. Instead of blocking the sun, the cloud made it brighter. He recalled standing on the roof of the church and how he'd longed to take off his guns. He remembered Fancy giving birth, how he'd cried out and how God had answered. And he remembered praying with Josh and calling God by name.

"I don't know how you can stand me, Lord Jesus," J.T. said to the cloud. "You know how weak I am, how stubborn and stupid. You saved Fancy Girl, and I turned my back on You. You gave Mary to me, and I walked out on her. And Gus—" He thought of the boy standing up to him. "I walked out on him, too."

J.T. tried to swallow but couldn't. There was nothing left in him, not even a drop of spit. He licked his lips, felt the dryness and spoke again to the unreachable sky.

"I don't deserve another chance, Lord. But I'm begging You to be good to Mary. I love her and I let her down. Keep her safe. And Gus—" he could barely speak. "Help him grow into a good man, a better man than me. And for Gertie, heal her nose and help her to grow up." He thought next of Fancy Girl. "Fancy's just a dog, but I love her. Make sure she has lots of bones and someone to scratch her."

He took comfort in knowing Mary would give his dog a good home. She'd always had a heart for strays. He thought of the way she loved him when he didn't deserve it and how she saw the good in him when there wasn't any. He took a final breath. "Spare Mary the pain of missing me, Lord. I have so many regrets—" He choked on his dry tongue. "I wish—I wish I'd trusted You."

Trust Him now.

The thought was in his head, but it seemed as loud as thunder. He thought of the hot bench, vengeance, darkness and turning the other cheek. He thought of Gus, boys eating hotcakes, puppies being born and Gertie running home to her family. Mostly he thought of Mary and the baby they'd lost, how much he loved her and how she'd forgiven him.

J.T. had asked God to show Himself, and He had. He was showing Himself now in a shaft of light that pierced the dark of this living grave. J.T. had taken fourteen lives. He'd hurt the people he loved. He'd done terrible things, yet the light had found him in the darkness, and he knew the light to be love. It pinned him to the ground and on his back. He couldn't fight and he didn't want to try. The light warmed him to the bones. It comforted him and promised hope. He felt the mercy of it on his face and knew he'd lost this final battle. He had no right to take another life, not even his own. Defeated by love, he shoved the gun out of reach.

He closed his eyes and murmured a prayer. He felt a tear on his cheek, except it wasn't warm. Another one trickled toward his ear. His eyelids flew open and he looked at the sky. Instead of a burning white mist, he saw the gray bottom of a thunderhead. A drop of water hit his cheek, then another…and another. Rain… blessed rain was falling from the sky.

Bolting upright, he stared at the sheen of water mixing with silvery light. Thunder rolled down the shaft. He blinked and the mist turned into a torrent of rain. Laughing crazily, he tipped his face upward and opened his mouth. He tasted the water on his tongue, felt the moisture on his lips and cheeks. The water was coming in buckets, running down the sides of the shaft and making puddles the size of wagon wheels. When he'd drunk his fill, he grabbed his hat and held it to catch a supply for later. He wouldn't die today and probably not tomorrow. He didn't know when he'd die, but he wouldn't die alone. God had shown Himself yet again, and J.T. wouldn't ever forget.

He pushed to his knees and lifted his face to the sky, feeling the rain on his skin as it washed him clean. With the storm raging and night approaching, he raised his arms and rejoiced.

Chapter Twenty-Three

On the morning of the third day, Mary closed the café after breakfast, borrowed a buggy from Adie and Josh and drove to J.T.'s boardinghouse. Desperate for a clue, she wanted to see the empty room for herself. No matter what she found, today she'd resume her search.

At the boardinghouse she asked the landlady to show her J.T.'s room. As the woman led her down the hall, Mary realized that not once had she seen where J.T. lived. In Abilene, he'd come to her. He'd had a room in the same hotel, but he'd never invited her inside.

"This is it," the landlady said.

Stepping into the room, Mary saw a wool blanket on the narrow bed, a mirror that had been wiped clean and a little book on the nightstand. She picked it up and recognized one of the chapbooks Josh sometimes gave to visitors. He'd given it to J.T., but J.T. had left it behind. It held no clues to his whereabouts, but its presence signaled he'd gone back to his old ways.

With her heart breaking, she surveyed the room and saw nothing except a few sheets of paper on a desk. On top of the stack sat a pencil. It was thick and round... and dull. Someone had used it. She crossed the room in four steps, lifted the top sheet of paper to the window and saw indentations. Most of the marks were faint, but she could make out a D and Gus. The rest of the words were fragments, but she recognized horse, sister, man and Fancy.

J.T. had written the note, but it hadn't been delivered. Something terrible had happened to him, she felt sure of it. Only one man could answer her questions, and that was Roy Desmond. She wanted to race to the theater and make him talk, but what threat did she pose? She needed help, and she needed it now. She thanked the landlady, climbed into the buggy and snapped the reins. The church was closer than the sheriff's office, so she went to find Josh. She reached the building in minutes. When she didn't see the minister, she called to one of the workers. "I need help. Where's Josh?"

"He went to buy paint."

Mary needed him now. She could almost hear J.T. calling her name. Surely she wouldn't feel such hope if he were dead. Her gaze shifted to the Newcastle Theater. She didn't dare go inside alone. She'd be putting herself in danger, and the risk would dishonor J.T. and his promise to protect her. She considered going for Deputy Morgan, but Josh would be back any minute.

Nervously she studied the theater. The new side door was ajar, as if someone had entered but not closed it for fear of being heard. She turned to the street, saw J.T.'s buckskin and gasped. She'd found him, but he was finally going after Roy. She had to stop him before he committed murder.

She leapt out of the buggy and ran through the door. The carpet muffled her steps, but a single gunshot shattered the silence. Terrified, she pressed herself against the wall. Had J.T. shot Roy? Or had Roy killed J.T.? She knew better than to go alone into Roy's office, but how could she wait? The man she loved could be dying this very minute.

With her heart pounding, she edged down the hall to the office. Trembling, she peeked around the corner and saw Roy facedown on his desk, blood pooling around his thinning hair and soaking into the blotter. She hated Roy for what he'd done to Gertie, but she couldn't abide shooting an unarmed man. Behind the desk she saw a wall safe left open and empty, an indication that J.T. had taken all the money. It seemed he'd returned fully to his old ways. She couldn't overlook the violence or the thievery. He'd have to pay for what he'd done, but she still loved him. He needed her more than ever, so she raced into the hall. She hadn't seen him leave through the side door, so she headed for the belly of theater.

"J.T.!" she shouted. "Talk to me."

As she rounded a corner, she glimpsed the shadow of a man turning down a hall. She charged after him, but he'd vanished down another corridor. Approaching slowly, she spoke in the low tones she'd use with a child. "I love you, Jonah. We'll go to the law together."

Snide laughter filled the hallway. J.T. never laughed like that. Confused, she stopped in midstep. She'd seen his horse in front of the theater. Who else could be in the hall? Before she could turn and run, a one-eyed man came around the corner with his gun aimed at her chest.

He cocked the hammer. "Take another step and I'll shoot you, too."

"You're not J.T.!"

"He's dead."

"He can't be." She could barely breathe.

"He's dead, all right." The man grinned. "If a bullet didn't kill him, the fall did."

"What are you talking about?" She had to know. Where was he? What had happened?

Lassen looked her up and down. "I got what I wanted. Quinn's dead and Desmond paid his debt. You're a pretty woman. If you want Quinn's body, you can have it."

No! No! No! She couldn't stand the thought of J.T. being gone. She hadn't told him she loved him. Gus needed him, and so did Fancy Girl. "Where is he?"

"At the bottom of the Slewfoot Mine." With a sly grin, he started to raise his gun. Knowing she'd become a witness who could identify this man, she turned and fled back into the theater.

She ran out the front door and hurried to the buggy, scanning the church for Josh. She didn't see him, but she spotted Deputy Morgan talking to Brick. She ran up to him, told him about Lassen and where she was going. Unwilling to wait another minute, she jumped into the buggy and drove as fast as she dared to the Slewfoot Mine.

J.T.'s third day in the mine dawned just like the second. When fear nipped at him, he looked at the sky and thought of Mary. He didn't know the words to the hymn she'd sung in church, but he remembered the tune and he hummed it now. If this hole in the ground turned into his grave, he'd die with the promise of loving her for eternity.

He dozed until the sun shined directly over the air shaft. In the silence he imagined Mary singing. He could hear her voice in his head, softly calling his name. Maybe God had sent an angel to fetch him up to the clouds. The cry grew louder, then louder still. His eyes flew open and he bolted to his feet. God hadn't sent an angel to take him to Heaven. He'd sent the woman he loved to take him home.

"J.T.!" she shouted again. The rig rattled to a stop.

"I'm down here," he shouted. "Stay back! The ground's not stable."

"You're alive!"

He could hardly wait to hold her in his arms. If she'd come in the buggy, there'd be a few tools under the seat. "Do you have a rope?"

"I'll get it."

With rescue just minutes away, J.T. took a last look around the mine. He saw his gun belt in the shadows and the Colt Navy lying next to it. The old J.T. had died in this place. The new one didn't want that gun to ever fill his hand again. It seemed a fitting end to a life he no longer wanted. He could only hope Mary would be a part of the new one. He had nothing to offer—no job, no money—but he loved her. He wanted to give her another child. To Gus he'd be a big brother, and for Gertie he'd be a pain in the neck to every man who came calling. Fancy would get an extra bone tonight, and he'd give her the longest scratch she'd ever had. He could hardly wait to see them all.

Mary finally called from the surface. "I've got the rope."

"Tie it off to the buggy and throw it down. But whatever you do, don't get too close."

"I won't."

He waited with his eyes on the sky, watching until she shouted, "Here it comes."

A coil of rope spiraled into the mine. He made a loop, hooked it under his arms and held on tight with his good hand. "My shoulder's hurt," he called to her. "The horse is going to have to do the work."

"We'll go slow," she answered.

The rope tightened around his chest, then lifted him to his toes and finally into the air. He used his legs to walk up the wall, being careful not to bang his bad side against the shaft. As the light intensified, the pain faded and he squinted in the brightness. He had ten feet to go, then five. He smelled dust and hot air and finally grass as the horse dragged him over the rim of the hole. The ground crumbled but only slightly. With the horse still pulling, J.T. waited until he was ten feet from danger before rolling to his back. Squinting because of the brightness, he took pleasure in the sunshine on his face. He heard footsteps and smelled cotton and rose-scented soap. When he opened his eyes, he saw Mary on her knees with tears streaming down her cheeks.

"You're alive," she murmured. "I thought you were dead."

"Me, too." He cupped her face. "How'd you find me?"

She told him about Lassen and Roy. The two scorpions had stung each other as J.T. had hoped, but he recoiled at the thought of Mary in harm's way and Lassen being on the loose. It troubled him until she told she'd seen Deputy Morgan at the church. "I told him Lassen was in the theater."

J.T. thought about his horse and the money. Maybe he'd get them back. "Morgan'll go after him."

Mary took a hankie from her pocket and wiped his brow. "You're a mess," she said, scolding him. "What happened?"

"Lassen left me to die." He sat up and told her about Roy tricking him, the gunfight, the fall and the rain that had made him a new man. He didn't mention the Colt and how he'd nearly used it, only that he'd left it behind. "Lassen got what he wanted." He cradled Mary's hand in his. "J. T. Quinn is dead and gone. From now on, I'm Jonah Taylor."

Tears filled her eyes. "I love you, Jonah."

"I love you, too."

She deserved far more than he had to give, but he'd already wasted too much time. He held Mary's hand in his, lifting it as he looked into her eyes. "I spent three days thinking I'd never see you again. I don't have much to offer, but whatever I have and whoever I am, I'd be honored if you'd be my wife."

She didn't say yes.

And she didn't say no.

Instead she kissed him full on the lips. It lasted so long that he started to laugh. "So you like that idea?"

"I do," she said. "But I have a condition of my own."

She could have anything she wanted. If she needed a dishwasher, he was the man for the job. If she needed a friend, he'd be there. He'd be her protector, her lover, the father of her children and the man who sometimes annoyed her, because he'd always be a bit of a scoundrel. He hardened his expression but just a little. "What's the condition?"

"I need a partner to help run the café." Her cheeks turned rosy. "What do you think of hiring someone else to wash dishes? Maybe one of the boys you impressed for Gus?"

"I like that idea."

"You can learn to cook." She looked pleased. "And someone has to fix things and paint the walls now and then. The chairs take a terrible beating. They get wobbly and—"

He stopped her with a kiss. "You know what else I want to do?"

She must have seen the shine in his eyes, because she blushed pinker than a rose. "What?"

"I want to have a baby with you." It wouldn't replace the child she'd lost, but he'd be glad to do what he could.

Mary blushed again. "I'd like that."

With the sun bright and the sky full of clouds, Jonah Taylor took his wife-to-be in his arms. His shoulder hurt, but that didn't stop him from kissing her the way he wanted. In that shining moment, he thought of his challenge to God to show Himself. J. T. Quinn had finally seen the light, and it was bright indeed.

Epilogue

August 1876
Swan's Nest

Mary and Jonah spoke their marriage vows on Sunday morning at Brick's saloon. Gertie stood up with Mary, swollen nose and all, and Gus stood with Jonah. Because she was part of their family, Fancy Girl joined them at the front of the church. In place of the bandanna she usually wore, Adie tied a pink ribbon around the dog's neck. Josh did the honors and then invited everyone to Swan's Nest to celebrate.

That's where they were now, surrounded by friends and family as Mary climbed the steps to toss the bouquet. A year ago Adie had done the honors, and Pearl had caught the flowers. She was here today with her husband and their two children, and earlier she'd told Mary she was expecting a baby in time for Christmas.

When Pearl's turn had come to throw the flowers at her own wedding nine months ago, she'd aimed them straight at Mary. Mary had nearly thrown them back, but today she felt only joy as she looked at her husband. Dressed in a new black suit and crisp white shirt, he was waiting not-so-patiently for the festivities to end. As soon as she tossed the flowers, they'd leave for the elegant hotel where he'd booked the bridal suite. Thanks to Deputy Morgan, Griff Lassen was in jail and Jonah had gotten his horse and money back. Yesterday he'd put the finishing touches on the bell tower, and he and Gus had tested the bell.

Mary was ready to leave the celebration, but she had to make sure Caroline caught the bouquet. She spotted Bessie, but she didn't see Caroline anywhere. She refused to throw the flowers to anyone else. Mary looked again at J.T. He mostly went by Jonah now, but she'd always love the scoundrel who'd first made her blush. He lifted his eyebrows as if to say, "What's taking so long?"

"I need Caroline," she called to him.

He nodded once, went to the kitchen and guided an unwilling Caroline into the crowd of women. Before she could protest, Mary walked up to her and put the flowers in her arms. The women applauded and hugged her, but Caroline barely smiled. "You shouldn't have done that."

"Why not?" Mary asked.

"It's time I faced facts. I'll never marry again."

"Caroline!"

"It's true." She took a breath. "I've accepted a position as a nanny for a rancher in Wyoming. He's a widower and he's ill. Bessie is going with me."

Mary nearly burst with curiosity. Just how ill was this man? Did his children need a nanny, or did they need a mother? And did the rancher need a nurse or a wife? She pushed the flowers into Caroline's arms. "I want you to have them."

"They *are* pretty." She sniffed a late-blooming rose and then forced a smile. "I'll write to you."

With the bouquet safely in Caroline's arms, Mary looked for Jonah. He'd slipped through the crowd and was two steps away. "Let's go," he said, offering his arm.

She grasped his elbow and smiled. "You sound like a man in hurry."

"I am." He gave her the look they'd first shared in Abilene, the one that had sent shivers down her spine and always would.

"Me, too," she whispered.

Arm in arm, they left Swan's Nest to the roar of thunderous applause. Mary thought of her days on the stage. She'd enjoyed that life, but it paled against the future waiting for her as Jonah Taylor's wife. She wanted to have children with him. She wanted to grow old together. He had returned to her, and she intended to cherish every moment of the starring role God had written just for her.

* * * * *

Florida native **Carla Capshaw** is a preacher's kid who grew up grateful for her Christian home and loving family. A two-time RWA Golden Heart® Award winner and double RITA® Award finalist, Carla loves passionate stories with compelling, nearly impossible conflicts. She's found inspirational historical romance is the perfect vehicle to combine lush settings, vivid characters and a Christian worldview.

Carla loves to hear from readers. To contact her, visit carlacapshaw.com or write to carla@carlacapshaw.com.

Books by Carla Capshaw

Love Inspired Historical

The Gladiator
The Duke's Redemption
The Protector
The Champion
Second Chance Cinderella

Visit the Author Profile page
at Harlequin.com for more titles.

THE PROTECTOR

Carla Capshaw

There is no fear in love, but perfect love casts out fear. For fear has to do with punishment, and whoever fears has not been perfected in love.
—*1 John* 4:18

To my sister, Nicolette Denton.
The saying "The sister everyone wishes she had"
was written about you. Thank you,
not only for being the best sister in the world,
but an incomparable sister in the Lord as well.

Prologue

Rome, 70 AD

"The General's come home, child. Put down your doll and go greet him like the proper daughter you've been taught to be."

Eager to obey her maid Prisca, the closest person to a mother she'd ever known, Adiona hastened to her feet.

A chilly morning breeze swept through the room. Adiona shivered, but not entirely from the cold. Her father was a stranger. He'd abandoned her to the care of servants when she was only three years old. Her sole memory of him was a vague recollection of his rigid back as he left for Britannia.

Filled with nervous energy, she draped a blue *palla* around her shoulders as she grappled to recall her father's face. Would the General recognize *her?* Would she please him? He'd been away on campaign for so long.

In the courtyard, the splash of fountains mingled with the smoky-sweet scent of incense as she and Prisca passed the family shrine. Praying she would make a good impression on her parent, she smoothed her dark hair back from her face and made her way across the mosaic tiles with brisk but anxious steps.

Down a short corridor, she heard men in conversation. She recognized neither voice, but assumed one was her sire. Her steps slowed and her stomach rolled. What if he found her lacking? What if he cast her away the same as he'd done her mother?

Light in the hall dimmed the farther she moved from the courtyard. The voices grew louder.

"I haven't seen Adiona," one of the men said. "I only returned to Rome three days past. After nine years away I've had more important matters to attend to."

Father? Why hadn't he come to her sooner? Did he have no care for her at all? Her questioning gaze darted to Prisca. Her brow pinched, the maid lifted a finger to her lips, warning Adiona not to speak.

"Naturally," the other man continued in a gravelly voice. "A daughter is less important than a favored pet."

"Right you are, Crassus. A son is the gods' blessing, but a daughter…"

"Is only as valuable as the marriage she makes. Of course, that's why I'm here. I understand Adiona will reach a marriageable age next week."

"She's going to be twelve already?" the General asked, a touch of surprise in his voice.

"According to your servants, she is. Let me be frank, General. I'm in need of a young and healthy wife to breed me sons. I believe the girl will suit my purpose."

A shudder ran through Adiona. She held her breath, willing her father to reject the stranger's offer.

"And if I agree to a marriage between you, how would the alliance benefit me?"

Adiona gasped. Would her father send her away without even seeing her first?

Prisca frowned and shushed her to silence. "Stay here. Don't follow me until I call you."

A dull ache spread through Adiona. Pressing back against the cool concrete wall, she wished she could disappear.

"Silver is in the bargain for you, General. I understand your last campaign didn't go well. I'll take the girl without a dowry and settle your debts, as well as sponsor your legions for the next year. Considering the sum you owe, who else besides the emperor could afford to be as generous?"

"The question is why you'd be so free with your coin?"

"She's the loveliest creature I've ever seen. With an ornament like her on my arm, I'll be the envy of every man in Rome."

In the silence that followed, Prisca went to the doorway and cleared her throat to make her presence known.

"What is it, woman?"

"The child is waiting in the hall."

"Bring her in. I'm anxious to see this girl whose face is worth a fortune."

Prisca poked her head around the door frame and waved her forward. "Come, Adiona, the General's ready to see you."

Chilled to the bone by her father's indifference, she remained frozen in place.

"Come *here,* child." Her maid walked toward her, extending a hand. "Come greet your sire and his important guest."

Adiona shook her head. She had no intention of placing herself on display like one of the prized cows her tutor had showed her at market.

Prisca fiddled with one of the curls tumbling over

her shoulder. "Don't shame me. What will your father think of the training I've given you if you prove to be willful and disobedient?"

Terrified, Adiona crossed her arms over her chest in a meager display of self-protection. "I won't go."

Her maid's lips thinned. The older woman's grip tightened on Adiona's upper arm. "*Yes,* you will." Prisca thrust her over the threshold and blocked the portal, Adiona's sole means of retreat. Caged like one of the beasts at the menagerie, she was flooded by a wave of panic. Too frightened to look at her sire, she turned on her heel and fought to push past the maid.

"Adiona!" The General's icy command froze her to the spot. "Present yourself."

She swirled around, taking in the faces of the two strangers on either side of the wide desk. The one dressed in an army red tunic was big, his face scarred. The other man was old and withered. He reminded her of a giant pockmarked bullfrog leaning on a gnarled cane. His jaundiced gaze was less than fatherly as it roamed over her in the same way the buyers sized up the heifers at market.

Only he wants a broodmare.

She shrank back.

"Come here, daughter."

Prisca shoved her forward. Gathering the remains of her courage, Adiona forced her heavy feet toward the huge man whose fisted hands and cold gaze promised retribution if she continued to embarrass him in front of his visitor.

She stopped several paces out of his reach, her chest aching for one kind gesture from him. With a sinking feeling, she realized the General would never be the father she longed for, a father who welcomed her with love and open arms.

"Well?" he demanded. "Have you gone mute since I left?"

She shook her head. Her chest tight, she answered as duty required. "Hello, Father. Wel…welcome home."

"That's better." He turned back to the bullfrog without offering her the slightest show of warmth. "I want you to meet Crassus Scipio. He's asked to wed you and I've decided to agree to his request."

Anger pierced through her heartbreak and rejection. Her rebellious gaze slid to the old man. The gleam in his eyes repulsed her until she feared she might retch at his feet.

Trembling, she turned to the General, the defender of Rome who did nothing to protect his own daughter. "Please don't," she begged him, "please don't give me to him."

His face hardened. "Ungrateful whelp. You should be honored that one of the richest men in Rome desires you for a wife."

Honored? Had years of war addled her father's wits?

"If Crassus agrees, I'll arrange your marriage to take place next week when you come of age."

"But—"

"No more interruptions, girl." He snapped his fingers, summoning Prisca. "Take her out of my sight and make the necessary preparations. It's time she set aside her dolls and learned to be a proper wife."

Chapter One

The Flavian Amphitheater, Rome, 81 AD

"Blood is sure to stain the sand today!"

Adiona Leonia shuddered at Claudia's gleeful prediction. As insidious as a spider, Claudia rarely approached anyone without nefarious intent. Unfortunately, the older matron had begun to spin her web around Adiona the moment she'd approached the entrance gate.

"The gladiators face war elephants and chariots this afternoon," Claudia continued. "I can hardly breathe with anticipation!"

Scanning the mob of enthusiastic spectators swarming into the massive arena, Adiona pretended not to hear the other woman over the roar of the crowd and motioned her bodyguards to clear a way to escape. Surrounded by the fragrance of burning pinecones meant to keep the stench of blood and death at bay, Adiona needed no reminder of who faced what in the arena. Her attraction to one particular gladiator both mystified and rattled her. Other than her friend the famed *lanista,* Caros Viriathos, she neither liked nor trusted men. Yet she'd been inexplicably drawn to Quintus Ambustus since the first time she'd seen him train at the *Ludus Maximus* five months earlier.

"One of the gladiator troupes is Viriathos's men." Claudia spoke louder, refusing to be ignored. "That should make the day more delightfully gruesome."

"It explains the crowds," Adiona agreed absently. "Caros trains the best."

"*You* would know."

Claudia's suggestive tone earned Adiona's full attention. Had the bloodhound somehow learned her guilty secret? Her pulse quickened with dread. All of Rome knew of her contempt for the opposite sex. She'd be a laughingstock if anyone—especially Claudia and her mindless patrons—discovered her unrequited fascination for one of Caros's slaves.

Irritated by the woman's nosiness, Adiona clenched her fists in the weighty folds of her blue *stola*. "What do you mean, Claudia? Everyone is aware of Caros's talents. I'm not special in that regard."

The spider's eyes gleamed with wicked pleasure. "True, but not all of Rome is on intimate terms with the great *lanista*."

"Are you jealous?" Adiona smiled, misleading her adversary on purpose. Eager to disappear before Claudia sniffed a hint of the real scandal clinging to her cloak, Adiona bid the other matron good day before she could be drawn into more uncomfortable conversation.

Glad to be free of Claudia's web, she relied on her trio of guards to lead her through the mob. At the top of the steps, she located her row. Reserved for senators, their families and other wealthy citizens, the prized seats closest to the arena floor were usually off-limits to women, but she and other rich matrons like Claudia were among the few privileged females whose wealth and social influence guaranteed them the best of everything the city offered.

Squelching the lust-filled glances men cast her way with a disdainful glare of her own, she took her place on the polished marble bench. The scent of cinnamon-roasted almonds infused the cool afternoon breezes, while wine flowed freely, encouraging the wildness that crackled in the air like heat lightning.

Adiona groaned inwardly when Claudia's rotund form appeared at the top of the steps. An overburdened slave carrying a large basket trailed her.

"We meet again!" Huffing from the exertion of her short climb, Claudia waved the wooden ticket she held. "It seems we've been assigned seats next to one another."

"Who did you bribe?" Adiona asked coolly. "I'd like to know who I should have whipped."

The spider chuckled as she plopped down on the bench, leaving Adiona no choice but to slide over or be crushed by the woman's girth. Within moments, Claudia's poisonous chatter made Adiona's head throb.

Dreading Quintus's arrival on the field, Adiona stared at the amphitheater's sandy floor. In the past few months Quintus had trained long and hard, but today he battled seasoned gladiators for the first time. Thanks to Claudia, she now knew he also faced war elephants and chariots...

A wave of anxiety swept over her. What if he died?

Her stomach twisted into a tight knot.

"Are you well, Adiona?" Claudia's sharp eyes probed her face as though searching for buried secrets. "You seem...troubled. Talk is, until Caros and his bride left for Umbria, you'd become quite a regular at the gladi-

ator practices. I assumed you'd come to enjoy the violence—"

"Talk?" Snapped out of her dark thoughts, her patience with the older matron vanished. "You know very
well I despise being talked about, Claudia. Or did you
seek me out today solely to dig up more dirt for your
discussion?"

Claudia wrinkled her nose and reached for a glass
bottle of water from the basket beside her feet. "Why
are you so sensitive about a little harmless chatter?"

Remembering all the times she'd been maimed by
gossip, Adiona snorted. "I'm not convinced there is
such a thing as 'harmless chatter.'"

"Of course there is." Claudia pulled the cork and
sipped from her bottle. "For instance, what's the harm
in wondering aloud if you're upset about the *lanista's*
marriage? It's common knowledge Caros Viriathos is
the one man you're fond of. Rumors say you're jealous
of his pretty new wife."

She blinked, suddenly understanding why Claudia
had sought her out. The other social matrons must be
riotous with the hope of her languishing from a broken
heart. They lived for gossip, sharpening their words
behind her back and spreading their vicious chatter
like a disease.

Happy to spoil their amusement at her expense, Adiona turned to the older woman and spoke loud enough
to be heard over the excited crowd all around them.
"Surely you jest. Caros is my friend. I wish him and
Pelonia eternal joy."

Disappointment flitted across Claudia's bulbous features before she hid her displeasure behind a sly grin.
"But he slighted you for a *slave* girl? If I were ever
abandoned so heinously, I'd—"

"Cease, Claudia. Pelonia is no mere slave girl. She's cousin by marriage to a senator. And though it's none of your business, let me be clear. Caros and I are friends, *nothing* more. As far as I'm concerned, he's one of the last decent men in the Empire. Even so, I'd slit my wrists before I wed him."

Claudia patted Adiona's tense shoulder. "Gods forbid you'd married him. He may be rich at present, but he spent years as a lowly *gladiator*. They're fine for trysts, mind you, but marriage? No—at least not for you. You may not have been born of noble blood, but who's to care when your beauty and riches can buy a royal husband?"

The trumpets' blast drowned out Adiona's tart reply. She'd vowed never to wed again. The six years of torture she'd endured in Crassus's depraved hands had cured her of any childish notions concerning love or marital bliss. She no longer prayed for a happy home filled with children or a husband who cared for her. For whatever reason, the gods had deemed her unlovable and she'd grown almost numb to the sting of loneliness she'd borne for as long as she could remember.

The announcer's voice echoed across the amphitheater, proclaiming the opponents of the afternoon's main event. The mob erupted as portals in the arena floor slid open. Lifts deployed gladiators onto the field. Gates at the far end of the amphitheater rose and a dozen war elephants, a beast master on each of their backs, charged onto the sun-drenched sand.

Adiona slid forward on the marble bench. Her lungs locked. Her heart hammered against her breastbone louder than the bellowing mob. Straining to see Quintus, she recognized him instantly. Black hair, square jaw, golden skin. His height, the breadth of his shoulders, his *presence* drew her attention to him with an immediacy that was both intoxicating and frightening.

The wild crowd jumped up in unison. Adiona surged to her feet. Her every muscle as tight as one of the archer's bows, she held her breath, promising the gods endless sacrifices if they kept Quintus safe. With her gaze fastened to Quintus on his troupe's front line, she watched him lead his men across the field toward her where they took up an attack position.

Dressed in a simple brown tunic, his bare feet buried in the sand, he carried a shield and spear, looking woefully unprotected against the war elephants' massive tusks.

One of the beasts charged toward Quintus and his men. Adiona clamped her hand across her mouth to contain the scream that burned in her throat. The huge animal raged on, tossing its head from side to side, its gold-covered tusks gleaming in the sun as they sliced through human flesh and bone.

Quintus's troupe attacked. Taking the brunt of the spears, the elephant faltered and fell. As the behemoth struggled to regain its footing, Quintus vaulted onto its back. He tossed the beast master to the ground and took up the reins, just as the animal lurched to its feet.

Another gate lifted. Chariots thundered into battle, deploying more archers. Arrows soared through the sky before finding their targets with horrible accuracy. Dead and wounded gladiators littered the sand.

Seemingly unconcerned for his own safety, Quintus positioned the elephant between the advancing chariots and his men. His muscles straining to control the enormous animal, he was so close she could almost see the green depths of his eyes.

Another wave of arrows pierced the elephant's hide.

One skewered Quintus in the leg, another in his shoulder. A cry erupted from deep inside her, as if the arrows had hit her instead of her man.

The elephant fell to its knees, its trunk trumpeting in one last painful wail. Giddy madness raced through the crowd. Despite the many battles taking place on the field, the mob focused on the drama unfolding around Quintus. Riveted, she watched him struggle to pull the arrow from his thigh.

She begged the gods to save him. Pinned atop the fallen elephant and exposed to the hateful whims of Fate, Quintus made a clear target for the archers taking aim. The sounds of rapid horses' hooves filled her ears, competing with the spectators' cries and fist-pumping demands for death.

In desperation she begged every deity she could think of for mercy, even the illegal one Quintus worshipped, "Jesus, *please*..." she whispered under her breath.

"Viriathos has lost a fortune in gladiators today!" Claudia cackled with amusement. She pointed toward Quintus. "Look at that one struggle. He'll never get away. The archers have him for certain."

The glee in Claudia's voice filled Adiona with rage, horror and a sinking sense of anguish. "Bite your tongue, you vicious crone! Quintus is an honorable man. How *dare* you delight in his death?"

Adiona's gaze flew back to the action in the arena. Quintus had disappeared in the mayhem. Panic seized her. She pressed past Claudia, raced down the steps and clung to the barrier, desperate to find him through the black smoke and crush of chariots forming a victorious circle around the few gladiators left alive.

As expected, the charioteers and their team were declared the victors. The mob jeered the decision and the unfair fight, then erupted into cheers as Quintus used the fallen elephant to slowly pull himself to his feet.

The game's referee dismissed the men who were able to walk. Quintus looked over his shoulder and scanned the crowd before limping to the edge of the field. His back to her, she couldn't see if he'd been able to pull the arrow from his shoulder. The other one remained in his thigh. Blood seeped down his leg and into the sand.

At least he lives. Relief as pure as a mountain stream flowed through Adiona, robbing her of strength. She braced against the barrier for support, promising herself she'd do whatever Caros required to ensure Quintus never entered the games again.

Turning to leave for the gladiator hospital where Quintus would be taken, she bumped into Claudia whom she hadn't noticed beside her. The spider's eyes gleamed bright and with dawning horror Adiona realized she'd given herself away.

"What a day!" her rival said with malicious satisfaction. "Not only was the sport amusing, but I learned *so* much. Little wonder you're happy for the *lanista* and his bride when you're enamored with a slave of your own."

Quintus Fabius Ambustus eased onto a bench in the gladiator hospital behind the amphitheater. Smoke from the torches lining the concrete walls burned his eyes. The stench of blood and sweat reeked in his nostrils. Delirious moans and cries for help from other wounded men ricocheted off the arched ceiling, but not even the chaos and bolts of pain radiating through his body failed to erase the image of Adiona's horrified gaze and frightened expression.

He rubbed his eyes, irritated by the beauty's hold

on him. Two months of near starvation in a disease-infested prison, a fortnight trekking through half of Italy in a slave caravan, and months of training in a gladiator *ludus* hadn't felled him. Yet one unexpected glimpse of Adiona's haunting visage in the stands of the arena had been enough to break his concentration and see him almost killed by arrows.

Dear God, what is wrong with me?

The question made him laugh, which made him groan as pain shot through his chest and bruised ribs. What *wasn't* wrong with him? In the last seven months he'd become *infamia*—disgraced, the lowest of the low. He'd lost his family, wealth, freedom, citizenship and reputation. Everything but his faith in Christ and that, he acknowledged, was hanging by a thread.

Whether he was being punished or tested like some other believers suggested, he knew he didn't need or want to be tempted by a vixen with an ability to sneak past his defenses and shred his self-control. No woman had ever done that, not even his wife.

He slammed the door on thoughts of Faustina. She was dead and memories of her filled him with guilt and eternal regret.

A solid blow jarred his wounded shoulder. "*There's* the mob's newest darling."

Quintus cracked open one eye. Alexius, the manager of the gladiator school, stood over him, a grin parting the Greek's swarthy face.

Rubbing the spot where he'd torn the arrow from his shoulder, Quintus pressed on the piece of cloth he'd used to cover the ragged flesh. "Was that necessary?" he asked, his tone as dry as dust.

"Of course. You don't think I'll go easy on you just because you're famous now, do you?"

"One lost battle isn't enough to make anyone remember my name."

"On the contrary." The tall Greek moved deeper into the small alcove. Pleased by the afternoon's events, he pulled up a stool and sat down. "Romans appreciate bravery above all else. The way you leaped on that elephant and protected your troupe… The whole city will know who you are by sundown."

Quintus grunted, unimpressed. "A lot of good it will do me if I bleed to death."

Alexius glanced at the arrow and growing ring of blood around the wound. "From that scratch? I doubt it."

A man's scream echoed down the corridor. A moment later, two of the hospital's attendants ran past.

"Where's the physician?" Quintus asked, weary of waiting when the deeply embedded arrow in his leg was making him light-headed from loss of blood.

"He'll be here soon. By the sound of it, the day's amputations are almost finished."

Quintus grimaced. He was thankful to God his injuries were relatively minor, but a part of him wished God had taken him and spared the other wounded in his troupe.

"You'd better get used to injury," Alexius warned. "You're not a coddled merchant anymore. You're a gladiator."

Quintus curled his lip at the veiled insult. He may have been a merchant, but he'd never been an idle man. "I'll try to remember that." To punctuate his disinterest in the lecture, he closed his eyes and leaned his head against the wall.

A stab of pain sliced through his thigh. His eyes flew open. Alexius had taken hold of the arrow and was slowly twisting the shaft. "Listen to me, Quintus. I know you're angry at the world and probably your God, though you deny it. But if you plan to live long enough in the arena to earn your freedom, understand these paltry wounds are only the first of many."

He threw off Alexius's hand. Let the Greek think what he liked. He wasn't concerned about his injuries. In truth, he didn't care if he lived or died. It was his reaction to the widow that had soured his mood.

"You *do* want your freedom, don't you?"

"You know I do." His freedom was the prize he longed for above all else. The goal he'd set for himself to return home and make certain the precious son he'd lost had received a proper burial.

"Then fear not. Today's games will bring you a wagonload of good. A messenger brought word Caros and his lady return from Umbria next week. Once Caros hears what happened, he'll see you're rewarded. Your price for each fight is bound to rise. Caros is a generous master. Mark my words, he'll see you benefit from your improved status for certain."

Alexius would know. As the premier champion and current manager of the *Ludus Maximus,* he possessed wealth, the freedom to do as he liked and the respect of his master, Rome's most feted *lanista,* Caros Viriathos.

"It won't be long before you have enough silver to buy your life back."

"We'll see." Weakness began to creep through him and his vision blurred. His eyes drifted closed.

"Stay with me, friend." Alexius gave him a light shake. "Widow Leonia attended the games this afternoon. She came to see you fight."

He opened his eyes, his focus hazy.

"I thought the mention of her might revive you."

Smirking, Alexius leaned forward on the stool and braced his wrists on his knees. "You know you might consider Adiona as a source of additional coin."

"I've nothing to offer as collateral."

"You could offer yourself. Everyone knows it's you she came to watch at training practice these last several months. Judging by her constant attempts to gain your notice, she'd pay a fortune to have you."

He doubted it. Rumor among his troupe said her true prey was Caros. That she flirted with Quintus to make the *lanista* jealous. Quintus had begun to suspect the gossip held merit when she stopped visiting the school the same day Caros and Pelonia left for Umbria. His brow arched with irritation. "You mean sell myself?"

"It's widely done. Wealthy matrons are known to offer a huge price for the attentions of a well-known gladiator. And there's no woman in Rome wealthier than the widow."

The thought of Adiona paying men for their favors hit him with the unexpected force of a blow to the chest. Rage and pain washed through him. He struggled to stand.

"Easy, Quintus." Alexius pressed him back onto the bench. "I meant to enliven you, not make you foolish. If you don't like women—"

"I like women fine," he said through gritted teeth, fighting the weakness that threatened to engulf him.

"All right, you like women. I believe you." Alexius shrugged. "I take it, then, it's only Adiona who leaves you cold? Why? She's exquisite to look upon. Most men would sacrifice their sword arm for a single smile from her luscious lips."

His eyelids heavy as bricks, he struggled to focus on Alexius. He couldn't deny Adiona Leonia affected him like no other woman he'd ever met, but she also reminded him of his wife. Not in looks, but in manner and her priorities in life. A decade of marriage to a faithless, self-centered woman who chased social recognition and vain pleasure had taught him much. Outward beauty meant little when the inner being was ugly. If God answered his prayers for deliverance from his current situation, he hoped one day to find a wife who possessed faith, kindness and honor.

"Widow Leonia is not for me." Too exhausted to frame his words with care, he answered honestly. "I don't want a woman whose sharp tongue resembles a knife blade and whose morals mimic a she-cat in heat."

A sharp gasp drew his attention to the edge of the alcove behind Alexius. Adiona stood in the arched doorway. Torchlight glimmered off her elaborately braided hair and the gold threads woven through the cloak she'd draped around her slender shoulders. To his blurred vision and pain-steeped brain she seemed like a bright morning star—just as beguiling and, for him, even more out of reach.

Words failed. He simply stared, grappling for an apology. He had no right to insult her. Never had he spoken of a woman with such disrespect. No matter if he believed he told the truth, he'd never intentionally hurt her.

Gutted by her stricken amber gaze and ashen complexion, he wished the arrow had missed his shoulder and skewered his heart.

And judging by the storm gathering on her flawless face, she agreed he deserved no less.

Chapter Two

He despises me.

Savaged by Quintus's brutal assessment, Adiona swallowed the hard lump of rejection in her throat. Determined he would never know how deep his derision cut, she refused to march off in a display of wounded pride.

"My lady—" Quintus said, his voice reed thin.

"Why are you here?" Alexius jumped to his feet, his expression sheepish.

Careful to avoid the slightest glance at Quintus, she masked her humiliation behind the haughty facade she'd perfected long ago to protect herself. "Have you called a physician, Alexius? Or did you think a long *chat* would dislodge the arrow from his thigh?"

"I asked for help when I came in," the Greek giant said defensively. "Quintus hasn't been here long and he's not the worst of the wounded."

"Then I'll fetch someone myself." Grabbing the excuse to leave, she rushed down the busy corridor. She'd arrived to hear Alexius prompting Quintus to seek her out for coin and Quintus's quick rejection of the idea.

That he preferred to risk his life in the arena rather than spend time with her pierced like a *gladius* to the heart.

Angry with Quintus, and furious with her own naïveté, she berated herself for the foolish compulsion to see about his welfare. She should have guessed he was no better than all the other men who forever misjudged her, yet she couldn't deny she had desperately wished he might be.

...Whose morals mimic a she-cat in heat.

The accusation went through her like a poisoned dart. If only he knew the truth. Every day was a struggle for her survival. All her life she'd fought off men who sought to use her, claim her, *abuse* her. Never had one looked past her outward appearance, fortune or social position to want her for herself.

Men are swine. She *hated* them. They could all rot for all she cared. Why did she think Quintus would be any different? What was it about him that made her forget she wanted *nothing* to do with *any* man?

She dabbed at her eyes with the edge of her *stola,* blaming the torch smoke for the sudden sheen that blurred her vision. *Idiota. Why did you let yourself hope?*

In the main surgery, dust motes danced in the light pouring through a series of arched windows along the concrete walls. Herbal scents mixed with the harsh odors of vinegar and blood. Several physicians bent over drugged patients who'd been laid out on flat couches. Except for the murmur of voiced instructions, soft moans and the occasional ping of metal surgical instruments, the room was surprisingly quiet, the opposite of the chaos in the halls.

She stepped deeper into the light. "You, there." She

pointed to a balding man she'd seen several times at Caros's compound. "Your name is Petronius, is it not?"

Petronius looked up from bandaging his unconscious patient. His eyes widened with recognition. "My lady Leonia, what are you doing here?"

"One of the gladiators from the *Ludus Maximus* needs your attention. He's been shot by arrows and continues to bleed. Finish quickly with your work here and I'll take you to him."

The physician wiped his hands on a bloodied towel and surveyed his patient with an air of uncertainty. "I've done all I can for this one. Fate will do the rest."

An assistant took over bandaging the unconscious gladiator while Petronius gathered a needle, stitching, a roll of clean linen and an arrow extractor. "I'm ready, my lady. Please lead the way."

Adiona relieved him of the linen and wasted no time taking the physician to the alcove. Alexius met them in the shadowed corridor.

"How is he?" Petronius asked.

"He lost consciousness moments after Lady Leonia left to fetch you."

The Greek's announcement sent a chill straight down Adiona's spine. Reason urged her toward the exit, but her feet refused to budge.

"How long has he been here?" Petronius knelt on the floor, his fingers testing the angry red wound on Quintus's thigh.

"Less than half an hour is my guess." Alexius took a torch off the wall and angled it to give the physician better light.

Adiona clutched the bundle of soft linen she held and bit her lip as every nerve in her body focused on Quintus and his treatment.

I should leave. I'm not wanted here. Quintus doesn't want me here.

She handed the bandages to Alexius. Once again she turned to go. A moan from Quintus tugged her back. Despite her resolve to cling to her anger and put him out of her mind, she found herself by his side before she realized she'd taken a single step forward.

Being this close to Quintus was rare. He was a slave, a *gladiator*. Always a battlefield stood between them.

Unbidden emotions filled her heart. Her fingers twitched with the need to touch him. Torchlight danced across the lean angles of his face, the smudge of dark bristles that shadowed the sharp cut of his jaw. Her gaze roamed over the thick muscles that roped his arms and broad chest, the bloody arrow wound in his shoulder.

Wishing she could ease his pain, she noted how he'd changed since she'd first seen him. Five months ago, he'd been little more than skin and bones. Caros's new slave with no more than a will to live and brooding green eyes. Green eyes that clashed with hers across a sea of golden sand and left her breathless.

She swallowed hard. "Will he recover?"

The physician shrugged. "It's a clean wound, but only the gods can say."

The pallor beneath Quintus's sun-bronzed skin scared her. Hesitant to touch him in case she caused him further pain, she brushed a thick lock of black hair from his brow and murmured his name.

"Don't bother, my lady. He can't hear you," Petronius said. "Until I get him stitched up, you don't want him to, either." He tossed the bloody arrow aside and it clacked against the cement floor. He set down the extractor, stemming the fresh spurts of blood with a piece of the linen bandage. "Hand me that bottle."

Adiona did as commanded, forgetting she took orders from no one. The physician poured the foul-smelling liquid over the wound, then began sewing together the hole's ragged edges.

Quintus's face contorted with pain. He groaned through his delirium. She spoke softly to him and soothed his brow until he calmed, deciding she would just have to wait and hate him tomorrow.

Caros Viriathos studied the training field below his bedchamber's second-story window. A bright winter sun had reached its zenith, flashing off his men's metal helmets and various pieces of weaponry. His pet, Cat, sat quietly beside him. The tiger's long tail swished on the mosaic-tiled floor as he sniffed the cool breeze carrying the scent of lamb meant for the noonday meal.

After a month away from the *Ludus Maximus,* it felt good to return, but since his marriage he acknowledged the gladiator school he owned and built no longer seemed like home.

His new wife, Pelonia, claimed that distinction in his heart. Wherever she was, he wanted to be. Together, they'd decided to start their lives afresh on the Umbrian hill estate once stolen from her father. Eager to leave for the villa and fertile lands he'd been able to return to her as a wedding gift, he had much to do to settle his affairs here in Rome.

He heard his wife's voice calling for him from out in the corridor. Assuming she had questions about the wedding feast they planned for Friday evening, he turned, a smile curving his lips. It quickly faded as she hurried through the door, her doe-brown eyes filled with distress. He and Cat both moved toward her. "What's wrong?" he asked.

"Did you know Quintus was injured while we were away? Alexius entered him in the games!"

He sighed. Home less than an hour and she'd already heard the bad news. He folded her in his embrace, enjoying how she fit against him, her floral scent, her cheek pressed against his chest. "I know. Alexius tried to help him—"

"By tossing him into the arena?" She pulled back and looked up at him with a dubious frown. "Quintus is a brother in the Lord. He's a slave because of his faith in Christ. You should *free* him, Caros. Not allow him to be maimed or worse in that horrid ring of torture."

He felt her shudder and knew she remembered the day she'd been cast into the arena for her faith. He kissed her brow, grateful the Lord has spared them both, yet wishing he could erase the nightmare for her. "I tried to free Quintus before we left for Umbria. I know he wants his liberty and I had no intention of sending him to fight."

"Then why—?"

"Because he declined my offer. If he accepted, he'd be indebted to me or so he claimed. He's a merchant, Pelonia, and a proud man with self-respect. He knows the value of a *denarius* and he's determined to pay his full debt himself."

"But how can he if he has no coin? Why not loan—?"

He shook his head. "I offered. Again, he declined. He won't take anything that isn't earned. When he leaves here, he intends to be free in every sense of the word."

"So Alexius entered him in the arena for the prize winnings." She searched his face. "But Quintus has only trained five months. How can he be ready?"

He tucked a soft tendril of black hair behind her ear. "Under normal conditions, I'd say he couldn't be, but Quintus is keenly intelligent and surprisingly agile for one of his class. After he'd been here only a matter of weeks he was already making progress with some of the more advanced battle stances. Alexius told me he fought well."

"What does that matter now that our friend is injured? His life is worth more than silver. He could have *died.*"

He lifted her chin with his index finger and looked deeply into her eyes. "Isn't it you who always reminds me God has a plan for everyone's life?"

She nodded, but her mouth drooped into a playful pout. "It isn't nice to throw my words back in my face."

"And it's such a beautiful face." He chuckled and kissed away her frown. "You should be thankful you have a husband who listens."

She hugged him tight and laughed. "Oh, I am, believe me."

"Then listen to *me,*" he said, pleased to see her smile again. "All will be well with Quintus. I've denied his request to reenter the ring—"

"What? He asked for *another* fight? Does he have no care at all for his life?"

"I admit his spirits seem much lower than when we left a month ago. He has the hardened look of a man who doesn't care if he lives or dies. That's to be expected after all he's suffered, but for the moment at least, I'll ensure he stays breathing. I'm confident the Lord will reveal a way for me to help him earn his freedom without the aid of the arena."

"Well, then," she said, resigned, "we shall just have to wait and see."

Cat bumped Pelonia, jolting her sideways, his patience for attention at an end. Laughing in surprise, she bent over the tiger and nuzzled the top of his striped head. She rubbed Cat's ears and grinned at Caros. "I think he missed me."

"I know I would if we were separated a month."

"A month?" She grimaced. "Don't think you'll ever be free of me that long."

"I'm glad to hear it." Watching her affectionate play with Cat, he marveled at how important she'd become to his happiness, his peace of mind. He tugged her back to him and kissed her tenderly. "A month would be an eternity I couldn't endure. I miss you the moment you leave my arms."

Quintus finished the letter he'd written to his brother and rolled up the scroll once it dried. Since his arrest, he'd lost track of the number of messages he'd sent Lucius. None of the correspondence had been answered and he despaired of hearing back from his good-natured but irresponsible twin.

For all he knew, Lucius had taken the gold Quintus entrusted to him after his arrest and traveled to Capri to waste it on dancing girls and honeyed wine. That Lucius had been the sole person Quintus had to rely upon from his prison cell testified to the bleakness of his situation at the time.

Praying Lucius wouldn't let him down again, he dressed and left the gladiator barracks. Caros's visit earlier in the morning had been a blessing. It pleased him to know his friends were content and encouraged his faith to see God's hand at work in their lives.

Drawing in a deep breath of cool, winter air, he crossed the training field, eager to get back to sword practice and regain his full strength. After four days, his wounds were healing. The twinge in his shoulder bothered him less and less, while the ache in his thigh caused no more than a slight limp. It was his dreams of Adiona's glorious amber eyes and flowing dark hair that conspired to torture him.

He searched the stands until he realized he was looking for those same amber eyes in person. Had he really believed she might be there just because Caros had returned to Rome? Disgusted by his disappointment in her absence, he despised the flaw in him that continued to crave a woman he couldn't have and shouldn't want.

"Why are you out here?" Alexius called from a short distance down field. "Go back to the barracks. You're supposed to rest at least another two days."

Quintus waited for Alexius to work his way through the maze of gladiators and other training apparatus. "I'd rather bleed to death out here than die of boredom inside that sweltering jail."

Alexius laughed and clapped him on his good shoulder. "Normally, I'd take pity on you, but Caros and Pelonia are hosting a wedding celebration Friday eve. I have strict instructions to make certain you're well enough to attend."

"I'm well enough now." He glanced over his shoulder toward the back of the main house. A sense of peace radiated from the *domus*. The open shutters welcomed the sunlight and laughter carried on the breeze from the second-story window.

A shaft of unexpected envy lanced through him. He didn't begrudge Caros and Pelonia's happiness, but he couldn't stop wondering why God had denied all his prayers for a loving wife and a joyful home. He'd spent years praying for Faustina to come to Christ.

He'd done his best to be a good and godly husband, but she'd shunned him and his beliefs. Now it was too late. Faustina had taken her own life after the tragic death of their son.

Quintus shrank away from thoughts of Fabius. His son had been his reason to wake each morning. Every detail from his mischievous smile to his boundless energy had been a wonder. Now all Quintus had left was an eternally broken heart.

"Quintus? Did you hear me?"

He blinked and focused on Alexius who watched him with intense silver eyes. "No. What did you say?"

"I said you might be interested to know the widow Leonia will be a guest at the master's fete Friday."

Quintus's heart kicked against his chest and his pulse quickened. He clawed his fingers through his hair, schooling his features to hide his reaction. "What does she have to do with me?"

"After what she overheard in the hospital, I'd wager you're not her favorite person."

"Most likely not. If I'm able to speak with her at the party, I'll apologize."

"I've known her a number of years," the Greek continued. "So take this as a friendly warning. Say nothing to her and stay clear of her presence. When she's riled, Adiona Leonia resembles one of the lions her family is named for."

Quintus ignored his sudden impatience for the party's arrival. Adiona may be a lioness, but he'd meet her at the gate when she arrived, before she had time to join the festivities and he, as a slave, lost the chance to speak with her. Despite the countless rumors among the men in his barracks, Quintus didn't believe the widow's heart was made of marble. He had no excuse for the cruel things he'd said about her and after all the mistakes he'd made in his own life, who was he to criticize her manner or her morals?

Alexius laughed suddenly. "But then, given the odd connection between you two, perhaps you're just the man to tame her."

Chapter Three

"Hurry with my hair, Nidia. I'm late for Caros's marriage fete. I must be on my way."

Her nerves stretched taut, Adiona fidgeted with the alabaster cosmetic jars and jewel-encrusted bottles lined across her dressing table. She should have left half an hour ago. She and Pelonia hadn't started out on the best of terms. If she were unreasonably tardy for the celebration, Caros would never believe she hadn't intended the slight against his new bride.

And Quintus will think you're more vain and rude than he already does...

"Hurry, Nidia. I *must* leave."

The glow of oil lamps in the polished silver mirror allowed her critical, kohl-rimmed eyes to study her blurry reflection and keep track of the maid's slow progress with the curling rod.

Thanks to the cosmetics, Adiona's skin was fashionably pale. A light dusting of rouge across her cheeks and a berry stain on her lips went well with the deep rose color of her embroidered *stola*. Long gold earrings set with pearls and garnets brushed her shoulders. A matching necklace, rings and bracelets glittered in the firelight. As always, she looked the part of a wealthy matron, deserving both honor and respect.

But you deserve neither, you fraud.

She dabbed scented oil behind her ears and across her inner wrists, but the cinnamon perfume failed to soothe her agitation.

Nidia pinned the last curl in place. "I'm finished, *domina.* You look beautiful."

Adiona jumped to her feet, as eager to escape the accusations in her own eyes as she was to be on her way. The quick movement jostled the dressing table. One of the perfume bottles crashed to the floor, spreading shards of glass and sweetly scented oil across the colorful tiles. With an uttered oath, she ordered Nidia to clean up the mess and raced into the hall.

Her steward, Felix, snapped to attention from where he'd been leaning against the frescoed wall. "Salonius Roscius awaits you in the inner courtyard, my lady. I told him you were on your way out for the evening, but he insists he has important news."

"He'll have to return tomorrow," she said without pausing her rapid pace toward the front of the palace. "The meeting with my property manager has made me late."

"But *domina*..." Her steward's steps gained ground behind her. "He says it's urgent."

"When is it not urgent, Felix?" she tossed over her shoulder. "And yet, when is it ever?"

"He brings word from your heir."

"Most likely Drusus means to beg more coin." She plucked a white silk *palla* from her maid's outstretched fingers and swirled the bejeweled shawl around her shoulders without missing a step. "If not for my cousin's sweet wife and lovely daughters, I swear on Jupiter's stone, I'd never send that worthless leech another copper *as*."

Without warning, the beaded curtain separating the corridor from the inner courtyard parted. Salonius's large frame filled the doorway. The epitome of a Roman upper-class male, he was freshly shaven and clothed in white linen. Dark curls were cropped close to his head and his manicured nails suggested many hours of leisure spent at the baths.

"My lady." He bowed and gave her one of the quick smiles she was certain he practiced in any reflective surface he came across. Why so many women found his studied seduction attractive, she couldn't guess.

"Salonius," she acknowledged with a quick nod. "You'll have to excuse me. I must be on my way."

His hand snaked out and caught her wrist in a light but unbreakable grip. "Surely you can take a few moments to see an old friend, my sweet?"

She tried to shake off his touch, but he held firm. "Unhand me," she said loftily.

"In a moment." He brushed his wet lips over her knuckles.

Repulsed, she yanked free of his hold and wiped the back of her hand on her *stola*.

Torchlight lent him the feral, yet amused, appearance of a hyena. "When are you going to stop this charade and admit you wish to wed me as much I want you to?"

"I suppose when the River Styx runs dry and Vulcan's forging fires extinguish."

His laughter echoed through the domed corridor. "Don't lie, precious. Everyone knows you're just waiting until I fall to my knees and beg for your hand."

"I've no doubt everyone *and* the little wife you keep

hidden away in the country would find that most amusing. As for me, I'd think you quite foolish."

His laughter faded, replaced by an ardent seriousness that caught her off guard. "You know I'd divorce her like this—" he snapped his fingers "—if you'd agree to be my wife."

"Then your wife has nothing to fear from me."

His expression soured as he slowly circled her. "You're off to the Viriathos reception, I imagine."

"Yes." Aware that wealthy, yet idle, men like Salonius both revered and despised the gladiators, she hid a smirk at his disgruntled tone and turned to leave.

"Wait." He held out a scroll as if it were a treat meant for an eager puppy. "I returned from Paestum by way of Neopolis this afternoon. You'll want to read this."

"Leave it with Felix. I'll see to it when I return."

"No, Drusus has important news. It can't wait."

Resigned and conscious of the passing time, she swiped the scroll from his outstretched hand and hurried away before he delayed her further. Outside, she cringed at the late hour. The sun had already set, its red-and-gold streaks fading into a deep purple sky.

A brisk breeze ruffled the curls piled high on her head and flowing over her shoulders as she crossed the columned portico to the litter awaiting her. Titus, her lead guard, drew the transport's heavy drapes aside. Her gold bracelets jangled as she climbed inside and breathed the scent of cloves her slaves had used to freshen the luxurious cushions. "Let's be on our way, Titus. Caros will never speak to me again if I don't show my face soon."

The litter lurched as four burly slaves lifted the conveyance and prepared for travel. Titus gave orders for her three other guards to take their positions surrounding the group.

The light dimmed as they carried her from her palace's torch-lit courtyard and into the dark streets of the Palatine Hill. With no lantern to read Drusus's message, she adjusted the heavy silk of her embroidered *stola* and reclined against the fringed feather pillows and mountain of furs.

"Gods below, I hate weddings." Only for Caros could she be swayed within a league of a marriage fete. She despised all reminders of her own marriage. Even now, eleven years later, she remembered the terror and helplessness she'd suffered that hideous day. And worse, later that night when Crassus ordered his guards to beat her for failing him.

A shudder of disgust rippled through her. Her fingers tightened on the scroll and she squeezed her eyes shut, glad the wicked old toad was dead. Reminding herself she was no longer that helpless twelve-year-old girl, but an independent woman in charge of her own life, she pushed the hateful memories to the back of her mind.

As the litter passed deeper into the maze of city streets, the sound of her slaves' swift steps mingled with the aroma of cook fires and the local inhabitants' bursts of laughter or occasional arguments.

Pleased by the litter's quick pace, she willed herself to relax. She'd spent the last several days dreading tonight. Given Caros and Pelonia's fondness for their Christian slave, Quintus was sure to be in attendance. Her attraction to him was over, she vowed, but the sting of his insults still smarted. With no desire to be further humiliated, she planned to avoid him at all costs.

Twisting one of the long curls flowing over her shoulder, Adiona tamped down her melancholy mood and forced her thoughts back to Caros. The fact that her friend was a Christian amazed her. When Caros confessed his belief in the illegal sect and their crucified God, he'd known she would keep his secret, just as he'd kept various secrets for her over the years. But she had trouble understanding why he'd put his life on the line when all gods were the same, and like most people, not to be trusted.

The litter slowed. She sat up. They couldn't have arrived already. They'd passed through the city gate and turned onto the lonely stretch of road leading to Caros's gladiator school mere moments ago. They had at least half a mile left to travel.

"Halt!" a commanding voice ordered.

The litter stopped. She reached for the curtain, annoyed by the delay that might squander the good time they'd made since leaving Palatine Hill.

"*Domina,* stay inside," Titus warned in a low voice meant for her ears alone. "We've met with a band of street rats. There may be trouble and you're easier to defend if you remain hidden."

"Let us pass," another of her guards demanded of the thieves. "We're guests of the *lanista,* Caros Viriathos. Cause us no trouble and we may allow you to live."

Tension sizzled through the night. The sound of ominous footsteps penetrated the thin layers of cloth cocooning her. A twinge of anxiety snaked through the darkness and across the back of her neck. She fought a desire to pull the drape aside and survey the situation, but she knew better than to endanger her men by ignoring Titus's instructions.

Her grip tightened on the scroll in her hand. She'd chosen her guards with care. All were ex-military men and formidable fighters. Along with the four other slaves carrying the litter, there should be plenty of hands to protect her and defend each other.

"Now!" someone barked. Yelling exploded through the blackness from all sides. Fear ripped through her. She screamed Titus's name.

"Stay inside, my lady!"

The litter swayed violently, tossing her against the poles supporting the transport's roof. She felt herself falling just before the litter hit the road with a bone-jarring thud. She fell back, the thick stack of pillows saving her from injury.

Outside, metal clashed against metal. "Kill the woman!" an enemy shouted.

Terror raked through her. She scrambled upright, hobbled by the furs and pillows snatching at her feet.

The clang of weapons grew louder. The number of strangers' voices outnumbered those of her own men. A sickening death cry erupted beside her. Shaking with fright, she bit back a scream.

Titus stuck his head through the drapes; his blood-spattered face increased her terror. "*Domina,* hurry! It's you they mean to have!"

Trembling, she rushed to leave the litter just as someone reached inside from behind and seized hold of her *palla*. A shriek burst from her throat. She cast off the garment and burst through the drapes onto the shadowed street. Titus's battered form towered over her. The strong odor of his sweat stung her nostrils. Quick, sideways glances told her they were hemmed in on both sides. Dilapidated buildings loomed behind them.

"*Domina,*" Titus whispered near her ear. "When I say run, follow the alley behind us. Appius and I will buy time, then follow you. Don't stop until you reach the school."

"It's the woman we want." One of the attackers stepped forward from the pack. "Give her to us and we may allow *you* to live."

Hearing their leader mimic her guard's earlier threat, the pack of rats skittered with laughter.

Titus shoved her behind him, the sword he held in his free hand raised to fight. "What has the lady done to deserve the dishonor of being assaulted in the street?"

Adiona strained to see through the dark. Her other remaining guard, Appius, stood a few paces forward and to her left. Moonlight glinted off her attackers' knives and the broken glass vessels they'd fashioned into weapons. The bodies of her men littered the barren road. Bile scratched her throat. Her stomach rolled with sickening shock and horror. Pity for her sorely outnumbered guards rose to choke her. Judging by the number of dead assailants that covered the ground, her men had fought with all their might.

Her teeth chattering uncontrollably, she turned back to back with Titus and located the narrow alley that offered her last hope for escape.

Impatient to finish her off, the rats moved closer by degrees like a tightening noose.

Titus's muscles flexed against her shoulder blades. *"Domina,"* he hissed, "Run!"

She hiked her tunic to her knees and raced. Mindless with fear, she sped down the alley without thought of what awaited her at the other end. Shouts raged and weapons clashed. Fast footsteps gained ground behind her, drowning her senses with panic.

She slipped on a wet spot and fell, scraping the fingers wrapped around the scroll. The smell of dust and mildew invaded her nose and gagged her. She shot to her feet. Hands clawed her shoulder and the loose curls tumbling to her waist. Her captor yanked her head back, nearly snapping her neck. She wheeled on the man, wincing from the pain of having her hair torn from her scalp. Her tunic ripped. The night air chilled her shoulders.

She raised the scroll and beat her attacker with the hard wooden knob at the end of the rolled parchment. She kicked with furious intent, catching the rat in the shin, the knee, the groin. He doubled over, shrieking with pain. More footsteps. Yelled profanities and insults shot through the night. The pack continued their chase. Her fingers tightened on the scroll now that she realized it made a decent weapon. Lungs burning from the added exertion, she ran ever harder, her bracelets rattling with each step like a frantic tambourine.

At the end of the alley, she turned right, disheartened to find another desolate road. Terror spurred her onward. The shouts of her assailants grew louder, closer. Her mouth dry, she panted for air, her chest tight and aching. Fatigue threatened to claim her.

Up ahead, torchlight glowed in the distance and began to grow brighter. The school! She ran toward the iron gates and the guards' darkened silhouettes. Spurred on by the sight, she summoned her second wind and pressed onward.

"I've got you, wench!"

Rough hands grabbed her around the neck. Her scream died in the vermin's tight grasp. She felt herself tumble. Pain exploded down her side where she landed, her face scraped the road's hard pavers.

The fall dislodged her attacker. She lurched upright, kicking the scum in the stomach, the face. The faint voices of Caros's men filled her with hope. She bolted toward the shelter in the distance.

With a rush of gratitude, she arrived at the gate. The party's music drifted on the cool night air. Weak with relief, she closed her eyes and sagged against the bars, pleading for help. Her labored breaths shook her whole body, clanking the scroll's wooden ends against the cold metal bars in her grasp.

"My lady!"

Her heart dropped. *No gods, please, not Quintus!* Her eyes widened with dread even as they roamed over his tall frame and broad shoulders to ascertain his wounds had healed as well as her steward reported.

"Guard, open the gate!" Quintus ordered. "You, there, fetch your master."

Why did the Fates toy with her? Of all the men in the *ludus,* why did *he* have to be the one to find her scorned and disgraced?

In Rome, no decent woman of rank was attacked in the street. People would blame her, judge her, believe she'd done something to *deserve* the dishonor. Quintus would be no different. How could he be when her shame supported the abysmal opinion he already held of her?

Hot tears burned her eyes.

The gate rattled open. She crossed into the courtyard and flinched as the heavy metal bars slammed shut behind her. A torch's flame reflected in Quintus's intense, unreadable gaze. Raw and exposed beneath his stoic inspection, she lifted her chin.

Her lips quivered as she grappled to maintain the last shreds of her dignity. Like her torn garments, the careful facade she cultivated to protect herself hung in tatters.

"My lady, what happened?"

His deep voice washed over her with a gentleness that unraveled the last of her control. Stripped of her pride, the armor she hid behind, she wished her attackers had caught her and finished her off.

The tears she'd fought spilled down her cheeks in hot rivulets, burning her with humiliation to the depths of her soul. She swiped at the moisture and swung away, furious with her weakness and that *he* should be the one to witness her shattered state.

She heard Quintus groan behind her. His footsteps crunched on the gravel. Assuming he'd gone to find someone else to deal with the embarrassment of her situation, she wrapped her arms around her middle, her right hand locked around the scroll.

Fear from the attack crowded around her. She heard the clash of weapons, saw the lifeless faces of her men. Eyes shut tight, she covered her mouth with her free palm, desperate to keep her sobs in check lest she fall apart at the seams.

"My lady." Strong fingers curved around her shoulders. She jerked at the contact, unused to being touched.

Quintus gently turned her toward him and with a sigh of resignation gathered her close. Surrounded by his scent of citrus and leather, she stood there rigid at first, ignorant of how to react because no one had ever held her. Always alone, always *lonely,* she was used to being abandoned, never cared for or comforted.

He stroked her mangled hair, offering her the solace she was loathe to refuse. The murmur of his deep voice soothed her. Warmed by his tenderness, she melted against him, accepting the first genuine embrace she'd ever known.

Surrounded by the security of Quintus's arms, she pressed closer against him and wept against his chest. Safety was foreign to her, but his quiet confidence made her believe he was the one man in existence meant to protect her from harm.

Voices drifted across the courtyard from the direction of the house. She stilled as reality invaded the haven she'd found. Suddenly ashamed of the flaw in her that enjoyed the solace offered by a man who thought the worst of her, she stepped back from Quintus, wishing he would leave her to cope with her humiliation and despair on her own. Awash with embarrassment, she made haste to repair her appearance.

Quintus let go of Adiona with reluctance. Clearly she'd been attacked. Suspecting thieves, he struggled to control his anger toward the jackals who hurt her.

The night's breeze ruffled her glossy black hair. He fisted his hand to control the urge to caress its softness once more. Both dazed and irritated by the sense of completeness he experienced while he held her, he despised the weakness that made it impossible for him to walk away as he ought to. He knew better than to court disaster, but her tears had chained him to the spot. His reason failed to quell his need to console and protect her.

Had he been wiser, he would never have touched her. Now, it was too late. Her scent and the feel of her in his arms were burned into his brain. Never again would he smell cinnamon or enjoy the texture of silk without thinking of Adiona Leonia.

Moonlight bathed her smooth skin with an ethereal glow. Moisture sparkled on the tips of her long lashes like diamond dust. Her beauty tormented him and pushed him to the edge of his endurance. If not for the bruises and scrapes, she might be mistaken for one of the sirens the Greeks believed tempted a man from his senses until he crashed against the rocks.

Lord, please help me keep my wits around this temptress.

"You ought to go inside," he said in a voice rough and hardly recognizable even to himself. His apology would have to wait. Besides the fact she was in no state to hear him, he was determined to see her safe before his control splintered and he lost his inner battle to return her to his arms. "You've been hurt. Your cuts need tending."

"I'm fine," she whispered. "Go back to the party without me."

He'd forgotten about the celebration the moment he saw her clinging to the gate. A quick glance showed the courtyard empty except for a few guards high on the watchtower. "No. I won't leave you."

"I want you to go." She had yet to look at him. "The gossips will roast me alive if I'm caught out here alone with a…a slave."

A wave of cynicism crashed over him. Here he was, reeling from the ferocity of his need to care for her, while she was embarrassed to be seen with him.

Let that be a lesson to you, fool.

His mouth twisted with self-mockery. He'd thought his pride had suffered every indignity imaginable since his enslavement. Leave it to this haughty, *haunting* beauty to prove him wrong again.

Although he supposed he should be grateful for the reminder of the chasm that spanned between them, bitterness hardened in his belly like a weight of lead. He was a slave because of his faith, not because of birth or low rank. Before his arrest, he and the widow would have been considered more than a worthy match. "You weren't embarrassed to be caught with a slave when you clung to me moments ago. Perhaps Alexius is right and you wealthy widows are just selective in how you spend time with slaves."

Her eyes flared, then narrowed at the veiled insult. Cheeks flushed, her breathing ragged, she transformed from weeping victim to an iron-spined matron of Rome. She thrust her shoulders back and pinned him with a glare so hot that he felt singed. "I've had enough of your insults, you ignorant, contemptible…*man!*"

His chest throbbed where she'd punctuated each word with a solid thump of the scroll she carried. He took hold of the rolled parchment and pried it from her death grip. "Don't hit me, mistress."

Her lip curled as she struggled to find a worse name to call him. He almost laughed when he realized she thought labeling him a man was the vilest of slurs. He was far from offended. After months of feeling caged like an animal, it was just what he needed to hear.

"Adiona!" Caros and Pelonia burst into the courtyard. The guard Quintus sent to fetch them trailed in their wake.

Caros pushed past him, his concern for the widow evident in his brusque manner. "What happened? Are you hurt?"

As Adiona explained how she was attacked, Pelonia wrapped her in a fur-lined cloak. Caros snapped orders to his guards to find the widow's men.

"I'll go," Quintus volunteered, eager to put distance between himself and Adiona.

"No, come with us," Caros said as he ushered the women back toward the main house.

A cheerful melody mingled with the aroma of lemons and smoked oysters, roasted lamb and fresh bread. The laughter and conversation of the guests in the *do-*

mus's inner courtyard contrasted sharply with the solemn air surrounding their hosts.

Inside the house, Quintus leaned against the back wall of Caros's office. The mosaic-tiled floor and expensive dark wood furniture reminded him of his own office before his imprisonment.

Cool evening air blew in through the large arched windows behind the *lanista*'s formidable desk. A mural of a setting sun dominated one wall. Ornate lanterns lit the space, providing Quintus with a clear view of Adiona on one of the blue cushioned couches across the room.

Pelonia sat down beside her and held the widow's hand. To Quintus's surprise, Adiona clutched her hostess's fingers like a lifeline. As far as he knew the two women were less than friends. The men in his barracks suggested a rivalry existed between them, that Adiona had been jealous when Caros wed the young woman who'd once been his slave.

He looked up to find Caros studying him with a frown. The *lanista*'s sharp blue eyes narrowed thoughtfully, before he turned his attention back to Adiona. "Why do you suppose someone wants to harm you? Was it simply thieves? Or did one of your enemies aim to dishonor you?"

"Dishonor wasn't their intention." She clenched her fist. "Some wretch means to murder me."

Murder her? Every nerve in Quintus's body went on alert.

"Why?" Caros asked. "What have you done this time?"

Adiona blanched. "Nothing!"

Quintus stepped forward. His grip tightened on the scroll as protective instincts surged through him.

"Caros." Pelonia stood and moved between her husband and Adiona before Quintus could reach them. Her calm presence defused the escalating tension. "Adiona is the one who's been hurt. Let's not add to her pain. No matter what she may or may not have done, it doesn't warrant murder."

Caros grunted in agreement, even though he seemed unconvinced.

Quintus stepped back to his place beside a potted palm. Rife with irritation, he watched Adiona, disturbed by the sway of his emotions and intentions toward a woman whose reputation was so sour that even her closest confidant wasn't surprised someone wished to harm her.

Never in his life had he been as irrational or distracted from his own goals. It was as though he rode a pendulum in a tempest. One moment his anger burned against the widow, her insults, and worse, her effect on him. The next he'd willingly vow to protect her. He was becoming a stranger to himself.

Eager to leave Adiona and the confusion she churned in him, he remembered the scroll he held and offered its return.

She waved the message away. "You open it. It's from my heir."

"Drusus?" Caros sneered.

She nodded and cupped her forehead in her palm. "Read it…if you're able, Quintus."

He grinned at her second failed attempt to insult him. He noted the serpent pressed into the wax seal as he broke it and scanned the script. "Bad news, I'm afraid."

"More?" Caros said, rounding his desk.

Adiona stood. "What? Is he whining for more silver?"

Quintus noticed the disdain in her tone and wondered why she'd chosen an heir she held in contempt. "The message was drafted three days ago. It seems your heir's wife has taken ill. The physician fears she'll pass on before the week is out. Drusus requests you attend her funeral."

Adiona paled. "Oh, gods, not Octavia." She sat heavily as though her knees were too weak to hold her slight weight.

Seeing her grief, Quintus's heart twisted with compassion. Again he wanted to comfort her, but he crushed the urge, determined not to lose himself in her pain-filled eyes. "For your own safety, you mustn't leave these walls."

"I agree," said Caros. "You'll have to send your condolences."

"No, I must go."

Pelonia crouched before the widow and cast a silencing glance over her shoulder to quiet both men. "Don't trouble yourself further tonight," she told Adiona in a gentle voice. "There's nothing more you can do. Come, let's tend your wounds and see you're made comfortable. Tomorrow, once you're rested, you can decide the best course."

Quintus watched Adiona's narrow back until Pelonia led her down a long torch-lit corridor and out of sight. A helpless yearning to soothe her warred with his need to guard his own interests. Only a fool would allow himself to be drawn to the temperamental shrew or embroiled in her many problems. Yet he'd known since the first time he'd seen her months ago that she was dangerous to his peace of mind. Tonight proved just how susceptible he was, both to her beauty and to her vulnerability. How could he continue to resist his attraction, as he must, if he didn't keep his distance?

He handed the scroll to Caros, disturbed to realize the *lanista* had been studying him again. "What do you plan to do?" he asked.

Caros shook his head. "I haven't decided."

"Do you really think someone means to kill her?"

"I don't know. Adiona can be…difficult. She doesn't act or hold her tongue like a proper woman should. I've seen her flay senators to the bone with a few well-aimed barbs. I can believe she's done something to make the wrong person angry enough to seek vengeance."

"Do you suspect anyone in particular? What about her heir? Neither of you seemed to think well of him."

"Drusus is the logical choice, but I have my doubts," Caros said. "It's true her cousin is a leech, but he's also a coward. If he wanted Adiona dead, he'd ply her with poison, not warn her of his intentions by having her attacked in the streets. He'd fear her dishonor might rub off on him. He's too fastidious for that."

"Unless his inheritance is more valuable to him than his self-respect or reputation."

"True."

Pelonia returned, her soft features marred by concern. Caros stood and met her in the middle of the room. "How is Adiona?"

"As well as can be expected. She's much calmer than I would be in the same situation. I suppose she's trying to put on a brave face, but I suspect her placid demeanor is no more than a thin layer of ice covering a turbulent winter pond."

Quintus silently agreed. He'd seen the widow's icy façade melt in the courtyard. The memory of her pain

washed through him until an unbearable need to seek
her out and make certain of her welfare sent him heading for the door.

"Quintus?" Caros stopped him. "Where are you
going?"

His hands curled into fists. Where *was* he going?
Adiona wasn't his woman to protect or care for. He
had no rights to her. Indeed, he was probably the last
person she wanted to see after the way he'd insulted
her. His jaw clenched, he scraped his fingers through
his hair in frustration.

Pelonia eyed him warily. He wished he could head
back to the barracks. He cleared his throat. "Do you
think Lady Leonia will listen to reason or insist on attending the funeral?"

"When I left her, she seemed determined to go,"
Pelonia said.

Caros frowned. "I'm not surprised. Adiona cares for
few people, but those who earn her trust have a friend
for life. Octavia happens to be one of those she loves."

"I don't know her well," Pelonia offered, "but Adiona seems stubborn enough to strike out on her own
if need be."

Fear spiked through Quintus. He suspected Adiona
was determined, proud and *rebellious* enough to leave
the safety of the *ludus* just to prove no one cowed or
controlled her.

"She just might." Caros caught Quintus's gaze. "I'll
do my best to convince her to stay until I can make inquiries and discover her attackers if possible. But if
she insists on leaving, I'll send guards to keep her as
safe as I can."

Pelonia sighed. "I suppose you'll send Alexius?"

"No," Caros said gravely. "I think Quintus is the best man for the task."

Relief and dread filled Quintus with equal measure. He closed his eyes, both savoring and despising the thought of being with Adiona for days, perhaps weeks on end.

Pelonia gasped. "You can't. He's still recovering from his fight in the arena."

I'm fine.

"He's fine," Caros said. "Haven't you noticed his limp is gone?"

Quick to begin making plans, Quintus listened with half an ear while the two of them discussed him as though he weren't there.

"Yes," Pelonia answered. "But he has no experience as a bodyguard."

He scowled, not happy to hear how weak Pelonia saw him. Did Adiona share the same view?

"No matter," Caros continued. "He has everything he needs. He's a natural leader. The other men I send for added defense will have no trouble following him. And if his time in the ring taught us anything, it's that he's intelligent, resourceful and battle-ready. He's strong and depends on the Lord for direction. We'll send them out in secrecy. If we're fortunate, they'll reach Neopolis before her attackers guess she's left our midst."

Satisfied to realize Caros didn't consider him a useless weakling, he had to admit the plan held merit. Of course, Caros didn't know about Quintus's gnawing fascination for the widow or the constant battle he waged to keep from handing her his heart on a plate.

Caros faced him. "What say you, Quintus? Are you willing to be Adiona's protector in exchange for your freedom?"

"I'd rather take my chances in the ring."

A smile twitched at the edge of Caros's mouth before he smothered it beneath a scowl. "I've already denied your request to reenter the games."

They both knew Caros possessed the power to reverse the decision and grant his approval. They also knew he would not. His friend cared more about Quintus's life than he did. Caros knew he longed for freedom, but wouldn't walk away without paying his debt. It was obvious the *lanista* saw the situation as a lesser of two evils, a way for both of them to win.

The anger he constantly fought because of his powerless position nearly blinded him. "I suppose I have little choice, then," he said tightly.

"Very little," Caros agreed.

"Then if you don't mind, I'll head back to the barracks. I have much to prepare."

In the corridor, he leaned against the wall and reined in his temper. The melodious music and laughter of the party mocked his agitated mood. Not for the first time, he wondered what he'd done to provoke God's wrath on him.

"Do you really think that was wise?" Pelonia's voice carried into the hall.

"What?"

"Forcing Quintus and Adiona into such close proximity. Have you seen the two of them together?"

Caros chuckled. "Why do you think I thought of Quintus? Who better to protect a woman than the man who can't keep his eyes off her?"

Chapter Four

"Have you lost your mind, Caros?" Incredulous, Adiona stared at her friend as though he'd grown two heads. The very idea of Quintus acting as her bodyguard made her tremble.

"No, I'm sane enough." Caros crossed his arms over his broad chest and leaned against the marble desktop. Morning sunlight streamed through the office's east-facing windows and glinted off the jewel-toned tiles in the mosaic floor. "You need a strong, trustworthy leader for your guard if you mean to leave for Neopolis anytime soon."

"Quintus is capable for certain, but he despises me. What makes you think he'll agree to your plan?"

"He doesn't despise you." He ignored her snort of disbelief. "He's already agreed."

Her heart skipped a hopeful beat. "He has?"

"He wants to earn funds to buy his freedom. Your situation provides a perfect solution to that end."

"Yes, perfect," she said tightly, wounded by the painful knowledge that Quintus had to be *bought* to spend time with her. She tugged the leaf off a potted plant, grateful Caros hadn't noticed the root of melancholy growing inside her. "Why force him to buy his freedom? You've released your other slaves and kept only volunteers since you became one of those Christians. Why not simply *release* him? You have no need of money."

"I've tried. He calls it charity and won't accept my offer. The two of you need each other."

She cringed at the idea of *needing* anyone. Unlike most men, Caros wasn't stupid. He possessed hawklike powers of observation. He was aware of how attracted she was to Quintus and just how much Quintus chafed at being within a mile of her. If she didn't know him better, she'd think her long-time friend was making a cruel joke at her expense. "I thought when you wed Pelonia you'd grow tired of meddling in my affairs."

His smirk slid into a full grin. She gritted her teeth, vexed she seemed incapable of sparking the tiniest flame of irritation in him when his plans had left her capsized and floundering.

She moved to the window, in need of air and something to focus on beside the conflicting mix of excitement, longing and fear that threatened to drive her mad.

Gladiators trained in the field below. She winced when she caught herself searching greedily for the tall Christian who tormented her thoughts by day and her dreams by night.

She twisted the end of her long braid around her finger. The clack of wooden practice swords and the glint of sunlight on shields reminded her of the attack the previous evening. She closed her eyes, absorbing the loss of her men, men she barely knew and shared no bond with beyond that of master and slave. What if Quintus were her protector and she was attacked again?

What if Quintus suffered the same deadly fate as Titus and her other guards?

She clutched her chest as a sudden rush of anguish robbed her of breath. She must keep him safe. How would she ever be able to live with herself if any harm came to him because of her?

"Adiona?" Caros asked.

"What?" Embarrassed by her overwrought reaction, she wrenched her eyes open and pretended interest in the gladiator practice.

"Are you well?"

"Of course," she whispered just as she spotted Quintus training with another gladiator in the center of the field.

Her traitorous heart leaped at the sight of him and his powerful movements mesmerized her. A voice of reason clamored in the back of her mind to leave the window before he saw her, but her feet seemed buried in the concrete floor.

Without warning, Quintus broke from the fight and glanced her way as though her presence called to him from across the sand. He turned slowly toward the house. The sharp, angular cut of his jaw was locked tight, his full lips unsmiling. Sweat poured down his temples and the bronze column of his throat, soaking the front of his dark tunic. His muscled arms and legs seemed relaxed in their stillness, but the intensity in his gaze exposed the turbulent inner man that both frightened and fascinated her.

As their eyes locked, tender feelings unfurled within her chest. Despite her best efforts to remember his disdain for her, she found her thoughts focused on the gentleness and security she'd found in his embrace the previous night.

Confused and aggravated by her reaction when she'd vowed to feel nothing but hate for the slave, she shivered, uncertain if it was the chill in the air or the coldness of Quintus's wintry gaze that spread ice through her veins.

Never had she felt more powerless to protect herself. Not when her father sold her off, not even when her husband locked her away in a damp cellar for days or when he ordered his minions to torment her for his amusement.

She swallowed the sharp lump in her throat and shoved the nightmares back into the dark recesses of her mind where the pain was more manageable.

Quintus's beautiful mouth compressed. He seemed irritated. As though he, too, had been caught unaware by the sight of her and was unable to sever the ever-tightening bonds that drew the two of them together.

Don't be an idiota. Scoffing at the fanciful idea of Quintus bearing her any emotion beyond dislike, she blamed the morning sun for the sudden flare of heat in her cheeks.

Caros gripped her shoulders and turned her to face him. "You know I'll concern myself with your affairs until I'm satisfied you're safe and no longer need me," he said, bringing her back to their conversation. "I've acted as your defender too long to leave you to the wolves now."

"I know." Every nerve in her body begged her to turn back to Quintus and she was grateful Caros was there to keep her from acting on the foolish impulse. "I'm truly thankful for your friendship."

He waved away her gratitude. "Will you trust me then? Quintus is the best man to keep you in one piece.

If I weren't convinced of his abilities, I wouldn't suggest him."

She eased from his grasp. With a fleeting glance out the window, she saw Quintus was gone. Her heart heavy with disappointment, she knew it wasn't Caros she didn't trust.

I don't trust myself.

She made her way to the couch across the room. Aware that she was being a coward, she found it infinitely safer for her peace of mind to indulge her fascination for Quintus from a distance.

"I'd prefer someone else."

"You're just being stubborn." He ran his scarred fingers through his hair. "You won't leave here without Quintus in command of your guards."

"You can't make my decisions for me."

"No, but I can lock you in a room upstairs until I discover your attackers and have them arrested."

"You wouldn't dare!" Furious he threatened her freedom, the one thing she valued most, she began to pace as though looking for a way of escape. "I'd never speak to you again."

"I'll take my chances."

She came to an abrupt stop in the middle of the office and glared at him. "Fine. Have the *slave* packed and ready to leave within the hour."

Caros's eyes narrowed with suspicion, but she managed not to flinch. He knew her too well. It wasn't like her to capitulate with ease. But why waste time arguing with the stubborn ox when she could simply agree, then order Quintus back to the *ludus* once they'd safely left the city? She had the other members of her guard to protect her if the need arose, while Quintus's absence assured he wouldn't come to harm because of his association with her.

"It wouldn't be wise of you to leave until late in the afternoon."

"You know I must reach Neopolis as soon as possible. If there's a chance to see Octavia before the end, I'd like to."

"I understand." He spoke gently as though she were one of his skittish Spanish mares. "But think, you may not reach her at all if you don't proceed with caution. Preparations must be made and new guards chosen if you're to be kept safe. Leaving later will provide the time we need to find the right men *and* ensure enough light for you to make the first tavern outside the city before nightfall."

"Fine," she snapped, rife with frustration, but unable to argue with the truth. "We'll wait. However, I *will* leave for Neopolis today, and gods protect you if you try to stop me."

When the sun began to wane and the afternoon turned cooler, Quintus made his way to the courtyard behind the main house. Most of the day had been spent in unbroken activity. After praying for wisdom, he and Caros had weighed various plans of escape and worked out the quickest, safest route to Neopolis. Quintus had overseen every detail of the trip's preparations himself. His own life meant little to him, but the thought of Adiona coming to harm chilled him to the marrow.

The pair of geldings he'd chosen for the road portion of the journey to the port town of Ostia waited to be hitched to the *raeda,* a small covered coach in the center of the courtyard.

Alexius hailed Quintus from where he sat on a bench

under an olive tree. The Greek joined him by the horses. He broke his half-eaten apple in two and fed a piece to each animal. "These scruffy beasts have certainly seen better days, no? With Caros's stable flung wide for you, why not choose horses with more…appeal?"

Eager to get the journey under way, Quintus cast a glance around the walled space until he located the assembly of formidable guards he'd selected based on their swordsmanship, speed and, most importantly, intelligence.

"These mounts are perfect for my purpose," he said, turning back to Alexius. "I picked them for strength, not beauty. If Lady Leonia's assassins are watching the compound, they'll expect her to leave in luxury, not cramped in the back of a shabby covered wagon."

"Good thinking, but I'm surprised Adiona agreed."

"I didn't ask her."

"I see." Amused disbelief crossed the Greek's dark features. "Do you mind if I stay until you *do* ask her? That ought to prove entertaining."

"She's an intelligent woman. She'll see reason."

"Usually I'd agree with you," Alexius said, trying not to laugh, "but the lady seems most *un*reasonable where you're concerned, my friend. In truth, I've considered lending you my armor for this venture."

Quintus offered a halfhearted smile. Alexius had a knack for turning every situation into a farce, but in this case he was too close to the truth for comfort. The next two weeks promised little but inevitable arguments and power plays. He didn't delude himself into thinking Adiona would be placid or agreeable, but he was determined to fulfill his duty and keep her safe no matter how often she tempted him to wring her slender neck.

Whatever it takes to earn my freedom.

Disgusted with himself to realize a part of him looked forward to being with her no matter how badly she behaved, he crawled under the *raeda* to ascertain the underpinnings were sound enough to hold the bounty of possessions a peacock like the widow was sure to require. Satisfied all was well, he slid out from under the vehicle, dusted off his tunic and went to check the supplies.

He opened the coach's back door, expecting the covered space to be stuffed with Adiona's frivolous trinkets and overabundance of clothing. To his surprise, no new chests had been added to the foodstuffs and *amphorae* filled with water he'd placed there earlier.

What is she waiting for?

He bristled, recalling the orders she'd sent for him and his men to be ready to leave when she commanded. The curt note still rankled. He should have ignored the missive like he'd intended. As he'd expected, she was the last to arrive.

Alexius said farewell and wished him a safe journey. Another hour passed and Adiona had yet to make an appearance. His temper rising, Quintus began to pace. He'd gone over his orders with his men and the horses were restless. He'd hoped to leave while there was enough light to see them safely beyond the city gates and installed in a *tabernae* before darkness made them prey for thieves and other riffraff. Not for the first time that day, he wondered if Adiona had any concept of the lengths he and her friends had gone to to ascertain her welfare.

A servant girl with a leather satchel approached from the direction of the main house. Quintus recognized her as the maid Adiona had sent for earlier in the afternoon. Tall and slim, the girl's wool tunic matched her dark brown hair and eyes. She seemed as timid as her mistress was untamed.

"I'm called Nidia," she said shyly, her eyes downcast. "My lady said she'll be along in a moment. These are her belongings."

Quintus took the satchel she held out to him. It was lighter than he expected. There must be some mistake.

"There's no more," Nidia said as though she guessed his thoughts. "My lady realizes you mustn't be weighted down if you mean to travel quickly."

Mystified but pleased by Adiona's good sense, he placed the satchel in the back of the covered cart and latched the wooden door just as Caros made his way through the gate that separated the courtyard from the private gardens of the main house.

"Are you ready to leave?" the *lanista* asked.

"Only for the last two hours."

Caros grinned. "No one claimed punctuality is one of Adiona's virtues."

Quintus snorted.

"She *does* have virtues, you know. She strives to keep them hidden, but I'm confident you'll see the truth once you've spent some time with her." Caros grinned at Quintus's dubious frown. "To be fair, I think she's tardy now because of a late delivery of tunics she ordered."

"That's understandable," Quintus said drily. "Wouldn't want to be unfashionable when we slink away in the dark."

The *lanista* chuckled. "There's plenty of light. You'll make it to the inn before night falls, just as you planned."

"Not if we don't leave soon."

Just then, Pelonia and Adiona came into view. Their

quiet conversation failed to carry across the courtyard, but their serious expressions warned of their concerns.

Quintus focused on Adiona, an unsettling yet unbreakable habit he'd developed over the last several months. The surprise of seeing her dressed in a slave's tunic and worn leather sandals left him momentarily speechless. She should have looked ordinary, drab, but the harsh, shapeless wool and rope belt failed to disguise her willowy frame or delicate bone structure.

His muscles tightened into knots along his shoulders. He closed his eyes, breathing in deep to clear his head. The image of her flawless face invaded his mind's eye. Clean of cosmetics, her skin shone like polished alabaster. Even now his fingers recalled the silken texture of the thick braid that spilled over her shoulder and past her slim waist.

She's not for you, Quintus!

He dragged air into his lungs and forced open his eyes. As usual of late, Caros was studying him as the women drew closer. Annoyed to think Caros suspected the widow's hold on him, he turned away only to fall into the amber flame of Adiona's contemptuous gaze. Her stare burned with challenge as she silently dared him to break his word and refuse to go with her.

His blood boiled. He wasn't afraid of any challenge she chose to throw his way. Since his son's death and Quintus's subsequent arrest for his faith, he'd walked through fire. His losses had left his heart broken and his soul scarred by grief, but his honor remained. It was all he possessed of his former self. He'd promised Caros to guard Adiona until her attackers were caught or until he drew his last breath. Nothing she said or did would detour him from his purpose.

"How kind of you to finally join us," he said in a

wooden voice that left no doubt he found her tardiness rude and arrogant. "Say your farewells and let's depart. The rest of us have been ready to leave for some time now."

Miffed by Quintus's commanding tone, Adiona arched her brow as she watched his proud back disappear around the opposite side of a tattered coach she wouldn't expect her slaves to ride in. How dare he presume to order her about as if *she* were the servant and he the master. He had much to learn if he thought she'd follow him around like a lamb. She'd ceased obeying *anyone* the moment her husband had done her the favor of dying.

"Shall I help you up?" Caros motioned toward the battered vehicle.

"I'm to ride in *that?*" She couldn't quite hide her disgust. The coach was so small. *So* closed in…

"I suspect Quintus will return rather quickly. You don't want to start your journey on the wrong foot by provoking him this early on, do you?"

Her irritation with her new bodyguard swelled to include Caros, as well. "By the gods, no. Whatever would we do if *Quintus* were provoked?"

"Don't be difficult," he warned, his humor at her expense barely concealed. "It's two days to Neopolis. Do you want to spend the journey fortifying his belief that you're a spoiled harpy?"

"I don't care about a slave's opinion of me in the least."

He burst out laughing. Cringing, she lifted her chin and studied the *raeda*. Like most coaches, it consisted of a flat bed, tall wooden sides and an arched oiled canvas cover. A small door at the back provided the only way of escape. She loathed enclosed spaces and the nightmarish memories they released within her. "I'll sit in the driver's seat with Quintus."

"That's not safe. It's best you stay hidden until you're certain no one is following you."

Her hands grew clammy at the reminder of how perilous the journey was. That someone wanted her dead. Pelonia placed an arm around her waist as though she suspected Adiona's rising unease. Grateful for the younger woman's friendship even though she'd done nothing to deserve it, Adiona promised herself to make amends if she managed to return to Rome alive.

She swallowed hard. "What if I'm locked in that... that *box* and my attackers decide to set it on fire with a few flaming arrows? I might be roasted alive. Or what if—"

Caros's incredulous expression silenced her rambling fears. "I never realized how colorful your imagination is."

Her head began to throb as the memories she fought to keep buried clamored for release. "Men are animals," she whispered. "They're capable of anything."

"Quintus isn't an animal, Adiona. Neither are these other men who've sworn to guard you with their lives."

Panic began to claw up her throat. She bit her bottom lip and looked beseechingly at her friend. "I can't get in that coach."

His mouth curved into an impatient frown. "Why?"

She glanced toward Pelonia. Had she and Caros been alone she may have told him the truth. Her friend already knew more of her past than anyone else, although not the worst parts. He was the only person she'd ever known who disagreed with the common wisdom that blamed a woman for the abuse she received.

But his wife's sympathetic expression filled her with

the familiar rush of shame she experienced when she recalled the vile acts her husband had subjected her to. Her pride smarted. She couldn't abide the thought of a *good* woman like Pelonia knowing about the vile treatment she suffered or the indignities she'd endured. After years spent cultivating an image of strength and separating herself from the weak girl she'd been before and during her marriage, she'd rather die than be pitied.

Quintus moved back into view as he checked the horses' bridles. She resented the way her heart quickened in response to a man who held her in contempt. At least she'd come up with a plan to keep him safe *and* release her from his company. Once they reached the port, she'd order Quintus to return to Rome, while she and the other guards sailed south to Neopolis.

Another sidelong glance in his direction showed his rapid progress toward her and the determined scowl creasing his dark features. By the look of him he just might toss her into the coach and slam the door.

"What will it be, Adiona?" Caros asked. "The way to the inn is a few hours, no more. Surely you can cope with a shabby *raeda* if the disguise will keep you safe? Or do you prefer to delay your trip longer by arguing with Quintus here in the yard?"

She wasn't afraid of an argument, but in this case, one seemed futile, not to mention detrimental to her ultimate goal of reaching Octavia before it was too late. She'd spent years taming the specters in her head and she refused to let them conquer her now. "I'll ride in the back. Help me up, will you?"

Pelonia walked with them to the covered wagon. Caros opened the back door and extracted a short ladder. Reminding herself that her husband was dead and no torture awaited her, she ascended into the shadowed interior. Inside, she was surprised to find the floor-boards in front of the supplies had been padded with cushions and blankets. A hint of smoked meat and the salty tang of fish sauce scented the air.

"Are you comfortable?" Pelonia stood in the doorway, a gentle smile curving her mouth. "Quintus worried he might not have gathered enough pillows. I can have someone fetch more of them if you'd like."

"No, I'm fine." She leaned up against a basket full of bread, feeling as though she'd conquered a mountain peak.

"Caros sent a trusted servant to prepare for your arrival at the inn. A warm meal and comfortable room awaits you," Pelonia said. "I'll be praying for you and a safe journey. I hope we'll have more time to become better acquainted once you return."

Adiona tried to smile back. Caros's wife truly was a kind woman, a rarity in her world. "Thank you." She didn't want to hurt Pelonia's feelings, but she doubted the Christians' God could be bothered to help her. "I believe we'll need any assistance your God is willing to give."

Quintus's orders to his men filtered through the wagon walls before he appeared in the open doorway. "If you're having second thoughts about this venture, now is the time to voice them, my lady. You can always send a messenger with your regrets if you'd prefer to stay here at the *ludus* where your safety is certain."

The flatness of his tone belied any concern the words might have implied. Angry and unreasonably hurt by his indifference, she was even more determined to put the plans she'd devised into action. "No, let's be off," she said, defying her rising anxiety of being trapped in the small coach. "We've waited long enough as it is."

Chapter Five

The setting sun shone like a fiery, red orb in the western sky. Quintus tugged on the reins, slowing the coach to a halt in front of a roadside *tabernae* a few miles outside of Rome's city gates. Smoke rose from the inn's cook fires and the smell of roasted pork tempted his empty stomach.

He rubbed a hand across his chin and worked the tightness from his jaw. After hours of bone-jarring travel along the Via Ostiense, every muscle in his body ached. He could only imagine Adiona's discomfort from being cramped in the back of the coach. At least they'd escaped the city unscathed.

He jumped down from the driver's bench and tossed the reins to Falco, a somber giant who said little, but was quick to follow orders. The other guards, Onesimus, Rufus and Otho, remained on horseback, surrounding the vehicle. "Have Rufus see the horses are watered and properly stabled before dinner," he told Falco. "Tell Otho and Onesimus to prepare for first watch. I'll see Lady Leonia settled while you bring in our supplies."

As Falco relayed his orders and the men dismounted

to carry out their tasks, Quintus rounded the back of the coach and knocked quietly. "My lady? May I open the door?"

Silence greeted his request. He waited a few moments and rapped louder. "My lady? How do you fare?"

She continued to ignore him and his impatience spiked. *So the battle of wills has begun.*

Irritated by her childishness, he undid the latch and cracked open the door. The gray shades of early evening offered little light. He couldn't see her in the coach's dark interior and a bolt of panic jolted him not unlike the one time he'd lost his son in a busy marketplace.

"My lady?" He yanked the door open wider to allow more light. Finally he found her curled against the left wall, her forehead lowered to her raised knees and her arms wrapped tightly around her shins.

"Adi…my lady, what's wrong? Are you hurt?"

She flinched from his touch and jerked upright, cringing flat against the carriage wall as though she feared he meant to strike her. Her wild, yet strangely empty eyes reminded him of a terrified colt's and filled him with deep concern.

"It's all right," he said, careful to keep his voice both firm and soothing. He hated the idea of her being frightened of him, but after the attack she'd suffered last night and assassins on her heels, it was little wonder she feared another assault.

It's not her fault. How can she trust anyone when she doesn't know who her friends are?

He eased closer, frowning at the bruise marring her reddened cheek. She'd been crying and the crescent of teeth marks in her swollen lower lip told him she'd done her best to stifle the sounds of her misery.

Until that moment, he hadn't considered Adiona capable of keeping anything that displeased her a secret. Used to women like his wife, Faustina, who never checked her need to pout, scream or throw a tantrum no matter how trivial the reason, he began to wonder if he'd compared and judged the widow unfairly.

"Let me help you, my lady."

She shook her head in adamant denial. "Go away! Leave me be."

The glow of early evening had given way to night, but the moon illuminated the inside of the coach enough for him to see Adiona's bloodless face and tortured eyes. The piteous way she slid down the wall and sat back in a crouch tugged at his heart. He'd done his best to be indifferent to her, but the sinking sensation in his belly forced him to acknowledge indifference was the one emotion he never experienced in her company.

An ox cart joined the other vehicles in front of the *tabernae,* offering him a momentary distraction from the confusion he suffered only around this particular woman. The cart's wizened driver and his hefty wife paid a boy to see to their animals before waddling up the torch-lit path toward the inn's arched front door. Laughter and music spilled from the main room as the couple made their way inside the large, three-storied building.

Quintus nodded to Falco who was guarding his back a few paces away. He took a deep breath and returned his attention to his charge. Refusing to examine his need to comfort her, he curved his fingers around her slim shoulder. "My lady, listen to me."

"Don't touch me!" She raised her head and flung off his hand as though his fingers burned her. "I told you to leave. I don't want you here."

"I can't leave you." He raked his fingers through his hair. "I *won't*."

"Why can't you understand? You mustn't see me like this!"

"What do you mean?" he asked tightly. "Is all of this…this ridiculous misery thanks to your *vanity?*"

Adiona winced at the edge of anger in his voice. A mere moment before, he'd sounded ardent when he declared he wouldn't leave her. Most likely she'd imagined his concern. Her mind had been playing tricks since the moment the *raeda's* door closed, trapping her in the darkness with nightmares that refused to be suppressed. Of course it made more sense for him to be angry. She wished it were otherwise, but no matter what she said or did, she always seemed to affect his temper for the worse.

She closed her eyes and dropped her head to her knees in an effort to calm the tremors shaking her body. She'd done her best to concentrate, to convince herself she had nothing to fear. But after what seemed like an eternity in the cramped darkness, she'd lost the battle until every sway of the vehicle and bump in the road became a tormented reminder of the beatings, insults and incessant cruelty her husband had subjected her to in the dark, moldy bowels of his palace.

Without warning, Quintus hoisted her into the air. A startled shriek burst from her throat as he slung her over his right shoulder. The wind knocked out of her, she gasped for air as she stared at his muscled claves and his sandaled feet, too stunned by his quick action to offer a protest.

"Put me down this instant!" she demanded once she got her breath back.

"When we're inside it will be my pleasure, believe

me." His forearm tightened across the back of her knees to stop her kicking. "But if you think I'll stand out here in the dark and miss my meal while you cry over your mussed hair and loss of silk gowns you're mistaken."

The censure in his voice made her cringe. Dangling over his shoulder like a sack of wheat, she yanked up her braid to keep it from dragging on the dusty path. She cursed him under her breath, but stopped pounding on his back or twisting to get free. It hurt that he always assumed the worst about her, but given the choice, she preferred he think her vain instead of fear-ridden and weak.

As he opened the front door, a wave of music and jovial voices flowed over her. The glow from a fire in the hearth illuminated the simple concrete floor and what she could see of the ocher-painted walls.

Quintus leaned forward and dropped her on her feet. Now that she was free of the darkness, she felt foolish. She dusted off her tunic as she gathered the remnants of her pride.

"Behave," he warned for her ears only. He swept off his cloak and handed it to her. "Put this on, keep your head down and try not to draw attention to yourself."

Her glare made it clear she didn't appreciate taking orders from a minion. She snatched the cloak from his hand and wrapped herself in the warm folds of wool. His delicious scent filled her head, making it twice as hard to calm her nerves.

"Having trouble with your wench, sir?" the innkeeper asked Quintus.

Quintus glanced at her and she smirked back. "She's spirited," he told the innkeeper without breaking eye contact with Adiona. "And more trouble than she's

worth, but I'm too fond of her to entrust her to someone else's care."

"She's a beauty." The innkeeper eyed her sugges-
tively and chuckled when she tugged the hood of the
cape up over her head. "She must be a handful if she
deserved that bruise. If you think she'll try to escape,
I have shackles in the stable."

Adiona didn't hear any more than the rush of blood
in her ears. The bravado she'd been slowly gaining back
evaporated. She broke eye contact with Quintus and
stared blindly at the floor, absently rubbing the faint
scars on her wrists as she remembered the burn of re-
straints chaining her to the cellar wall.

The clink of coins exchanging hands broke through
her private torment. She looked up to find Quintus
frowning at her.

"Come this way." Quintus gently grasped her elbow
as he led her up a flight of stairs and down an arched
corridor. Hanging oil lamps brightened the vaulted
space but did little to tame the draft. Simple frescoes of
fruit and vines lent bright color to the pale plaster walls.

He opened a door at the end of the hall and checked
the space before waving her inside. "It's safe to leave the
door open. Falco will be here soon with your satchel."

As Pelonia promised, the room was comfortable and
well prepared. Someone from the inn had lit several
lamps. A sleeping couch formed of concrete and covered with pillows and furs took up one corner. A rough
wooden chair, small table, basin and pitcher made up
the rest of the furniture.

"There's no window," she murmured, trying to keep
her dread hidden.

"I asked for a room without one," Quintus told her.
"If we don't have to worry about intruders entering

from the street, it will take fewer of us to guard you at one time. My men will get more rest and be better prepared for the journey tomorrow."

"Then I suppose it's adequate," she said, her throat tightening with renewed panic. She'd traded the coach for another airless box. With all the hours until sunrise how was she to keep her sanity?

"I'm glad you approve." His dry tone made it clear he didn't care if she was pleased with the accommodations.

She bristled. "Order a bath for me. Also, see if the inn has a maid I can hire for the night. I'll need help with my hair."

"I'll have Otho and Rufus bring you a bath." He gripped the back of the chair. "But there will be no maid. For your safety we need as few people as possible to know you're here. You'll have to manage on your own."

She'd never dealt with her own hair before. Unbound, the thick mass hung to her knees. It was already coming loose from the braid Nidia had woven before they left Rome. If the braid wasn't repaired, it would degrade into a tangled mess. Her ignorance over what should be a simple, personal task made her feel useless, but she'd rather bite off her tongue than admit she was helpless.

"You *are* able to see to your own hair, aren't you?" he asked, studying her.

She lifted her chin. "Of course."

Falco's massive frame filled the doorway, her satchel hanging from one hand. The gladiator always gave her pause. Not only was Falco as big as a titan, his pockmarked face, chipped teeth and scarred, tattooed arms made him look like a monster.

Quintus retrieved the leather satchel and placed it on the table. "I'm going to fetch your meal, my lady. Falco will be right outside your door if you encounter any trouble."

His assurance did little to soothe her. Falco's narrowed gaze and disturbing disposition brought her more anxiety. "Close the door," she told the frightening gladiator. Alone, she had to face down her nightmares, but that was better than having to stare one in the face.

Chapter Six

By the second hour, the inn's patrons were abed for the night. All was silent except for the occasional squeak or scurry of a rodent.

Quintus shifted on the chair he'd placed in front of Adiona's chamber. A single oil lamp burned on a low stool beside him, casting tall shadows on the facing wall and down the long corridor where Otho and Rufus kept watch at the top of the stairs.

He pulled his cloak tighter around him. With the fires banked in the inn's common areas, the cold night air crept through the halls unhindered. Not for the first time, he considered asking Adiona if she had enough furs to keep warm.

Something was wrong with her. It was nearly sunrise and he could still hear her footsteps behind the closed door as she crossed the chamber from one end to the other.

According to Falco, she'd eaten little of the meal Quintus brought earlier. Once the tub and hot water were delivered, she'd taken a long bath. Other than Adiona's manner being unusually subdued, Falco assured him the night had been uneventful until the pacing began shortly before Quintus arrived for guard duty just after midnight.

So why doesn't she sleep?

Wide-awake, due to the few fitful hours of rest he'd gotten after eating his own meal, he tried to lose himself in prayers for wisdom and safety. The journey that stretched before them was perilous, their enemy unknown. The miles of road until they reached Ostia were well-traveled, but with no hint of who might be friend or foe, there was no one he could fully trust except the Lord.

Another hour passed before the endless rhythm of Adiona's steps stopped on the other side of the door. He felt her presence and her indecision, heard the slight rattle when she placed her hand on the latch.

"Quintus?" she asked, her anxiety palpable through the wood. "Have you come back?"

"Yes, my lady." He stood and placed his palm flat against the rough oak, the strain in her voice more than he could resist. "I'm here. What do you wish?"

"Nothing." The word was little more than a whisper through the filter of the door. "All is well now."

An odd ache pierced his chest. "You ought to rest, my lady. You're safe here. Your enemies can't harm you."

He thought he heard her sigh before her footsteps trailed away. He suspected it was his imagination, but she seemed soothed by his presence as she settled for the night. Hopeful she'd find some peace from her worries in slumber, he began to do some pacing of his own.

Certain he'd been too rough with her when they arrived at the inn, he wished he'd been more patient or said something to relieve her distress. She may be spoiled and her vanity irksome, but she was also being hunted by assassins and her friend lay dying in Neopolis.

Whatever her behavior, it was no excuse for him to act like a barbarian. As the head of his family, he'd been raised to treat women with honor. More importantly, as a follower of Christ he knew he should let compassion guide his actions.

A scream shattered the night. The hackles spiked on the back of his neck. He shot to his feet, *gladius* drawn in instant preparation for battle.

Another scream. This one not as loud but even more tormented than the first. He shoved the chair aside as he beat on the locked door.

"Adiona, are you hurt? Let me in!"

No response. Had someone managed to sneak past Falco and hide in her room? Dread fueled him onward. He shouted for his men. Leading with his shoulder, he threw himself against the door like a battering ram.

After two tries, the latch splintered and the door sprang wide. He rushed across the threshold, noting the pair of lit oil lamps on the table as his gaze circled the chamber for any sign of his lady.

A slight movement drew his attention to the floor at the foot of the bed. His heart twisted painfully when he saw Adiona against the wall in a fearful crouch, a fur pulled over her head like a cowl and clutched tightly under her chin.

His swift steps carried him across the room until the terror in her wide eyes made him pause a few paces in front of her. Uncertain of what to say or do to reassure her, he bent down on one knee and promised she was safe.

Her panic appeared to lessen until her gaze darted to something behind him and her eyes flared with alarm.

He spun on the balls of his feet and sprang upright, bracing to fight off an attacker. Instead, he saw his men struggling to bar the doorway against a stream of curious guests.

Exasperated by the gawkers, he sent the inn's patrons back to their beds. The situation once again under control, he gave swift instructions for Otho to prop the door against the jamb and guard the entry while Rufus located the tools to repair the latch and broken hinge.

Dragging in a ragged breath, Quintus waited for a reaction from Adiona, uncertain what to expect.

Until tonight, he'd had few reasons to question his impression of her. Since his first glimpse of the beauty five months ago, she'd portrayed herself as wanton, superior or insulting. She made it easy to believe she was no more than an icy lioness on the prowl.

Yet three times in as many days he'd seen her veneer melt before his eyes, exposing a vulnerable woman with hurts and fears. He was no liar: she'd always fascinated him, but her haughty manner aided his ability to resist her. As it was, the mysterious woman behind the glacial facade beckoned him like a freezing man drawn to a flame.

As a successful merchant, he'd perfected the art of dividing traders from their many secrets, but Adiona was different. She had nothing to sell and no apparent reason to portray herself as anyone other than whom she claimed to be. Yet, if not for her terror, he was convinced she never would have allowed him to glimpse behind her persona.

So who was the real Adiona? A paradox or a Pandora's box? A beautiful young woman who sought to protect herself behind a wall of pride and wealth or a flagrant, razor-tongued vixen who delighted in causing trouble?

She tipped her head back against the wall behind her. The fur slipped down and bunched around her slender shoulders, revealing the smooth, slender column of her throat. Her sorrow-filled eyes watched his every move, the bruise from her attack a faint purple on her pale cheek.

Careful not to further frighten her, he made slow progress across the room, half-afraid she might bolt. He offered his hand to help her to her feet. She shook her head and lowered her face against her raised knees. Her entire manner spoke of deep humiliation.

He wanted to say something to reassure her, but the words locked in his throat. There was no friendship between them and he was no mentor to give advice, but he had to do something. The grief etched in her face would haunt his dreams to the end of his days if he walked away and ignored her pain.

Determined not to leave or make matters worse, he sat down beside her, his back to the wall, his legs spread out and crossed at the ankles in front of him.

One of the lamps had gone out on the table and the other burned low, lending just enough light for him to see her lift her head and watch him with trepidation. Her beautiful face was stained with tears. The glow from the corridor illuminated the corner around the broken door, while the rest of the room remained wreathed in darkness.

To his surprise, she slowly wove her arm through his and leaned against his shoulder. He stiffened, regretting the mistake of moving this close to her. Her cinnamon scent clouded his senses, innocently tempting him to brush his lips across the top of her head and steal the kiss he craved, the only one he was ever likely to have from her.

Needing a distraction from the feel of her softness pressed along his side, he tipped his head back against the frescoed wall and listened for any disruptions Otho might need assistance with in the hall.

"I'm sorry," Adiona murmured into the stillness.

"For what, my lady? You've done nothing wrong."

She hung her head, clearly disagreeing with him.

He lifted her chin with his index finger and waited for her to meet his gaze. "Tell me what frightened you? Did you dream of another attack? If so, I assure you, you're safe. I've given my word, I'll defend you with my life."

He felt her tremble. The thick fringe of her lashes dropped to conceal the war of emotions raging in her eyes. "I have… I have nightmares."

"And today in the *raeda?* Was it the same nightmare or were you afraid your assassins might find us?"

"The same one."

Amazed she feared her nightmares more than she feared her assassins, he pulled the fur up over her shoulders, concerned she might catch a chill.

She drew closer as if seeking his warmth. "Is there anything *you* fear, Quintus?"

A humorless smile curved his lips. He feared a great many things whenever he was in her presence. The loss of his sanity and self-control chief among them. "Everyone is afraid of something from time to time."

"I know," she said in a small voice. "But…is there something in *particular* that frightens you?"

He concentrated on the scratch of her wool tunic against his arm to block out her nearness. It went against the grain to admit his weaker points, but he sensed telling the truth might alleviate some of her torment. He swallowed hard. "I'm afraid of failure, my lady."

She lifted her face to his, her surprised eyes the color of liquid gold in the fire's glow. "I can't imagine you failing at anything."

Her sincerity made him wince. She didn't know him. If she did learn the truth about him, she'd curse him as a fraud. His son and wife were dead because of his incompetence. No matter what he did or accomplished with the rest of his life, he'd carry that unforgivable burden to his grave.

Her fingers tightened on his forearm and she lowered her head back to his shoulder. "I believe in you, Quintus. I know you won't fail me."

Her trust was a salve to the festering wound in his heart. He deeply regretted his aversion to guarding her when Caros first broached the subject. Since his arrest, he'd questioned God's will and allowed the pain of his losses to fill his soul with resentment.

Remorse settled over him. He offered a silent prayer for forgiveness. The texts promised the Lord always had a plan for His children. If he trusted God as he claimed, then he had to believe each situation he faced happened for a reason. Was it possible the Lord had nurtured him back to health in a gladiator school just to learn the skills required of him to defend Adiona?

In that moment, earning his freedom became secondary. Adiona needed him and the Lord had seen fit he be made her protector. He vowed not to let either of them down.

"Quintus?" she asked quietly.

"Yes?"

"Thank you."

"For what?"

"For not leaving me when I know you must want to."

There was no self-pity in her tone, just a resigned sense of loneliness that called to the empty recesses of his own heart. "You're mistaken, my lady. I've no wish to be elsewhere. You have my word before God I will be here until you send me away. As long as you need me, I'm yours."

Adiona woke from an untroubled slumber. Buried under soft furs and cradled by pillows, she was cocooned in comfort and warmth. Eyes still closed, she stretched her tight muscles. Quintus must have put her to bed after she'd fallen asleep against his shoulder. A drowsy smile tugged at her lips. His gentleness seemed like a dream after the many months he'd rebuffed her attempts to win his notice.

A knock sounded on the door. "My lady, it's time to rise."

A pleasant frisson of awareness made her smile when she heard Quintus's deep voice. She opened her eyes and…collided with the dark.

Another knock. "My lady? Did you hear me?"

"The lamps have burned out," she called, already ill at ease and feeling trapped. After yesterday and the previous night, she had no reserves to battle her memories. Panic simmered just beneath the surface of her control.

Eager to escape her cage, she threw off the covers, instantly regretting the motion as chilled air whispered across her skin and under her silk-lined tunic. She ignored the cold cement floor beneath her feet as she ran toward the ribbon of light around the newly repaired door.

The portal opened before she reached it, illuminating the darkness. Quintus stood before her, one hand on the latch, a fat beeswax candle in the other. "Don't be frightened."

Whether he cautioned her to be unafraid of him or the dark, she wasn't certain, but his presence calmed her rising fear. She didn't understand her absurd re-action or the intrinsic trust she placed in him, but not even her friend Caros, an undefeated champion, man-aged to give her more peace of mind.

Quintus handed her the candle. Hoarding the mea-ger warmth, she cupped her palm around the flame.

"I should have left a light burning," he said. "But after your unease last night I thought it might disrupt your rest when you needed to sleep."

"That was considerate of you. Thank you." She low-ered her head, embarrassed by his knowledge of her weakness. Having anyone—*especially* Quintus—aware of her darkest secrets made her feel strangely raw and off kilter. As if he had some sort of power over her that she could never recover.

She moved to the table and lit the three oil lamps. The windowless room filled with a golden glow. She returned her attention to Quintus, struggling for some-thing to say when his effect on her had always been disconcerting.

Neither of them moved. The air between them grew thick with tension. Her eyes roved over him, taking in his tousled black hair and clean-shaven face.

A frown pleated his chiseled features. She knew she must look frightful fresh from slumber with her braid in a tangle and her face unwashed. She raised her free hand to brush loose tendrils behind her ear.

The voices of the other guards filtered in from the hallway, but Quintus consumed her attention. His unsolicited promise not to leave her infused her with a budding sense of security previously unknown to her experience. She dreaded the thought of sending him away once they reached Ostia, but the longer she stayed in his presence, the more she wanted him safe.

"Did you mean what you said last night?" she asked, determined to learn the truth. Having been burned by life so many times in the past, she found it difficult to believe a truce had miraculously formed between them. "You'll stay with me until I send you away?"

His jaw clenched, leaving her to suspect he regretted his vow. "I don't make promises I don't intend to keep."

A chill in the air caused her to shiver. He stepped forward, lifted her cloak off the back of the chair and draped it around her shoulders.

He was so close that she smelled the clean, masculine scent of his body and the tinge of smoke on his tunic. She wanted to wrap her arms around him and soak in the heat of his skin. She wondered if he felt the connection between them the same as she did, then brushed away the notion, certain she was just deluding herself.

She turned away, desperate to regain her concentration. "I think you're a rarity—an honorable man—so I'm asking you for the truth."

"You'll have it. I assure you I don't lie."

Facing him, she nodded, choosing to believe him. "What I want to know is *why* you added to your vow. You're already bound to Caros to protect me until my assassins are captured. If you want your freedom as much as I've been led to believe, why promise to stay until *I* release you?"

"Simple, my lady. You need me."

She frowned. He was wrong. She'd spent too many

years proving her independence in a world filled with predators bent on ripping her apart. "I don't *need* anyone."

He shrugged. "I disagree."

"Don't be condescending, Quintus. If you had an *inkling* of what I've survived, you'd realize there's nothing I can't handle myself."

His dark eyebrow arched. "Like you handle being alone in the dark?"

Already embarrassed that he knew about her debility, she felt ambushed. "It's not the dark I fear, you wretched man! It's…"

She bit her lower lip. He stepped closer. "It's what, my lady? What do you fear?"

Infuriated by the pity in his eyes, she glanced away.

"You can tell me," he said, his deep voice soft and gentle.

"Why?" Her gaze darted back to his. "So you can use my vulnerability against me?"

"How would I use the knowledge against you? I'd never seek to harm you."

"You think your insults in the hospital brought me no pain?" she scoffed. "I assure you being called a razor-tongued she-cat hurt my feelings."

He jerked as though she'd slapped him. Dark color stained his high cheekbones. "Adiona, I—"

A knock sounded on the door frame. They both turned to find Rufus standing in the open portal. Eyes averted, the young gladiator tugged at his right ear. It was easy to see he'd drawn the short straw when the decision was made to interrupt them. "I beg your pardon. Falco sent me to ask how much longer you think you'll be. He made porridge. It's growing cold."

"We won't be much longer," Quintus said tersely.

"The rest of you eat and prepare for the day's travel. The lady and I will have something once we've started on the road."

Adiona watched Rufus disappear, mortified to realize she'd forgotten the other guards were right outside. Rufus's awkward behavior made it plain they'd overheard every word between her and Quintus.

She crossed to the table and rummaged through her satchel, humiliated to realize her private fears were exposed to men who were virtual strangers.

Quintus stood across the table from her, his hands fisted by his sides. "I want to apologize for what I said in the hospital—"

"Don't bother." She pasted on a disinterested smile and forced herself to look at him while inside she was bleeding. "Your opinion of me is no worse than a hundred other men's. I admit I found your honesty a bit harsh at the time, but I've since recovered. In truth, most people compliment me to my face, then weave lies behind my back. In a way it was almost refreshing to learn your true thoughts straight from your own lips."

He raked his fingers through his thick black hair. Sensing a war raged inside him, she longed to soothe the strands back into place and give him peace. But the table between them might as well have been a brick wall she had no idea how to breach.

His intense green eyes studied her face until she wished to flee. What was he looking for...or worse, what did he see *in* her when he examined her that closely? Using a dismissive tactic she'd learned long ago, she pulled one of the long wool garments from her satchel and injected ice into her voice. "Go along,

Quintus. As you know, a murderer may be on my trail.
I'd hate to give him the chance to catch me just because
you'd rather stand there gaping."

Chapter Seven

Unused to being dismissed like the slave he'd become, Quintus burned with the need to smash something. Always quick to anger, he'd become more temperate since believing in the Way, but without Divine assistance, Adiona's mercurial behavior was bound to ruin the progress he'd made.

He passed Onesimus in the hall. With a curt order for the younger guard to see Adiona safely to the coach, he left the inn to find Falco and his other two men.

Outside, it was no longer first light, but still early. A heavy gray sky promised rain. Cook fires dotted the wheel-rutted field between the inn's small front garden and the Ostian road. The usual morning aromas of bread and fish mingled with the stench of oxen and horses as travelers from all walks of life readied themselves for their day's journey.

Searching for anyone who looked dangerous or out of place, Quintus dragged in deep breaths of cold air, berating himself. From the moment he'd entered Adiona's chamber, he'd been at a sore disadvantage. He usually had more time to steel himself for the ravaging effect she played on his senses. But soft, warm and fresh from her slumber, she was a vision, a devastating temptress even a eunuch couldn't ignore.

And he was no eunuch. He was a healthy man who'd spent the past five months denying he craved the impetuous beauty the same as food and air.

He prayed for more strength. He didn't want to sin in deed or in his thoughts, but Adiona was as much a test to his self-control as she was to his patience.

Discovering Falco had set up a makeshift camp by positioning the coach under a protective copse of olive trees, he set out across the muddy field.

Adiona's tormented visage flashed across his mind's eye. He groaned inwardly. He had much to learn about the widow, but he hoped he was beginning to understand her, if only a little. The squabble in her room had been enlightening, shedding a light on the source of her terror as well as her past.

He suspected she'd revealed more of her inner self than she intended. Her reminder of his insults in the hospital was a measure of just how much he'd hurt her. He regretted his harsh assessment and the pain his careless words had caused. She claimed not to want an apology, but somehow he'd convince her he was sorry to the depths of his marrow.

Seeing the way she retreated behind a wall of ice when she felt threatened, he no longer believed she was a shallow vixen, but a tender woman of deep, tormented depths.

But who had hurt her? A husband? A lover? Whoever the mongrel was deserved to be whipped.

He spotted Falco sitting on a campstool near the back wheel of the coach. A few paces away, a black iron pot hung from a tripod over a stone circle of dying embers.

As Quintus approached, the titan jumped to his

feet and offered a greeting. "Is all well? Before he and Rufus left to fetch bread, Otho said you and the lady were sparring."

"Everything is fine," Quintus said more sharply than he intended. He went to the wagon and began to assess its safety.

Falco stood and crossed to the fire. "It looks like we're in for a downpour today."

Quintus studied the stormy gray sky that matched his mood to perfection. "Excellent," he said drily. "All we need is rain to slow us down."

"You know," Falco said, not bothering to hide his amusement. "I warned you when you came to me about this mission that woman wasn't going to be easy. Truth to tell, I wasn't surprised to learn someone wants to kill the shrew."

"Why?" As always, the need to defend Adiona rose to the fore. "I'll grant you she's not meek or pliant, but from what I know of her, she's far from evil."

"She's worse." Falco stirred the pot. "She's the kind of woman who worms her way into a man's soul, then eats away at him little by little until there's nothing left except a hollow core."

Quintus opened the *raeda*'s back door and frowned. "So you think her assassin might be a rejected admirer?"

The snaggle-toothed gladiator scrubbed his bald head. "It's a possibility I'd consider. I've seen Her Highness parade around the *ludus* for years. She never once acknowledged the broken-hearted fools she left in her wake."

Quintus checked the seals on the water casks as he considered Falco's theory. "The widow's not to blame for any man's reaction to her."

"Perhaps not, but her face and form are a lure few men can or want to resist."

Suffering from his own bout of attraction to Adiona, Quintus rubbed the bunched muscles at the base of his neck.

"Given what she did to her husband," Falco continued, "the Fates might be amused to see that haughty wench brought down by a man she considered beneath her."

Quintus resisted asking about Adiona's husband, just as he refused to acknowledge the pinch of jealousy he experienced when he thought of her belonging to someone else.

"Word is she poisoned the poor fool she married—a good and honorable man," Falco said without prompting. "Then she bribed his lawyers to help her lay claim to his fortune."

"Enough of your gossip, Falco. I don't believe Adiona is capable of murder."

"I think she is," Falco disagreed mulishly. He took the iron pot from its hook and used a large wooden spoon to scoop the ruined porridge into the embers. "From all accounts, she has a heart made of brass. Even insults the master on occasion. I don't know why he puts up with it."

"From what I can tell, she and Caros are good friends."

"Yes, *very* good friends if what the men say is true."

"Falco, do you hear yourself? How can you say Adiona hates men on one hand, then paint her as a soon-to-be adulteress with the other?"

"Adiona?" Falco tipped his head to one side, his eyes narrowing. "Since when are you on a first-name basis with the woman?"

"I'm not." Quintus waved away the slip. "Caros is happily married and—"

"That doesn't mean she's given up on having him. For all we know she may have planned that attack in the street to regain his notice and his sympathy."

"Don't be insane." Quintus yanked on the rope tightening the wagon's canvas roof into place. He'd sought to choose intelligent as well as able-bodied men to guard Adiona. Falco was able enough, but to suspect the woman of planning her own assault was madness. He'd seen her directly after the attack. Her terror had been too real to be a hoax.

Even so, he couldn't dismiss the idea that Adiona wanted Caros for herself. He'd heard similar rumors among his own troupe since the first week of his arrival at the *ludus*. Her flirtation with Quintus had abruptly ended once Caros left for Umbria. If it wasn't the *lanista* she sought, why stop visiting the school? Alexius and the other trainers knew her well. No one cared to deny her entrance if she chose to attend the practice sessions.

He looked up from checking one of the back wheels to find Adiona and Onesimus crossing the open field. His pulse quickened. Even dressed in a slave's garb of gray wool, her head covered with a cloak she'd formed into a cowl, she embodied the grace and bearing of a queen…or a siren.

He forced himself to look away just to prove he possessed the ability, but her presence was a magnet stronger than his will.

His gaze slid back to find she'd stopped several paces from the coach. A gust of wind pushed back the cowl to reveal her flawless features and the yellowed bruise on her smooth cheek. The scrapes were healing

and her soft black hair was held back from her face
with wooden combs.

Eager to get her out of the open, he wiped the mud
from his hands with a rag, tossed it into a wooden
bucket and started forward.

Her sudden deathlike stillness warned him of im-
pending trouble. Her eyes were riveted to the *raeda*'s
open back door as if it were a trap waiting to be a
sprung or a snake about to strike. She seemed swept up
in another place and time, a living statue with a strand
of hair blowing like a glossy banner in the wind.

Quintus's long strides swallowed the distance to her
side. "My lady, what is it?"

"I… I can't get in the coach."

He took her icy hand in his. "You're trembling."

She tried to pull away, but he held firm. Glancing
over his shoulder, he located the source of alarm. The
raeda was an ordinary vehicle as far as he could tell,
a bit tattered in places, but not a monstrosity. "Why
does the coach distress you? Whatever it is, tell me.
I'll fix it for you."

"It's so small, so *confined*," she rasped. Her lovely
face was pale, her full lips pinched into a colorless line.
She tugged the cowl back into place, hiding. "The torture. I remember… I remember it all too well."

Torture? His chest tightened with compassion as the
mist clouding the situation began to clear. He should
have known no simple fear of the dark had the power
to intimidate a spirited woman like his lioness.

He led her to one of the olive trees, snapping up a
campstool on the way. Once she was settled, he ordered
his men to turn their backs and keep watch over their
small makeshift camp.

Certain the men were close enough to provide protection but out of earshot, he knelt before Adiona, one bare knee sinking into the layer of cool, damp leaves by her feet.

Breathing in the scent of cinnamon she favored, he took her hand, expecting her to flinch away. She held steady, her fingers bloodless from the tightness of her grip.

In that moment, the last sparks of anger he'd brought with him from her room died away, smothered by his need to soothe her. "My lady, you know you have to ride in the coach. There's no help for it."

"I *can't*." Her whole body quivered like the tree's slender branches overhead.

"It's not my intent to be cruel, but you must be aware you'll be safer out of sight. Not one of us will harm you, but out in the open you're an easy target if your enemy chooses to make a move."

"I'd rather be dead than locked away again." Her throat worked convulsively. "If I ride all the way to Ostia in that prison, I may keep my life, but I will *lose* my mind."

Convinced this was no display of temper or manipulative fit of feminine dramatics, Quintus weighed their options. Her previous reactions to being confined tipped the scale. "I'll take you back to Rome."

"Rome?" She sprang to her feet. "No! Octavia *needs* me."

He stood, calmly brushing sprigs of debris from his knee. "If you won't take shelter in the coach, then you'll have to ride with me on the driver's seat. Rome is two hours away. Ostia is ten. If you refuse to be hidden, you're going to be exposed for the shortest possible time."

Her brows puckered with the arguments forming in

her head. She began to pace. With each hectic step, the long wool tunic whipped around her shapely ankles and the straps of her plain leather sandals.

"Adiona, I won't debate this with you. I promised Caros—and you—I'd see you safely to Neopolis. If you won't let me do what I know to protect you, I'll return you to Caros and *he* can try to keep you out of danger."

"No. I won't be dictated to by a slave." She lifted her chin. "Neither does Caros make my choices for me. No man does."

"Perhaps one should if this is the kind of rash decision you make on your own."

Her shoulders straightened. "I'm not rash. I'm determined."

"You're as stubborn as a goat."

"You would know. After all, like recognizes like."

An involuntary smile tugged at his lips, but he promptly squelched it. The situation was too serious to find humor in any of it. "Woman, you are in danger. You must see reason."

"I'm not unreasonable. If you had ever experienced the death of a loved one—"

"Say no more. You know *nothing* about me." The death of his son was a bottomless well of grief in his chest, an open sore that refused to heal. "I'm acquainted with death as well as the next man."

"Then how can you deny my plea?"

"I'm willing to shoulder your anger, but I won't have your blood on my hands."

"You'll either do as I tell you or you can return to Rome on your own." She made a wide, sweeping gesture. "You chose these other guards. They can see me safely to my heir."

"You know I won't leave you here."

She shrugged. "It's your choice."

"I made my choice before we left Rome."

"Yes, and since you want your freedom *so* badly, I suggest you see me as far as Ostia. If it's any consolation, I won't burden you much longer. I already planned to send you back to Caros before my ship sailed."

Incredulous, he gripped her shoulders, barely suppressing the need to shake some sense into her. Fury fueled by a pain he didn't understand wrestled with his disbelief for supremacy inside him. He opened his mouth, ready to lay down the law, to inform her that *she* was in *his* care, not the other way around. But her horrified expression sent a wave of shame crashing over him. After years of learning to control his temper, he'd acted like a baited badger most of the morning.

"Release me." She slapped his hands away, her voice thick with equal measures of indignation and panic.

He let go of her instantly, dazed by his aggressive reaction when he could neither comprehend nor explain it.

Her color high, Adiona backed away until she bumped into the campstool he'd placed beside the tree trunk. He watched, fascinated, as she struggled to replace her fear with her favored mask of frigid disdain.

"Don't hide away from me," he said, silently promising to earn her trust. "I don't want you to be afraid."

Indecision notched her brows. Dark clouds rolled across the early-morning sky. "I'm always afraid," she admitted so softly he thought he'd misheard.

Her honesty surprised him, considering his behavior. "But you weren't afraid of me until now, were you?"

Her silent affirmation cut him to his core.

"Adiona, you must believe me," he said, his voice ragged with repentance. "I will *never* harm you no matter what happens between us."

She remained leery, but her expression lightened, seeming to give him the benefit of the doubt. "Tell me what happened. Why react as you did when I told you I planned to send you back to Rome? If you're worried about your freedom, you needn't be—"

"My freedom isn't what concerns me at the moment. I want it, don't misunderstand, but the thought of you plotting to rid yourself of me is more than I can stomach."

Her amber eyes clouded with confusion. "I know you're convinced I need you—"

"No," he interrupted, realizing she was the first person to matter to him since the death of his son. "*I* need *you*. I must know you're safe before I can rest or have any peace."

"I don't understand. You barely tolerate me."

A humorless laugh clogged his throat. She had no idea how he felt about her. How could she when he was so conflicted himself? He was far from inexperienced with women. He thought he'd met her kind before, but he was wrong. Never had he met a woman who called to his heart and soul the way she did. The longer he spent with Adiona the more he realized how unique she was; the more he wished to claim her for his own. But other than prayer, he had nothing to offer her.

He glanced skyward, noting the advance of more storm clouds as he searched for the right words to explain himself. Save Caros and Pelonia, he'd told no one about his son or wife's death, and then only out of necessity. He rubbed the back of his neck and swallowed deep, determined to make Adiona see why he wanted to stay with her, to protect her.

"The day before my arrest," he said, his voice roughened with grief even though he sought to sound emotionless, "I had business in a neighboring town. I was gone overnight. When I returned home, I learned my only son was dead, trampled by a runaway chariot. In her grief, my wife had committed suicide a few hours later."

Adiona gasped. "I'm *so* sorry," she whispered.

He closed the space between them. "Don't you see? I wasn't there to protect my family—"

"Their deaths weren't your fault," she assured him. Her hesitant fingers cupped his cheek. "You're *not* to blame, Quintus."

Longing to believe her, he closed his eyes, absorbing the bittersweetness of her touch. Grateful for the comfort she offered when most of his friends and family had deserted him, he covered her hand with his larger one and brushed her fingertips with his lips. "What I'm trying to say—not very well, I admit—is that even though I failed to protect my family, I believe God has brought you into my life to give me a second chance. I refuse to disappoint Him...or you."

She slipped her hand from his and bowed her head, fidgeting with the edge of her cloak. "I understand your concerns and I'm grateful you believe your God cares enough to send you to me, but time may be running out. If you mean to be my protector, so be it. I want no other. But be warned, if I have to walk to Neopolis, I will. I'm not going back to Rome until after I've seen Octavia."

Frustrated, irritated, *afraid* for Adiona, Quintus sought to change her mind one last time. "Why? I understand she's your friend. It's admirable you care for her, but with your own life at stake, why *must* you go?"

"Octavia needs me...if she's still alive. And if she's passed into the afterlife, she needs me even more."

He threw the end of his cape over his shoulder to ward off the morning's chill. "How so?"

She plucked an olive leaf off the tree next to her. Her slender fingers quivered as she tore it apart and pitched the pieces aside. "I know my heir. Drusus is an ignorant miser who won't do the right things to see that Octavia isn't forced to wander unhappily throughout eternity."

She picked and decimated another leaf before tossing the remains to the wind. "Drusus will skimp on hiring mourners, he'll cut the number of visitation days to save having to feed the guests. He's even crass enough to steal the coin from Octavia's mouth without regard for how she'll cross the River Styx with no gold to pay the ferryman."

Her expression wilted into tragedy. "You have to understand. Octavia was a lovely hostess—she never gossiped or hurt anyone. She was the kindest mother, faithful, virtuous, always spoke well of even the most undeserving creature. She was ideal in every way. In life she was chained to Drusus, but in death she deserves a grand procession and a vaulted place in Elysium. If I leave matters in Drusus's incapable hands, he's liable to toss Octavia onto a pyre as if she were rubbish just so he can return to his wine and mistress."

Quintus scanned the dwindling number of travelers in the open field. The inn looked empty and abandoned against the backdrop of the dark gray sky stretching out to eternity.

Adiona's commitment to the mission she'd set for herself was admirable. Far from being self-centered as he'd once thought, she was as loyal and true a friend as he had ever come across. Her concern for the defenseless Octavia resounded through him like a flash of lightning. All the harsh uncertainty of not knowing if his own son had been properly buried rose up to choke him.

Fabius. He closed his eyes, driving back the pain that welled in his chest until his ribs ached. How could he condemn Adiona to even a tithe of his own suffering when the journey to Neopolis *was* possible?

"I'll take you." The approaching storm carried a sense of foreboding Quintus couldn't quite shake despite his belief in God's protection. "But if you're going to ride in the open, for your own safety, you must promise to do as I say."

Her face brightened with a smile that knocked the breath from his lungs. "I'm out of practice when it comes to obeying men. But for you, Quintus, I'm willing to negotiate."

Chapter Eight

Adiona shifted on the driver's bench next to Quintus. Several hours of bone-rattling road travel made her long for the ship they planned to board in Ostia. A cold rain had started within a mile of their departure from the *tabernae*. Dark clouds continued to lurk above them. The pelts Quintus gathered from the back of the coach and insisted she use for cover sheltered her from the constant drizzle.

"Tell me more about your heir," Quintus said, flicking the reins. "He seems the most likely candidate to hire assassins. Caros and I agree he has the most to gain from your death."

"I don't think he's guilty. He knows he'd be the first suspect." She shrugged. "Besides, he's aware he'll be disinherited if I die under mysterious circumstances."

Quintus cast her a sidelong glance. "How insightful of you."

"Once you meet Drusus you'll understand my caution. He has a small intellect, but he's as poisonous as the vipers he collects."

A silky black brow arched in question. "Your heir collects snakes?"

"Yes, repulsive, isn't it?" She shivered, but not from the cold. "The more exotic and toxic the creature, the more he prizes it."

"Why did you choose an heir you abhor?"

She watched the road ahead as she considered whether she'd have to divulge her past to give him an accurate answer.

Falco rode in the lead. Every so often the big gladiator ventured ahead to assess the route and look for any ambush. Otho and Rufus flanked each side of the coach, while Onesimus brought up the rear.

A rut in the road tossed her sideways into Quintus's unyielding shoulder. His long fingers gripped her arm as he steadied her. He jerked his hand back, as though touching her caused him acute discomfort. Sadness settled over her. Why did he find her so repellent?

She cleared her throat. "Drusus is my cousin and last, although distantly related, relative. He is a drunk and as trustworthy as a thief in a gold mine. I didn't choose him as my heir for his own merits. He has none. But as much as I loathe him, I love Octavia and their three daughters. I would have made Octavia or the girls my heirs, but Drusus had to do because he holds all legal rights over them."

Quintus's brows drew together as he considered the information. "If you were gone, who's to say Drusus would honor your wishes and share your fortune with his children?"

"Before I made him my heir, he agreed to bestow a handsome portion on each of the girls. He signed contracts and my lawyers will see the matter is carried out as I desire."

"Unless you perish by questionable means?"

She gripped the side of the bench as the carriage

swayed like a lumbering elephant. "Yes. In that case, Caros will inherit. He's promised me each of the children will receive a third of my wealth once she marries and Drusus no longer controls her."

"Why not cut out Drusus altogether and make Caros your heir in the first place?"

"Because of Octavia. There's nothing I can do to see that she inherits directly, but it was…*is* my hope that if Drusus gained my fortune, she'd benefit in *some* way."

"You're a good friend, my lady."

Warmed more by his compliment than the thick furs wrapped around her, she looked at him through the veil of her lashes. Her breath feathered in her throat and stopped altogether as she fell into a penetrating gaze the color of rare green glass.

"Quintus," Falco called, drawing his horse alongside them. "This stretch of road seems quiet enough. I'm going on up ahead. I'll return within half an hour."

"Fine," Quintus said, dragging his attention to the fierce gladiator. "Make note if you see a decent spot for us to rest."

With a nod, Falco left. Rain splashed on the road's stone pavers, nearly drowning out the clip-clop of horse's hooves and the rattle of the coach.

Olive and cyprus trees lined both sides of the road. The sky stretched in an endless foreboding pattern of dark gray clouds and filtered light. Occasionally travelers headed in the opposite direction nodded or waved as they passed by, but the weather discouraged any verbal contact.

Quintus didn't seem to mind the lack of conversation. Except for a few remarks to his men, he remained silent, his eyes focused on the course in front of them. His large hands deftly managed the reins.

Drowsy from lack of sleep the previous night, Adiona held on to the driver's bench and fought to stay awake. The temptation to lean against Quintus beckoned her like a fire on a cold night. She resisted, certain he'd resent the task of holding her even if he didn't push her away.

"What?" Her head jerked up and her eyes snapped open as strong fingers gripped her upper arm.

"You fell asleep," Quintus told her. "You almost toppled off the bench."

"I'm sorry," she whispered, her eyelids as heavy as stones.

"You didn't sleep enough last night."

"More than you."

He shrugged. "I haven't slept well in months. Are you sure you don't prefer to rest in the back of the coach? You'll be more comfortable."

"No," she said with a vigorous shake of her head.

He sighed. "Then come here." Somehow he managed to hold her steady as he adjusted his right arm around her shoulders. The pelt he'd wrapped around himself encircled her, creating a warm, protective bubble.

Snuggled against him, she ignored the scratch of his tunic beneath her cheek and breathed in his spicy scent. The sway of the coach lulled her into a peaceful half-dream state where Quintus brushed a kiss across her temple and whispered gentle words like, "Sleep, my lioness, I'll keep you safe."

The reins in his left hand, Quintus held Adiona close with his right arm. He understood she wasn't a woman who relied easily on others. The unintentional glimpses she'd given of her past revealed she had good reason to be wary. That she placed her confidence in him at a time when he trusted himself least of all, both honored and humbled him.

The rain had lessened to a sprinkle. The damp wool of his garb had rubbed him raw along the neckline. Not for the first time, he promised himself he'd buy a trunkful of soft linen tunics the same day he regained his freedom.

He consulted the mile marker as they passed by. A mere eight miles—about four hours if all went well—until they reached Ostia.

Falco should have returned long ago. A mix of concern and apprehension crawled up the back of his neck. The possibility that something nefarious had happened to the gladiator on his latest circuit couldn't be discounted. But after their conversation this morning, Quintus realized Falco was far from sympathetic to Adiona's plight—an opinion he'd taken great pains to hide before they'd left Rome.

As he always did, Quintus prayed for wisdom and for the truth to come to light. He clung to his faith, striving to believe God held them in His capable hands. Yet an insidious voice in the back of his mind refused to let him forget the Lord had ignored his prayers for his son's safety and good health.

Now Fabius was dead.

What if God took Adiona, as well? His arm tightened around her slim form. He broke out in a cold sweat as rising fear warred with his faith. Endless torment-filled moments passed before his belief in God's mercy won out.

Guilt snaked through him. Empty and wary, Quintus knew the Lord deserved more trust than he had to give. Fabius's death had marooned him on an island of despair. He knew in his head the facts of faith—God had a plan for everyone who gave their life to Him, but that knowledge wouldn't bring his son back to life or keep Adiona with him if He chose to take her down a different path.

"Quintus." Otho drew up alongside the coach. "Falco seems gone overlong, no?"

Snapped out of his bleak thoughts, Quintus nodded. "The same occurred to me."

The younger man looked away, shamefaced. "I didn't mention it before because I didn't believe he was serious…now I have to reconsider."

"What is it?" Quintus demanded. He drew back on the reins, slowing the horses to a stop. Otho followed suit while Onesimus and Rufus allowed their horses to drink from the ditch beside the road.

"Is the lady asleep?"

Quintus angled a glance at Adiona. She raised her hand to rest in the center of his chest. Her delicate fingertips stuck out from under the pelt covering the rest of her hand and arm. A slight smile curved her lips as she sighed and snuggled closer. Protective instincts surged through him. His heart thundered with tender emotions and yearnings so powerful it was as though Adiona was the reason his heart beat at all.

"Quintus? Is she sleeping?"

Stunned by the depths of his feelings for her, he tore his gaze away from Adiona and pinned Otho with a glare. "Yes, she is. What can you tell me?"

Otho's eyes shifted nervously. "Falco went drinking after you relieved him from guard duty last night. I guess he'd had a few mugs too many when he approached me and Rufus at our post on the steps."

"And?" Quintus prompted when the younger man hesitated. "What did he say?"

"He said we ought to kidnap the lady ourselves and demand a king's ransom because she's worth a fortune. He said she deserved to be shaken up a bit after what she did to her husband."

The horses nickered and stomped their feet as though they sensed Quintus's fury.

"Of course we told him we weren't interested," Otho assured him in a rush. "Falco tried to laugh it off like he was joking, but…"

"Now he's disappeared," Quintus said, his rage brewing. "For all we know he joined the lady's enemies and the lot of them are lying in wait up ahead."

Otho nodded gravely.

A million thoughts vied for precedence in Quintus's mind. He swiftly shifted through the mire, deciding the best course to keep Adiona safe. "You and Rufus switch places with the lady and me. She and I will ride the rest of the way and meet up with the three of you in Ostia. Give us an hour's lead. If anyone *is* waiting to attack us they'll be expecting the coach, not looking for their prey to be on horseback."

Otho nodded and went to explain the situation to the other pair of guards. Quintus tied off the reins.

"My lady, wake up." He shook her gently. The cloak fell back, revealing her mussed hair and unraveling braid. The thick black curve of her eyelashes rested against a soft ivory cheek. He ran his fingertip along her delicate jawbone and across the pout of her full bottom lip.

"Quintus."

The way she whispered his name in her sleep made his pulse speed. He resented having to give up the pleasure of holding her. "Adiona, we must leave."

Her eyes fluttered open and she blinked several

times as she took in the wooded area to the left of the road and the lemon grove on the right. "Where are we?"

"Less than eight miles to Ostia."

She clutched his arm beneath the pelt and pushed herself into a full sitting position. "What's happened? Why have we stopped?"

Quintus rapidly apprised her of the situation. "It's unconventional, I know, but can you ride?"

Pale and distraught, she nodded and swallowed hard. "What did I do to make Falco wish to harm me?"

"You did nothing." He jumped down from the coach and raised his hands to help her down from the driver's bench.

She placed her hands on his shoulders. Her brow creased with disbelief. "I must have done something."

"He wants money." He placed her on the ground beside him. "You're not responsible for his greed."

Otho cleared his throat nearby. "My lady, Quintus is right. You're not to blame. Falco's excuse to ransom you is based on rumors and—"

"Enough, Otho," Quintus warned. "We've no more time to waste on speculation."

"I want to hear the rest," Adiona said stubbornly.

Quintus clenched his jaw. "I'll tell you later. Otho, bring me your horse."

Irritated by Quintus's high-handed behavior, Adiona swore to learn the truth. All her life people had blamed her for the pain they caused her until sometimes she believed she *deserved* to be hurt. But Falco was different. Until they'd left Rome yesterday, she'd never even spoken to the monster.

Otho brought his mount forward, then returned to help Rufus gather a few supplies from the back of the coach. Adiona patted the horse's sleek brown neck and introduced herself.

Quintus chuckled. "Don't expect Spiro to understand you. He's one of Caros's Spanish geldings. I doubt he speaks much Latin."

She grinned and repeated herself in the Iberian tongue.

"Impressive, my lady. Are there other languages you speak?"

"Yes, two German dialects and Greek, but don't tell Alexius." Mischief sparkled in her amber eyes. "I find it humorous when he rattles on in his native tongue thinking no one understands him."

Quintus laughed. "Your secret is safe with me."

"I knew I could trust you the first moment I saw you."

The admission caught him off guard, and judging by the rising color in her cheeks, she'd surprised herself, as well.

Of course, he remembered their first meeting—if indeed it could be called a meeting. He'd been at the *ludus* only a matter of weeks. Still weak and skeletal after his arrest and time in prison, he'd seen her enter the stands overlooking the practice field. She'd worn blue, her hair piled on her head and anchored with gold clips. To a man desperate for release from bondage in the hot dry sands of a gladiator school, she'd reminded him of the sky, fresh air and life-sustaining water.

He cleared his throat. "Your father must have prized you to make certain you were well educated."

She turned her attention back to Spiro and straightened the pelt beneath the four-horned saddle. "I had my share of tutors. One taught me Greek, in fact. The other languages I learned from the slaves."

"Then I'm doubly impressed by your intelligence. I had tutors and foreigners in my house, yet I learned only passable Greek."

"I'm not surprised. You seem like you'd be a lazy student."

Seeing she teased him, he arched his eyebrow in mock seriousness. "I preferred other subjects."

"Such as? Chasing women—?"

"Philosophy and—"

"Wine tasting—?"

"Mathematics." He frowned at her. "I also enjoyed learning the intricacies of trade."

"I see," she said.

"What?"

"You've always been a serious man. That makes me feel better."

"Why?" he asked suspiciously.

"Because I feared I'm the only person you scowl at. Now I understand frowning is a natural talent in which you excel."

His lips quirked with a smile.

He gripped her slim waist and lifted her into the saddle. Her tunic rode up above her knees as she swung her leg over the pummels and straddled the horse. Seeing the wealth of supple limbs, he stifled a groan and sought refuge from temptation in the mundane task of checking his own mount.

"Perhaps I ought to leave my legs uncovered—"

"No!" Quintus croaked. The brief glimpse of her shapely calves was etched indelibly in his mind.

"Why ever not?" she asked in an innocent tone. "Onlookers will think I'm a man."

"No, they won't."

"A boy, then?"

He shook his head, desperate for a lifeline as though he were drowning. He massaged the bunched muscles at the back of his neck. "You'll fool no one. Nothing about you is remotely male. Now cover up."

Snippets of the other guards' conversation near the wagon filled the silence. The gray midday sky had darkened again with the promise of more rain. "You know, Quintus, you're awfully dictatorial for a slave."

The reminder of his lowered status should have rankled. Instead, her censure made him laugh. "My friends usually call me commanding."

She gave an inelegant snort. Fabric rustled as she arranged her billowy cloak. "I'm ready," she said.

He turned, relieved to find her covered from head to toe in ugly gray wool.

"Tell me the truth." She readjusted the cowl. "What chance do we really have to slip past Falco and his cohorts?"

"We'll be fine." He glanced at the other gladiators a short distance away. "I've told no one of our change of plans, but there is a side road you and I will follow to Ostia." He handed her her satchel. Intrigued by the sheen on the underside of her cloak, Quintus reached for the upturned edge of the garment. "What's this?"

"Silk. I had all my wool clothing lined with it. Why should I have to mar my skin just because some hateful miscreant wants me dead?"

He shook his head, incredulous.

"I suppose this proves to you I'm spoiled and vain beyond redemption?"

"No one's beyond redemption." He rubbed the soft cloth between his thumb and fingers, its smooth texture the same as Adiona's creamy skin. "Truthfully, I admire your foresight."

A wry smile crossed her lips. "I don't know if it was wise or not, but if I'm killed at least I'll die comfortable."

On the outskirts of Ostia the secondary road Quintus and Adiona travelled merged with the Ostian Way. Traffic began to thicken and slow as pedestrians, chariots, litters and oxcarts competed for the quickest entrance into the walled city. The clack of wheels, horses' hooves and human chatter mixed with mooing cows and the distressed bleats of disgruntled sheep.

Food stalls lined both sides of the congested road, filling the air with the pungent aromas of spices, smoked meats and fish sauce.

Inside the city walls, Quintus took the reins of Adiona's horse and led them through the lively grid of streets toward the port district.

"I have friends who own a *tabernae* down by the shore," Quintus said. "They have a large family to help me keep watch over you and each room has a window with a view of the sea. I think you'll like it."

Darkness was descending by the time they stabled their horses and walked to the waterfront. The *Mare Internum* stretched to the horizon on their right. Waves crashed against the seawall, spewing foam high into the air. The sinking sun splashed bright flames of red and gold across the deep blue sky. Anchored sailing ships dotted the liquid expanse, their sails and oars put to rest for the night.

"There it is." Quintus pointed to a stout, tile-roofed building of whitewashed cement. Long wooden tables and chairs had been brought out into the street in front of the two-story structure, creating a makeshift terrace. A young boy was busy lighting oil lamps on each table where a crowd of jovial patrons shared huge bowls overflowing with prawns and fried squid.

Inside the main dining room someone strummed a *cithara*. The soft music drifted aimlessly toward the four windows evenly spaced along the second floor. A flower box dripping with bougainvillea and sweet-smelling jasmine hung beneath each of the open arches.

Another servant brought out two large platters of oysters. She set them on separate tables and wiped her hands on her apron. Petite and curvaceous with thick dark hair, the girl interacted easily with the guests. She balanced a stack of dirty platters on one arm and swatted overly familiar male hands even as she seemed to catalog customers' requests in her head.

"That young lady is Josephina." Quintus quickened the pace, his excitement over a reunion with his friends obvious. "Her parents, Joseph and Sapphira, own the *tabernae*."

"What is everyone looking at?" Adiona clutched his arm. The majority of customers seemed focused on something out to sea. She glanced over her shoulder, interested to learn what held their attention. A dark moonless sky stretched into oblivion.

All of a sudden the group clapped and cheered as one. Some of the patrons whistled, a few others rattled tambourines. She looked to Quintus, confused. "What happened? What's the clamor about?"

"It's a long-standing tradition. Every night people gather to celebrate the exact moment the sun goes down."

"Ah, they must be followers of Apollo. Do they come out each morning to see his chariot rise, as well?"

"Some," he said evasively. "Not all."

"Do you suppose a few of them are *Christians?*"

she asked just to see his reaction. Ever since Caros told her Quintus belonged to the illegal sect, she'd been intrigued by his choice of religion.

"Possibly."

She could tell by the way he stiffened she'd surprised him with the question, but he kept up his pace without missing a step.

Josephina recognized Quintus the moment he stepped into the circle of light surrounding the front of the building. Her expression filled with wonder and she squealed his name. The dirty dishes she held clattered as she dumped them on a nearby table. She flew across the space between them and launched herself into Quintus's arms, pushing Adiona out of the way.

Josephina promptly burst into tears. "Lucius told us you were dead! I cried and cried for you," she said between muffled sobs. "Praise Jesus you've returned to us!"

Praise Jesus? Adiona's interest perked. More Christians? Who was Lucius?

"It's all right, little one." Quintus stroked the girl's hair. "The Lord saw fit to keep me alive. It was only a matter of time before I came back for a visit."

Adiona noticed the bemused glances some of the customers cast toward Quintus and the girl. She turned her back on them and angled her body as best she could to provide Quintus with a modicum of privacy.

Josephina finally stopped crying and stepped back, wiping her eyes with the edge of her tunic. She clasped Quintus's hand and tugged him toward the *tabernae*'s front door. "Come, we have to let Mother and Father know you're here. They're going to be so happy."

"Wait." He untangled his fingers from the girl's. "Josephina, this is Adiona Leonia."

Josephina's smile dimmed. She perused Adiona from head to foot, taking in the dusty, road-weary garb. Her mouth tightened into a straight line. "Are you Quintus's new servant?"

Adiona gasped. "No! He's my—"

"Friend," Quintus interrupted swiftly. He frowned at Josephina. "And you'll be nice if you know what's good for you, brat."

Adiona recognized the competitive light in Josephina's dark eyes. Other females perpetually saw Adiona as a rival in spite of her well-earned reputation as a man-hater. Until that moment, she'd never understood a woman's need to fight for her man, but the girl's silent challenge set Adiona's teeth on edge. She clutched Quintus's arm and, as she'd seen other women do when declaring battle, staked her own claim.

Half an hour later a steady stream of Josephina's family had come to see for themselves that Quintus was alive and well. Much sympathy was offered for his wife's death and tears were shed for his son.

Adiona watched events from the sidelines. The women wept all over Quintus, while the men thumped him on the back until his entire torso must be bruised. Joseph, the family's patriarch, was a short, curly haired Jew from Palestine. He helpfully sent servants to find Otho and Adiona's other guards. Joy reigned and the entire *tabernae* seemed to sigh with contentment.

Having never enjoyed the warmth of a familial bond, Adiona found the commotion made over Quintus sweetly amusing. The news of his arrest had been tragic for his friends, his safe return a cause for celebration and prayers of thanksgiving. It occurred to her that if her enemies succeeded in their plans, no one would care if she were gone, but Quintus's friends genuinely loved him. She understood why. He was a good man, the very *best* man she'd ever met. Steadfast, kind, gentle and true to his word, he personified honor.

His tolerant expression as yet-another female fussed over him released a wellspring of tender emotions she hadn't known was buried inside her. Raw and over-powered by the ferocity of her ill-timed epiphany, she blinked back the sting of tears. She sought out a quiet corner as far away from the reunion as possible without drawing undue attention.

Eventually, Sapphira shooed away the last few relatives and drew Adiona back toward Quintus. "Now you two must eat." The tiny Greek lady bustled each of them into a chair in a quiet alcove of the main dining room. Candles flickered on well-scrubbed table-tops. Adiona's mouth watered from the scents of roast fish and fresh herbs.

"I realize my family can be a bit much." Sapphira smiled proudly. "I've told everyone to leave you alone and let you breathe. Of course, Josephina won't listen because Quintus is hers, but the others will heed my warning."

Adiona watched Sapphira scurry away to fetch a loaf of bread, a flurry of orders to the servants flying in her wake. The musician strummed his *cithara* and the melodious notes drifted through the dining room like the sea breeze, blending with the low murmur of conversation.

Curious and more disturbed by Sapphira's claim than she cared to admit, Adiona leaned back in the chair. "So, Quintus, what did she mean you *belong* to Josephina?"

Chapter Nine

Quintus leaned forward, his elbows on the arms of the chair, his long fingers clasped loosely between his body and the table. Here among Christian brothers and sisters who knew him as more than a slave, he felt rejuvenated.

Through the front window he glimpsed a group of merry diners outside on the street beneath the star-filled sky. He returned his attention to Adiona's expectant face, the loveliest sight in the room—no, the entire city. "Why do you want to know about Josephina? Are you jealous?"

"Of that…that hussy?" she scoffed, glancing away. "Don't be ridiculous."

"That's good to know." His tone took on a sharp edge. "But I'd appreciate a little respect for that 'hussy' because I happen to love her dearly."

Her gaze swung back to his. "Love?" she whispered.

"Of course," he said, unable to credit her stricken expression. "She's lively, charming, lovely—"

"And a Christian?" Adiona injected with a sour twist of her lips.

Quintus hesitated. He didn't care who knew about

his own beliefs. It was no secret he'd been condemned to die because of them. But he wasn't prepared to give Adiona, a pagan woman with vast civic connections in Rome, any information about his loved ones.

"You needn't go all silent and brooding," she said, regaining some of her color. "I won't expose your friends. Caros told me months ago you're one of those deviants and your secret has been safe with me ever since."

He relaxed and leaned back in his chair. "A deviant, huh?"

"Yes, and I can't believe you corrupted *Caros,* of all people, to your odd little sect."

He laughed. "Caros is a contented man since he found his way to the Lord."

"It would seem so," she said, mystified. "But some of that is due to Pelonia's influence, I'm sure. I didn't like Pelonia at first," she mused. "I thought she seemed rather weak and insipid. I still don't know her well, but after the way she handled me…following the attack Friday night, I realize she has the spine of iron she'll need to keep Caros in order."

Sapphira returned with a basket of bread, a shallow dish of olive oil and a short stack of colorful ceramic plates. Her easy laughter and sparkling eyes proclaimed her happiness over Quintus's return from the grave. "Watch your fingers, the loaf is fresh from the oven. Don't burn yourself," she added as she hastened to the next table.

Quintus reached for the bread. He tore one of the crusty loaves in two. Steam rose from the soft center. He offered the first half to Adiona. A subtle shock of sensation danced across his skin when their fingers touched, tempting him to drop the bread and simply hold her hand.

"I agree about Pelonia's effect on Caros," he said, steering their conversation back on course. "She's an excellent woman and an intelligent man values a good wife above all the riches in the world."

Her expression went blank. Her thick lashes fluttered down. Her slender fingers absently shredded the bread. "Did you love your wife that much, Quintus?"

Soft music filled the lull. He was grateful for the distraction when Josephina brought mugs of water and a chalice of new wine for each of them. She lingered by their table, sharing bits of news, until another customer called her away. He noticed Josephina's cold manner toward Adiona and he didn't care for it. He'd have a talk with the younger girl later.

Quintus lifted the chalice to his lips, stalling for more time. Given a choice, he never spoke of Faustina. A husband was always supposed to honor his wife with praise, especially after her death. Not given to lying, he considered it for the first time in years, then quickly rejected the notion. There was enough darkness and ambiguity between him and Adiona. At least in this he could offer some light.

He swallowed a mouthful of sweet nectar and cleared his throat. "I'm ashamed to say I never loved her, although I did try. Faustina and I were wed as part of a business agreement. We were supposed to bring peace to our rival families, but we were ill suited from the start."

Sapphira appeared with a huge tray of fragrant fish roasted with lemons and capers. "This is Quintus's favorite." Seemingly oblivious to the tension in the air, she winked at Quintus, then whispered in an aside to Adiona. "I once watched in amazement while he ate a whole swordfish by himself."

Adiona laughed politely at the jest, but there was no real humor in her eyes. Sapphira left, pulled along by the needs of her other customers. Adiona busied herself cutting the tender fish. He suspected he'd shocked her with his honesty. "Did I offend you, my lady?"

"Offend me?" She set down the knife. "How? By telling me the truth?"

He nodded.

"No," she said. "I always prefer the truth, but it's rare to hear and often more difficult to address than lies."

The music shifted tempo to become a whisper in the background. Using her fingers, Adiona raised a bite of the fish to her lips. She closed her eyes, savoring the earthy flavors of herbs and citrus.

Watching her, Quintus stopped breathing. With every moment and action, she became somehow more fascinating. She opened her eyes and smiled at him, her amber gaze bright with satisfaction. "The fish is delicious. No wonder it's your favorite."

"Yes." He cleared his throat and drank deeply from his chalice. "Joseph's men went to find Otho and the others," he said, hungry for a change of topic. "God willing, we'll all leave at first sail tomorrow. You'll arrive in Neopolis by noon."

"Just as you planned," she said woodenly. "I still think it's a good idea for you to see me to the ship tomorrow and then return to Rome."

"No. I won't discuss that nonsense again." He almost laughed at her reaction to his decree. If she were a child, she would have stuck her tongue out at him. As it was, she took another bite of fish and glanced away, her nose stuck in the air.

He studied her. She wasn't the Roman matron he'd first seen at the *ludus*. Gone was the gilded peacock.

Travel-worn, she looked embattled and exhausted, but still beautiful enough to make him ache for her.

She reached for her mug of water. "Who is Lucius?"

"My younger twin brother." He reached for his own bite of fish.

"I overheard you discussing him with Joseph."

"Yes, I'm pleased to learn he passed by here on his way down the coast."

"Do you plan to look for him?"

"I'd like to."

"What are we going to do if the men don't return or can't be found tonight?"

"Joseph's two older sons will guard your door upstairs. I'll stay down here beneath your window."

"When will you sleep?"

He shrugged. "Tomorrow. We're going to hire a private boat. There's no way your enemies will be on board. I'll nap on deck."

"I don't like it," she said, meeting his eyes. "I'm going to stay awake tonight down here with you."

"No, that's ridiculous."

She frowned. "I see."

"What?"

"You want privacy with Josephina."

He laughed. "She's just a child."

"How old is she?"

Still chuckling, he shrugged. "Fifteen."

"I was twelve when my father married me off to a man twice your age."

The news sobered him instantly. Wedding a child to a man in his fifties wasn't unheard of, but that didn't make the practice any less repellant. "It's not like that between Josephina and me."

"Then how is it? Even her mother says you *belong*

to the girl. Don't think I didn't notice how you avoided my question when I asked about the *child* earlier."

He released a deep breath. "I'm a merchant by trade, Adiona. A successful one…at least I was until my arrest. My business brought me to the port here in Ostia at least four times a year. Seven years ago, when I was twenty, I found this *tabernae*. Joseph and Sapphira's kindness drew me back again and again. They shared their faith in Christ with me and led me to the Lord."

"I thought Joseph was a Jew," she said.

"He is. He believes Jesus is the Messiah foretold by the Hebrew Prophets."

She picked at her bread, thoughtful. "You were arrested for your religion, were you not? Did you know what it would cost you to believe in your Jesus?"

"At the time… I suppose not."

"And now that you're a condemned man?"

He combed his fingers through his hair. "I'd do it all the same."

"I don't understand, Quintus. Why can't you believe in a god that won't see you thrown into the arena?"

He tried not to smile. "I believe my God is the one true and living God. He isn't interchangeable."

"But I don't want you to die," she whispered.

Something deep inside him shifted, like a broken bone set back into place. For months he'd been too despondent to care if he was alive or dead, but Adiona's concern breathed new life into his veins. "Don't worry. I don't plan to die anytime soon."

Adiona's attention turned to Sapphira who was laughing with a patron at a table nearby. "She and Joseph are lovely. Sapphira reminds me of Octavia. She's open and kind. It's plain to see why you love them— even Josephina," she added grudgingly.

"Yes, I consider them as much a part of my family as my blood kin, perhaps more so. Josephina came along to them late in life, the only daughter after half a dozen sons. She's young and well-loved. I'll even concede she *may* be a little bit spoiled."

Adiona snorted. "More than a little."

He grinned. "When she was eight years old, I stopped here on the way to my villa farther down the coast. She crawled in my lap and proclaimed I was hers. The family finds it amusing and it's a running joke. But believe me, regardless of how she feels, I think of her as a little sister, nothing else."

"Then why can't I stay with you?"

"You need to sleep."

"Shall I remind you, that *you* are my protector? I don't like being surrounded by strange men."

"I'll be right here. If you need me just call out your window." He didn't consider Joseph's sons "strange men." Obviously, Adiona did. Then again, she was known for her hatred of the opposite sex. When had that loathing begun? "After all your questions of me tonight, do you mind if I ask you one of my own?"

She shifted on her chair uncomfortably. "That depends."

"How long were you married?"

Her mouth tightened. "Six years."

"Were you content?"

"That's two questions, Quintus."

He waited. The hour was growing late and the throng of diners began to thin. She pushed a piece of bread around her plate with the tip of her index finger. "No, I was far from content."

Just as he'd thought. How much of her fears stemmed from her marriage? When she finally met his gaze, he knew he should seek a different topic, but when his mouth opened he found himself asking, "Was your husband the brute who hurt you?"

She gasped as though he'd stabbed her. Her color high, she closed her eyes, then nodded once. Her chair scraped on the cement floor as she stood and fled.

Taken aback by her sudden flight, he followed her outside, past the few empty tables left to be stored away for the night. Her swift steps carried her across the street and the short distance to the seawall.

He stopped a few paces behind her and scraped his hand through his hair. He should change the subject, he realized, but a rampant need to know every facet of her being drove him on. "Adiona, what happened? I have an idea, but I'd like you to tell me for certain."

"Why are you doing this?" She swung around to face him. Bitterness flowed off her in waves. The shadows hid all but her strained eyes, the tip of her nose and the curve of her stubborn chin. "You've no great affection for me. No reason to care."

She couldn't be more wrong. He'd spent months fighting her hold on him, desperately trying to convince himself his attraction was no more than a carnal reaction to a beautiful woman. But every day, every hour he spent in her company wore away his resistance until his mind was forced to accept what his heart already knew.

He loved her.

Restive tension sparked between them. He had no more fight in him where his feelings for her were concerned. She burned like a fever in his blood—a fever that his prayers, his reason and the lessons of his past had all failed to cure.

Pulse racing, he stepped closer until they almost

touched. Every nerve in his body begged him to take her in his arms, to kiss and hold her until he'd convinced her she loved him, too.

Instead, he placed a gentle hand on her shoulder. She trembled. The pad of his thumb brushed the soft silken skin below her ear, the one concession he made to his craving to touch her. "I care, Adiona. I want to help you."

"I don't *need* help," she said with stony insistence.

"Then you're the only soul in Creation who doesn't."

Between the starlight and the faint lamplight from the *tabernae* behind them, he saw her eyes close. "What's to tell?" she whispered. "I was married to a beast who tortured me almost every day for six years."

Even worse than he'd suspected.

"He kept you in a small room."

"A cage."

Pain knifed him through the heart. Taking him by surprise, she folded into him, unaware she inflicted her own brand of torture when she pressed innocently against him. His heart hammering, his breathing constricted, he wrapped his arms around her, not from a selfish desire to hold her, but because she needed his comfort.

"I *hated* him," she murmured against his chest. A tremor rippled through her slender body.

"Understandable." He pressed a kiss to the top of her head. "Did you poison him?"

"What?" she gasped, leaning back.

"That is the rumor, the reason Falco used to justify his plan to ransom you."

"I didn't poison Crassus." She pulled away. Arms wrapped protectively about her waist, she leaned back against the seawall, her tall, slender body as taut as an oar. Wrapped in the darkness, it was as if they were the only two people on some long-deserted island. "By the gods, I wish I *had* had the mettle to murder him. Believe me, I'd have chosen something more painful than poison. And I wouldn't have waited six long years to finish him off."

Unable to blame her for wanting freedom from an abuser, he wished there was some way to erase the anguish from her memory. "I'm sorry," he said. "I'm sorry you endured such grief. But not all men are fiends. Perhaps someday you'll remarry—"

"No!" she spat vehemently. "I will *never* marry again. I will *never* risk my freedom or give a man control over me."

"What if you loved him?"

She shook her head, pale and rife with denial. "Not even then."

Loud voices and a commotion in front of the *tabernae* filtered across the street. Quintus paid no attention. In that moment, nothing mattered more than Adiona or the long-buried secrets she was finally willing to share.

"Quintus!" Joseph called. "Quintus, hurry! We found your men. They're hurt."

Chapter Ten

"Oh, no!" Adiona cried, her eyes widening with alarm. She lifted the hem of her tunic and darted off ahead of him, leaving Quintus to follow her mad dash back to the now-closed *tabernae*.

Joseph waited with several members of his family around the first of two horse carts. The *raeda* was nowhere in sight. A handful of servants held torches, allowing Quintus an unhindered view of Otho and Rufus. The two gladiators were laid flat on their backs in the cart. Bloodied and bruised, they were as still as death.

"These two should be fine by morning," Joseph said. "They were awake when we found them. Their injuries are minor."

Relieved, Quintus scrubbed a hand across his eyes. "There were three of them."

"Yes," Joseph indicated the second wagon. "The third one is hurt the worst. He might not make it."

Adiona hung her head. "This is all my fault."

"No," Quintus denied, heading to check on Onesimus. "Don't even think it."

Sickened by the needless violence that left Onesimus with a gaping chest wound and deep cuts on his arms, Quintus returned to Adiona.

"Where were they found?" Adiona asked thickly. Stress lined her delicate features.

"On the side of the road about three miles out of town," Joseph said. "The coach you mentioned was gone. I've sent for a physician and the women are preparing beds upstairs."

Rufus's eyes fluttered open. Disoriented, he groaned and fought to sit up.

Calling for a cup of water, Quintus stayed the young gladiator with a hand on his shoulder. "Don't move, my friend. We'll have you comfortable in moments."

"Is Onesimus dead?" Rufus's voice was as thin as air.

"No, he lives," Quintus assured him.

"It…was Falco," Rufus fought to add. "We killed him."

"How many men were with him?"

"Too many." The gladiator's eyes slipped closed.

"We found six on the ground," Joseph added. "I've sent men back to bury them."

Quintus thanked him and moved out of the way when servants arrived to carry the three wounded gladiators upstairs. Fury and a wild need for vengeance raged through him. He wasn't sorry Falco was dead. Falco had duped both him and Caros, not an easy task. Worse and unforgivably, Quintus had allowed the savage near Adiona.

He watched Sapphira place an arm around Adiona's bowed shoulders and whisk her through the *tavernae*'s arched front door. Framed by the dining-room window, Adiona was a picture of unhappiness. The lamps' golden glow highlighted her air of misery.

Joseph came to stand beside him. "Your man will be safe here while he recovers."

"Thank you, my friend."

Joseph nodded toward Adiona. "She reminds me of you when you first came here. Sapphira and I prayed a long time you'd find the Lord and shed that look of emptiness."

Quintus remembered how lost and lonely he'd been nine years ago. How his life had changed for the better once he accepted Christ into his heart. "I thank Him often for guiding me here."

Joseph thumped him on the shoulder. A huge grin covered half his swarthy face. "We thank Him often He brought you to us, as well."

The waves crashed against the seawall. Joseph turned contemplative. "Adiona is special to you, no?"

"More than special," he admitted.

"Would you like us to pray for her with you?"

Grateful for good friends, he nodded. "We both need all the prayers we can get."

The next morning, Adiona woke before sunrise in her own room. She didn't remember falling asleep. She suspected Quintus had shared her abhorrence of small spaces with Sapphira since the older woman kept her talking late into the night. She'd even helped her wash and braid her hair, a task that had taken hours.

She dressed with haste and made her way downstairs in search of Quintus. After asking a servant, she found him with Joseph and Sapphira's family in a private garden behind the *tabernae*. Seth, Joseph and Sapphira's oldest son, was reading from a scroll. Too intrigued to leave, but unwilling to disturb the gathering, she found a sheltered spot behind a brightly painted pillar.

When Seth finished, a younger son, David, sang a song of thanksgiving to the Christian God. Josephina accompanied him on a lyre. The others joined in, their mingled voices confident in Whom they worshiped.

The atmosphere shifted. A peace like Adiona had never experienced settled over the garden. As the voices faded, the flow of the fountain and a soft melody of birdsong filled the tranquil stillness.

Quintus stood. He selected a scroll from a basket sitting on a low wooden bench. He unrolled the parchment and scanned the document. Locating the place he sought, he cleared his throat and began to read in a deep, clear voice: "Who shall separate us from the love of Christ? Shall trouble or hardship or persecution or famine or nakedness or danger or sword?"

She listened intently. Reading from the text he lived by, he was opening a window into his soul and she was fascinated by the view. His commitment to his God had perplexed her. Nothing in her life was important enough to die for, yet when he read about trials and persecution he'd lived them. Just last night he'd told her he would face every hardship again. But why…?

"For I am persuaded," he continued, "that neither death nor life, neither angels nor demons, neither the present nor the future, nor any powers, neither height nor depth, nor anything else in all creation, will be able to separate us from the love of God that is in Christ Jesus our Lord."

When he was finished he looked directly at Adiona. She was still contemplating the text and reeling from shock. Now she knew why Quintus believed as he did. No wonder she'd never really understood. The bond he'd forged with his God wasn't based on guilt, duty or fear. He *loved* his God and was convinced his God loved him.

She wished she had the faith to believe for herself. But how could she? No *person* had ever loved or wanted her enough to stay in her life. How was she supposed to accept that a *God* considered her worthy enough to care?

Trembling, she broke eye contact with Quintus and left. Back inside the *tabernae,* guests were preparing for the day. Servants scurried by with brooms and buckets. The smell of sausage made her stomach churn.

Of course a man like Quintus found that text believable. Everywhere he went people cared about him. Pelonia and Caros. Joseph, Sapphira and their family. Even she had loved him from the first moment she'd seen him.

The admission brought her up short. She stalled in the middle of the corridor. Tears scratched at the back of her eyes. She'd tried so hard not to love him, but it might have been easier to fight her need for air.

A short time later, when the sunrise was no more than a few pink streaks in the eastern sky, Adiona, Quintus, two of Joseph's sons as well as a bandaged Otho and Rufus prepared to leave for the wharf. Gripped by an inexplicable sadness, Adiona threw her arms around Sapphira and hugged her tight.

"You're welcome to come back here anytime," Sapphira said. The tiny Greek cupped Adiona's face with both of her hands. She stood on tiptoes and kissed Adiona's forehead. "I've considered Quintus my son for years. If you don't mind, from now on I'd like to consider you my daughter."

Touched to the heart, Adiona embraced Sapphira again. "I'd be honored. I've never had a mother."

"Then the honor is mine."

The men made quick work of saddling the horses one of Joseph's sons had fetched from the stables. As she stroked her mount's long neck, she noticed Josephina took overlong in her farewells to Quintus. After Josephina smothered Quintus in a second hug, Adiona itched to pinch the younger girl. An unfamiliar emotion settled over her like a murky, green fog. She wanted to pull Josephina's hair out by the roots or push her over the seawall. Most of all, she wanted Josephina's hands off her man!

She knew she was being childish. She believed Quintus's explanation of the relationship, but the fact that he admitted to loving the younger girl in any fashion when he didn't love *her* tied Adiona's heart in a knot.

Another hug and Adiona was boiling. "Are you ready to go, Quintus?" she asked coolly. "Or shall we all head back inside the *tabernae* and plan to leave tomorrow?"

Quintus, the infuriating man, dared to laugh. Joseph's sons snickered. Quintus lifted Adiona into her saddle and climbed into his own. "By all means, let's travel."

Seething, she noticed Josephina's smirk as they left.

What is that girl up to? she wondered, just as they turned the corner.

Chapter Eleven

What is wrong with you? Adiona mused to herself as their group made slow progress through the street's morning throng. *Josephina is a sheltered fifteen-year-old, not a devious matron out to ruin you.*

Musing she needed a change from the intrigues of Rome, she felt absurd for suspecting the girl of nefarious activity and was more than a little embarrassed by her waspish behavior at the inn. Still shaken by the knowledge that she loved Quintus, she willed her tight muscles to relax. The attack from her unknown enemy, Falco's scheming and the uncertainty of where and when her assassins might catch up with her, if indeed they were even following her, must be taking a toll on her nerves.

"It's a good day to sail."

Adiona glanced at Quintus. His eyes were a deep shade of heart-stirring green in the lean, bronzed planes of his face. "What?"

"It's windy." He gestured toward the colorful flags stretched taut by the strong gusts of air. "It's a good day for a sail."

Caught up in her thoughts, she hadn't noticed they'd

arrived at the wharf. Busy and thriving, Ostia was Rome's main port, providing the landlocked capital with goods from all over the world. In the half-light provided by the rising sun, galleys and sailing ships were being loaded at the docks. Some ships had already sailed or put oars to water as they navigated the man-made channel that led farther out to sea.

Joseph's son, David, drew his horse alongside Quintus. "Horatius is waiting for us at the last dock."

"You're sure he's an adequate captain?"

"The best I know, besides you," David said with a grin. "His boat isn't large, but it's swift. If the weather holds, you'll make Neopolis by midmorning."

The closer they got to the water, the stronger the wind. The air was heavy with a sharp hint of salt and strong stench of fish. White-capped waves marched toward shore, jostling the vessels moored in the docks.

A large, heavily bearded man met them on the wharf. Dressed in a stained brown tunic, he wore a gold hoop pierced through each ear. David introduced him as Horatius, their captain.

Horatius led them to a well-maintained sailing ship, its sail lashed tightly to the cross mast. Once on board the vessel, the men talked amicably. All seemed well until the captain glanced at Adiona with the kind of lascivious intent that left her longing for a bath.

Disgusted but used to male aggression of that sort, she ignored him as though he were dirt. Still talking, Quintus turned and looked over his shoulder, following the other man's gaze across to the deck toward her.

He gave her a reassuring smile, then turned back to Horatius, his hands clenched into fists. The wind swept across the deck stealing Quintus's words, but she understood by the captain's sudden shamefaced expression that Quintus had defended her honor.

Lighthearted, Adiona gripped the ship's rail. She pressed into the wind, her cloak whipping around her, and made her way across the rocking deck to a long, wide bench near the blunt-shaped stern. Chilled by the cold sea air, she shivered. She placed her satchel on the bench beside her and bundled deeper into her cloak.

Flocks of birds in vee formations filled the cerulean sky. Their calls vied for precedence over the snatches of foreign languages drifting to her from the nearby piers. She leaned back against the bulkhead. Her hopes for an uneventful journey began to rise. Whether Falco had been in league with her assassins or formed his own band of thugs, the attack on Onesimus and the others proved the murderers didn't know her whereabouts. The knowledge was a heavy weight lifted off her shoulders. The danger was far from over, but for now it seemed routed.

Her thoughts returned to Octavia and the three precious girls who'd be motherless if she failed to recover. A need to make haste for Neopolis gripped her. She wanted to pray for her friend, but rejected the notion. Except for the day she asked the gods to keep Quintus safe in the arena, she hadn't sought their help in years.

A shadow fell across the deck. "You look sad, my lady. If it has to do with the captain, don't be troubled. He won't bother you again."

She grinned. "Thanks to you, my protector."

"That's what I'm being paid for," he said.

She realized he was joking, but the undeniable truth caused her heart to sink like an anchor. Looking out to sea, she brushed loose tendrils of hair behind her ear. "I'm worried about Octavia."

"We'll be under way soon."

"It can't be soon enough."

He leaned back against the rail across from her, his arms folded across his broad chest, his legs braced against the sway of the boat. The sun glinted on his black hair and darkened his skin to a deep burnished bronze.

"I wanted to pray for her," she said.

He dropped his hands and gripped the rail behind him. "Why don't you?"

"Except for once recently, I haven't prayed for a long while. I don't think the gods even exist," she whispered, aware she spoke blasphemy.

He leaned toward her in a conspiratorial manner. "Don't be shocked, but I don't believe in them, either."

She worked her lower lip to keep from laughing. "Yes, but you do believe in *your* God."

"Why don't you believe in Him, too?" he invited pragmatically.

When she didn't answer right away, he offered, "Would you like me to pray for your friend, my lady?"

She raised her hand to her forehead, shielding the sun from her eyes. "Yes," she said, reassured and comforted by his ability to pray even when she found she could not.

He sat next to her and took her hand in his warm grasp. He bowed his dark head. "Dear Heavenly Father, Adiona and I come to You concerning her friend, Octavia. We've been told she's unwell and may perish. We don't know the future, but You do. If she's not already recovered, and if it be Your will, we ask that You heal her in Jesus's name, amen."

Stunned, Adiona blinked in confusion. "You address your God as Father?"

"Yes."

"Why?" she asked more sharply than she intended.

"Our texts say that as believers in Christ we're adopted into God's family. That we're no longer spiritual slaves, but are His sons and daughters."

She pulled her hand away. "I already had a father. I don't need another one."

His brows drew together. She saw the questions forming in his too-quick mind. She refused to speak of the General. It was bad enough she'd told Quintus about her husband.

The boat lurched as it was cast loose from its mooring. David and Seth wrestled with the square canvas sail, while Otho and Rufus pulled up the anchor. Frantic to change the subject, Adiona latched on to the first thought that came to her head. "What did David mean when he said you're a captain?"

His mouth tightened. He settled back on the bench and rubbed his palm over his tired eyes. She hadn't fooled him. She'd have to be careful or he'd steer the conversation back to her father before she realized what he'd done.

"I used to own a fleet." His eyes were bloodshot, his handsome face lined with fatigue. He'd said he planned to sleep today on deck. She was keeping him awake. "I found it boosted my profits to own my ships," he continued. "There was no middleman to pay and where there was room, my captains were instructed to rent out the space."

"You were very rich."

"My family and I were comfortable enough, though I doubt I was as rich as you."

"Yes, well, my husband had several more decades than you've had to make his fortune."

"I suppose so." He shrugged and leaned against the bulkhead. His eyelids grew heavy. He struggled to keep them open. "It doesn't matter. It's only money. I'll make more." His eyes closed. Thick black lashes fanned out like miniature arches across his high cheekbones.

Adiona waited, careful not to disturb him. When his breathing turned deep and even, she reached for her satchel and removed one of the silk tunics she'd brought to wear once she reached her destination. She folded it into a soft pillow. Coaxing him into a reclined position, she placed the tunic under his head, then used all her strength to lift his muscular legs onto the bench. She stepped away, breathing heavily. Stretched out on his back, Quintus slept with his left palm flat on his chest, his right arm dangling to the deck. Her chest tightened. He looked boyish, the lines of stress banished by slumber.

She thought to take off his sandals, but changed her mind. The movement was certain to disturb him. She lovingly brushed his hair off his brow and, unable to resist the temptation, buried her fingers in the soft, thick strands.

When she'd done all she could to make him comfortable, she sat on the deck, leaning against the lip of the bench like a bolster in case the ship rolled and pitched him forward. Taking his right hand off the deck, she kissed each of his callused fingers and the center of his palm. "Sleep, my love. I'll be your guard and keep *you* safe for once."

The Bay of Neopolis sparkled like sapphires in the midmorning sun. Adiona brushed a loving hand over Quintus's lightly bristled jaw before calling his name.

He woke instantly, pushing himself into a sitting position, his sandaled feet hitting the deck with a thud.

Adiona snatched her tunic off the bench and stuffed it into her satchel before he realized she'd made a pillow for him. Quintus rubbed his face with his palms and stood.

"Did you sleep well?" Adiona asked.

"Remarkably well." He grinned, adjusting his tunic and the *gladius* strapped to his belt. "Did I miss anything?"

"The view was gorgeous," she said, thinking of his face as she'd watched him sleep. "But the voyage was calm and uneventful."

Once on land, Quintus paid Horatius. He waited with her and the others while David inquired about directions. Usually, a whole host of servants traveled with her. Under normal circumstances, one would have been sent to Drusus's household to inform them of her arrival. Horses would have been provided for her as well as a guide for her party. However, Quintus stubbornly refused to send word to her heir, reasoning that if Drusus *were* embroiled in the assassination attempt on her life, the fiend didn't need extra warning in which to make plans.

Although administered by Rome, Neopolis rejoiced in its Greek roots. Inhabitants thrived on the classical arts: music, theater and literature despite the economic decline that had hit the city decades earlier. The eruption of Vesuvius and the destruction of Pompeii and the surrounding town two years previously had not helped matters, but Adiona suspected people paid little heed if the colorful posters advertising a plethora of entertainments was anything to go by.

The lively but dirty street that led to Drusus's home

was lined with brightly painted houses. A salty breeze blew in from the bay as people sat in arched doorways playing dice or board games of twelve lines or lucky sixes.

The uncertainty of Octavia's condition caused Adiona's head to drum with tension. Hope for Octavia's recovery wrestled with a fear that Adiona might be too late. The need to see her friend became paramount. Quintus's steady pace frustrated her until she wanted to scream.

Adiona noticed that with each step their horses took, Quintus grew quieter, tenser. Alert and cautious, he sat rigid in his saddle, the reins clenched tight in his fists. His profile was hard and unyielding, as though his chiseled features had been cast in bronze.

"I know this place," she said when they came to a short row of market stalls selling bread and other dry goods. "We need to go left. We're almost there."

She bristled when Quintus looked to David for confirmation before heading in the direction she'd indicated. *Typical man!*

Two blocks ahead, Adiona recognized the *domus* Drusus rented from her. The largest residence on the street, the stucco, two-story building was surrounded by a high protective wall and massive front gates. Stripped of the colorful potted flowers and hanging baskets Octavia used to soften the exterior, the stark facade radiated a sense of foreboding.

Adiona's stomach churned sickly. She feared the worst.

A guard met them at the gate. Quintus explained who they were and offered the scroll Salonius had given Adiona in Rome as proof of their identities. The gate opened. A slave appeared on the front steps, then quickly retreated.

Once inside the courtyard, Quintus dismounted. He helped Adiona do the same. He took her satchel, carrying it for her as she moved swiftly toward the columned portico.

Drusus arrived in the doorway just as Adiona started up the steps. Short and shaped like an egg on legs, Drusus clapped his chubby ring-bedecked hands in welcome. "My lady Adiona! Gods be praised. You've finally arrived! The girls and I feared you'd met with harm as each day ticked by without your gracious presence."

"I left Rome as soon as possible."

Adiona searched her heir's round face and small brown eyes for any trace of bereavement. When she found none a fountain of hope sprang up inside her. "Octavia? Is she well? Has she recovered?"

A feigned expression of sadness pulled his ungenerous mouth into a frown. "Sadly, you're too late. Octavia is dead."

Chapter Twelve

Numb from the heavy weight of grief, Adiona entered the house. The sweet aroma of incense nearly overpowered her in the grand entryway. A mosaic of a serpent-draped Bacchus enjoying a feast covered the floor. The walls were painted in a fresco of a forest filled with romping nymphs and fauns. How like Drusus to surround himself with pictures of parties and excess.

"When did Octavia pass into the afterlife?"

"Sadly enough, the day after Salonius left us for Rome."

"I'm truly sorry. I know you must have been devastated by her untimely passing."

"The children will miss her," he said, unconcerned. "I, on the other hand, had to cancel a hunting trip."

"A hunting trip?"

"Yes, I can't tell you how vexed I was when Octavia didn't have the decency to live until after I'd returned… or at least until after I'd gone."

Every nerve in her body taut with indignation for Octavia's sake, she itched to slap him.

"Where are the girls? I'd very much like to see them."

His brow crinkled as though she'd asked him to calculate a difficult mathematical equation. "I believe they were sent to their grandmother."

Adiona's jaw tightened in frustration. How could any decent man not know where his children were located?

Disgusted a gem like Octavia had been wasted on a lout who bore her so little regard, Adiona struggled to maintain a mask of politeness out of respect for her departed friend.

Drusus reached for her hand, then thought better of touching her. With a derisive glance at Quintus and their small traveling party, he called for his steward. "Have someone take these men to the slave quarters."

"No," Adiona snapped. "Install Quintus in a room next to mine and provide these other fine men with chambers of their own."

"You can't be serious," Drusus denied like an affronted rooster. "Slaves and gladiators as guests in my *home?*"

Adiona felt Quintus stiffen beside her. "Shall I remind you, Drusus, that *I* own this house? You're as much a guest here as anyone else."

Impotent fury burned in Drusus's narrowed eyes. His hostile gaze flicked to Quintus, before raking over Adiona. "So the ice maiden has finally taken a lover. How charming. I'm sure Salonius will be interested to know you're sleeping with a *slave* behind his back."

A sound very much like a growl emanated from Quintus's throat. Adiona sidled in front of him, worried he might attack her heir before she learned the information she sought. "Salonius? What does he have to do with me?"

"He was here a week ago. I know you saw him in Rome. You wouldn't know about Octavia otherwise."

"I did see him—"

"Of course, you did. You're betrothed to him."

She laughed so hard, she gasped for breath. "Excuse me? Me marry Salonius? Either you're jesting or you've lost your mind."

"I don't believe you. He told me himself."

A subtle breeze blew away all hints of amusement from the entryway. She straightened her spine and leveled him with glacial stare. "You believe Salonius… over *me?*"

For once Drusus had the wit to back down. He studied the toe of his sandal. "Of course not, my dear. That would be foolish of me."

And you're the biggest fool I know. "Look at me, Drusus."

He slowly raised his eyes to meet hers.

"Have you conspired to murder me?"

Every man in the room gasped. Drusus's eyes bugged and he paled. He looked as though he might choke…or worse, faint. "Of course not, Adiona! I'm not an imbecile. I know the terms of your will."

"Fine, then. Show us to our rooms and let's forget this unpleasant discussion ever happened. I wish to see Octavia. Where have you placed her?"

He seemed to relax, but his hand shook as he combed back his thinning hair. "In the garden just as she asked. You know how she loved to waste time on her flowers."

Adiona swallowed the sudden lump in her throat. "Yes, too bad she was surrounded by so many weeds."

The household steward showed Adiona to her room on the second floor. Quintus was given the room next door, while the other four men were installed in two separate rooms across the hall.

The warmth of the large chamber's deep red walls welcomed her. A comfortable-looking sleeping couch dominated one corner. To her left, against the wall, a beautifully carved chest waited for her clothes. Pleased to let in more light, she had the steward place her satchel on the marble-topped desk and open the double doors that overlooked the house's back garden.

A short time later, a maid, Caelina, arrived with a selection of Octavia's jewelry, cosmetics and floral perfumes to help her bathe and dress.

After her bath, Adiona wrapped herself in a length of soft linen and waited while Caelina curled and arranged her hair in an upswept style pinned with gold clips.

As Adiona reached for the jars of cosmetics, she caught her reflection in the looking glass and stilled, confused by the sensation that she'd never seen herself clearly. The black hair and curved brows were the same. The amber, slightly up-slanted eyes, straight nose and full lips were familiar, as well. But, as if a miracle had happened somewhere along the Ostian Way, gone was the need to hide behind a thick mask of face paint and kohl. With a light hand, she applied a soft gloss to her lips and just enough cosmetics to disguise the trace of bruises on her cheeks.

She reached for her satchel. She'd brought two tunics and *pallas* with her from Rome. One, a cheerful yellow in hopes she arrived to find a healthy Octavia, the other in mournful black.

Her chest swelled with grief as she donned the flowing black silk. The maid opened the alabaster jewelry box. Adiona blinked back tears, recognizing several pieces she'd sent as gifts to Octavia over the years. Normally, she would have worn most of the baubles as befit her wealth, station and the expectations of everyone around her. Instead, she chose a simple pair of long gold earrings, a delicate bracelet and an obsidian ring she slid onto her right index finger.

"Is that all, *domina?*" the maid asked, obviously confused by a woman who ignored a feast in favor of a morsel.

A knock sounded on the door. Caelina set down the box and rushed to answer it. "It's your bodyguard, *domina.*"

"Let him—"

"What were you thinking?" Quintus interrupted as he stalked across the threshold. He froze when he saw her. The lines of irritation faded from his face. He seemed to catch his breath.

"When?" she asked, pleased by his reaction more than she could say.

He shook his head and rallied. "Downstairs when you confronted that piece of slime you call an heir. Did you expect him to admit he'd tried to kill you?"

Aware there was a good chance Caelina was her slimy heir's spy, she offered Quintus a calm smile and entwined her arm with his. "Walk me to the garden, will you?"

His frustration unconcealed, he led her into the hall. She patted his hand in an effort to soothe him. "What you don't understand about Drusus," she said once they were alone, "is that for all his bluster, he's much too slow of mind to form a believable lie when asked a direct question."

"What if you're wrong?"

"I'm not," she assured him as they descended the stairs. "I know Drusus."

"I don't trust him," he said.

Soft music drifted to them from the inner peristyle

surrounding the central garden. She forced a grin in an effort to ease his discontent. "I never said *I* trusted him, either. I promise you I'll be careful."

He sighed and tugged his hand through his hair. "I just don't want you harmed."

Her confidence bloomed, fed and watered by his blatant concern for her. She feigned an air of haughty grace and winked at him. "I'm Adiona Leonia, Lioness of Rome. No one can touch me."

He ran a fingertip along the smooth curve of her jaw and leaned closer to brush a curl behind her ear. He frowned. "What scent are you wearing, lioness?"

The question startled her. "Do I smell?" She pressed her nose to her shoulder and drew in a delicate sniff, certain by his expression she must reek.

"Mmm…like flowers."

Relieved, she laughed. "You had me worried. Caelina put rose oil in my bath."

"I'm used to you smelling of cinnamon."

"And you prefer that?" she asked, thinking she'd order a vat of the potion once she returned to Rome.

He nodded. "It suits you better."

"How so?" She leaned into him.

"It's sweet—"

She wrinkled her nose. "I'm not *sweet*."

"—with a healthy dose of spice."

She rolled her eyes.

He cupped her cheek with his palm, his voice turned kind. "I'm truly sorry about your friend."

Mesmerized by the tenderness in his eyes, she whispered, "Thank you. Now I must go to her."

He reluctantly let her go and stepped back. "I'll be right here if you need me."

* * *

Lifting the hem of her black tunic and billowy *palla,* Adiona entered the villa's inner courtyard. In life, Octavia had loved the rectangular space and filled it with a wealth of flowers that bloomed in every season.

The haunting melody of a panpipe mingled with the gentle splash of the central fountain and the conversation of a small group of visitors. Her eyes misted with tears of sadness and burned from the sweet cloud of incense as she crossed the verdant garden to the slim linen-covered body laid out in wake.

Already the sixth and final day of mourning, she'd nearly missed the chance to pay her respects. Guests were already arriving for Octavia's procession outside the city where she would be cremated.

She rested a hand on Octavia's shrouded arm. Remembering how the gentle woman had always been quick to give a hug or lend a hand in need, she bit her lower lip to keep from sobbing. She would always regret not arriving in time to care for her friend during her sickness or to offer a final goodbye.

Through the thick haze of incense smoke, she saw Drusus immersed in conversation with an elegant older woman.

Drusus left his guest and weaved his way toward Adiona. In the hour since their confrontation in the entryway, he'd changed his light tunic to one of black. Carrying a gold chalice in his hand, he came to a stop on the other side of his wife's corpse.

"See, Adiona, I followed all the cus…customs just like I knew you'd expect."

"Really? Moments after Octavia died, you closed her eyes and called out her name?"

He nodded, smug.

"Then you had her body washed and—"

"Yes, of course!"

"You placed a coin in her mouth for the ferryman?"

"I need to speak with you about that…"

"As I expected."

"I did everything," he defended hotly. "I even wasted more spices to…to keep the stench down."

Drusus snapped his fingers at a passing slave to pour him more wine. Noting the slight slur in his words, she frowned, disturbed as much by his glassy gaze as the rancor in his voice.

Her eyes narrowed. "Are you drunk, Drusus?"

"I? At my own wife's funeral?" He smirked, lifting the chalice to his lips to drink deeply. "I assure you, if I'm drunk it's s…solely from grief."

Liar.

She bit her tongue. Everyone knew the importance of following the proper rituals if a departed soul was to cross into the afterlife unhindered. To her surprise, Drusus seemed to have followed those customs. *At least most of them.* She didn't want to start an argument at the wake when it might cause Octavia problems in the underworld.

"Octavia was a special woman, Drusus. You didn't deserve her."

He shrugged, unoffended. "I treated her well enough."

She gritted her teeth. "I pray her journey across the River Styx is smooth and the Judges honor her with a favored place in the Elysian Fields."

"I doubt she earned a *favored* place," he said, taking another drink. "She was an adequate wife, but failed in her ultimate duty to give me sons."

She gasped. "She gave you *three* beautiful daughters."

"What are daughters but mouths to feed and eventual dowries to empty my purse?"

Adiona bristled. He sounded so *male* and unforgivably ignorant. Exactly like her father and her toad of a husband. "Be wise, Drusus, and hold your tongue before you vex me beyond endurance. *Your* daughters are the reason *you* are heir to a fortune."

"Excuse me." The elegant woman who she'd seen speaking with Drusus joined them beside Octavia's body. "I apologize for the interruption but it's time."

Adiona paled. Mortified by her loss of temper in the circumstances, she dragged in a calming breath before offering a silent apology to Octavia. She squeezed her friend's stiff fingers through the shroud as her body was carried away by four members of the funerary *collegia*.

The procession to the outskirts of the city was long. Hours of mournful wailing, the heat of the pyre and the sad trek back to the house left Adiona drained of all but her grief. Thankfully, her bodyguards had been beside her, but it was Quintus's stalwart presence that gave her the strength to endure.

Slaves had set up a feast for the returning mourners. Drusus wasted no time refilling his glass, not that he'd been overlong without wine. If anything, he was more inebriated now than when she'd last spoken with him.

Too upset to eat, Adiona had the slaves carry food to her guards. Just as he had earlier in the day, Quintus waited in the hall within easy striking distance in case she needed him.

"I don't believe we've met," the elegant older woman she'd seen with Drusus approached her. An affable smile lit the woman's dark brown eyes. "I'm Gaia. A friend of Drusus…and, of course, dear Octavia."

"I'm Adiona Leonia."

"Yes, I know. Octavia spoke of you often. She admired you greatly and praised your strength of will. She proclaimed you the most beautiful woman in the Empire. I see she didn't exaggerate."

"As always, Octavia was too kind."

Dressed in fine black silk edged with silver fringe that matched the silver hair at her temples, Gaia motioned toward the garden's exit. "Drusus asked me to have you meet him in his office. Apparently, the two of you have much to discuss. I'll stay here and see to his other guests."

Thinking the woman was a bit presumptuous, Adiona was too unhappy to be offended. She left the garden and found Drusus already in his office, sitting behind his desk. Tall floor candelabras were placed in each of the room's corners. A seamless, brightly painted mural of Diana leading a hunt dominated all four walls, but instead of the goddess being the focal point of the piece, a large golden serpent coiled in a tree behind Drusus. Rubies had been imbedded in the wall to give the painted reptile the look of glowing red eyes. Used to her heir's eccentricities, she shrugged off the eerie feeling that slithered down her spine.

Aware that Drusus meant to claim a position of power by placing himself behind the desk, Adiona took control of the conversation and spoke first. "Who is Gaia and what is she to you?"

He blinked several times as though trying to clear his head. "She's a…a neighbor. A friend of Octavia. She helped me with the children during Octavia's sickness and then with the funeral arrangements."

For that she owed Gaia a favor. "Why don't you allow the girls to live with me in Rome?" Eager to give Octavia's daughters a home filled with appreciation and love, she expected Drusus to give them to her for the right price. "With no family of my own I'd enjoy the company. You know I'd hire the best tutors for them when they're old enough. They'll want for nothing."

He leaned forward in his chair, lacing his fingers atop the desk. "No, I couldn't allow them to go with you."

"Why ever not?" He had no appreciation for his offspring. After an hour or two, she doubted he'd remember their names.

"No offense, my dear cous…cousin, but they'll end up poisoned against men and marriage the same as you are. I'll never get them wed and they'll be stones around my neck for all eternity."

Incensed, she arched a brow at his wine-induced bluntness. How was she *not* to take offense at being told she'd poison his children?

She lifted her chin and looked at him as though he were a bug she'd like to smash beneath her sandal. "I don't hate *good* men, Drusus. Unfortunately, they're just more difficult to come by than gold coins in a pauper's hovel."

His cheeks flushed, he glanced away, suitably chastised. He cleared his throat after a long, uncomfortable pause. "Speaking of gold coins. I'm wondering if you might pay me back for the one Octavia took to the pyre."

"You're a worm, Drusus."

"Don't be unkind, Adiona. You keep me on a tight leash."

She gave a derisive snort. For the children's sake,

she paid him an allowance twice what he deserved. Although comfortable in his own right, her cousin was a spendthrift who was rumored to make his slaves go hungry if it meant having a few extra *sestertii* to spend on himself.

"Not tight enough if I go by the rings you're sporting."

His glassy eyes grew wide. "Don't misunderstand me. I'm *not* complaining."

"Of course not," she scoffed. She stood and aimed for the door. "Let's finish this tomorrow, shall we? I suspect we'll accomplish more than running in circles once you're sober."

Her temper boiling just beneath the surface of her skin, she marched back to the garden. Music and a hearty dose of wine had erased all sadness from the guests. They danced and laughed as if they'd attended a wedding instead of a funeral.

Disgusted by the lack of respect for Octavia, she left the garden the way she'd come. Quintus was waiting for her.

"Are you well?" he asked. "You look exhausted."

"Exhausted? No, I'm madder than a barbarian horde. I'd so hoped to arrive to a recovered Octavia. Instead, I'm cursed to deal with Drusus, that maggot. I wish he'd died instead!"

"What did he say to upset you?"

"I need a few moments. As of yet, I'm too angry to speak of it." His steady presence had a soothing effect on her temper as they ascended the steps to the second floor. Servants had lit oil lamps to banish the night's darkness. A chill swept through the stairwell.

"He said," she began once they reached the threshold, "that I'm not fit to raise his daughters. That allowing them to live with me would ruin them. That I'd *poison* them against men."

"And?" Quintus prompted when she offered no more.

Furious, she demanded, "What do you mean, *and?* Isn't that bad enough? Do you agree with him?"

"I have no opinion whatsoever." He opened the chamber door for her. Slaves had been there to close the balcony doors and light candles. "From what I've seen, he's a mockery of a man, but I don't know how he is with his children or how he wants to raise them."

"Then let me enlighten you." She stormed into her room. "He thinks girls are worthless. Just like my *own* father did!"

Silence fell. She whirled around to find Quintus in the doorway. Arms crossed over his muscular chest, he leaned against the jamb. His intense green eyes appraised her as though the final piece of a complicated puzzle had just been snapped into place.

"I see," he said, his expression intent and filled with understanding. "You do know both of them are wrong, don't you?"

"Of course!"

"Then why have you let their ignorance distress you?"

"Because it's hurtful and unfair." She began to pace a circle around the desk. "It's a horrible lie!"

"Yes, and look who's perpetuating the falsehood. Drusus, a slug of no account who needs to feel important, and your father. I didn't know him, but if he treated you as less than the treasure you are, then he is of no account, as well."

She gaped at him.

"I hope you know your own worth by now, but if you need a man's opinion, ask a real one."

Fascinated, she walked toward him, her gaze locked with his. "All right, Quintus. What *do* you think of me?"

Chapter Thirteen

Quintus groaned inwardly. He'd known better than to throw Adiona a challenge if he didn't want her to take him up on it. His fingers slashed through his hair. "I think you're…exceptional."

Her eyes brightened. She started to smile, then her lush mouth drooped into a frown. "Exceptional in what way? Spoiled? Difficult? Sharp-tongued? Unlovable?"

Unlovable? Was she mad? "My, what a high opinion you have of yourself."

"I know I'm those things. Everyone says so."

"That doesn't make them true. In fact, I—"

A shadow moved on the wall above the sleeping couch behind Adiona. Not the flicker of a candle's flame, but an odd undulation. A warning crept up the back of his neck. The pelts covering the couch moved.

He pulled her behind him, shoving her through the open doorway and out into the hall.

"Quintus, what—?"

"Be still." The covers rustled. Something was *in* her bed.

He didn't want to frighten her. Getting her to sleep in unfamiliar surroundings was difficult enough as it was. "Don't ask why, just trust me. Go fetch one of my men. Then go sit with David and Seth."

"But—"

"No," he said, firmly. "Do as I say."

He expected an argument, but as usual, she surprised him and did as he asked. Her knock sounded on the door across the hall.

The door swung open instantly. "My lady?" Otho's surprised voice filtered into the hall. "What is it?"

"*Emperor* Quintus commands your attention."

Quintus's lips twitched, but the covers rustled again, banishing all amusement.

Otho stepped up beside him. "What's going on?"

"Where is the lady?" Quintus asked without taking his eyes off the bed.

The shadows shifted on the walls as Otho leaned back to see around the door frame and locate her whereabouts. "She's almost to David and Seth's door."

"Good." Quintus pulled the *gladius* from the sheath on his belt and stepped deeper into the room. Otho followed, picking up a candle on the way to the bed. The ridge beneath the covers rippled.

"What *is* it?" Otho asked.

"I believe it's one of the snakes our host collects." Quintus raised his *gladius* and sank the blade through the pelt and into the creature's thick flesh. The serpent thrashed and hissed. Quintus slashed again, hitting his mark a second time. Blood oozed into the covering. Finally, the reptile stopped twitching.

"The balcony doors are closed," Otho pointed out. "The snake couldn't have found its way in here by accident."

A deadly calm came over Quintus. "No, I highly doubt it was an accident."

"Another assassination attempt, then," Otho surmised. "Do you think the serpent's poisonous?"

"Drusus prizes no other kind according to widow Leonia." He pulled the short sword free of the carcass and wiped the blade clean on the pillow.

"Are you going to tell her about this?"

"I'd rather not, but I must. She needs to know exactly what her heir is capable of."

Otho eased back the pelt and lifted the candle.

Rage spread through Quintus like venom. Snakes weren't his specialty, but as a boy he'd learned the most dangerous types. Judging by the 'horn' on the viper's snout and the wavy pattern of light and dark scales, the adder was one of the most lethal in all of Italy.

"I'm going to get Drusus," Quintus said through clenched teeth.

Otho stopped him. "I think Rufus and I need to find him. We want him to explain how this happened. In the mood you're in, he might not live long enough to make it up here."

Quintus agreed with a curt nod. Otho left. His breathing heavy, Quintus focused on the bloodied adder twisted across the sleeping couch. Its milky white belly glowed in the dim light. As long and thick as Quintus's arm, the snake wasn't yet full-grown, but that didn't make it any less deadly. What if Adiona had returned to her room on her own and pulled back the cover? What if she'd climbed into bed without investigating beforehand? One strike from the serpent and he would have lost her.

Twin knives of panic and pain sliced through him. His stomach swirled sickly. The prospect of losing Adiona filled him with a white-hot terror that threatened his reason.

He focused on the serpent, but Drusus's face loomed in his mind's eye. A bonfire of fury ignited inside him. He'd never yearned to kill anyone until that moment. Quintus yanked the pelts over the snake. Now fully convinced Drusus was behind a plot to harm Adiona, he closed his eyes and prayed for restraint. Without the Lord's intervention Drusus's hours were numbered.

Drusus's protests rang from the hallway long before Otho and Rufus shoved the squirming drunk across the threshold. Glassy inebriated eyes struggled to focus on Quintus. "What's the meaning of this, slave?" Drusus demanded thickly. "How dare you snatch me from my wife's fu…funeral."

Anger vibrated through Quintus in waves. Drusus's miserable life hung by an unraveling thread. "How dare *you?*" he asked with deceptive calm. He ripped back the pelts, exposing the dead serpent.

Drusus blanched and moaned, "What have you done to my *baby?*" He sank to his knees by the bed, grasping the viper and clutching the scaly tail to his chest.

Disgusted by a man who wept over a dead reptile, yet shed not a tear for his late wife, Quintus grabbed Drusus by the scruff of his neck and yanked him to his feet. He caught him up by the front of his tunic and slammed him against the wall. "You miserable cur!" he growled. "You'd best thank my God I don't end your useless existence."

"My baby, my precious baby!" Drusus continued to sob. His eyes closed, his head rocked back and forth like a rattle.

Vaguely aware of David's voice calling Adiona in the hallway, Quintus drew back his fist. "Cease your sniveling!"

Drusus continued to whine inconsolably.

"Why are you yowling like a cat with its tail on fire, Drusus?" Adiona breezed into the chamber, David close on her heels. Seeing the byplay, she stopped in the center of the room, a quizzical expression pleating her elegant features. "Quintus? What are you doing? What's going on?"

"You!" Drusus squealed through the chokehold Quintus held on his throat. His bug-eyed gaze settled on Adiona, vivid with accusation. "You're responsible for this tragedy! Have you seen what your minions did to my little one?"

"What are you talking about?" she snapped, offended by his censure. "What *tragedy?*"

Otho stepped forward. "My lady—"

"What *is* that?" Adiona interrupted as she peered through the half-light toward her bed. She took a curious step forward.

"Don't!" Quintus groaned. He shoved Drusus over to Otho and reached for Adiona, but it was too late. She'd seen the snake. She looked to Quintus with dawning horror, her lovely face pale as moonlight.

"Is that—?"

"My *baby,*" Drusus wailed. "They've murdered her."

She shrank back, her eyes bright with appalled disgust. She closed her eyes and pressed a hand over her quivering mouth.

Quintus moved forward, compelled to comfort her. "My lady—"

"Wait!" She stretched out her palm to warn him off. "Come no closer. I fear I'm going to retch."

"What are you going to do about this?" Drusus complained. "Your slaves have murder—"

"Silence!" She pressed trembling fingers to her temples. The ring she wore glistened like black fire in the

candles' glow. She eased her hands back to her sides and looked to Quintus with troubled eyes. "Tell me what happened."

He related the details in a flat voice as he fought to contain his fury toward Drusus.

"*Noooo!* He's a vicious liar. I'm not guilty!" Her heir fell to the floor before her, his arms around her legs, his head bent and pressed to her knees. "I'm innocent, my lady! I swear I'd never harm you! Never, never!"

Quintus lunged forward. He grabbed Drusus by the hair and slid his knife along the swine's throat. "Release her or you're dead."

"Quintus, stop!" Adiona gasped.

He ignored her and pressed the blade tighter. A fine line of blood trickled down Drusus's fleshy neck.

Drusus let her go. Quintus removed the knife and Drusus fell forward, facedown on the tiled floor by her feet. "I didn't do it, I didn't!" he sobbed in a pathetic crescendo.

"That's enough!" Quintus ordered his men to take Drusus to his own chamber. "Don't let him out of your sight. We have yet to learn his accomplices."

Trapped in appalled stasis, Adiona wasn't sure if the room was shaking or if she was trembling so hard it just seemed to be. Drusus's cries for mercy came to her as though she were under water. From the moment Quintus explained the situation, she'd been unable to take her eyes off the adder on her bed or form a coherent sentence.

Questions rolled through her mind in malignant waves. What if Quintus hadn't been there to see the creature? What if she'd blown out the candles and crawled into bed...?

She shivered as a smoke-tinged draft from the hall brushed across her skin. Only vaguely aware of Drusus being dragged from the chamber, she marveled at her own gullibility. How had she misjudged her heir to such an extent? She believed him witless, not murderous. Now, it seemed, *she* was the fool.

"Adiona." Quintus placed himself between her and the adder. The bronzed column of his throat, the width of his broad shoulders and muscled chest filled her line of vision like a mountain of reliability and strength. He took her hands in his, banishing the insidious chill overtaking her with the warmth of his touch. "Come with me, my lady."

Still in shock, she allowed him to lead her to a sitting room downstairs. He closed the door, muffling the music and laughter of the funeral guests.

"I wish someone would send them on their way," she murmured. "It's the middle of the night. Their behavior is a mockery of Octavia's sedate nature."

"I'll see to it." He turned to do her bidding.

"No." She grabbed his hand. "Please…don't leave me."

Without question, he guided her to a cushioned seat near the window. He knelt before her on the tiled floor, his long fingers grasping the armrests on either side of her chair. "I'm taking you from here at first light."

"No—"

"Yes." He placed his index finger over her lips. "Listen to me. We're leaving at first light. I'd take you from here sooner, but the roads at night are as dangerous as this house. At least here, I know who some of our enemies are."

Her thoughts were becoming clearer due to Quintus's calming influence. "I'm not yet convinced Drusus is part of the plot."

His intense green eyes flared with disbelief, but he didn't belittle her. "Why not?"

"Instinct."

"Adiona—"

"He prizes his serpents. I don't think he'd risk the adder's life."

"Unless he reasons he can purchase a new one with the fortune your death will drop in his lap."

"My will—"

"Magistrates and lawyers are more easily bought than snakes," he said flatly. "Once you're dead, your will can be rewritten and forged for the right amount of coin."

She nodded in resignation.

"Tell me this," he said, dragging an impatient hand through his hair. "Do the terms of your will change if you wed and have children of your own?"

"Yes, but…that won't happen."

His jaw clenched. "You can't know that for certain."

"Yes, I do."

"How old are you?"

"None of your business."

He seemed to do a quick summation in his head. "Based on what you told me of your life, I'll say you're three and twenty."

She nodded begrudgingly. "Yes, I'm twenty-three. Old enough to decide for myself that I'll *never* marry again."

"*Never* is a word that carries the weight of eternity with it and few things last that long."

"Perhaps not, but my decision will stand." For her, marriage was too frightening to contemplate. Her husband had condemned her as a waste of a woman. He'd abused her for her failure to tempt him to the marriage bed, let alone give him the son he'd purchased her to bear.

As a child bride, she'd believed him because she had no one to teach her differently. Now, a woman full-grown, she understood Crassus was the animal who deserved to be caged, not her. But that knowledge did not erase the scars she carried inside or silence the constant voice that whispered she was worthless and intrinsically undesirable.

"Stubborn," Quintus said under his breath. "But consider Drusus *believed* you were betrothed. You won't convince me a man of his ilk would simply let his inheritance slip through his fingers."

He had a point and it was sharp as a knife. "What do you propose we do?"

"I'm sending David and Seth to Rome with a message for Caros informing him what's happened here. On swift horses they can be there by tomorrow night to request reinforcements. Otho and Rufus will stay here to guard Drusus."

"And you and I?" she asked.

"I'm taking you home."

"Home? How will I be safer in Rome?"

"We're not going to Rome," he clarified. "I told you I have a villa farther down the coast. We can be there in a matter of hours. No one will know you're there or be able to guess your whereabouts. I'm certain you'll be safe while we learn the depths of Drusus's treachery."

"Your brother will be there?"

He nodded. "I'm hopeful."

She bit her lower lip as she mulled over his plan. If he found his brother, he'd have the chance to lay hold of his fortune. With his wealth restored, he'd purchase his freedom and her value to him would end.

He'll leave me for certain.

The thought stung like acid on thin skin. "Do you promise you'll see me safely back to Rome…even if you find your brother?"

"Of course," he said, eyeing her closely. "I told you I'll stay with you until you no longer need me."

She forced herself to smile. She didn't doubt his sincerity at the moment, but she had no illusions, either. Life had taught her vows were easily made and even more easily broken. Intentions shifted like the breeze blowing through the open window. People did what they wanted.

Naturally, Quintus wanted his life back. His freedom was precious. Why stay a slave to a woman with nothing of value to offer? He didn't need her fortune and he'd made it clear in the hospital he didn't want her body. Given the option of regaining his freedom or remaining with her, why wouldn't he choose gold over dross?

Chapter Fourteen

Just as Quintus insisted, he and Adiona sailed from Neopolis at sunrise. The short voyage offered splendid views of the southern coast. A narrow ribbon of white beach separated the azure sea from the jagged mountain peaks that stretched toward an equally blue sky. Colorful villages fanned out along the mountain face only to fade into terraced groves of citrus and olive trees. Wildflowers in bright hues of yellow, orange and fuchsia added a riot of color to the sun-dappled greenery of the lush valleys.

At Quintus's direction, the hired captain steered the sailboat into a private cove and docked at a long pier constructed of a series of cement arches.

The pier led to the beach and a winding set of stairs cut into the mountainside. The villa at the end of the stairs halfway up the mountain was nothing short of magnificent. Constructed of stone with marble columns, arched doors, and balconies overlooking the sea, the palatial residence seemed carved from its surroundings.

"This is all *yours*?" Adiona asked as Quintus lifted

her from the boat. The villa rivaled any of her properties and surpassed most.

"It was," he said impassively, taking their satchels from the captain and slinging them over his shoulder. "Now it belongs to my brother."

Sensing unease in Quintus, Adiona hooked her arm with his as they walked up the pier. He raised his eyebrow at her familiarity. "What?" she asked innocently.

"I'm still a slave," he said. "At the marriage fete last Friday you said you'd be embarrassed to be seen touching me."

"Yes, well, things have changed."

"Why?" he asked with a dubious smile. "Because you know I'm rich?"

Because I love you, she thought, looking up into his gleaming green eyes. "Of course, it's because you're rich. Why else?"

His expression soured. "At least you're honest."

A flock of birds landed on the beach, running to and fro in time to the gentle melody of the surf. A cool breeze tempered the warmth of the sun on her face. Adiona wished she knew how to tell him how much she cared for him. How he'd brought her heart to life. But love was new to her experience and although Quintus no longer seemed to despise her, he'd made no declaration of any softer emotions, either. Riddled with frustration and lacking enough bravado on this one particular subject to simply state her piece, she said the first thing that came to mind. "You don't seem happy to be here, Quintus."

"I'm...pleased." He led her across the short stretch of beach between the pier and the steps. "In fact, it's the first time I've felt like myself in months."

"Then why the dour expression?" she asked as they started up the stairs.

"Something is wrong, though I'm not sure what."

"Do you think my enemies—?"

"No, no," he said, quick to reassure her. "You're safe here."

The higher they rose on the steps, the stronger the wind. The slave's garb she'd donned as a disguise before leaving Neopolis fluttered like a sail in a storm. She clasped the whipping tendrils of her hair back with her hand. "Then what's troubling you? All looks well. The villa is beautiful."

"Normally, this cove is alive with activity. Boats are docked up and down the pier. People coming and going. A phalanx of servants would have met me on the beach when I arrived…now, the place is deserted."

"How many slaves did you keep?" she asked, thinking how strange and difficult his loss of status must have been for a proud man like Quintus. Judging by the grandiose villa before her, a winter residence at most, he must have relinquished an even greater fortune for his beliefs than she'd realized. A part of him must regret his decision. How could he not?

On the sail to Neopolis, he'd spoken of earning riches as if it were a game, but obtaining wealth was more than a trivial pursuit. She worked incessantly to maintain her fortune and place in society because money and position meant safety and security in a world that offered too little of either.

"I stopped keeping slaves not long after I became a believer in the Way."

Her forehead puckered at the odd notion. "Why?"

They reached the top of the stairs. A brick terrace covered the expanse between the villa's wide front steps and the intricately carved stone railing that provided a protective barrier from the cliff's edge.

"When I studied our texts, I realized God loves and sees everyone as equals."

"Even slaves?" she asked, intrigued enough by the novel idea to drag her eyes from the awe-inspiring view of the sea and mountainous cliffs that formed the cove. "What about women?"

"Yes. Slaves and women, too," he said.

Perplexed, she tried to internalize the concept of equality as they crossed the terrace and mounted the villa's front steps. In truth, she'd never heard such a radical notion. All of society thought females were on par with chattel. A woman's value was defined by the honor she brought to her father through the status of her marriage and the number of children she bore for her husband.

Adiona had failed to give her husband children, dishonoring Crassus, and in turn, her father. When Crassus condemned her as worthless, he'd maimed her, but he'd said no more than what everyone else considered the truth because she'd broken the natural order.

"I've wondered why you seem untouched by your slave status? It's because you don't think of yourself as inferior, do you?"

"No. I try to see myself, and everyone else, through God's eyes. People judge a man by his circumstances, but God's opinion doesn't alter with the change of my clothes or the amount of coin I have from one day to the next."

Afraid of how his God viewed her, she lifted her chin in a show of indifference even though her heart raced. "So you freed your people and, what…paid them a wage?"

"Yes," he admitted. "There was no other option if I intended to stay true to my beliefs."

She stared at him, incredulous. He was even more out of step with society than she was and her admiration for him knew no bounds. Hypocrites infested Rome at every level. To find someone so true left her stunned.

"I suppose you think my actions were foolish."

"From a financial standpoint? Most certainly."

He laughed. "What would you have done?"

Her brows puckered. "I suppose if I wish to court your good opinion—"

"Which, of course, you don't."

She grinned. "But *if* I did, I should pretend to be altruistic and say I agree with you, but to be honest… I don't know."

Quintus led her up the steps and tried to open the front door. The massive portal was locked. He groaned. "Barred from my own home."

Her eyes rounded. "What will we do?"

"Wait and see." He knocked on the door. A few moments later a voice sounded from inside the house.

"Libo," Quintus called, relieved. "It's Quintus Ambustus. Open the door."

"Take your pranks somewhere else," a reedy voice wheezed. "You're not welcome here."

Color scored Quintus's lean cheeks. Whether he was angry or embarrassed, Adiona didn't know which.

He pounded on the door again. "Libo, this is no joke. Where is my brother? I know Lucius passed by here recently."

A long moment passed. The door opened a crack and a man's craggy face appeared. "Master Quintus?" Libo's voice shook. "Is it really you?"

Quintus laughed. "It is, my friend. Let me in and you can see for yourself."

Shock rippled across the old man's leathered features. To Adiona's amazement, tears welled in Libo's eyes. He yanked open the door. "Praise be to God, our prayers have been answered!" The old man threw his arms around Quintus and Adiona stifled a laugh at his startled reaction.

"Forgive me, *dominus*." Libo collected himself and scrubbed the moisture from his face. "Your brother told us you were dead. Everyone's gone, save the wife and me."

"How is Bernice?"

"She lives, but things have been better."

Quintus reached for Adiona without taking his attention off Libo, who continued a sorrowful account of the numerous woes that had befallen the villa since Quintus's arrest. Adiona grimaced as Quintus's grip tightened with each new complaint. Loath to pull away when he seemed to need her, she distracted herself from the pain in her hand by nudging him into the villa.

Sunlight and the distant crash of waves on the shore streamed into the space through large westward-facing windows. The splash of a fountain drew her eyes to an interior garden that was lush to the point of being overgrown.

Quintus introduced her to Libo as his guest once they were inside the spacious, circular reception hall. Even though he was polite, the servant paid her little attention. As the men continued their discussion, she admired the multicolored tiled floor and the intricate gardenscape painted on the walls. She also noted the empty niches and lack of furniture that spoke of the family's shifting fortune.

"Let me understand this," Quintus said, sounding incredulous once Libo finished his rambling. "Lucius has been staying here for months, but he's failed to pay you and the others?"

Libo noticed the satchels Quintus carried and took them from him. "That's so, *dominus*. Bernice and me had funds saved from the healthy wages you always paid us, but Dacien's wife delivered their fourth child and Maro wished to get married. Tullia's father died… she had to get work at the bakery in town to help her mother. Pul—"

"I understand." Quintus interrupted with a wave of his hand. "They were right to seek out other work. I'm sorry I let them down."

Adiona bit her lower lip. She doubted the servant heard the pain of failure in Quintus's voice, but *she* did. She slipped her hand into his callused palm, hoping to lend him support. He didn't reject her and she basked in the knowledge that he needed her for a few moments longer at least. He brushed the pad of his thumb across her fingertips, sending a delightful shiver up her arm.

A short time later, Libo returned to his work. Quintus led Adiona to a room on the second floor overlooking the cove. Awash with light, the chamber's unfashionable white walls gave the space an airy feel that Adiona instantly favored. Rare purple textiles draped the bed and windows. Gleaming white tiles covered the entire floor. "This is a beautiful room, Quintus."

He nodded. "It was my mother's. She had simple tastes, but everything she touched became a thing of beauty."

Looking at Quintus, she found it easy to believe his mother had been a remarkable woman. Her son was exceptional—honest, responsible, loyal, proud in the best possible sense.

She moved deeper into the chamber. A carved wood desk sat in front of the window, covered by alabaster jars and jeweled boxes. "Thank you for letting me stay here. It's an honor."

"I meant it as such." He tugged at his hair. A smile curved his lips as he hooked the strap of her satchel on the back of the desk's chair. "That and the fact I knew it would be the last room my brother ransacked for heirlooms to pilfer."

She moved to the window, uncertain of his mood since he seemed equal parts amused and aggravated. "Is your brother like Drusus? Always interested in gaining coin for himself?"

Quintus released a deep breath. "No, Lucius has little in common with your heir. He's light of heart and a friend to all."

"Is that the problem?" she asked. "Too many friends, too little purse?"

"Something like that."

"What are you going to do, Quintus?"

"I'm going to pray and put the situation in God's hands." He walked to the door. "Then I'm going to find Lucius and try not to put my new gladiatorial skills to good use."

Four days later, Caros Viriathos and ten of his best gladiators arrived in Neopolis. Vexed for having to leave Pelonia in Rome while he dealt with Adiona's weak-minded heir, Caros led his men through the winding streets to Drusus's villa. In the week since Adiona's attack, none of the spies he or Adiona's steward kept on retainer had failed to find the first clue to her assassin's identity. Frustrated, he prayed that if Drusus *was* responsible he'd discover the necessary evidence to prove the man's guilt and see the matter put to rest.

As he and his men dismounted in the villa's front yard, the afternoon was rife with the odor of horses and sweat caused by the driving pace the group had set from Rome.

Otho met them on the front steps. "*Lanista,* good to see you, sir. The lady's heir has been screeching for justice these last four days. Me and Rufus are nearly deaf from all the racket."

Caros chuckled. "David and Seth returned to Ostia on the journey back here. They told me of the adder in the widow's bed and Quintus's wisdom in removing the lady to safety. Is there anything else to report?"

"Neh. Except for the whining, it's been as uneventful as a grave."

Inside the villa's reception hall, Caros curled his lip at the repugnant display of snakes painted on the walls and tiled onto the floor. "Where is the viper?"

"Drusus was locked in his room on Quintus's order. He's had no visitors save one of his neighbors. An older woman who brought food and water."

"Tell me, does Drusus seem repentant?"

"He says he was framed."

"You've observed him these last few days," Caros said. "What do you think of his claim?"

Otho drummed his fingers on the table beside him. "I think he's half-crazed."

"And the other half?"

"I don't know." The young gladiator shrugged. "The old dog doesn't seem savvy enough to plot murder. If he was upset the widow escaped unharmed, he didn't show it. In fact, he's barely mentioned her, but he's still grieving the death of his 'pet.'"

Deep in contemplation, Caros turned to leave.

"He's adamant to talk to you, sir. Shall I bring him down?" Otho asked.

Caros paused and rubbed his chin. "Since he's *adamant,* by all means, bring him down. He can wait in his office."

An hour later, Caros made his way to meet Drusus. Having washed off the travel dust and eaten a meal, he now felt confident he could speak to the man without harming him.

Long before he reached the office, he heard Drusus's high-pitched complaints. "Who does he think he is to make me wait? He's nothing but a worthless *lanista!* How dare he—"

"How dare I what?" Caros asked from the doorway, his tone flinty calm.

Drusus ceased his ranting and stopped cold in the center of the room. He colored as though he'd swallowed his tongue. "I—"

Ignoring Otho's struggle not to laugh, Caros took the master's chair behind the desk. "Have a seat, Drusus."

Drusus did as he was told, although he was clearly irate to be displaced in his own office. "This is an outrage! What have I done that Adiona sends her lapdog to chastise me?"

Caros arched his brow and almost laughed when Drusus shrank back in his chair. "You're suspected of attempted murder, Drusus. Adiona's murder. Understandably, she's none too pleased with you. And neither am I."

Drusus swallowed hard. "I told Adiona *and* her minions, I'm innocent!"

"Yes, well, no one expects you to shout your guilt in the Forum, do they?"

"You suggest I'm *lying?*"

Caros shrugged eloquently. "I *suggest* you prove to me you're telling the truth. Otherwise, I'll be forced to call in the magistrate and let him decide the case."

Drusus paled. Torture was legal and its brutality was expected in judicial matters. He slid down in his chair, a petulant expression creasing his fleshy face. "You're already set against me. How can I prove something when you refuse to listen?"

"For a start, why don't you tell me your side of the matter," Caros said. "Go ahead and even up the balance. At the moment, the adder found in Adiona's bed has the scale heavily weighed against you."

The mention of his snake brought Drusus flying from his chair. "I didn't put my pet in her room! And I want to know who's going to compensate me for my loss? It was your man who murdered her. *You* should—"

"Cease, Drusus! Let the matter go. It's over."

Round-eyed and sputtering, Drusus dropped back into his seat. Caros studied him. "Let's say I believe you didn't intend to harm your benefactress. Who *do* you think put the snake in her room?"

"It could have been anyone." Drusus frowned. "One of my servants or a funeral guest. How should I know? It's not as though Adiona is loved. Some even consider her more poisonous than my adder."

"You ungrateful weasel." Caros ached to strike the wretch, but as a Christian, he'd been working to control the violent tendencies he'd learned in the arena. "Adiona has been kind and generous to you and yours. How can you speak ill of her?"

Drusus glanced away, shamefaced but unrepentant.

"I suppose," he said grudgingly. "My beauty might have even escaped her cage and accidentally found her way to Adiona's room."

"Accidentally, eh? From what I understand the balcony was locked and the chamber door closed when Adiona arrived back from the funeral."

"I told you, I don't know. Whatever the case, I didn't do it."

To his amazement, Caros found himself believing the other man. It galled him to do so, but his instincts rarely led him wrong. Until he held solid proof against Drusus, he had to follow his gut. He rose from the chair and rounded the desk. "Here's what is going to happen. I'm going back to Rome—"

"Gods be praised," Drusus muttered under his breath.

"My men will stay here and keep an eye on you."

Drusus's thin lips twisted. "You mean imprison me in my own villa."

"Take it as you like," Caros said, unconcerned. "If you're as innocent as you say, you'll send word to me if you learn the smallest detail of who is trying to harm Adiona."

"I'll consider it." Drusus raised his hand and studied his fingernails.

Caros's eyes narrowed. His fingers itched to close around the weasel's throat and twist. "Good. Because if you don't and I learn you've lied to me, you'll be begging for the magistrate's mercy before I'm finished with you."

Chapter Fifteen

Always an early riser, Adiona woke to the sound of the sea and birdsong. She wrapped a *palla* around her shoulders and slipped her feet into the sandals she'd left by the bed.

Leaning out of the open window, she breathed in the fresh sea air. She turned to prepare for the day when the sight of Quintus walking alone on the beach caught her eye. Her heart picked up speed. With the distance between them, she was too far away to guess his mood or see his handsome features, but he'd rid himself of the slave's garb in favor of a light-colored tunic just as he'd said he would.

Smiling because he never failed to keep his word even on the most trivial matters, she dragged herself from the window and dressed with haste. Washed and wearing her yellow tunic, she dabbed cinnamon perfume behind her ears before making her way into the corridor, down the stairs and out the front door.

Her quick pace continued all the way to the beach. At the last step before reaching the sand, she slowed and raised her chin to a regal angle. Quintus had his back to her, giving her a chance to catch her breath.

She admired the cut of his short black hair and the small birthmark at the nape of his neck. Muscles rippled across his broad shoulders as he skimmed stones across the surface of the sea.

Brushing the sand off his hands, he faced her. Caught staring, she felt her cheeks flame.

"Good morning, my lady." His eyes were the same intense green as the limes growing in the villa's central garden. "You look like a ray of sunshine in that tunic."

"Thank you." She caught her bottom lip between her teeth. The blood rushing in her ears was louder than the surf breaking on shore. Slightly dizzy from his warm regard, she felt as though a tide had rode in and she was drowning. "Your new garb suits you, as well."

He smiled. "My clothes are more snug than when I was here to wear them last, but *anything* is better than the prickly wool of a slave's tunic."

She laughed. The white cotton he wore was a sharp contrast to his bronzed skin. His gladiatorial training had built his physique and long hours in the sun had only added to his appearance of health and vitality. "Of all the indignities of slavery, I do believe that wool is the one you complain of the most."

He rubbed the back of his neck. "You're probably right. Likely because its chafing is a constant reminder of my losses."

A wave crashed loudly, drawing her attention to the shore a short distance away. Quintus rarely spoke of his past and then only when she inquired about it. "What is the first thing you'll do once you're a free man again?" She held her breath, hoping he planned to include her in his future.

"I'm returning to Amiternum," he said without pause. "My son. I have to see that he was properly buried. I was arrested and taken to prison before I was able to make certain."

His worry for his son all these months must have tormented him. Her concern for Octavia had been overwhelming, yet Octavia was only a friend, not her child. "I'm sorry, Quintus. I can't imagine how awful these past months have been for you."

His jaw flexed. He turned away and looked out to sea. "My God has sustained me. I have faith He'll continue to do so."

She longed to go to him. She admired Quintus's certainty in his God, but he didn't fool her. His pain was too strong to hide. She wished she knew what to say to offer him comfort, but mere words seemed trite after all he'd suffered.

She went to stand beside him. He continued to look out over the sparkling sea. It was clear he didn't want to discuss his past or his son any longer.

"You're up early," she said, striving for a change of subject. "Were you going somewhere?"

"No, I was praying."

"Praying?" She glanced around. "Where is your shrine?"

Some of the tension left his body. He motioned with his hand to the sea and sky. "I don't need a shrine when all of creation testifies to God's glory."

She remembered his prayer for Octavia on the way to Neopolis. The way he'd spoken to his God as though He were a trusted friend.

"What did you speak to Him about?"

"You're nosy."

"I'm sorry." She flushed. "I'm intrigued."

"I'm teasing you." He grinned. "I don't mind you asking. I sent Libo off to town for supplies and a few messages, one of which I hope will find Lucius. I asked the Lord for Libo's protection and to bring Lucius back here quickly."

"Ah. When will Libo return?"

"Tonight, I imagine."

She looked out over the water. A school of dolphins played a short distance from shore. "It's beautiful here," she murmured.

"Yes," he agreed. "It is."

She glanced over to find him watching her. Her face heated again, and she feared her cheeks were going to become permanently red if she didn't control her reactions to him.

"Come." He offered his hand to help her down from the step. "Take a walk with me. I want to show you something."

Such an easy thing, taking hold of his hand, but this morning the simple action seemed monumental. Telling herself she was being foolish, that the frisson of excitement in the air was her imagination, she accepted his outstretched palm.

He led her across the beach, the wind whipping at her tunic. When they reached the mountainside that formed the southern end of the cove, Adiona thought they would return the way they'd come or head back to the villa. Quintus surprised her. "Follow me," he said, smiling.

A little uncertain but enjoying the adventure, she allowed him to tow her along the base of the mountain.

"There it is." He pointed ahead of them.

"I don't see anything," she admitted, feeling a bit duped and wondering if he was making a joke at her expense.

"Good. You're not supposed to."

"You're starting to vex me, Quintus," she said with mock seriousness. "If you're playing some sort of trick on me, I'll—"

He laughed. "You'll what?"

"I don't know. I'll have to think about it," she said coolly.

Grinning, he made a sharp right turn and tugged her into a hidden passage in the rock face. The sheer walls muffled the pounding of the waves on the beach. His warm hand clasping hers, Quintus reassured her with a smile. "It's not far now."

Eager to see where he was taking her, she followed him along the damp, sandy path, her blood humming with excitement.

"There it is." Quintus pointed to what looked like a cave.

Adiona pulled back instantly. "I don't want to go in there."

He studied her for a moment. Had he forgotten her fear of small spaces? He combed his free hand through his hair. "Adiona, please trust me. I would never endanger you—"

"I know, but…"

"Don't allow your husband to hurt you any longer."

She gasped and pulled her hand from his grasp. "How dare you? You know nothing of it."

"I know what you've told me. Is there more?"

She turned away. "I want to go back to the villa."

"All right."

His easy capitulation miffed her. "Is that all?"

"Is what all? You're not making sense."

"I know."

"Then explain," he said gently. "I want to understand."

She released the breath locked in her chest. "I… I'm afraid, but I don't want to be. I want to see why you've brought me here, but what if I panic again and act like a fool?"

He eased her closer. "No matter what you do, I won't think you're a fool. I'll think you're brave if you try. And if you find you're afraid, we'll leave."

She glanced away, her vision blurring as she stared at the rock face. Indecision tugged at her until she thought she might rip in two. She closed her eyes. What did she have to lose? "All right. If you promise…"

"I do."

He gave her no time to change her mind and hastened their pace up the path and through the covered channel. Inside the cave, the air grew cooler. Adiona's heart pounded and her hands grew clammy, but her trust in Quintus prodded her on. Strange green lights flickered on the walls, growing brighter with each step forward.

A bend in the path found them in a grotto bathed in shimmering green light. Adiona caught her breath, marveling at the pool of seawater that glowed like an emerald backlit by sunshine.

"What do you think?" Quintus asked.

Speechless, Adiona knelt by the water's edge and swept her hand through the cold water, watching the play of light on her fingers. "It's the most beautiful place I've ever seen." She looked up at Quintus and nearly drowned in the tenderness she found in his eyes. "How did this happen? What makes the water so clear and green?"

He shrugged. "No one knows."

"How did you find this place?"

"My brother and I used to play here as children when

my parents brought us to the villa each winter. It's one of my favorite places."

"I can see why." She stood and rubbed her hands together to dry them. "It's like being transported to paradise."

"My thoughts exactly." He drew her over to a bench. She sat on the damp marble and leaned against the cool stone wall. "How are you?" he asked.

In truth, the anxiety she usually experienced in confined spaces was perplexingly absent. "I'm fine... I think."

"Good, but make sure to tell me if you need to leave."

As always, his concern melted her heart. She patted the bench beside her. "Won't you sit with me?"

He hesitated, but did as she asked. For long moments they sat in companionable silence, enjoying the sounds of the sea and the play of green light.

"The color reminds me of your eyes," she said. "The first time I saw you, I remember thinking I'd never seen their like."

"Yes, they're an odd color, all right."

"Don't be dim. Surely, you know how handsome you are?"

He raked a hand through his hair, an action Adiona realized he did when he was uncomfortable. "That's not for me to say."

Amused by his modesty, she grinned. "Come now, you must have had females chasing you since childhood."

He shrugged. "A few, perhaps. Surely less than the number of boys who chased after you."

She glanced away, the game no longer amusing. "No one ever chased me. I was married off at twelve, remember? Crassus would have killed any man who looked twice in my direction."

"Perhaps he loved you in a twisted sort of way."

She gave a bitter laugh. "No one's ever loved me. Certainly not Crassus."

Quintus took hold of her hand. The matter-of-fact way she spoke of never being loved pierced him like an arrow to the heart. He longed to take her in his arms, to convince her of how much *he* loved her. But what would be the point? He'd sent Caros the money he owed for his freedom the day he'd arrived at the villa, but until he heard back from the lanista he was still a slave.

And she isn't a Christian, he reminded himself.

He remembered Pelonia had encountered a similar problem before her marriage to Caros. Until now, he hadn't fully appreciated the faith and strength of will his friend had employed to leave the man she loved. Fearing he lacked the same strength when it came to leaving Adiona, he pushed the thought from his mind.

"I think you're more loved than you realize," he said.

"Really?" she asked, her voice flat. "What makes you think so?"

Realizing how dangerously close he was to declaring himself, he swallowed hard and sought a diversion. "Your father must—"

"Hardly," she scoffed. "He abandoned me for war and sold me to Crassus for a fortune to cover his debts. I never saw him again after my wedding day. He died half a decade ago and I couldn't care less."

The note of pain in her voice told him otherwise. "You deserved better. What of your mother?"

"Father sent her away soon after I was born. I never knew why. I tried to find her after Crassus died, but all my inquiries proved futile. My old maid told me she died, but I don't know for certain."

"I'm sorry," he said quietly.

She shrugged. "It was all a long time ago."

Contemplating her confession, he stood and walked to the water's edge where the play of colors was especially bright. The level of trust Adiona displayed in telling him her secrets honored him. Ever since that first night in the *tabernae* when he glimpsed the sensitive woman behind the mask she showed the world, Adiona had been an enigma he longed to explore.

He faced her. Thinking how lovely she was and how blessed any man would be to call her his wife, he asked, "If you're certain Crassus bore you no affection, why pay a fortune for you? If he'd simply wanted a child bride, he could have bought one for a pittance."

She glanced down at the folded hands in her lap. "I'd rather not say."

Frustrated, but leery of pushing her, he nodded. "I understand."

"Do you?" Adiona studied him from under her lashes. In the years she'd spent vying for social prominence among the Roman elite, she'd seen all manner of lascivious behavior. Nothing shocked her because she'd seen every vice imaginable, not that she'd ever participated. Always holding herself apart from the men who sought to use her, she'd been determined no one would ever have the chance to abuse her the way Crassus had during her marriage. The thought of submitting to any man's touch sickened her.

Until Quintus.

She stood, gathering every ounce of courage she possessed, and walked toward him. For years, she'd watched other women use seduction as a game or a weapon to glean a man's affections. She wanted neither to toy with Quintus nor to harm him, but she did want him to love her.

Struggling to ignore the voice in her head that whispered she was a failure unworthy of affection, she clung to the hope that her husband was wrong and that somehow Quintus might find her appealing. Noting Quintus was trapped between her and the pool's edge, she stopped a breath away from his broad chest. Terrified he'd ridicule her or reject her at any moment, she stood on tiptoes and wrapped her arms around his neck.

She felt his breathing quicken and saw his eyes dilate. Trembling, she closed her eyes and pressed her lips to the warmth of his.

He froze. His fingers clutched the silk at her ribs. In the exact moment she felt certain he meant to push her away, he groaned and pulled her against him.

Chapter Sixteen

It would have taken less strength to move a mountain, but somehow Quintus managed to break the kiss and set Adiona away from him. His breathing ragged, he fought the need to drag her back into his arms.

Adiona's eyes fluttered open. In a blink, her wistful gaze changed to one of confusion. "Did I do something wrong?"

Desperate for greater distance between him and temptation, he sidestepped her, careful not to fall back into the pool, although a plunge in the cold water might be good for him.

"No," he choked. "You did nothing wrong. I did."

"What do you mean?"

He raked his fingers through his hair. Her scent of cinnamon and sea air teased his senses. Every instinct he possessed clamored with a riotous need to claim her as his own. "I shouldn't have touched you."

"*I* kissed you," she said. "You've rejected me often enough. I should have saved us both this uncomfortable situation and just accepted you don't want me."

His gaze shot to her face. What game was she playing at? *Want* was a ridiculous, tepid feeling when compared to how much he *craved* her.

"I understand." She took a step backward. "I really do."

Was she insane?

"I know it's not your fault," she whispered.

His eyes narrowed as he considered her. By now he understood her well enough to sense when there was a deeper meaning behind her words. "What isn't my fault?"

She locked her arms around her waist defensively. She looked away, her cheeks darkening with color. "You don't find me appealing."

"Appealing?" he choked on a humorless laugh. He closed his eyes, unable to get himself under control when the sight of her called to him like a mirage after months of exile in a desert. "I find you *more* than appealing, Adiona. You are without a doubt the most beautiful woman I've ever seen. How can you possibly think otherwise?"

She bit her lower lip. Indecision clouded her expression. Her eyes seemed to glisten in the shifting green light of the grotto. "You pushed me away. Just as my husband did."

"Your husband was an old man. Was he blind, too? I can't imagine any man with breath in his lungs not willing to give up his right arm to have you."

She stared at him, her bewildered eyes wide and genuinely amazed. He thought he saw her tremble, but it might have been the filtered light rippling over her skin.

She crossed to the bench and sat down without her usual grace, pondering him as though he were on trial. "Then why…?"

"Because you're not mine. Because I'm *not* your

husband. I don't have the right to claim you no matter how much I'd like to."

"How does marriage enter into this? Everyone I know does whatever he likes, with whomever, whenever the mood strikes."

He could imagine. The social circle she inhabited was notorious for its vice and she was notorious within that social circle. "That may be, but I'm a Christian."

"And Christians don't believe in passion?"

"Adiona," he said, "If you were mine, you'd have *no* reason to doubt my ardor for you."

Her eyes rounded and her lips formed a silent "Oh." "Then you do want me?"

He sighed. "Yes, I'd have to be dead not to, but I want to live by my God's standards even more, no matter how difficult that may be."

She ducked her head and studied her clenched hands in her lap. She cleared her throat. "You said whatever happened in this grotto, you won't think ill of me because of it."

"Of course, I won't think badly of you."

"You might. You don't know the truth about me."

"Whatever you may or may not have done, it's in the past. I'm not proud of every action or decision I've made, either."

Looking at him, she tilted her head, a wan smile curving her lips. "I don't know how you do it, but you make me *want* to tell you things I've never told anyone."

Quintus suspected it was the Spirit in him that drew her.

"I trust you like I've never trusted another person. If I tell you something, will you vow to take my secret to your grave?"

Keenly interested in learning every detail she was

willing to share about herself, he nodded. "You have my word, Adiona. To the grave."

She glanced away, seeming to accept his promise. "You asked me why my husband paid a fortune to wed me. Crassus was almost sixty and childless. He told my father I was the most beautiful creature he'd ever seen and my youth assured him many sons. He disgusted me, but at twelve years old what was I to do but accept my fate and my father's commands?"

Her profile was tense and pale. "On our wedding night, Crassus refused to consummate our vows. I was glad until…later."

She released a shaky breath. "He called me a witch and a deceiver. He accused me of putting a spell on him. He claimed I'd beguiled him into marriage to steal his fortune, but the spell had ended when I didn't…excite him in our marriage bed."

Quintus worked at keeping his face emotionless, but rage brewed inside him. The old goat was broken. Rather than accept responsibility for his failure as a man he'd blamed an innocent child.

"He cursed me as a useless woman and said that I deserved to be punished like the dog I was for tricking him."

A red haze clouded Quintus's vision. The man deserved to be tortured. Slowly and by intensifying degrees. "The cage?"

She nodded, her throat working. "He left me there for days at a time, whenever the fancy took him. His slaves weren't allowed to scar or touch me. You see, he didn't want to have his ornament marred," she said bitterly. "But he encouraged them in all other manner of cruelty against me."

Quintus ached to take her in his arms, but he hesitated in case she stopped talking.

Her eyes slid closed and her chin quivered. She rubbed her temples with her fingertips. "They heckled me, spat on me, poked me with sticks. Rotten food was left out to draw rats. After that first night I learned not to scream because my fear made Crassus laugh… and laugh."

She covered her ears with her palms, her face pinched with remembered agony. Unable to keep himself from comforting her, Quintus crossed the grotto's sandy floor. Sitting down on the bench beside her, he drew her against his side and waited patiently while she decided whether to continue.

Countless moments passed before she spoke. "I tried to escape—once."

His arm tightened around her narrow shoulders. He didn't need her to elaborate.

"When Crassus *finally* died, men swarmed to me like vultures all vying for the carcass of my husband's fortune. Because Crassus had no children and hadn't declared an heir, they assumed he'd leave his money to me. They tried to woo me into marriage with honeyed words and gifts like I was a simpleton unable to see through their designs. When the lawyers read Crassus's will, I learned he left every *denari* to the son of one of his friends.

"In the end, I bribed the lawyers to rewrite the will with me as sole beneficiary. I learned then I needed to protect myself or I might end up another man's whipping post. Frankly, I'd have rather drunk poison than allow one of those pigs to touch me."

"I understand," Quintus said over the pain lodged in his throat. The knowledge of her suffering tormented him. It was no wonder she hated men and refused to remarry. She'd had no decent male examples. Instead of protecting her, her father had betrayed her into the hands of a madman. And the madman hadn't only abused her body, he'd wounded her to the depths of her soul. Quintus didn't doubt her beauty and wealth had made her the target of every fortune hunter from Rome to Dalmatia. No wonder she'd adopted the facade of an iron she-wolf, impervious to the hunters' arrows. A flesh-and-blood woman could bleed.

"I'm proud of you, my lady."

"*Proud* of me?" She pulled away and looked up at him, her slim body stiff with disbelief. "How can you be when my whole life is a sham?"

"Explain," he said, leery of taking her thoughts for granted. She didn't think like other women. Each time he imagined he understood her, she proved him wrong.

"I'm a fraud. Even Caros, my most trusted confidant, doesn't know the whole truth about me. He knows I had a bad marriage, but no more. All of Rome believes I'm a wealthy widow when the truth is, I don't qualify to wear the *stola* of a married woman and the money isn't rightfully mine."

He stood and gathered her hands in his, drawing her to her feet. "I'm proud of you because you're strong. Another woman who suffered as you have may have turned into a dormouse, but you, you're a lioness. You survived. After what I've lived through these past months, strength is something I appreciate. All the while, you stayed kind—"

"Kind? That's not the description people usually use when discussing me."

He grinned. "It's true you do a fine job of hiding it. But your care for Octavia and her children prove your sweetness and fidelity. As does your friendship with Caros. In fact, now that I think about it—"

"What?" she asked.

"I recall something Pelonia told me. A couple of months ago, before she and Caros wed, they were separated. As I remember it, he walked around like a man on the edge of dying."

"Yes, he was rather pathetic," she agreed.

He laughed. "Then you just *happened* to host a party for Pelonia's newly wedded cousin, didn't you?"

"Yes." She fidgeted with her *stola.*

Assured all the rumors had been false and that she and Caros had never been more than friends, his smile grew wider. "The party wasn't for her cousin, was it? It was an excuse to draw Caros and Pelonia back together."

Her mouth tightened. "*Someone* had to help them." She rolled her eyes. "All that drama was better suited for the stage."

He chuckled. "Once again you prove my point." He brushed his fingertip across her soft cheek, loving her more with each crash of the waves outside the grotto. "As for the money, if having it bothers you, return it to its rightful owner."

Her brow arched. "It doesn't bother me *that* much. Even if it did, Crassus's heir and his two remaining sons died in Herculaneum after Vesuvius erupted two years ago."

"Then find people in need you can bless. Think of the orphans on Rome's streets whose lives would be forever changed if they had a benefactress to provide them with basic necessities and education."

Her eyes sparkled with excitement. "Yes," she said. "I'd very much like to help children. Ease their suffering if possible. Perhaps…perhaps you could ask your God to show us a way to bring that about."

"I'll be happy to ask Him, but I'm certain He'd love to hear from you, as well."

A knock on Adiona's bedroom door woke her from a sound sleep. The angle of the sun streaming through the open shutters signaled the time as midmorning. She usually rose at first light, a habit left over from her marriage because Crassus always slept late.

Another light knock. "Who is it?" she called, raising her arms above her head to stretch her tight muscles.

"Bernice, my lady. Shall I come back?"

"No, just a moment." Adiona pushed off the warm silk bedcovers and pulled a *palla* around her shoulders before answering the door.

Bernice, a young woman no more than a handful of years older than Adiona, waited on the threshold with a basket of cloth in her arms. "Were you sleeping, my lady? I'm sorry. You're always awake before the rest of us."

"Yes, I slept overlong today."

"I hope you're not falling ill."

"No, I feel fit. Quite good, actually."

Pleased, Bernice smiled. She indicated the basket on her hip. "Master Quintus asked me to bring these to you. They're tunics the females of his family left here over the years for guests to use. Some of them may be too short, but I told him there might be a few long enough for your height. Even if there aren't, no one here will care if your ankles show." She colored. "I mean, that is, if you don't mind, my lady."

Adiona grinned. "Thank you. You can put the basket on the table. I'll look through them after I wash."

Bernice did as she was told and went back to the door. "I made cinnamon rolls this morning. You seemed to enjoy them a few days ago when you first arrived. I thought you might like some more."

"I did," Adiona said, brushing her hand over the soft cotton lying on top of the basket. "I have a friend in Rome whose cook is famous for his cinnamon rolls. Truth to tell, yours are even better."

Bernice blushed and beamed. "Thank you, my lady! The secret is the date paste I put in them. Most people just use the cinnamon and let the honey add all the sweetness, but the dates *and* honey, now that's the trick."

Adiona grinned, pleased that her compliment made the other woman happy.

"Shall I bring some up here for you?" Bernice asked. "Or do you want me to leave them on the breakfast table in the garden?"

"Where is Quin...your master?"

"He's in his office."

"Ah, then leave the rolls in the garden, I think. I'll be down soon."

Once Bernice left, Adiona searched through the basket of tunics. How thoughtful of Quintus to realize she'd like a change from the few garments she'd brought along with her. She chose one off the top, shook it out and raised the neckline to her throat to test the length. Too short. She repeated the process, noting that all the tunics were made of the softest cotton, silk or fine linen. Each was embroidered with masterful detail.

By the time she reached the bottom of the basket, she'd found three of the tunics were long enough, while a handful of others would do.

After she'd washed, she donned a white tunic with

blue embroidery around the neck, wrists and hem. There was little to do for her hair except brush it out and pin it back from her face with the wooden combs she'd brought with her from Rome.

Downstairs, she made her way to the villa's central garden. Dense shrubbery and trees filled the open-air courtyard with a rainbow of exotic fruit: red pomegranates, orange tangerines, bright yellow lemons, green limes and purple figs. Tall date palms reached to the sky from the middle of the rectangular space, surrounding a mosaic-tiled fountain.

Just as Bernice promised, Adiona found the sweet rolls and a selection of fruit waiting for her on a small table in the center of the garden. She chose one of the sticky cinnamon rolls and poured extra honey over the top before taking a bite of her favorite treat. She closed her eyes, savoring the added sweetness of the dates.

Footsteps drew her attention to the covered peristyle. The sight of Quintus smiling at her infused her with joy. Leaning against a red pillar, his arms crossed over his broad chest, he wore a dark tunic that turned his eyes a vivid green in his bronzed face. Clean-shaven, his black hair newly shorn, he was so handsome he stole her breath.

"Have you eaten?" she managed to say over the sudden dryness of her throat.

"Hours ago." He straightened and walked toward her.

"Then you should eat something else."

"I'll take one of those if you'll share."

She glanced at the platter piled with enough cinnamon rolls to feed a legion. "No, I'm sorry. I planned to eat them all myself."

He eyed the stack and muttered drily, "All right, if

you insist. Good thing the doors are wide. I may have to roll you out."

She burst out laughing. "Silly man." She lifted the platter and held it toward him. "Bernice assures me this is a special recipe, but I suppose you know that."

"Yes, I think it has something to do with the dates." He grinned and chose one of the treats. Obviously, Bernice had shared her unique take on the rolls before.

A huge smile tugged at her lips. Just being with Quintus brought her joy. "Personally, I like the added honey best."

He tried her suggestion and drizzled extra honey over the top of the roll before popping it into his mouth. He chewed with exaggerated enjoyment until he swallowed.

"You're right. It's delicious." He reached up and softly brushed a crumb from the corner of her mouth with his thumb. "Almost as sweet as the kiss you gave me last week."

Her face flamed. Caught off guard, she felt certain her hot cheeks must rival the redness of the pomegranates sitting on the table. She ducked her head, unused to light banter or having her tongue tied in a knot.

Chuckling, Quintus picked up the plate of rolls and bowl of fruit. He tipped his head to indicate two glasses and a pitcher of fruit juice on the table beside her. "Bring those, will you, and sit with me while you eat. I have some good news."

She followed him to the rectangular fountain covered in a mosaic pattern of colorful flowers and vines. They sat on the benchlike ledge surrounding the clear pool with the food situated between them.

"What's happened?" she asked, handing him a glass of nectar.

"I've received word concerning my brother."

"Ah." Her stomach clenched. She set the pitcher down and feigned interest in the bowl of fruit. "Such good news, indeed. When will he arrive?"

"Therein lies my problem. Lucius sent word to Libo and a messenger brought it this morning. My brother has a penchant for drinking and gambling. It seems he was involved in a…situation a few towns south of here. The local magistrate is holding him in the jail."

"Can you send Libo to fetch him? If you need money to pay a fine, I have it in my satchel."

"No, I don't need your coin." He gave her a crooked smile. "But thank you for the offer."

She licked her bottom lip and chose a section of pomegranate. "If ever I can help you, you need only to ask."

"That's kind of you, my lady."

"Adiona," she stressed. "You've been calling me by my given name of late. I prefer that."

"As you wish, Adiona." He raised the glass to his lips and drank deeply before he continued. "Libo can't fetch Lucius for me. I need to go myself."

Adiona ate the tangy pieces of fruit she held, pretending a calm that eluded her. "Must it be you?"

"Unfortunately, yes. Libo's not practiced enough to sail the necessary distance and my other servants have yet to be rehired." He reached across the space between them and clasped her hand. "Look at me, lioness."

Her mouth tightened, but she lifted her gaze. "What?"

"I wouldn't consider going if I thought you were in the least bit of danger."

"I know," she said, trying to keep a petulant tone from her voice.

"If you're frightened, I won't leave you."

Her heart melted. Defeated by her love, she realized she had to let him go. Her capitulation might pave the way for him to regain his fortune and leave her, but his happiness meant more to her than her own. "How long do you think you'll be gone?"

The lines in his forehead eased. "I'll be back this evening. The winds this time of year will take me down the coast in no time. The magistrate is a friend of mine. I'm certain I can convince him to release Lucius into my care. The return sail will take a few hours, but all will be well."

She worked her hand free of his and stood. There were too many dangers to count. Freak storms and boating accidents were all too common. Her fears began to multiply. If she didn't let him go now, she'd never be able to. She turned away. "I suppose you must leave, then. The sooner you go, the sooner you can come back."

A pigeon landed on a limb of the tangerine tree nearby. She focused on the cooing bird to help maintain her calm appearance. Quintus came up behind her and placed his hands on her shoulders. She caught the sweet scent of cinnamon on his fingertips. His warm breath fanned her ear. "You mustn't be worried. I *will* return."

Her eyes drifted shut. She didn't doubt his intentions, nor did she understand her reaction. She'd never been this weak. But now that she had someone to love, she understood all that she had to lose. "You promise?"

"You have my word."

She released a pent up breath. "Then hurry. I'll miss you."

She felt him smile against her temple. "Will you?"

"Of course," she said, struggling for a light tone, but feeling drearier by the moment. "Who else will amuse me while you're gone?"

He laughed and pressed a lingering kiss to the top of her head.

Fighting the need to call him back, she listened to his footsteps until they were gone.

Chapter Seventeen

Adiona took a deep breath of sea air and dug her bare toes into the beach's soft white sand. The afternoon sun sparkled on the water's surface as though an unseen hand had scattered diamonds from the shore to the dark line of the horizon.

Quintus was due to arrive soon. The hours since he'd gone had stretched like days. In an effort to pass the time more quickly, she'd recruited Libo to help her in the garden. They'd weeded most of the beds, but many of the trees still needed pruning. She planned to continue her efforts tomorrow.

Her sandals dangling by the laces she held, she crossed the beach to a peninsula on the south side of the cove.

Intrigued by the watery nests of sea urchins and starfish in between the rocks, she left her sandals on the beach and climbed to the top of the outcropping.

She gingerly made her way across the slick surface to the farthest point. Surrounded by the churning sea on three sides, she sat down and leaned back on her braced arms. A gust of wind whipped the long tendrils of her hair and the dampness of the rocks seeped through her tunic. Cold sea spray soaked her face and chest, but she laughed, enjoying the untamed quality of the elements.

Raising her hand to shield her eyes from the sun's glare, she noticed a lone crag not too far offshore. Like a sentinel guarding the mouth of the cove, the monolith reminded her of Quintus. He was solid and dependable, impervious to the wind and waves of life that stormed against him.

The better she knew Quintus, the more she realized his faith in his God sustained and strengthened him. For some reason the knowledge comforted her. She longed to find that confidence for herself.

The thought reminded her of what Quintus said about prayer. There was no need for a priest or even a temple. Her arms locked around her shins, she lowered her forehead to her knees.

"Quintus's God," she whispered. "If You're there, please hear me. Thank You for bringing him to me. Please deliver him back safely."

Not sure of what she expected, she waited a long moment for any kind of reaction. When none came, she lay back on the rocks and closed her eyes, soaking in the warmth of the sun. The ebb and flow of the waves made her sleepy. She wished Quintus was there to bask in the moment with her.

An icy blast of water woke her. Sputtering and a little disorientated, she sat up and rubbed the sting of salt from her eyes. A quick glance out to sea told her she'd slept long enough for the tide to start rolling in. The dark line on the horizon had widened and the waves were rough. The heavy atmosphere promised a storm.

With another prayer for her man's safe return, she stood and headed for the villa. Thunder rumbled and the rising wind tested her balance. Her hair whipped in wild disarray as she struggled not to slip. Regretting the decision to investigate the peninsula, she secured her unruly tresses back from her face with one hand and kept her eyes on the slick rocks at her feet.

When the beach appeared in her periphery, she looked up to judge the remaining distance to the villa. She froze. A small sailboat was moored to the pier and a stranger was striding toward to her. Panic jolted her. She tried to stifle her fear, but after weeks of being chased by an assassin she fought a losing battle. Her protector was gone and neither Libo nor Bernice were anywhere in sight, not that either of them would be much help against the tall stranger or the knife sheathed on his belt.

Her thoughts raced. Caught between a possible killer and the oncoming storm, she was fraught with indecision. If she sought refuge in the sea, the inescapable waves would grind her against the rocks, whereas she might have a chance to escape capture if she took her chances on the beach.

Determined to fight for her life if need be, she stooped to pick up a sharp rock before forcing her feet forward. Quintus had called her a lioness and she refused to cower like a lamb.

Weapon tight in hand, she climbed off the peninsula, the jagged stones cutting into her palms and feet. By the time she reached the beach, there was nowhere to go and no use to scream. The stranger was too close to outrun and the stretch of open shore offered no place to hide. Her blood racing with fear, she braced her feet in the sand like a gladiator waiting for battle.

Her nemesis stopped several paces away. His dark eyes roamed over her from head to toe, his glance stopping momentarily at the rock she held. He gave her the slow, calculated smile of a practiced seducer. "Just the woman I've been looking for."

Her knees began to shake. There was only one person looking for her—her assassin. Her fingers tightened around the rock. She lifted her chin. "I could have gone forever without seeing you."

"Arrows to my heart, my lady." He pressed his right palm against his chest in a dramatic display. "Neptune finally sends me a gift from the sea and instead of a nymph to use for my pleasure, I get a siren who disdains me."

Her eyes narrowed. "What is your name, fool?"

"Lucius Ambustus at your service." He gave a small bow. "Since you're on my property, perhaps you'd be good enough to tell me your name, as well."

"Lucius?" Her gaze darted past him, searching the near-darkness for any sign of Quintus. Her fright evaporated. "Where is your brother? Isn't he with you? Has he already gone to the villa?"

Lucius lost all traces of humor or warmth. "Who are you?" he demanded over a clap of thunder. "What game do you play? Quintus is dead."

"No, no, he's not," she said in a rush. "He received word you were in jail. He went to look for you this morning."

"Gods be praised." Lucius closed his eyes to fully absorb the news. "How did he survive? Where has he been? Who are you to him?"

Seeing his genuine shock and concern, she dropped the rock she held. The sky had darkened ominously and the first drops of rain began to fall. "Let's go inside. I'll tell you all once we're indoors."

The storm began in earnest as they raced across the

beach and up the stone steps. Bernice met them in the entryway. She handed Adiona a large square of cloth to dry herself, while ignoring the pool of water collecting at Lucius's feet.

Lucius laughed at the mess. "You might as well know now, my lady, Bernice has a bone to pick with me."

"Hmmph!" Bernice grunted as she left to fetch another drying cloth.

Unused to servants showing disapproval of their master, Adiona glanced between him and Bernice's departing back. "From what I understand, she has a whole skeleton of justified complaints against you."

Lucius grinned. "True. But all will be well now that Quintus is back to straighten us out."

Bernice returned with the cloth. Lucius dried his hair and patted down his tunic before showing Adiona into an office on the north side of the house. She knew instantly the room belonged to Quintus. The deep green walls and masculine, expertly carved wood furniture spoke of a man with understated taste and refinement. She took a seat in front of the desk, noting the set of unopened scrolls a messenger brought earlier that day, the ivory stylus and bronze oil lamp. Lucius sat in the chair beside her.

"That hulk is not mine," he tilted his head toward the desk. "After what I've done to the family fortune, I'm not fit to sit behind it."

"No head for sums?" she asked.

"None at all. Thank the gods Quintus is back or I'd end up in the streets."

Adiona studied Lucius's pleasant, open expression. She began to realize what Quintus meant about his jovial brother. Lucius might be full-grown, but he was a boy in a man's body. There was no guile in him, but neither was there any hint of maturity.

"Now tell me what happened. Why are you here?" he said, his eyes keen with interest. "When will Quintus return?"

She sat back in her leather chair and explained the situation, including her reasons for being there. "Quintus received word of your whereabouts earlier today. He promised to be back by this evening, but with the storm, I don't see how."

Her gaze drifted to the open window and the sheets of rain pouring off the eaves. On land, the storm was relatively minor so far, with little thunder and no lightning. But at sea, in a small sailboat… She shuddered. Quintus and his safety were paramount. *Please, God, bring him home.*

Bernice's footsteps echoed in the hall. The maid crossed through the office's open door carrying a tray. She'd draped a *palla* over her left arm. "I've brought you both some hot lemon water. I don't want either of you to fall ill."

"See, she can't stay mad at me." Lucius winked at Bernice. "Did you sweeten it with honey, my honey?"

Bernice snorted and rolled her eyes, but her manner softened a little. She set the tray on the desk and shook out the *palla*. "I thought you might want this to keep warm, my lady."

Adiona murmured her thanks. With her hair and tunic damp, she had begun to feel chilled. Wrapped in the *palla,* she cupped her hands around the warm glass and sipped the hot, sweetened water. Bernice lit several more oil lamps before she left.

Lucius eyed her over the rim of his drink. "Don't

worry about Quintus, my lady. Nothing bad ever happens to him."

Incredulous, Adiona set her glass down with a thunk. Already fretful over Quintus's whereabouts, she lost her temper. "*Really?* You don't think the death of his son was bad? Or being arrested and tossed into prison? Perhaps you'd consider it a *good* thing to be made a slave or to fight for your life in the arena?"

Lucius shrank back in his seat, clearly unused to facing serious anger. "Of course, Fabius's death was a tragedy," he said sadly. "We all felt it. The child was a joy. Always laughing. Quintus had just bought him his first pony last spring. But the rest?" He shrugged. "My brother is golden. Always has been. Look how he's recovered. I find I can't be distressed when he's alive and all is well."

She glared at Lucius. "All is *well?* I beg to differ. All *was* well until word of your whereabouts came this morning. If not for your lackadaisical ways, Quintus would be here with me now."

His face fell. She refused to feel guilty, even though he made her feel like she'd kicked a puppy.

"You're right," he said, full of woe. "I'm sorry. I always cause trouble. Did you know Quintus and I are twins?"

"Yes, he mentioned it," she answered, taken off guard by the unexpected question. Although both men were handsome, Lucius was a duller version of his brother. His hair was brown not black, his eyes mossy-green instead of emerald. They shared a similar height, but Quintus was more muscular. Most of all, Lucius possessed none of his brother's presence. When Quintus entered a room, he owned it. Even in the chaos of the arena, he'd become a focal point for the mob.

"Since boyhood he's watched my back and cleaned up my messes," Lucius shared without a hint of reserve. "I've been overwhelmed without him these many months thinking he was dead. I've missed him more than I can say."

"I understand," she said, thinking how dejected she'd been after a single day without Quintus.

Some time later, Bernice returned to the office and delivered roasted fish with an herb sauce for dinner. The delicious scent made Adiona's nervous stomach roll sickly.

She cast another glance out the window. Night had come early thanks to the storm that continued to build. Flashes of lightning lit the darkness, thunder crashing quickly on its heels.

Raw with worry, Adiona jumped to her feet and began to pace. Lucius chattered on while he ate. She ignored him until she realized she'd been given a chance to learn more about Quintus from his talkative twin.

She faced the man-child and gave him a winsome smile. "Are you married, Lucius?"

He finished chewing a bite of fish. "Twice divorced. I have no trouble getting wed. It's the knack of keeping a wife that escapes me."

"And Quintus? He was married, yes?"

His mouth tightened and he quieted for the first time that evening. Frustrated, Adiona wanted to kick him. Why, when they were finally discussing something of interest, did he have to go sullen and silent?

"He told me a little of his marriage," she said. "I take it he wasn't happy. I confess I'm curious to know what Quintus did to make the poor woman miserable enough to…" She sliced a finger across her throat and let the implication hang in the air.

"It wasn't *his* fault," Lucius said taking the bait in his brother's defense. He pushed back his tray of half-eaten fare. His shoulders slumped. "Actually, it's mine in a roundabout way."

"*Your* fault? How?"

"We were only eighteen," he offered as an excuse. "I gambled myself into a corner with the son of a rival family. I ended up owing Faustinus more than a year of my allowance. For once, I didn't want to embroil Quintus in my problems, but when Faustinus sent his lackeys to collect my debt, I didn't have a way of hiding the broken bones they left behind."

Thinking he deserved a few broken bones for being stupid enough to gamble away his inheritance, she said nothing and waited for him to continue.

"When Quintus found out what happened, he offered to loan me the money, but I owed too much. It was late in the year and he didn't have enough funds on hand, either."

He ran his fingers through his hair in a way that reminded her of Quintus. "He tried to reason with Faustinus, but the rat wasn't interested. Quintus went to our parents for me, but they refused to pay the debt. Neither of us realized they declined because Faustinus had petitioned them for a marriage between Quintus and Faustinus's sister, Faustina."

Adiona's anger burned brighter toward Lucius by the moment.

"You see, all the ladies of Amiternum wanted Quintus. Our family is prosperous and Quintus has been blessed since birth. Faustina knew she'd be the envy of every woman in the province if he married her."

An alarm sounded in Adiona's head. She sank into the chair behind her. The story sounded eerily similar to how Crassus had chosen her. "I can understand any woman wanting to marry Quintus, but why did he agree to Faustina?"

"As the oldest son, it was Quintus's responsibility to marry well and for connections. Our father saw the agreement as ideal and agreed without discussion. The union combined the families' fortunes, ended a century-old rivalry, plus my debt was erased in the bargain. Faustina was beautiful and cultured. On the surface, she seemed the kind of woman a man like Quintus could grow to love."

"I see," Adiona said, jealous even when she knew there was no need to be.

"Quintus doesn't speak ill of anyone," Lucius continued, warming to his subject. "You won't ever hear him complain about the shrew, but there's never been a more vain or selfish woman since time began. Faustina spent every waking hour chasing her own pleasures. She was always attending some party or hosting one. After Fabius was born, it got worse. For months she abandoned them both for an opium pipe. Quintus tried to help her. She refused. He prayed for her for a long time, but she scorned his God and turned to other men just to prove she wanted nothing to do with his new religion. The whole situation was intolerable. He was going to divorce her. Even his Christian texts said he had the right to. But the Fates removed the choice from his hand."

Dread began to rise in Adiona. She didn't want to hear the rest, but a driving need to better understand Quintus compelled her to listen.

"Normally, Quintus took his son everywhere, but he had unavoidable business in a nearby town and Fabius had a stomachache. Not wanting to tire the boy or make him more ill, Quintus left him with the nurse-maid. Faustina was gone with friends as usual. After that no one knows for sure what happened except that Faustina returned and dismissed the maid. Somehow the child ended up by himself in the street.

"When Quintus returned the next morning, his son was dead. Faustina had killed herself out of guilt or so she claimed in the missive she left."

Adiona wiped tears from her cheeks. Her chest ached for Quintus and the pain he'd suffered. In a different way, he'd been abused in his marriage just as she had been in hers. No wonder he seemed to understand her plight.

"Who reported him to the authorities?" she asked, her throat tight.

"None of us know for certain. I suspect it was Faustina's brother, although I have no proof. He's petty enough to see it as a way of regaining some of his sister's honor if he can paint Quintus as a villain."

"What will happen if Quintus returns to Amiternum?"

"I don't know. Truth to tell, I don't know why he was arrested in the first place."

"Because he's a Christian, or so I thought," she said, confused.

"He was. I suppose every Christian lives with a sword over his head, but what I meant is, I don't understand why he happened to be arrested at that precise moment in time. He'd never hidden his beliefs and there was no purge going on in the region. He'd been a respected merchant for years. After Quintus's arrest, I went to the magistrate, but he refused to even see me."

Adiona frowned. She'd never heard of a magistrate

refusing an audience with a prominent family. "Perhaps he was honest and not open to bribery?"

"Hardly. If anything, he knew of Quintus's scruples and thought bribery wasn't an option," he scorned. "But that argument fails to make sense. *I* was doing the negotiating. From past...incidents, the magistrate knew money wasn't a concern of mine when I go after something I want."

Bernice returned to collect the dinner dishes.

Adiona moved to the window in need of air. Her fingers clutched the wet marble windowsill as she searched the blackness for any sign of Quintus's return.

Bernice joined her. "He'll be all right, my lady. Master Quintus is wise and I'm certain he's stopped in a nearby town. He'll come home first thing in the morning."

"I hope you're right," Adiona said, her chin quivering.

Hours passed. Adiona prayed, uncertain if Quintus's God heard her, but she had to try.

Lucius sighed. "Would you care to play a game of cards or dice to pass the time?"

She stopped pacing and pinned him with a glare rife with impatience.

"All right, all right," he said, his hands raised in self-defense. "I just thought I'd ask."

"Yes, well, don't."

Lamplight flickered across his discomforted features. "If anything happens to Quintus, I swear I'll make amends."

"And how will you do that?" The man-child wasn't worth one of Quintus's sandal laces. "Your brother is unique among men. The finest there is. If he dies..." Her voice broke. She closed her eyes until she calmed herself enough to speak. "If he dies there will be no amends great enough to make up for his loss."

Somewhere in the house a door opened and closed. "Adiona!"

She stilled. Her heart stopped. Quintus's voice.

"Adiona, where are you?" he called.

"We're in your office," Lucius yelled. He jumped to his feet, seeming to understand she'd lost the ability to answer.

Laughing, Lucius flew across the tiled floor and out into the entryway. Adiona listened to the brothers' joyful reunion.

"Where is my guest?" she heard Quintus ask.

"She's been prowling in your office since the storm began."

Hearing footsteps on the tiles, she tried to compose herself. She sat down in her chair and affected an air of serenity. But the sight of Quintus on the threshold flooded her with sweet relief. Before she knew what she was doing, she jumped from her seat and ran to him.

He caught her around the waist, and up off the floor, his arms tight as a sail's lashing. "I guess you did miss me," he murmured against her hair.

He smelled of salt and the sea. He was soaking wet and freezing cold, but her heart had never been warmer toward him. "Not at all," she said, hugging him fiercely.

"I'm glad." He laughed and buried his face in the curve of her throat. "I didn't miss you, either."

Lucius pushed passed them. "Liars, the both of you."

Quintus and Adiona ignored him. "I prayed to your God He'd return you to me," she whispered.

He tilted her face up to his. The firelight made his skin appear a burnished bronze. He searched her face. "You prayed for me?"

She nodded. "The storm. I was so worried you wouldn't come back."

"I promised I'd be here tonight."

"I know." She wrapped her arms around his waist and pressed her cheek to his chest. "That's why I didn't give up hope. You always tell the truth."

A short time later, Quintus headed to his room to change his tunic. Warm and dry, he returned to the office. Still marveling that Adiona had prayed for him, he thanked the Lord for the work He was doing in her life.

He took his place behind the large desk. Adiona and Lucius sat across from him.

"So, brother." Lucius spoke first. "Where have you been? Your woman here has been beside herself with worry and I haven't been too calm, either."

Quintus's gaze drifted back to Adiona's exquisite face. The lamp's glow caressed her smooth skin and soft features. A blush stained her cheeks. The storm had sent his boat into the rocks. He'd barely made it to shore before walking several miles through a mountain pass to get back to her. Had he guessed the sweetness of her reaction to his return, he would have run. Barefoot. Over broken glass.

"Once I learned you'd been released, I started back," he explained. "The storm hit without much warning and I had a little trouble with my boat about five miles south of here."

"Hmm…" Lucius said. "Let me translate, my lady. When Quintus says he had 'a little trouble' it means the boat either capsized, sank or hit the rocks—"

Adiona gasped. Her anxious gaze roved over Quintus. "Is that true?"

Quintus glared at his brother. "It hit the rocks."

White as chalk, she jumped to her feet. "Are you hurt? You looked fit when you arrived, but—"

"I'm fine," he said, basking in her concern. "Truly."

She dropped back into the chair, her relief unconcealed. "How did you get back with no boat? You're not a fish. You couldn't have swum."

"He must have walked," Lucius guessed.

Her eyes flared. "You walked? In this rain? How?"

"It's a simple matter," Lucius injected drily. "You place one foot in front of the other."

"Just ignore him," Quintus told her. "I do all the time."

"Gladly." She didn't take her eyes from Quintus. "Now tell me how you walked here. I thought the cove was only accessible by sea."

"No. There's a mountain pass similar to the one that took us to the grotto."

"You took her to the grotto?" Lucius whistled between his teeth. "You must be madly in lo—"

"Quiet!" Quintus commanded. "Better yet, leave us. I'll speak to you later."

"Fine. I know when I'm not wanted." Lucius chuckled all the way out the door, for once doing as he was told without making a fuss.

"I'm sorry," he said once Lucius left. "My brother can be a bit much."

"I don't care about him," she dismissed. "I care about you and the danger you faced tonight. Why didn't you stay somewhere you'd be safe? Don't you know by now that if anything happened to you, I'd…?"

"You'd what, lioness?"

I'd never recover. She swallowed thickly. "I'd be sad, naturally."

He eased back in his seat. "That's good to know."

The sound of pouring rain filled the quiet. Thunder rolled overhead. Nervous energy danced between them. She rose from her chair and closed the shutters, eager to break the tension. There was so much to say, so many emotions to confess, but she didn't know how.

She turned and fell into a ravaging gaze of green fire. Her mouth ran dry and her knees grew weak. She felt consumed.

Quintus blinked. The emotion raging in his eyes disappeared as though it never existed. Bereft and breathless from the loss, she wondered if she'd imagined his intensity toward her or if she'd simply wished it were so.

"A messenger brought those scrolls soon after you left this morning," she murmured in need of defensive measures.

He reached for the rolls of parchment and studied the seals with interest. He frowned. "They're from Caros," he said, breaking the blob of wax. "This one's addressed to both of us."

His deft fingers unrolled the scroll and he scanned the message. His expression darkened with each word. "I think you should sit down."

Intrigued and anxious, she sat in one of the chairs before the desk. "What's happened?"

"It seems your assassin has been apprehended."

"*What?* Who?"

"Someone named Salonius Roscius—"

"Salonius? I don't believe it."

"Wait. He's the married fortune hunter you told me of in Neopolis."

Numb with shock, she nodded. "The last time I spoke to him was the night of Caros and Pelonia's fete. He delivered the message from Drusus concerning Octavia's illness."

"How convenient. He planned to be the last person to see you alive."

Nausea swirled in her stomach. "How was he discovered?"

"Caros didn't give details. I imagine one of his or your steward's spies uncovered the lout."

"I suppose now we have to return to Rome."

"Yes." He rolled up the scroll. "Your testimony is needed to press charges and prepare for a trial."

She knew her assassin's capture should make her happy or bring her relief, but anger bubbled inside her instead. Salonius and his murderous plans infuriated her, but the unfairness of having Quintus in her life only to lose him was a cruelty that burned her with impotent rage.

"Congratulations." She strove for an even tone despite the hard lump of grief in her throat. "You're a free man now."

He set down the scroll and rounded the desk. She didn't understand the tension in his body or his less-than-gratified expression.

"Are you releasing me, then?"

She knew Quintus was a man of specifics who always kept his word. He wanted a clear declaration that she no longer needed him. But if she had her way, she'd never let him go. "Yes, our agreement is finished. I have no further use for you."

"Is that so?" he asked, the sharp edge of his voice undisguised. "Have you grown wings all of a sudden that you can fly back to Rome?"

Why was he angry? She was the one being abandoned. "If you'd be kind enough to hire a boat for me, I'd appreciate it. Once I'm in Neopolis I can make my own way home."

He raked his fingers through his hair. "No. That's not an option. You'll have to put up with me a few more days. I'll see you safely back to Rome myself."

The reprieve ushered in a swell of hope. He wasn't leaving her yet. "If you insist on accompanying me, who am I to argue?"

He eyed her dubiously. "I appreciate your wisdom."

She snorted and stood. "Then if you'll excuse me, I'll go pack my satchel."

Without waiting for his answer, she turned and left the office, his gaze burning a hole in her back.

Chapter Eighteen

❧

"Do you wish to go home?" Quintus asked Adiona as Rome's massive gate came into view. "Or do you prefer to visit Caros and Pelonia at the *ludus* first?"

"The *ludus*," she said, keeping her eyes on the crowded road ahead of them. Quintus's imminent departure loomed closer with each beat of the horses' hooves.

She'd spent the last three days since they'd left the villa trying to wean herself from the pleasure of being able to look at him whenever she wanted. So far, the experiment had proven a catastrophe, but failure wasn't an option. She had to be strong. She had no choice. Quintus was leaving her. She'd be an *idiota* to pretend otherwise. Trying to convince him to stay wasn't possible when his son's funeral rites were in question. All that was left for her to do was get used to being alone again.

The press of travelers slowed their progress to a halt. The journey back to the capital had been uneventful with a stop in Neopolis to collect the gladiators Caros left to guard Drusus. Her heir had been relieved, and too self-satisfied for her liking, to have his innocence confirmed. And even though Adiona was sad not to see Drusus's daughters, she'd been delighted to learn the girls would be living with their grandmother indefinitely.

In Ostia, the group stayed with Joseph's family at the *tabernae* for a night. She and Quintus had checked on Onesimus's recovery. His wounds were healing, but the young gladiator remained bedridden—and much fussed over by Josephina.

At a fork in the road, the group followed a path that circled the city, rather than taking the direct route inside Rome's massive walls.

The good mood of the gladiators rose the closer they came to the *ludus*. Clearly, the men were as happy to be home as Adiona was miserable.

All too soon, they arrived at the *Ludus Maximus*. Guards opened the heavy iron gates. Caros and Pelonia joined them in the courtyard before Quintus had time to help Adiona down from her horse.

Once Adiona touched the ground, Caros snatched her up in a tight embrace. "Thank God you're back safe. You and your prickly ways have been missed."

She hugged him back, holding on a moment longer than necessary when she saw Quintus's eyes narrow on the exchange.

Pelonia linked arms with Adiona and walked her through the peach orchard back to the main house. "I'm happy you've returned to us, as well," Pelonia said. "We've been sorely worried about you."

"Thank you," she murmured, embarrassed but touched by her friends' concern, especially Pelonia's because the two of them had not started on the best of terms. "Quintus protected me well."

"I'm sure he *did*." Pelonia grinned. "He's the type of man who excels at all he attempts."

"True. He's exceptional in every way." Noticing Pelonia's pleased smirk, she hastened to add, "What I mean is, his quick thinking saved me several times from certain danger."

"That's what I thought you meant," Pelonia said, leading Adiona to a guest room where a basin of water awaited. After she'd washed off the travel dust, Adiona returned to the sitting room to find Pelonia. The splash of the fountains in the inner courtyard flowed through the large, airy chamber. "Have you eaten?" Pelonia asked. "Are you thirsty?"

Adiona asked for water, but declined food. She and Quintus had breakfasted on fresh bread and cheese before leaving the *tabernae* at sunrise. The noonday meal wasn't due for at least another hour.

"I must say," Pelonia began once the two of them were comfortably seated, "Caros and I were surprised when the messenger announced you and Quintus were arriving together this morning. After Quintus sent his slave's price last week, we assumed you'd hired a new guard and Quintus had headed directly for Amiternum."

"What do you mean he sent the money last week?" Adiona's brow pleated with confusion. "His freedom was to be compensation for guarding me."

"That's what I thought as well, but… I'm sorry, I think I've spoken out of turn."

A servant entered the sitting room with a tray of rolls and the cups of water Pelonia ordered. Setting the refreshments on a low table in front of the couch where the women were seated, the girl left at the same time Quintus and Caros strode through the door.

Adiona rose to her feet. "Quintus, I need to speak with you. Right now, if you please."

Quintus frowned. "All right. Just a moment. Let me say goodbye to Pelonia. I'll be leaving soon."

Winded by the punch of pain the announcement brought, she started blindly for the garden.

"Wait, Adiona," Caros said. "There's been a development. You need to sit down."

She did as he said. "What's happened?"

"Salonius. He's dead."

"How?" she asked, only half-interested in the worm's demise when she had so few moments left with Quintus. "Was he killed in prison?"

"Trying to escape," Caros clarified.

"Good riddance." Adiona glanced at Quintus who was watching her intently. She stood and turned for the garden, needing fresh air to clear her head. "Quintus, I'll be outside when you're finished here."

Aware of the silence she left behind, she reached the courtyard and sat heavily on a carved stone bench near the largest fountain. She rubbed her upper arms to ward off the chill. The peaceful flow of the water did nothing to soothe her misery as she listened to the renewed camaraderie and muted laughter of Caros, Pelonia and Quintus saying their farewells.

Grief pressed down on her like a slab of marble. How could anyone laugh when the occasion of Quintus leaving warranted sackcloth and ashes? Didn't Caros and Pelonia realize Quintus might never return? Hot tears scratched the back of her eyes and her head throbbed with tension.

Quintus's strong presence alerted her of his arrival in the garden even before she heard his sandals on the floor tiles behind her. Force of habit warned her to brace herself, to hide her true feelings behind a glib facade, but sadness drained her of the will to pretend all was well.

"Adiona?"

She stood and faced him. "Quintus."

"Are you truly as indifferent to Salonius's death as you seem?"

"Should I be upset the man who tried to kill me is dead?"

"You have a tendency to blame yourself for others' actions against you. I want to make certain you know this business with Salonius is his doing, not yours."

She nodded. Unable to look at him when tears clouded her vision, she developed a sudden interest in the knotted end of her leather belt. Never in her life had anyone understood her or cared for her like Quintus did.

And now he's leaving.

"Why do you wish to speak to me?" he asked when she stayed quiet for several long moments.

A breeze rustled the trees in the garden and brought a faint hint of smoke. She cleared her throat. "Why did you send funds to Caros to buy your freedom?"

"That's none of your concern."

"Not true." She lifted her gaze back to his face. "Guarding me was supposed to ensure your liberty. How did you afford it? Lucius admitted he squandered your family's fortune."

"You may have noticed my brother talks too much."

"All right," she said, irritated by the distance he wedged between them, but unwilling to drop the matter. "Perhaps it's not my concern, but I'd like to know. Did Caros refuse to honor his promise?"

"Of course not."

"I see."

His eyes narrowed. "What do you see, Adiona?"

"That your pride is threatened."

"Explain."

She was surprised he didn't disagree with her outright. "You don't want the return of your freedom tied to me in any way. You're afraid that by accepting the bargain, I'll have some future hold on you and you won't take the risk."

"Your mind is a wonder," he said. "But here is the truth, if you must know it. My brother spent most of the gold I gave him in Amiternum, but that was merely a portion of my wealth. Once I reached my villa the situation was better than I expected. I had written to Lucius to tell him of the money I had stored there, but he never received my letters. With the gold still in the villa, money was no longer an issue. I sent the funds I owed Caros because I wanted him to know I was protecting you by *choice,* not because I had no other way to earn my freedom."

"You *chose* to stay with me when you could have gone to your son?" she asked, unable to fathom the idea when she knew how much he loved his child.

He moved closer. His large palms cupped her shoulders. "Adiona, you think I fear some future hold you might have on me, but you're wrong. Although I tried to deny it, your hold on me began the first moment I saw you and it's grown tenfold every day since. When my life was at its most ugly, the Lord brought you to me and filled it with your beauty. There isn't a day that passes when I don't thank Him for you or an hour that goes by when I don't think how special you are to me."

Quintus was too honest for her not to believe him. The last seeds of shame and fear her husband implanted in her shriveled up at the roots and died under the force of Quintus's high regard.

Tears blurred her vision and slipped down her cheeks. She locked her arms around his waist and pressed against his chest. For years she'd taught herself to ignore pain, but this was an agony beyond anything she'd endured, as though her heart were being removed from her chest while she watched. "I can't bear for you to leave me."

He pressed a kiss to the top of her head and held her tight. "You know I must. Fabius—"

"I know," she said over the rock of pain lodged in her throat. "Just promise you'll come back to me."

He lifted her chin and gently brushed the tears from under her eyes before touching her lips with a kiss.

"I won't make a promise I'm not certain I can keep. I don't plan to court trouble, but I still don't know who reported me to the authorities."

She placed her hand over his mouth, unable to consider him being rearrested or worse. "Please, stop," she begged.

He brushed his lips across her palm and kissed the tip of each of her fingers. "I have to go, lioness. Amiternum is a ten-day journey from here. I want to get a head start before night falls."

A thousand things to say bubbled to her lips, but silence lingered as she watched him stride through the arched doorway, her heart going with him.

Adiona glanced at the sundial of her villa's private garden. It was almost noon, not that the hour made much difference when each moment was as empty as the next.

In the twelve days since she'd returned to Rome,

she'd grown to hate the copper timepiece. More often than she cared to count, she'd been tempted to have it removed and melted down. A just punishment for mocking her with the reminder of how long Quintus had been gone.

Not that she needed a reminder when even the weather seemed to mourn his absence. The early January rains brought shorter days and longer nights filled with a cold, depressing dampness that seeped into the bones.

"Domina?"

Adiona looked up from the sundial to find her steward, Felix, wringing his hands near a pot of winter crocus a short distance in front of her. Lost in thoughts of Quintus, she hadn't heard the older man's approach.

"Domina, I'm sorry to trouble you, but Claudia Arvina is at the door. I thought I'd best ask if you want to see her before I send her away."

"Yes, send the spider back to her web," she said, thinking of the last time she'd spoken with Claudia and the woman's glee over Quintus's near-death in the arena.

"As you wish, *Domina."* Felix was almost to the edge of the garden when Adiona called him back. The other matrons usually respected her long-established perimeter of privacy. If Claudia intruded without an invitation, there might be an emergency.

Adiona met Claudia in a large reception room near the front of the villa. "Thank the gods it's warm in here," Claudia said, handing Felix her *palla.* "The north winds have blown in early this year. I thought I'd freeze waiting on your doorstep."

"I don't think the gods deserve the credit," Adiona said, trying to ignore the other woman's sickly sweet perfume. "Whoever the genius was that invented the hypocaust deserves your thanks. Without the hot water running beneath the floor and the steam rising between the walls, we'd all need to head south for the winter."

A maid entered the room with a tray of fruit and cups of warm lemon water.

"What brings you here, Claudia?" Adiona asked once the matron lowered her rotund form into a chair near one of the shuttered windows. "I trust all is well."

Claudia sipped water from a rare blue glass cup. "That's for you to tell me. You've been gone for weeks. Rumors are running rampant about you, yet there's been nary a word from your camp to refute them." The spider peered over the rim at Adiona. "Isn't it about time you cleared the air? It wouldn't be prudent to let people think you've gone soft."

Adiona arched an eyebrow. She didn't need advice from her rival. Her steward kept spies all over the city to keep her informed of Rome's current events and latest scandals, but she found she lacked the interest to care about matters that now seemed trivial. "What gossip do you mean, Claudia?"

"Well," she said, setting down her cup. "There's a full-blown scandal about you and Salonius Roscius. He told everyone you were on the cusp of agreeing to wed him."

"Lying mongrel," Adiona snorted, making no attempt to hide her disgust for the man who'd conspired to murder her. "As if I'd be desperate enough to wed that flea-bitten hound."

"That's what *I* told everyone," Claudia said in a commiserative tone that belied the calculation in her eyes. "You've made it clear you'll *never* remarry. And since I saw how enamored you were with that gladiator in the arena, I knew love wasn't clouding your vision enough to draw you to Salonius."

Schooling her features to betray none of her inner turmoil, Adiona sat back in her chair. The gossip concerning Salonius was an irritant much like the incessant buzzing of a fly, but if anyone spoke an ill word about Quintus she refused to be held responsible for her actions.

"When we all heard you were accosted like some common street wench—"

"Where did you hear of the matter? No one knew about the attack outside of a few who'd never prattle about me."

Claudia grew thoughtful. "I don't know where the rumor began, if truth be told. It…it just was. Salonius meant to murder you. When that plot failed, maybe he started the scandal as an attempt to discredit you instead."

The explanation seemed plausible. A few well-placed rumours was all it took to spark a wildfire. Adiona picked up her cup and sipped the hot, lemon water. "What I don't understand is why Salonius wished me dead in the first place."

"You humiliated him," Claudia said without hesitation. "All of Rome was aware of how you spat on his every proposal of marriage. No one knew how to react when he told us you'd changed your mind."

"Even if he weren't so irksome, he was *already* married."

"Divorce is a simple matter." Claudia's bracelets jangled as she waved away the issue. "Everyone knows the real reason you rejected Salonius and every other suitor over the years is because you despise men. At least you *did* hate them. How goes it with your gladiator?"

"He's not a gladiator. And he's none of your concern."

"I understand." Claudia eyed her with feigned sympathy. "We've all enjoyed a dalliance or two with the lower orders, but you're right, it's best not to speak of our forays in the mud."

Adiona slowly rose to her feet, ice flowing through her veins. "You're wrong, you poisonous shrew. Quintus is the finest man I've ever met. If he'd have me, I'd consider myself truly blessed. I'd take hold of his arm in the Forum and raise my head high with the knowledge that I was the most fortunate woman to ever walk the earth."

Claudia's eyes glittered. "Oh, my! So a slave rejected you, eh? How dreadful for you."

"He didn't reject me and he's no longer a slave," she muttered, disappointed in herself for allowing Claudia to bait her.

"Then you'll be marrying him?" Claudia asked, clearly excited by the scandal Adiona's marriage to a former gladiator would create. "Or will an affair have to suffice?"

"Neither, Claudia. He's no longer in Rome."

"What a shame. You must be devastated." Claudia sipped her lemon water. "Still, the ocean is full of other fish. Now that you're no longer averse to men, we'll find someone suitable for you and your social position."

Adiona bristled. There was no one more suitable for her than Quintus. Her social position was worthless compared to him. Even the thought of marriage no longer terrified her when she imagined herself as his wife.

Felix cleared his throat discreetly in the doorway. "Forgive me, *Domina,* but—"

"What is it?" Adiona asked, grateful for the interruption.

"The *lanista*'s wife is here. Shall I tell her you're occupied?"

"Caros's new wife is here? I'd love to meet her," Claudia said. "She's become quite famous since Caros fought for her in the arena."

Thinking of the unassuming and gentle-spirited Pelonia, Adiona hesitated to put her in close proximity with Claudia. Still, there was no way to ignore Pelonia without being rude. She would just have to protect the younger woman from Claudia's poisonous tongue. "Show her in, Felix. And order more lemon water. I don't want Pelonia catching a chill."

The steward disappeared. Claudia's smile widened. "This is why you're competition for the rest of us matrons, Adiona. You always know the most interesting people."

A few moments later, Felix showed Pelonia into the sitting room. A tiny dark beauty with huge brown eyes and ruby pins in her expertly arranged hair, Pelonia was dressed in a red *stola* trimmed with prized white ermine.

Adiona stood and greeted Pelonia with a kiss on the cheek. "Be careful of Claudia," she whispered for only Pelonia to hear.

Pelonia showed no sign she'd heard the warning. Adiona groaned inwardly, concerned she was leading a lamb to a butcher.

"Hello." Pelonia smiled. She moved deeper into the room as Adiona introduced the two women. "It's lovely to meet you."

"I agree," said Claudia. "I've been wanting to make your acquaintance for weeks, but you and the *lani-*

sta have denied your company to all of Rome. Given your husband and Adiona's…history together I'm surprised the two of you are friends. You must be very open-minded."

Adiona frowned. "Claudia—"

"I assure you," Pelonia said with a laugh that hid any offence she may have taken. "I'm not open-minded in the least when it comes to my husband and other women. Thankfully, Caros is trustworthy and I've no cause for concern on that score. As for Adiona, she's been an excellent friend to both of us. Without her, my husband and I might have lost each other after we became separated for a time before we married. I'll never be anything but grateful to her and her kindness toward us."

Claudia opened her mouth to speak, but thought better of whatever she planned to say. Instead, she set her cup on the low table in front of her and stood. "It was a pleasure to meet you, Pelonia. Adiona, as always it was good to see you, but I must be on my way. So many other friends to visit and the morning is on the wane."

"Indeed," Adiona said, calling for the older woman's *palla*.

Claudia wrapped the shawl around her shoulders. "We must meet again sometime."

"Absolutely," Adiona agreed, thinking once every other decade would suffice.

When she returned after seeing the older woman out, she found Pelonia standing in the center of the sitting room, her head tipped back as she admired the painted ceiling.

"It's so lovely," Pelonia said, turning to face Adiona. "The way the artist made it look as if it's a cloudless blue sky at all times."

"Mmm… I gave Octavia free rein. She said I needed some sunshine in my life."

"Octavia? Your friend who just passed away?"

"Yes, she wanted to be an artist, but Drusus refused to allow her. He said painting was a man's trade."

"How sad," Pelonia said.

"Yes. Octavia turned her hand to flowers instead. Her garden was a beauty to behold."

"I'm glad she found a way to use her talents."

Adiona smiled. "I'm also glad."

Both women returned to their seats across the room. Pelonia straightened the frothy folds of her red *stola*. "I apologize for interrupting the visit with your friend when I stopped by unannounced today. I was on my way to the Forum. I thought you might like to go with me."

"I don't think so. I'm very tired."

"Tired or depressed?" Pelonia said, wide-eyed and innocent.

"Why would I be depressed?" Adiona hedged. "I'm home, my attacker is no longer a concern and I even have a new friend who can put Claudia Arvina in her place."

Pelonia chuckled. "I'm glad you think of me as a friend. It's my sincere hope that we become close. I meant what I said to that…that sly woman when I told her how grateful I am to you."

"There's no need. You and Caros are fated. I'm certain your God would have provided another track to bring you together had I not intervened."

She turned to find Pelonia studying her, a smile curving her lips. "You've been talking to Quintus about the Lord."

"Yes," she hedged.

"Have you accepted the Lord in your heart?"

Adiona shook her head. "What do you mean?"

Pelonia moved to sit by her on the couch. "Have you spoken with Jesus and asked Him to be your God?"

"No. I've only asked him to protect Quintus and bring him back to me."

"I see." Pelonia beamed. "If you speak with Him, I think you must believe in Him."

"Perhaps." Adiona picked a stray thread from her tunic. "But I have no idea if He hears me."

"He does. He adores you. He loves to hear from you. Our texts say He cares for you so much He even numbers the hairs on your head."

"I think He might love other people that much, but not me."

"Why would you think that?" Pelonia asked so genuinely perplexed that Adiona didn't have an answer.

"Whoever tells you Jesus doesn't love you is a liar, even if that person is yourself," Pelonia continued. "The truth is He loves you so much He gave His life for you. He wants to fill you with joy and a peace so pure it's beyond your understanding."

"I want that," Adiona admitted quietly, "but I'm not certain I can believe you fully yet."

Pelonia squeezed Adiona's hand. "That's wonderful. Don't worry if you can't believe yet. Just keep talking to the Lord. He'll reveal Himself to you. And if you need a friend, please come to me whenever you like."

Adiona gave a hesitant nod.

"Promise? Even if it's the middle of the night."

Adiona laughed. "I'm sure Caros would love that. He'll think I'm insane."

"No, he'll be overjoyed. We both pray for you daily."

"Thank you." Touched that her friends prayed for

her, Adiona smiled for the first time since Quintus left. "If you still plan to visit the Forum, I'd be happy to go with you."

"Excellent. I've been having the most incredible craving for apples and I'm sure you need to get out of this palace."

"Why do you think so?"

"Quintus has been gone almost two weeks."

"What does he have to do with me?"

"You don't have to put on a brave face," Pelonia said, gently clasping Adiona's clenched hand. "It wasn't so long ago that I was in your place."

"What place is that?" Adiona asked, dreading the answer.

"The place where your heart feels like it's shattered into a thousand pieces and life without the man you love looks like a lonely, hopeless road stretching into a dismal eternity."

"Yes," she said, unable to pretend otherwise. "That would be the place. Except my heart isn't shattered. It's gone. Quintus took it with him."

Chapter Nineteen

Adiona, Pelonia and their handful of guards made their way to the fruit stands located on the first floor of the Forum's central market. An icy wind blew through the open colonnade, making Adiona wish she'd traded her wool cloak for a warmer, fur-lined one. The dark gray sky signaled the onslaught of another afternoon rain.

Adiona's guard created a path through the crush of patrons buying produce for their evening meal. After visiting several fruit sellers, Pelonia was still looking for apples. This late in the season, Adiona secretly believed there were none to be found, but she admired the younger girl's determination.

Spotting a large basket of pomegranates, Adiona selected several ripe pieces before following the scent of roasted chestnuts to a wagon outside.

Once her steward paid for the items she chose, she wandered through the citrus market. The tangerines reminded her of Quintus's garden at the coastal villa. She bought a dozen of the ripest fruits more for sentimental value than because she enjoyed the taste of them. Meandering past a large display of various kinds of figs, she located Pelonia near an exotic fruit stand, speaking with an older woman who looked vaguely familiar.

Pelonia lifted her basket. "I found my apples," she said happily. "Cook will have a few brown spots to cut off, but they'll do well enough." She turned to the elegant, silver-haired lady beside her. "Adiona, this is my friend, Annia. She owns a textile and ladies' goods shop on the second floor."

"Yes, I've seen you before," Adiona said. "Your shop has the best silk in the Forum."

"Thank you," Annia murmured. "I've waited on you before in the shop, but it's a pleasure to make your formal acquaintance. Pelonia's told me wonderful things about you. My thanks for your hand in bringing her and Caros back together."

Adiona rolled her eyes at Pelonia. "Have you told everyone in Rome that story?"

"Oh, no, there's at least three or four people I've yet to share it with."

Laughing, the three ladies made their way to a small *thermopolium* that served beverages and light snacks of hot sausages, cheese and dates. The smells of smoked meat and fresh bread teased Adiona's nose, making her realize she hadn't eaten since the previous evening. Street musicians played various instruments, seeking to fill the overcast afternoon with a sense of merriment.

While the ladies ate, they discussed the latest fashions and colors. "I've ordered a new shade of soft linen from North Africa," said Annia. "The samples I saw are a pale orange, similar to a ripe peach. It should be lovely on lighter skin tones."

Pelonia groaned and set down the apple she'd been unable to resist. "That leaves me out. I always look too sallow in shades of orange or brown. But the color sounds perfect for my cousin, Tibi. She has beautiful flaxen hair, alabaster skin and the darkest eyes you've ever seen."

"I'll tell you when my shipment arrives," Annia said. "You can bring her by the shop and we'll see how she likes it."

Adiona finished her smoked sausage and dabbed her mouth with a facecloth. Shivering and ready to go home, she looked out the open window and down the long, crowd-filled courtyard between two multistory wings of the Forum's shops. The swarm of people shifted and Adiona caught sight of a woman who reminded her of Octavia and Drusus's neighbor, Gaia. "I'll be right back," she told her companions. "I think I recognize someone."

Her guards surrounding her, Adiona lost track of her quarry thanks to the hectic masses. She was about to give up and return to the *thermopolium* when she caught one more glimpse of the woman.

After failing for the third time to get the lady's attention, Adiona turned to her closest guard. "See that woman in the green *palla* near the apothecary? I want you to follow her. All day if you must. Learn her name and report her address to my steward."

"Yes, my lady," he said, venturing into the sea of shoppers.

Adiona returned to her companions. Annia was standing over Pelonia, a worried frown on the shopkeeper's face.

"What's wrong?" Adiona asked.

"I've gotten frightfully dizzy," Pelonia said, her eyes closed and her fingertips rubbing her temples.

Annia went to fetch a cup of cool water from the service counter.

"Do you suppose it was the apple?" mused Adiona.

"I don't know. It's possible. It tasted good. A bit soft, but far from rotten."

When Annia came back with the water, Adiona sent one of her men to prepare her litter.

"We need to take her home," she told Annia. "Caros will feed us to Cat if anything bad happens to his wife."

An hour later the rains arrived. A physician had been summoned to the *ludus* to examine Pelonia. A tormented colossus, Caros prowled his office where he, Annia and Adiona waited for a report on Pelonia's health.

Adiona watched Caros with a mix of confusion and astonishment. A shared understanding of life's cruelties had forged their friendship over the past three years, but the last few months had altered Caros at his core. Pelonia had brought him true happiness and his new religion had healed the inner torment his past had caused to fester for far too long.

The physician returned. "You can go to your wife now, *lanista.*"

"What's wrong with her?" Caros said, failing to hide his anxiety.

A smile curved the doctor's thin lips. "Go ask her yourself."

Caros broke into a run, shocking Adiona with his haste.

"My word," the physician said. "To look at him now, one would never know he used to murder for sport."

"Not fair," Adiona refuted, always quick to defend her friend. "As a gladiator, he didn't have much choice except to fight or end up dead. What would you have done in his place?"

Caros and Pelonia returned within a short time. To

Adiona, they looked as though someone had lit a lamp inside each of them.

"We're having a child," Caros said without preamble. The pride and wonder in his announcement filled every crevice of the room. His happiness was blinding. Like staring directly at the sun, it hurt to look at him.

Annia squealed and hurried forward to offer heartfelt congratulations, while Adiona hung back, struggling to find the right words. She didn't resent her friends' joy; she was thrilled for them, but for the first time in years, the lies she'd convinced herself to believe refused to stifle the truth of how much she longed for a happy marriage and children of her own.

But Quintus was gone.

She moved forward, a well-practiced smile learned from years of disguising her feelings was plastered on her face. She clasped Pelonia's hand. "I'm so pleased for you, both of you," she said to Caros. "What a pleasure it will be to have a little one to spoil."

Pelonia hugged her. "How fortunate our child will be to have you for an aunt."

Caros pulled Adiona into his bearlike embrace. "Can you believe it?" he asked, his deep voice marked by amazement. "Me, a father."

"I can." She laughed, his good mood infectious. "I have no doubt you'll be the very best."

Hours later, Adiona wandered through the vaulted corridors that wound through her palace. Alabaster sconces cast flickering light across the elaborately painted ceiling and mosaic-tiled floors.

In her bedchamber the shutters were fastened tight against the earlier storm. Her terror of being trapped in closed spaces was a mere shadow of the monster that once plagued her, but the residual fear forced her to open a window. The damp night carried in a whiff of smoke and the sound of dripping rain.

Having grown used to caring for her own needs while she traveled with Quintus, she dressed in a soft wool tunic and prepared for bed before calling her maid.

While Nidia brushed out the long strands and plaited Adiona's hair, Adiona allowed her thoughts to wander back to the happy events of the afternoon. Caros's joy made her smile. He truly was a man reborn, as the Christians were fond of saying. She'd known Pelonia and Quintus only as Christians. Both of them acknowledged their faults and failings, while thanking their God for bringing them through difficult times. But Caros she'd known before he became a follower of the Nazarene and his transformation was as complete as a caterpillar's metamorphosis into a butterfly.

Adiona envied Caros's newfound freedom and wished for her own. Quintus's kindness and understanding had helped to heal the wounds inflicted by her husband's evil, but there was a darkness that still lurked inside her soul.

The soft click of the door signaled the maid had finished her task and left Adiona alone. The candlelight illuminated the glass bottles and mirror in front of her. The polished metal was higher quality than most, but the reflection it offered was distorted at best.

She wanted to see herself clearly. Not her face and outward appearance, but her inner being. She remembered Quintus telling her that he tried to see people the way his God saw them. Pelonia had said their God loved her enough to die for her. Marveling at the concept of a love that true, she twisted the end of her long braid, wondering if it was possible that He genuinely cared enough to count the hairs on her head.

She thought of the prayers she heard Quintus say and the words Pelonia used when speaking of their God. She cleared her throat, hoping their God would accept her into His fold.

"Dear Heavenly Father." To her surprise the word *father* came more easily than she'd anticipated. "I'm Adiona. We've spoken a few times before when I asked you to protect Quintus. I'm here to plead for his safety again, but also to do as Pelonia suggested and ask You to be my Lord."

She stood from her chair and walked to the open window where the breeze ruffled her hair. "My friend Caros became Your follower recently and You've done a fine job helping him to be a better person. I'm not kind and gentle like Pelonia or as honest and wonderful as Quintus, but if You'll have me, perhaps You can place some good in me."

As an afterthought, she realized she'd forgotten to ask for forgiveness. "I also pray that You forgive me for the wrong I've done in my life. Please help me to do...to *be* a person worthy of Your love." Remembering how Quintus prayed for Octavia, she added, "In Jesus's name, amen."

She waited. There were no lightning bolts, no claps of thunder or celestial music. But a sense of tranquility pervaded her being until there was no room left for fear or doubts.

She closed the window. Crawling into bed, she covered herself with furs and burrowed into the soft pillows, feeling very much like a caterpillar who'd just been given a glorious pair of wings.

* * *

Verging off the Via Caecilla, Quintus rode into Amiternum ten days after he left his heart in Rome with Adiona. Built in a fertile valley at the junction of four roads, his birthplace was a thriving city based on commerce and trade. For centuries his family had been among the area's civic leaders, contributing to and overseeing the various public works like the theater, aqueduct, public baths and even the amphitheater.

Until his arrest, he'd owned myriad acres of fertile farmland, a vineyard and a hillside estate along with the large city residence where he'd been born. Now all of it was gone, stripped from him by an unnamed accuser and a greedy magistrate who'd worked in tandem.

He rode his horse through the energetic heart of town—a way he'd traversed thousands of times to find his way home. Given the mountainous region and the season, the weather was remarkably pleasant—cold but clear. The street vendors were taking advantage of the blue skies and the greater number of patrons enjoying a bit of sun.

After eight months away, he noted the new storefronts and the disappearance of shops he'd patronized over the years. Tempted to stop and speak with old friends, he kept riding. The need to know about Fabius compelled him onward.

He turned a corner and followed the street up the slope of a hill. His familial residence came into sight. A high wall surrounded the large two-story villa, but the gate was open, allowing him a voyeur's view of his home. Beech trees and mountain pine lined the front of the house. Painted in a mellow hue of gold, its arched windows and doors, as well as a covered balcony gave the place a stately yet welcoming appearance.

The front door opened. For a moment, he was transported back eight months in time. He held his breath, expecting his five-year-old in his little tunic and sandals to run onto the wide steps to greet him.

Instead, an old man in slave's garb tottered onto the portico, a broom in hand. He closed the door behind him and began to sweep the tiles.

Quintus choked in air and blinked rapidly to clear the moisture from his eyes. Fabius, with his sweet, ever-present smile, was gone. Never again would he hear his son's bright laughter or feel his chubby little arms squeezing his neck in a too-tight hug.

The loss gutted him. His chest ached and his throat convulsed as he worked to keep his emotions in check. He'd known his son was dead, but the events leading up to Quintus's arrest and sale to the slaver's wagon had happened rapidly, making it easier to deny the truths he didn't want to face.

Now he had no choice but to fully accept what he could not change. *Why, Lord?* clamored over and over in his mind. All of his losses combined failed to compare with the death of his son.

Another slave closed the gate. Quintus turned away. His old life was over and done. Oddly, his only regret was Fabius. Grateful for the peace of knowing his son was with the Lord, that he would be reunited with him in heaven one day, he tugged on the reins and sent his horse in the direction of his former brother-in-law's villa. He and Faustinus had never been friends, but they'd always been civil. There was no reason for Faustinus not to answer his questions.

As Quintus climbed the steps of his in-law's villa, black memories of his wife assailed him. Her tantrums and insatiable vices had brought misery to both families although her kin made endless excuses for her actions.

He'd been a fool to ever compare Adiona with Faustina. On the surface the two women seemed similar, but in heart matters, they were as different as summer from winter.

The steward of the house opened the door. Mencius blinked, his only show of surprise before ushering Quintus into the incense-sweetened entryway. The steward left to consult with his master a few moments, but quickly returned to show Quintus to Faustinus's office.

A tall, thin man with brown hair and a thickening waist, Faustinus was standing in front of his desk when Quintus crossed the threshold. Tension was a third being in the room.

"Is that really you, Quintus? How is it possible you've returned to us? Where have you been?"

"In Rome." In quick fashion, he told Faustinus of his time away. "Thankfully, my Lord saw fit to let me live."

"Then I'm glad for your God's kindness."

"Really?" Quintus said, unable to hide his doubt. "Lucius thinks you're the one who turned me over to the authorities."

"Me? That half-wit brother of yours is wrong once again."

"Then who? I'm certain you know something of the person who's responsible."

Faustinus glanced away guiltily. "Why? How would I know?"

"Just a hunch," Quintus said. "If you can tell me, I hope you will. The episode is over as far as I'm concerned, but I'd still like to know the truth. It's an odd way to live when you don't know if the person you're speaking to wishes you were dead."

"How is any of this over? You're *infamia*. Your life is wasted."

"No, my freedom's been restored and much of my wealth is intact. If I ever thought my faith might not stand the truest test, I learned otherwise. My son's death is all I regret."

"And Faustina? Do you mourn her?"

"I'm sorry I was never able to make her happy. You may not agree, but I did my best with her. I will forever be grateful for the son she gave me and I never once wished her dead. But given the circumstances and difficulties between us, I'd be a liar if I said I wasn't grateful to be free of her."

Faustinus hung his head. His shoulders slumped. "It's not good to speak ill of those who've passed on and you know I loved my sister, but I must tell you this. I know you tried, Quintus. My sister's behavior wasn't your fault. I've felt guilty all these years because I forced the arrangement between the two of you. My parents and I were always aware something was…not right." He pointed to his head, indicating a sickness of the mind. "She liked your looks and I knew enough about you to appreciate your loyalty and strength of character. When your brother played into my hand, I knew your father could be convinced to join our families. I believed…*hoped* that if she were content, she'd be easier to live with. I thought if anyone could make her happy, it was you."

Sick in the pit of his stomach, Quintus glanced away, unable to look at the other man without wishing him harm. As a gladiator Quintus had learned many ways to kill and his rising temper goaded him to maim Faustinus at least.

"I know you'd probably like to hurt me—"

"You can't imagine," Quintus said. "Just know that if I weren't a Christian, you'd be dead."

Faustinus blanched and sought refuge behind his large desk. "I didn't know she was as bad off as she was or that having a child would make things worse."

"Just tell me where Fabius is. I hope you respected me and my beliefs enough to have him buried."

"Yes, of course. I knew how you felt on that score and I wanted to honor your memory. Faustina was cremated, but Fabius is here."

"Here?"

"Yes, I had him buried in the garden under the evergreen tree he loved to climb when he visited. None of the funerary *collegia* challenged me or insisted he be buried outside the city because he was such a young child. Believe it or not, I loved him, too. I thought if he were buried here at least he'd be surrounded by family."

Cold air swept through the open window, carrying the scent of smoke and pine.

"My thanks," Quintus said, his throat raw and tight. He realized Faustinus had tried to honor both him and Fabius. Wanting to let go of his anger as he always strived to do, he focused on that kindness. "I want to see him."

"Of course, I'll take you to him."

Outside the villa, Quintus stopped on the steps and pulled his cape closer around him. He knew the way to his son's favorite tree. "I'll go from here alone."

Faustinus nodded, the lines on his face pronounced. "Don't leave without seeing me. I have more to confess."

Quintus followed the winding path. His breaths curled into white mist in the cold air. Winter's fingers had plucked the shrubs and bushes clean of any greenery, leaving pine trees and evergreen alone in their task of providing color.

The tall evergreen he sought waited at the end of the path; snow-capped mountains stood majestically in the distance. A grave marker brought unquenchable tears to his eyes. He dropped to his knees. The frozen earth was as unyielding as death itself. Riddled by grief, he covered his face with his palms. Visions of his son's sweet face played through his mind, making him laugh and weep by turns.

When he was empty, he gathered up a handful of soil and sat back on his heels. He waited until the cold had seeped through the layers of his clothes before he whispered a final goodbye.

Taking his time to return to the villa, he thanked the Lord for the blessing of his son and the time he'd been given with him. He prayed for Adiona as he'd done continuously since leaving Rome. With every breath in his body he longed to return to her, to claim her for his own. She was the keeper of his heart, the woman he'd longed for, the wife he'd dreamed of for more years than he cared to count.

But she isn't a Christian and she's sworn off marriage, he reminded himself. He still wanted her. If she never accepted the Lord as her own and he could never have her for his wife then he'd be her friend or remain her protector. Either way, he knew without a doubt he'd spend the rest of his days loving her.

He found Faustinus waiting for him on the steps. "I'm leaving for Rome."

"Back to Rome? Why? If you have your fortune as you say…"

"My heart is no longer here."

"I see," Faustinus said.

"What was it you planned to tell me?"

"You asked who turned you in."

Quintus tensed, certain Faustinus meant to confess.

"It was Faustina. I didn't tell you because I didn't want to be disloyal."

"Then why tell me now?" Quintus said, disgusted by his wife's perfidy when he'd never once sought to harm her.

Faustinus shrugged. "After all you've suffered, it seemed wrong for you not to know the whole truth."

"My thanks," Quintus said sincerely. "I can live my life without the constant need to look over my shoulder."

"Yes."

Quintus turned to leave, then paused. "Do you know why she hated me so much?"

"She didn't hate you. She loved you."

"No," Quintus said, biting back a harsh laugh. "She never had the first drop of love in her heart for me."

"I only attest to the message she wrote just before she died."

"What message? Where is it?"

"The wax tablet she used was ruined, but your brother can vouch for me. I showed Lucius the message after we thought you were dead."

"What did it say?"

"She said she loved you. That Fabius's death filled her with shame for the kind of woman she'd been. She knew you'd never take your own life as she planned to take hers. Turning you in was the only way to ensure you met her and Fabius in the afterlife. She paid the magistrate to condemn you."

"She *was* crazed," Quintus said, his mind reeling with the duplicity of her plan.

"I told you. Perhaps now you'll believe me."

All the guilt he'd carried because of Faustina drained away, leaving him with a clean conscience and the hope that he could be a good husband to Adiona—once he convinced her to marry him.

"Peace go with you," Faustinus called with a wave as Quintus mounted his horse.

"And to you," Quintus said, turning for Rome and the new life he hoped and prayed awaited him.

Chapter Twenty

Adiona was reading a wax tablet from her property manager when Pelonia arrived the next morning. Dressed in an understated fashion, the *lanista's* young wife wore a blue *stola,* matching *palla* and simple wooden combs in her hair.

"Should you be up and out this early?" Adiona asked as Pelonia sat down across from her at the table. "Aren't pregnant women supposed to rest?"

"I don't know." Pelonia's brow furrowed. "I've never been pregnant before. I feel fine."

"Good, but be certain you don't overdo."

"You're sounding like Caros." Pelonia grinned. "At dinner last night, I was lifting a bowl of broth. He asked me if it was too heavy. I thought he was joking, but he was serious."

"I fear it's going to be a long nine months for you." Adiona laughed and indicated the selection of food on the table. "Care for some fruit or water?"

Pelonia chose a wedge of tangerine and a spoonful of pomegranate seeds.

"Why are you here?" Adiona asked.

"Can't I drop by to say hello?"

Adiona laughed self-consciously. "You'll have to forgive me. I'm not used to friends who come to visit with no agenda."

"Then I'm glad you're changing the company you keep."

"I am also."

Pelonia ate a section of tangerine. "In truth, I woke this morning with an unction to see you. It was even worse than my need for those apples yesterday."

"That was urgent, indeed."

Pelonia grinned. "Just wait until you're pregnant. You won't be laughing at my cravings then."

Adiona's amusement dimmed. "I won't be having children."

"I'm so sorry," Pelonia said. "I didn't realize you're barren."

"I'm not. At least I don't think I am. What I mean is, I don't plan to marry."

"But what about Quintus? Surely you won't abandon him. You love him and he's madly in love with you."

Hope swelled in Adiona's chest before she could squelch it. "Did he say so?"

"He doesn't need to. Anyone with eyes can see it's the truth. I thought you knew." Pelonia's pretty face puckered with confusion. "How could you not?"

"He said I was special to him, but he never mentioned love. I didn't assume."

"But it's *so* obvious."

Adiona shredded the roll on her plate. "Not to me."

"Yes, well, when two people are in love they're often the last to know."

"Perhaps." A dove cooed nearby and Adiona tossed it a few scraps of bread. "What does it matter anyway?

Quintus isn't here. Who knows if or when he'll come back. I asked for his promise to return, but he refused."

"He'll be back. I have no doubt. Do you know why he wouldn't give his word?"

"Yes. He didn't know who reported him to the authorities or if it might happen again. I wanted to beg him not to go, but his son…"

"I understand," Pelonia said full of sympathy. "It's a harsh reality for us Christians, but the possibility of punishment is an ever-present reality. Thankfully, the mob assumed I was only a slave being used for their amusement when I was sentenced to the arena. If not, Caros and I would have no safe place to go. As it is, once again the Lord proved his promise that all will work for our good when we trust in Him."

Adiona ate a spoonful of pomegranate seeds, the usual tang of the fruit tasteless on her tongue. When she'd accepted Christ, she hadn't considered that sometime in the future she might have to face the arena for her faith. Hesitating, she realized she didn't have to tell Pelonia about the change in her and no one would ever have to know. Instead, she drew in a deep breath and released it slowly. "I prayed again last night."

"You did?" Pelonia smiled.

"Yes," Adiona admitted in a whisper. "I asked Jesus to be my Lord."

"How wonderful!" Pelonia fairly buzzed with excitement. She jumped to her feet, rounded the table and before Adiona had time to brace herself, threw her arms around her in a hug. "Praise be the Lord. Welcome to the family!"

"Thank you," she said, radiating with her own sense

of joy. "I must admit I feel somewhat different this morning. As if I'm no longer alone in the world."

"You're never alone. Our texts say He never leaves us."

"That neither height nor depth can separate us from His love," Adiona supplied.

Pelonia looked at her with wonder. "You know the texts?"

"Just a line of two," she said. "I heard Quintus read that passage once. That bit stayed with me."

"You're welcome to the *ludus* anytime, of course, but I hope you'll come the first day of the week when several of us Christians meet to read the texts and worship the Lord."

Adiona shook her head in disbelief. "Christians meeting in a gladiator school? How marvelously clever."

"Caros didn't think so the first time he saw us there. Of course, that was before he was a Christian himself. He couldn't decide if we were brave or suicidal."

Thinking back to the hard and violent man Caros had been just a few short months ago, she laughed. "I can imagine."

Pelonia stood. "I must go. Annia is expecting me. I'm helping her with some orphans today. My mother died giving birth to me and I've no experience with children. Annia thinks it will be good practice for when the baby comes."

As always, Pelonia spoke with an accompanying smile, but Adiona sensed a tinge of anxiety in her friend. "You're going to be a wonderful mother, Pelonia. I have no doubt. You have the natural warmth children need in a parent."

"How kind. Thank you for saying so. I'm going to do

my best. Of course, Caros will be there. He'll be *such* a good father. I'm going to have to work day and night to keep him from spoiling the child."

"I agree." Laughing, Adiona stood. "Would you mind if I came with you today?"

"Of course not. I should have invited you myself."

"It's just that Quintus suggested I use my resources to help others and I like children very much. Perhaps I can help in some way."

"I think that's a lovely idea. I'm ready to leave when you are."

Surprise brightened Annia's face when Pelonia and Adiona arrived at the small *domus* inside Rome's city gates. The house, with its low ceilings and plain cement floors, was dry, but cold, despite the small cooking fire. A dozen dirty children of various ages had assembled in hopes of receiving a noonday meal. Annia and another woman, Vergilia, had organized the group into two camps. Half the children were setting rough-hewn tables with colorful, but mostly chipped ceramic dishes and cups, while the other half helped to wash vegetables for a savory lamb stew.

Fresh bread that Adiona and Pelonia brought with them rounded out the meal. Adiona wished she'd thought to bring the extra fruit she'd bought at the Forum the previous day. She made a mental note to have one of her people send it and a round of cheese over for the dinner hour.

After the children ate, they washed and dried the dishes. Several of them slept on pallets on the floor. "They're desperate for a safe place to sleep," Annia whispered to keep from waking them.

"Is this house yours?" Adiona asked the older woman.

"No, it belongs to another Christian brother of ours. He's letting us use it until he can find new tenants."

"Then where will the children go?"

"I don't know," Annia said. "I trust the Lord will provide us with somewhere else to use."

Within a week, Adiona bought an abandoned *domus* a short distance from the Forum. Large and multistoried, the building needed repair, but there was an adequate kitchen and large rooms for a number of children to sleep.

Caros and Pelonia arrived to inspect the place. "This is marvelous," Pelonia said.

"It is," Caros agreed as he knocked on a wall to test its sturdiness. "If you'd like, I'll hire an engineer to come and check the foundations and the soundness of the place."

"I did that before I bought it," Adiona said wryly. "I was going to offer one of the properties I already own, but this one is closer to the Forum. I'm hoping beggar children will find us and we can get them off the streets. It can't be safe for them wherever they're staying now."

"What are you going to do with all of them?" Caros asked. "You can't feed every orphan in Rome."

"Who says we can't?" Adiona lifted her chin. "You should know by now, Caros, I don't do things in half measures. With my income unlimited as it is thanks to my various investments, and the sizable donations you and others like you will make, I'm thinking we can help quite a few children for a long time to come."

"What sizable donation?" he asked.

Pelonia laughed and elbowed him gently in the ribs. "Don't be a miser, my love. Adiona has made amazing plans."

"I'm sure she has. Everything she sets her mind to, she does well."

Warmed by the compliment, Adiona showed them the rest of the house. "The garden is a mess, but I'm thinking we can grow herbs and vegetables, and plant fruit-bearing trees here. It would lessen the food expenses and give the children fresh produce. The ornamental fountains can be replaced with more practical ones to ensure the children have clean water to drink and bathe.

"There are ten bedrooms upstairs. I thought we could have beds built like those in your gladiator barracks to give even more children a place to sleep. I'm already looking to hire several people to keep the place clean. We'll also need a gardener and a cook or two. As things progress perhaps others will be needed or the children can take on chores. I noticed the other day, Annia had them setting the table and helping prepare the meal."

Caros grinned. "You've worked it all out. Has Annia offered any other advice?"

"Yes. She's in charge. I'm only trying to give aid. She suggested we put the older children to work in the garden to help them learn a trade. The same with cooking and repairing the building. She says so many of them end up in brothels or thieving because they have no useful knowledge to help them when they're older. Of course, so much has to be done, but perhaps in the future we can even hire tutors and…" She flushed, embarrassed to realize she was rambling.

Caros wrapped an arm around her shoulders. "This is excellent work. If anyone can make it succeed, you can."

It was dark when Quintus arrived at the *ludus*. His only stops had been to change horses or to sleep for a few hours. With the promise of seeing Adiona as his goal, he'd shortened the ten-day journey from Amit-ernum to eight.

Guards opened the gate, and he made his way to the *domus*. Caros and Pelonia were sitting down to their evening meal.

"Come and join us," Pelonia said. "You must be fam-ished. You look like you've been through a war."

"Not quite," Quintus said, declining the offer. He scrubbed his bearded chin. "I'm road-weary and filthy."

"Then go take a bath and change," Caros insisted. "We'll wait. Hurry, we have much to tell you."

Once he was clean and dressed, Quintus went back to the inner garden where his friends were waiting. Surrounded by torches to ward off the cold, couches had been set up in the peristyle. The aroma of various dishes teased his hungry stomach.

"What news is there?" Quintus asked as they ate a first course of steaming fish chowder.

"News in general?" Pelonia asked. "Or news of Adi-ona?"

Quintus dropped his spoon, splashing drops of the hot liquid on his hand. "Is Adiona well? Has something happened to her?"

"Several excellent things," Caros said, grinning at his wife. "Too bad her news isn't ours to tell."

"Yes, you must go see her tomorrow without delay," Pelonia agreed. "She's not the same person she was when you left. First, though, I think you should rest and shave. I'm sure she'll be happy to see you in any form, but as a woman, I'd suggest you go to see her looking less like something Cat dragged in."

Relieved to learn Adiona was well and receptive to

seeing him, he was a little annoyed by the couple's obvious fun at his expense.

"Since you won't tell me more of Adiona, what is the general news? I've been gone almost three weeks. What's happened?"

"We're having a baby," Caros said, his smile brighter than the oil lamps lighting the garden.

"Congratulations!" Quintus exclaimed, happy for his friends, even though talk of children reminded him of Fabius. "God be praised."

"There's also a new orphanage Annia is opening. With the help of a new benefactress, they've bought a house to shelter at least fifty children."

His thoughts constantly on Adiona, he remembered the talk they'd had and her interest in helping orphans. "Do you think Adiona might be welcome in such a venture? She told me once she'd like to help in something like this."

"Oh, I'm certain she'd be welcome," Pelonia said. "Without a doubt."

Chapter Twenty-One

✦

"*D*omina," Felix said, "The lady, Gaia, is here."

Adiona set down her glass of orange nectar. "Welcome her in."

When Octavia's friend entered the courtyard, Adiona stood and left the breakfast table to greet her with a kiss on each cheek.

"How good of you to come. I feared you hadn't received my invitation."

"I've been visiting friends outside the city this week. I didn't know you wished to see me until I returned last night."

"No matter, you're here now. All is well." Adiona swept her hand toward the table, laden with her favorite cinnamon rolls, orange juice and dates. "Have you eaten this morning? Do you care to join me?"

"I ate earlier," Gaia said, "But I'm parched. A glass of water would do well for me."

"Of course." She led Gaia to the table. "Sit here. There's a charcoal pot on the floor to warm your feet." When the older woman was comfortably seated, Adiona went to the door and called for Felix to fetch a glass.

Adiona returned to her chair and took a drink of

juice. Her mouth puckered at the extreme tartness, but after eating honey on the rolls, she expected as much. "I've wanted to speak with you since Octavia's funeral," she said. "I was sorry to leave Neopolis in such haste without thanking you, but the situation was unavoidable. Octavia was a dear friend to me. I feared Drusus wouldn't do her justice, so your guidance with the rites was most appreciated."

"It was no trouble. Octavia was a friend to all. It was she who first welcomed me to Neopolis when I moved there two months ago."

Adiona swallowed a bite of cinnamon roll. She said nothing, but it surprised her to learn the shortness of Gaia's acquaintance with Octavia. After seeing Gaia and Drusus at the funeral, she'd thought them long-time friends.

She took another drink of juice and angled the top of her sandaled foot near the warmth of the coal pot. "Yes, Octavia was the best woman I've ever met. Have you been in Rome long?"

"No," Gaia replied, "I arrived midweek last. I'm preparing for my wedding."

"Your wedding?" Adiona smiled politely. "Much happiness and blessings to you."

"Thank you. My husband died almost a month ago—"

"My condolences," Adiona said, careful not to show her distaste at Gaia's rush to remarry.

"Condolences aren't necessary. As far as I'm concerned, his death was well-deserved."

Taken aback by the woman's candor, Adiona hid her surprise behind another sip of juice.

Gaia sat back in her chair, as amiable as if the topic were the arrival of spring. "My husband planned to divorce me for a younger, wealthier woman. He'd done the same to his first wife when he married me two years ago, so I recognized the signs. I should have known better than to wed him, but I believed his lies when he said he loved me. After he wasted most of the money my first husband left to me, he thought to move on to someone else." Her voice took on a flinty tone. "What galls me is that his paramour didn't care that I was an excellent wife or that he was even married. She's a spoiled seductress who thinks her money can buy her whatever she desires. I plan to enlighten her soon."

Gaia's contempt made Adiona fear for the younger woman's safety. "I don't mean to add to your pain, but men are quite duplicitous when they choose to be. Perhaps your husband didn't tell her he was married."

"No," Gaia said stonily. "She knew."

"Then shame be upon them both. I hope your new husband will be worthy of you."

Gaia sipped her water and seemed to rein in her anger. "He's sure to please me. My new betrothed is a malleable man and heir to a large fortune." She smiled. "I expect to be quite content."

"If one *must* marry," Adiona said in response to Gaia's prosaic attitude, "those are commendable traits in a husband."

Gaia nodded. "The best. I find honor is wasted on men because the sight of any young beauty will challenge their wedding vows."

Adiona chose a slice of fig and ate the sweet fruit, trying to ignore the bitterness behind the woman's smile. "I agree, most men prove themselves worthless. However, of late I've learned a very few are worth their weight in gold."

"Surely a woman like you is the object of a great many men's affections."

Adiona smirked. "My wealth is."

Gaia cocked her head as though considering Adiona in a new light. "You don't mind a man desiring you for your coin?"

"Certainly I do." Adiona sipped her juice. "My intolerance for men is well-known. Especially those with lucrative intentions."

"I hadn't heard that." Gaia drank her water. Her hand shook slightly. "Most wealthy women will buy love if they can't find it for free."

"Many do, but I'm not one of them." Uncomfortable with the course of the conversation, Adiona changed the subject. "When will you marry?"

"A few weeks at most," Gaia said. "My betrothed's benefactress is on her death bed. I don't want to be accused of poor taste by marrying too quickly after she leaves us."

"That's wise." Adiona shivered at the coldness of Gaia's calculations. Claudia was a poisonous spider, but Gaia could teach the Roman matron a thing or two. "Will you be living in Rome? I think you'll blend in well with the society here."

"I'm not certain. My former husband loved Rome and spent most of his time here wooing his new lover," she said bitterly. "But my betrothed prefers Neopolis."

"Does he know my heir, Drusus?"

"Yes, they're well-acquainted." Gaia circled the rim of her glass with her fingertip. A slight smile turned her lips. "Drusus prides himself on knowing everyone of importance in Neopolis. Of course, he only considers the men important. The way he treated Octavia was disgraceful."

"I've always thought so," Adiona agreed. She finished her juice.

Gaia smiled at the empty glass Adiona set on the table. "I'd like to tell you a story. It's important. I hope you'll indulge me."

Perplexed by her heightened sense of danger, Adiona decided to listen before making an excuse to send the woman on her way as soon as possible. "All right."

"Six months ago, my husband and I moved to Neopolis. He was a business acquaintance of your heir, so naturally he attended a party Drusus invited him to. I wasn't feeling well, so I stayed home. As it turned out, my husband met the woman who was to become his mistress. She lives here in Rome, but happened to be visiting Octavia at the time.

"When I learned of the affair, I befriended Octavia and told her I was a widow. I planned to learn all I could in order to rid my husband of his latest…interest."

Adiona continued to listen in rapt silence. Gaia took another drink of water. "I decided to do myself and the city a favor by doing away with such an unscrupulous she-dog."

"Why punish the woman and not your husband? He's the one who owed you loyalty."

"Yes, I had plans for him, as well. Not what he deserved because I preferred to put an end to both of them, but I'm no longer the beauty I once was and my husband squandered most of my fortune, leaving me unable to attract a new spouse with my money or buy the protection an unmarried woman needs to survive.

"When Octavia became ill all those weeks ago, it occurred to me that if she were gone I'd have the perfect solution to all my problems."

The hairs on the back of Adiona's neck stood to attention. Her heart began to pound rapidly and her gums tingled. "You evil cow! What did you do?"

"With the help of some hemlock I aided her journey to Elysium, but not before I hired thugs to dispatch my husband's mistress."

"Felix!" Adiona shouted, jumping to her feet. "Felix!"

"Don't excite yourself. Your steward can't hear you. My men have trussed him up in the kitchen with the rest of your household slaves. They're waiting by the doors if you think to run." She studied her fingernails. "Besides, I'm not finished with my story."

Deciding it was better to listen to the lunatic while she considered her options, Adiona sank back into her seat. The coal pot scraped the tiles beneath the table. She'd been enthralled enough by Gaia's story not to feel the hot pot when she bumped it.

"That's better." Gaia smiled. "Once Octavia was gone, I thought all was going according to my plans. Octavia was no longer an impediment between Drusus and me. He proved easy enough to seduce. You were supposed to have died in the street, providing Drusus with his inheritance. Salonius was my last concern. I was debating whether to divorce him or have him dispatched like he deserved."

"Salonius?" Adiona began to tremble. She ran her tongue over her teeth and gums. Numbness was creeping over her. "I never had anything to do with Salonius."

"Don't! Everyone from Rome to Neopolis knew of your affair."

"Because your husband propagated the lie. I rejected his interest and advances more times than I can count. I told him to go back to his wife—to you!"

"I don't believe you. With his charm and handsomeness, Salonius could have had any woman he wanted. I knew he married me for my money, but until you, he'd never attempted to leave me."

"You're insane."

"No," she said, her voice flat. "I've been used, robbed and scorned. I won't be abused any longer."

"I never wanted your husband. I'm in love with someone else!"

"A woman like you is incapable of love. When you arrived at Octavia's funeral, I realized my plans were in shambles."

As the horror of the situation compounded, Adiona blanched at Gaia's evil. "*You* put the viper in my bed."

"My servant did."

"It's the same thing."

Gaia shrugged. "When you escaped again, I realized I'd have to end your life myself because everyone else proved inept at the task."

Adiona gripped the arms of her chair until her fingers turned white. Perspiration broke out on her brow.

"After you and your watchdog disappeared from the funeral, I needed you to expose yourself. When Caros Viriathos traveled to Neopolis and threatened Drusus, I knew Salonius could be made to look guilty for your attack with some well-placed evidence. My plan succeeded beyond my expectations. My fool husband did me the favor of trying to escape jail and dying in the process. The situation made his guilt in your attempted murder unquestioned. Within a short time you did as I anticipated and returned to Rome."

"What do you plan to do to me?"

Gaia smiled. "I've already done it." She picked up Adiona's empty cup and studied the residual rings of orange nectar on the glass. "Didn't the hemlock taste sour to you? I added it when you left to order my water. I worried you might notice when you returned."

Adiona felt the blood leach from her face. Her heart kicked. To survive in Rome, one had to have a basic knowledge of poisons. Its use was so common most wealthy households kept a food taster. Hemlock was slow-acting, starting in the extremities and closing down the body as it worked its way to the lungs. Perfect for killing, especially if a murderer had a story to tell before her victim died.

Adiona bolted from her chair. Unable to feel her feet, she stumbled the few steps to the garden's nearest flowerpot where she stuck her finger down her throat and forced herself to retch.

"That won't help you. I can see you're already having trouble walking."

Adiona eyed the knife on the table. There was no way to reach it before Gaia did. Her hatred of the other woman was almost as intense as her love for Quintus.

"I'll be going," Gaia said, her voice warm with the satisfaction of a woman whose fondest plans were fulfilled. "Considering Octavia's goodness, it's unlikely you'll see her in the afterlife, but if you do, please apologize for me. Her death is my only regret. Unfortunately, it was necessary."

Adiona didn't try to stop her. As much as she wanted retribution, she wanted to live more. Hemlock had no antidote that Adiona knew of, but it was important she stay calm. The more excitable she became the quicker the poison saturated her blood.

Using the peristyle's columns, then the corridor walls for support, she worked her way to the kitchen. Gaia's men were gone. Her own people were bound and gagged. Despite the roaring cook fire, she was so cold she was shivering. She found a knife and cut the ropes from her steward's wrists.

Felix ripped the cloth off his mouth. "*Domina,* we tried to fight them. What's happened?"

She quickly related the details as he cut the other slaves free. "Please, Felix. Go to the *ludus.* Tell Caros and Pelonia I need them. Someone else fetch a physician."

On his way out the door, Felix ordered one of the house slaves to carry Adiona to her bedchamber. A brawny slave placed her on her sleeping couch. Her maid, Nidia, covered her with furs to fight the insidious chill.

Shaking, her teeth chattering, Adiona began to pray. She thanked the Lord for Caros and Pelonia. She asked for blessings on their baby and long lives filled with joy. She asked that He give special care to the orphans and wished she'd had time to change her will to include them.

Mostly she prayed for Quintus. Her heart swelled with love for him. She thanked the Lord that Quintus existed, that she'd been allowed to know him. She regretted the shortness of their time together, aware that even a thousand years wouldn't be long enough for her to love him.

Her eyelids grew too heavy to keep open. For most of her life she'd been alone. To know the Lord was with her at the end brought her peace.

Chapter Twenty-Two

Surrounded by the smells of hay and leather, Quintus led his horse from the stable. Caros and Pelonia waited in the *ludus*'s courtyard.

"You look exceptional today, Quintus." Pelonia grinned up at him, her warm, friendly expression contrasting with the day's sharp cold. "A shave and a good night's rest did wonders for you. Adiona will think you're the handsomest of men."

He frowned. "You're certain you don't want to tell me about what I'll find this morning?"

"Oh, no. You'll have to discover it for yourself. You'd best hurry."

"You're sure you have the correct directions?" Caros asked.

"You can always ask someone if you get lost," Pelonia said, stroking the gelding's smooth black neck.

The two men exchanged a dubious glance at the suggestion.

Pelonia laughed. "Of course, I know you won't."

"I'll find it," Quintus assured them. Saying good-bye to his friends, he gathered the reins and turned his horse toward the school's iron gates. "Until later, then."

Inside Rome's city walls, he turned his horse onto the road leading to the Palatine Hill where Adiona's palatial villa overlooked the Forum. Lined by thick foliage and numerous trees, the road wound up a steep incline. At the top of the hill, he followed the road past the villas of Rome's most exalted and wealthiest families.

At the end of a wide thoroughfare, he found the palace Caros described as belonging to Adiona. To Quintus, the lavish three-story structure with its marble Corinthian columns and precisely arranged statuary looked more like a public building than a home. Its marble facade was as cold and self-contained as a tomb, exuding none of the vitality his lioness possessed in abundance.

Taking the mountain of steps two at a time, he reached the columned portico and knocked on the front door. No one answered. He knocked again, listening for any indication of life. When the silence stretched, he turned to leave, disappointed and chagrined by his impatience to see Adiona when she wasn't even home.

He was halfway down the first flight of steps when he heard the door open behind him.

"Wait! Are you the physician?" a woman's voice called. "My lady Leonia is dying. *Please* help us!"

Dying? Hammered by fear, Quintus raced back up the steps. "What happened?" he demanded of the maid. "Where is she?"

"This way." The maid's shorter stride frustrated Quintus as she led him to Adiona down a long-corridor. "A woman named Gaia visited this morning," the girl panted, her breathing labored as she worked to keep up with his driving pace.

Growing sicker to his stomach with each word of the maid's explanation, he began to pray, begging for

Adiona's life. His anger burned toward Gaia. He blamed himself for not recognizing her malevolence. He rejected the possibility that Adiona might not recover. That would be the same as his own heart dying and he cherished the hope of a lifetime with her. Every drop of faith inside him cried out to the Lord for mercy.

"Where is the steward of the house?"

"Felix went to the *Ludus Maximus* to fetch the *lanista* and his wife."

"When did he leave?"

"Almost an hour ago. He should return soon."

Quintus clawed his fingers through his hair. He must have missed the steward by moments. At least Caros and Pelonia's arrival was imminent. He needed their prayers.

"Who went for the physician?"

"I thought you—"

"No."

The maid stopped midstride. "Then who...?"

He grabbed the girl's wrist and towed her along, ignoring her protests. "I'm no one to concern yourself with. Who went for the physician?"

Overrun by distress, the maid stopped struggling against his hold. "It was Pulus. He left the same time as Felix. I don't know why he isn't here yet."

At the end of the long corridor, the maid pushed open a heavy door. Barely registering the vibrant colors and rare Eastern textiles, Quintus raced across the room to the slender bump reclining on the large sleeping couch.

"Adiona?" He grabbed her hand and pressed his lips to her cold knuckles. Breathing in her scent of cinnamon, he tested the inside of her wrist and felt the weak pulse. He pressed his lips to the faint tick beneath her translucent skin and web of delicate blue veins. Molding her fingers to the curve of his cheek, he squeezed his eyes shut, silently begging God to heal her. After Fabius's death, he'd go mad if he lost Adiona, too.

Unexpectedly, Adiona's fingers curled, one catching his ear. His eyes flew open. He rejoiced to see her amber gaze riveted to his face.

"Have I…died?" she asked, her voice barely a whisper.

"No, you're going to live, my love. I won't let you leave me."

Her eyes slid closed. A hint of a smile curved her lips. "You came back."

"Open your eyes, Adiona." His voice broke. "Stay with me. The physician is coming soon. You *have* to stay with me."

She was so cold she felt like snow. Quintus ordered more pelts. He was covering her with a blanket of mink when her eyes slipped opened again.

"You…certain I haven't died?"

"No, I'm here. We're in Rome."

She nodded imperceptibly. "If I die, don't worry—"

"Don't speak of your death. I won't hear it. I don't accept it."

"Shh…come." Her index finger tapped the place beside her.

He sat on the edge of the couch. "I'm listening."

"If I die. I'll see you in…in heaven."

"Heaven? Not Elysium?"

"No. I prayed—"

"You're a Christian?" he asked, trying to speak for her, to help her conserve her strength.

"Yes."

His throat tightened. Joy competed with his terror. God had heard his prayers for her soul and answered.

Surely, He wouldn't give with one hand and take her from him with the other?

"I love you," he said, kissing her palm. "I love you."

Her eyes slid open and her pulse quickened beneath his fingers. "You...love me?"

"Yes. I've missed you every moment I was gone. You've been in my thoughts and prayers every day since I left. I will wait for you as long as it takes to win your heart and your consent to be my wife. And if you never agree to be mine, I will love you forever anyway, whether it's in this life or the next."

Her eyes slid closed.

"Adiona, *please* don't go."

A commotion in the corridor signaled the physician's arrival. "Where is the patient?"

"She's here," Quintus called, waving the newcomer into the room and over to the bed.

"Are you the lady's husband?"

"I will be."

The physician, a stocky older man with dark curly hair and pockmarked cheeks, motioned toward the clutch of slaves in the hallway. "The boy said she was given hemlock. There's no cure, you know."

"There must be something we can do," Quintus said with steely determination.

"Nothing certain. The idea is to stir the heart. I've seen a few victims survive by eating certain fruits and nuts, but I can't promise it will work."

"What do we feed her?" Quintus asked, desperate.

"Pomegranates, hazelnuts, crushed mustard seeds, cinnamon—"

"Fetch them all," Quintus ordered the maid. "Bring a mortar and pestle. Hurry!"

Pelonia arrived, her face etched with anxiety.

"Caros, Felix and several of the gladiators have gone to search for Gaia," she told Quintus. "Felix had her followed before. He knows where she's staying. I've sent word to Annia and several of my other Christian friends. I thought the more prayers, the better."

The maid returned with the fruit, mortar and pestle. Quintus reached for them instantly, wasting no time in grinding the spices together. Next he cut open a pomegranate and crushed the seeds into a juicy, gritty broth. He took the mixture to Adiona.

With Pelonia, Annia and several other ladies praying quietly across the chamber, Quintus sat next to Adiona on the couch. He held her against his side, one arm propping her head. With his free hand, he coaxed her to drink the spicy concoction. She made a face. "Drink it, lioness," he said. "Drink it all. Then I'm going to get you some more."

She drank slowly, but eventually got the first dosage down. While Adiona drank, the maid prepared more of the liquid. Quintus forced Adiona to drink it and more. When they began to run out of the ingredients, Quintus sent one of the maids to the Forum. "Get enough to feed an army."

Quintus held Adiona for hours, never tiring in his task. "Drink some more," he said, willing to bully her if necessary.

"No, no, I can't." Her head rocked against his shoulder. "I'm going to be sick."

"That's a good way to get the poison out of you."

"I made myself retch as soon as that evil cow told me what she'd done."

Quintus smiled. Adiona was getting stronger. She no longer stuttered with weakness. Some of her usual fire had reignited in her eyes.

The sun was setting by the time Adiona needed privacy. Pelonia and her friends forced Quintus from the room, leaving Adiona with the physician and her maid. Quintus paced up and down the long hallway like a threatening storm cloud until the maid called him back in the room at Adiona's insistence.

Inside the chamber, Quintus froze. Adiona was sitting up. She wore a fresh white tunic and bright red *palla,* her black hair was brushed and draped over her left shoulder. She looked exhausted with dark purple smudges beneath her amber eyes and pale chapped lips, but she was more beautiful than any woman had a right to be, especially one who'd spent the day fighting poison.

He looked to the physician. "Is she well?"

"Seems to be. I've told her to keep drinking the juice you made. I don't know if helped, but I doubt it will hurt. I'm going to recommend it for other patients in the future."

Once the physician left, Quintus went back to Adiona. "What?" she asked when he drew near.

"Nothing." Relief pouring through him, he knelt by the edge of the sleeping couch and ran the pad of his thumb over the dark circle beneath her right eye. "Do you feel recovered?"

"For the most part. I can feel my toes and the tips of my fingers again. I had a burn on my foot the physician treated."

"A burn? From what?"

"When the poison set in, I lost feeling in my foot. There was a charcoal pot beneath the table. I didn't realize I was touching it."

"My poor lioness. Anything else?"

"The cold plagues me despite all these furs. And my

vision is a mite blurry. The physician said all should be well within a few days."

"Praise the Lord." Quintus kissed her palm, struggling to keep his voice steady. "Do you remember anything of what I told you today?"

She smiled, surprising him with uncharacteristic shyness. "You told me you love me."

He stroked a ribbon of her hair between his thumb and index finger. "Do you believe me?"

"Yes." She lowered her eyes to the mink covering her. "You never lie."

"Do you know I'll never hurt you, that I'll cherish you until my dying day?"

She tossed her hair playfully. "I don't recall you saying that. However, I do remember something about you waiting an eternity if that's how long it takes to win me."

He trapped her gaze with his. "I'll wait five eternities if necessary. Ten. Twenty."

She glanced toward the other ladies talking across the chamber. "Kiss me before the ladies come over here," she whispered.

He brushed his lips across hers, leaving her heart to ache for more of him. "You don't have to wait," she said. "I love you. I've loved you from the first moment I saw you—even before I knew what true love was. I'll marry you today, if possible."

His eyes widened and his lips parted. He kissed her again, this time sealing the promises between them. "You know," he said, "I left my heart here with you when I left for Amiternum."

"But you took mine," she said softly. "I don't know what I would have done if you hadn't come back. I think I would have hunted you down."

"A lioness for certain." He laughed. "You were never in any danger of me not coming back. I didn't want to leave you in the first place."

"You needed to care for Fabius. Did all go well?"

"It did. I'll tell you the whole story once your full health is restored."

Hours after dark that same night, Caros, Pelonia, Quintus and Adiona sat on couches in one of Adiona's main salons. Adiona continued to suffer from the cold, but Quintus kept her buried in furs and tucked against the heat of his side. Caros and Pelonia were sitting in a similar fashion across from them.

"I must know what happened with Gaia," Adiona said, aware that everyone was treating her like a breakable piece of glass. "If not, I'll worry she's out there somewhere plotting against me."

Caros glanced toward his wife before he spoke. "Felix led my men and me to the *tabernae* where she was staying. We almost missed her. I'm convinced the Lord allowed us to arrive in time. When she saw us, she sought refuge on the top floor. When we informed her the plot she planned against you had failed and that we intended to take her to the authorities, she—"

"She jumped, didn't she?" said Adiona, cringing.

Caros nodded. "She didn't survive the fall."

Adiona shuddered and burrowed tighter against Quintus. "I'm sorry about her."

"The whole situation is terribly sad," Pelonia added.

"Yes. I can see much of myself in Gaia. Without good friends to show me to the Lord and a wonderful man to bring my heart to life, I may have ended up bitter and angry like she did. I was certainly on that road."

Quintus frowned against Adiona's hair. "I saw nothing of her in you."

Caros chuckled. "I did."

Adiona arched a brow. "What do you mean?"

"You both could be shrewish and opinionated, overly independent—"

Adiona threw a pillow at Caros's head. Laughing, he ducked, the weak toss missing him by a mile.

"Adiona is none of those things," Quintus declared. "She's sweet, kind, loving, generous to a fault—"

Caros chuckled. "Oh, he's definitely a man in love."

Pelonia elbowed her husband in the ribs. "Be kind, Caros. Quintus is right. Look at Adiona's interest in the orphans, and don't forget what she did to help you and me."

"What orphans?" Quintus asked.

When Adiona tried to downplay her role in helping the children, Pelonia interrupted to tell him all of Adiona's deeds and the plans she'd made in his absence.

"I'm not surprised," Quintus's said, smiling into Adiona's eyes. "As lovely as you are to look upon, it's your soul that's most beautiful."

Held securely in Quintus's arms, Adiona barely noticed when Caros and Pelonia excused themselves to take a walk in the garden.

"How are you feeling, lioness?" he asked again, his worry for her health undiminished.

"Cherished and loved," she said, overflowing with contentment for the first time in her life. "I can't wait to be your wife."

"I can't wait either. You're the answer to all my prayers."

She smiled. "I am?"

"Definitely. For years I asked the Lord for a wife of faith and honor. He gave me those things and more when He brought you to me."

She looked at him from beneath her lashes and grinned. "I think He brought you to me. I was already here in Rome."

"True." He laughed. "When I first came here, I didn't think there was anything worse than being a gladiator. But the Lord knew differently. Now that I have you, I can see it was one of the best things to ever happen to me."

She blinked back tears. "*You're* the best thing that ever happened to me. In case you didn't know it, you're everything I've ever wanted and never thought to find."

"Good." Quintus stroked her hair and settled her closer to his heart. "Because I'm never leaving you, lioness. I love you more than life itself."

* * * * *

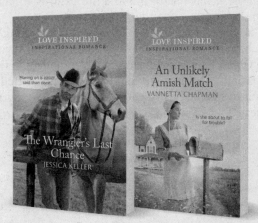